W9-BST-020

Thorn recognized the strength it had taken for her to come this far and her fierce desire to provide a better life for her baby, but he also knew how vulnerable she was.

As much as he wanted to have Hank reassign him so that he didn't have to dig his own emotional grave deeper, he was stuck. He'd gone way past being able to hand her off to someone else. So far past, that all he wanted was to hold her in his arms and keep her safe from anyone who wanted to hurt her.

"I can leave. You don't have to help me." Her fingers dug into his shirt, belying her suggested solution.

"You know damn well I can't let you leave." Thorn pulled her into his arms, crushing her mouth with his. He dragged her body close to his, melding them together in an embrace far more flammable than a lit match to a stack of dry tinder.

ABOUT THE AUTHOR

A Golden Heart Award winner for Best Paranormal Romance in 2004, Elle James started writing when her sister issued a Y2K challenge to write a romance novel. She has managed a full-time job and raised three wonderful children, and she and her husband even tried their hands at ranching exotic birds (ostriches, emus and rheas) in the Texas Hill Country. Ask her, and she'll tell you what it's like to go toe-to-toe with an angry 350-pound bird! After leaving her successful career in information technology management, Elle is now pursuing her writing full-time. Elle loves to hear from fans. You can contact her at ellejames@earthlink.net or visit her website at www.ellejames.com.

Books by Elle James

COWBOY RESURRECTED

& KILLER BODY

—

Elle James

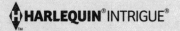
HARLEQUIN® INTRIGUE®

ISBN-13: 978-0-373-69718-2

COWBOY RESURRECTED
Copyright © 2013 by Mary Jernigan

KILLER BODY
Copyright © 2010 by Mary Jernigan

This edition published by arrangement with Harlequin Books S.A.

For questions and comments about the quality of this book,
please contact us at CustomerService@Harlequin.com.

Printed in U.S.A.

CONTENTS

COWBOY RESURRECTED

CAST OF CHARACTERS

Thorn Drennan—Undercover agent for Covert Cowboys, Inc. battling guilt over the deaths of his wife and unborn child.

Sophia Carranza—On the run from her abusive ex-fiancé, a drug-cartel leader with connections on both sides of the border.

Hank Derringer—Billionaire willing to take the fight for justice into his own hands by setting up CCI—Covert Cowboys, Inc.

Antonio Martinez—One of the leaders of _la Familia Diablos_ drug cartel.

Grant Lehmann—FBI regional director and old friend of Hank's.

Scott Walden—Forman of the Raging Bull Ranch.

Cara Jo Smithson—Pretty single woman who owns the diner in Wild Oak Canyon.

Pj Franks—Hank's grown daughter.

Brandon Pendley—Hank Derringer's computer guru.

Zach Adams—Former FBI special agent tortured and broken by _Los Lobos_ cartel.

Jacie Kosart—Big Elk Ranch big game hunting trail guide desperate to find her twin sister.

Ben Harding—Former cop with the Austin police department.

Kate Langsdon—Inherited the Flying K Ranch from the father she'd never known. Husband killed in Afghanistan a month before their daughter was born. Just looking to provide a safe home for her little girl.

Chuck Bolton—Wounded soldier returning to Wild Oak Canyon to join Hank Derringer's team, Covert Cowboys, Inc.

This book is dedicated to my husband, whose love and support helped clear my schedule to write!

Chapter One

Elena Sophia Carranza gunned the throttle to make it up the steep, rocky slope, doing her best to keep up with Hector. Thank God he'd taken the precious extra time to train her on how to ride a dirt bike in rough terrain. There was no more treacherous landscape than the border crossing between Mexico and the United States leading into the Big Bend National Park.

"You can do this, Señorita Elena, but you must be brave," Hector had insisted when they'd set off on their desperate escape. "Once we leave, we cannot return."

She'd known that from the start. Her ex-fiancé, Antonio, would not stop until he found her. And if he did catch her, there would be the devil to pay.

Squeezing Hector's hand, she'd whispered, "You must call me Sophia from now on. Elena no longer exists."

"*Sí,*" he'd agreed before mounting his bike and taking off.

It was imperative Sophia commit to her goal, or she'd die. Others had risked too much to help her break out of the compound. Hector had risked his life and his future to get her this far. The least she could do was hold up her end by keeping pace with him, not going so slow as to put them both in jeopardy. They had come across the United

States border without being detected thus far. Now all they had to do was find help.

They'd splashed through the Rio Grande at a low-water crossing before dawn and headed into the canyons, zig-zagging through the trails, climbing, dropping down into the shadows, heading north as far as they could before Antonio discovered their betrayal and came after them.

No matter what, Sophia couldn't go back. Even if she could withstand another day of physical and mental abuse, she refused to let the tiny life growing inside her suffer the same.

Escape seemed impossible from the far-reaching Mexican Mafia *la Familia Diablos.* As soon as Antonio realized she'd left, he'd send a gang of his *sicarios,* enforcers, to find and return her to Mexico or leave it for the Americans or the vultures to clean up her body.

As far as Sophia was concerned, she'd rather die and take her baby to heaven with her than subject another innocent life to the evil of Antonio Martinez and the drug cartel he called family.

Anna, her only friend in *la Fuerte del Diablo,* the Chihuahuan compound, had compromised her safety and that of her young son to get Sophia out. Sophia couldn't fail. Too many had risked too much.

Deep in the canyons of the far edges of Big Bend National Park, Sophia dared to hope she could evade Antonio and his band of killers long enough to find a place to hide, a place she could live her life in peace and raise her child.

Sophia had been born in Mexico, and her mother was an American citizen, ensuring Sophia had dual citizenship and could speak English fluently. Unfortunately, she no longer had her passport. Antonio had stripped her of identification after he'd lured her away from her family in Monterrey.

Once she found a safe haven, she'd do whatever it took

to reinstate her citizenship and ask for asylum. In exchange, she'd give the Americans any information they wanted on the whereabouts of Antonio's cartel stronghold on the Mexican side of the border. Not that it would do them much good. The Mexican government struggled to control their own citizens. What could the Americans do across the border?

Sophia knew that Antonio had contacts on the American side. High-powered, armed contacts that guaranteed safe passage of his people and products for distribution. Since the death of the former cartel boss, Xavier Salazar, Antonio had taken over, amassing a fortune in the illicit drug trade of cocaine, methamphetamines, heroin and marijuana. His power had grown tenfold, his arrogance exponentially, but he reported to a higher boss, a mysterious man not many of the cartel had actually seen. Rumor had it that he was an American of great influence. True or not, every time he visited, cartel members who'd betrayed *la Familia* were executed.

Sophia's only hope was to get far enough onto American soil and reach Hank Derringer. Anna said he would help her and protect her from Antonio. She'd said Señor Derringer was an honest, good man who had many connections on both sides of the border.

Her motorcycle hit a rock, jerking the handlebar sharply to her left. Sophia's arms ached with the constant struggle to keep the vehicle upright. She slowed, dropping farther behind Hector as they climbed yet another steep trail. They'd been traveling for hours, stopping to rest only once.

Her stomach rumbled, the nausea she'd fought hard to hide from Antonio surfacing, telling her she needed to eat or her body would set off a round of dry heaves that would leave her empty and weak.

When she thought she could take it no more, the beating sound of chopper rotors swept into the canyon, the roar bouncing off the vertical walls.

Adrenaline spiked through her, giving her the strength to continue on.

Ahead, Hector climbed a trail leading to the rim of the canyon.

Sophia shouted, wanting him to wait, seek cover and hide from the approaching aircraft. She feared Antonio had discovered her escape and sent his enforcers to find her and bring her back. He had the firepower and access to aircraft that would enable him to extract her from the canyon. Sophia had seen the airplanes and helicopters near the compound's landing field. Money truly could buy anything.

Hector cleared the top of the trail, then leaped over the edge and out of Sophia's sight. The helicopter pulled up out of the canyon headed straight for Hector.

Sophia prayed the aircraft was the bright green and white of the American border patrol. The setting sun cast the vehicle in shadow. When it moved close enough, Sophia gasped. The helicopter was the dull black of those she'd seen at *la Fuerte del Diablo*. Her daring escape had been discovered.

She skidded to a stop, hiding her bike beneath an overhang of rocks. Her entire body shaking, she killed the engine and waited, the shadows and the encroaching nightfall providing as much cover as she could hope to find until the helicopter moved on.

As the chopper passed over her without slowing, Sophia let out the breath she'd held, then gasped as sounds of gunfire ripped through the air.

Madre de Dios. Hector.

Her foot on the kick start, Sophia fought the urge to race to the top of the canyon rim to help Hector. Nausea held her back, reminding her she wasn't alone. The child inside her womb deserved a chance to live.

Sophia waited fifteen, twenty minutes, maybe more, for the helicopter to rise again into the sky, then realized it must have landed and the crew might be searching for her. She remained hidden for all those agonizing minutes, while the sun melted into the horizon. Storm clouds built to the west, catching the dying rays and staining the sky mauve, magenta, purple and gray.

When the helicopter finally lifted and circled back, Sophia pressed her body and the bike up against the canyon wall, sinking as far back into the darkest shadows as possible. The chopper hovered, moving slowly along the trail they'd just traveled, searching.

For her.

After what seemed like hours but was in fact only minutes, the aircraft moved on, traveling back the way it had come.

The smoky darkness of dusk edged deeper into the canyon, making the trail hard to find. Sophia eased her dirt bike out from the shadow of the overhang. Tired beyond anything she'd ever experienced, she managed to sling a stiff leg over the seat and cranked the engine with a hard kick on the starter. At first, the bike refused to start. On the fifth attempt, the engine growled to life. With a quick glance behind her, she was off, climbing the trail more slowly than she'd like in the limited light from encroaching nightfall.

At the rim of the canyon, her heart sank into her shoes.

The other motorcycle came into view first, lying on its side a couple hundred yards down the steep slope. Ahead on the trail lay the crumpled body of Hector, her ally, her only friend willing to help her out of a deadly situation.

She stopped beside Hector's inert form, dismounted and leaned over the man to check for a pulse.

The blood soaking into the ground told the tale, and the lack of a pulse confirmed it. Hector Garza was dead.

Sophia bent double as a sob rose up her throat. Tears flowed freely down her cheeks, dropping to the dry earth, where they were immediately absorbed in the dust.

Anna had sent Hector to guide her. Hector had been the one to encourage her along the way. He'd arranged to buy the bikes from a cousin in Juárez and had hidden them in a shed behind his brother's house in Paraíso.

The hopelessness of the situation threatened to overwhelm Sophia. The only thought that kept her going was that Anna and Hector would have wanted her to continue on. Sophia brushed away the tears and looked around, not sure which way to go. Instinct told her to head north. With only a compass to guide her, and the few provisions she'd loaded into her backpack, she was on her own. Alone and pregnant.

Afraid the helicopter would return, Sophia removed the rolled blanket tied to the back of Hector's bike and secured it to her backpack. She forced herself to climb back on the bike, the insides of her thighs and her bottom aching from the full day of riding and the strain of remaining seated on the motorcycle across the rough terrain.

She removed the compass from her pocket and clicked the button illuminating the dial. She set her course for north and took off across the desert, the night sky full of stars guiding her. With the threat of rain fast approaching, she increased her speed, refusing to give up when she'd come this far.

Before long, she came across a barbed-wire fence. If she hadn't seen the silhouettes of the fence posts standing straight and tall in a land of short, rounded and oddly shaped cacti, saw palmetto and sagebrush, she would have run right into the razor-sharp barbed wire.

Hector had armed her with wire cutters for just such an occasion. He'd warned her that the wire was stretched taut and not to get too close or, when she cut it, she'd be wrapped in the sharp barbs, unable to extricate herself without grave harm.

Sophia held her arm out as far as she could when she cut through the bottom strand. The wire snapped, retracting into a coil farther down the fence line.

She cut the other two strands and drove her bike through, exhaustion making her movements slow and sluggish. If she didn't find a place to hide soon, she'd drive off a bluff or wreck.

With only the stars and her compass to guide her, Sophia picked her way across the terrain, dodging vegetation not nearly large enough to hide a dirt bike or a woman, but large enough to cause serious damage should she hit it.

After the third near miss with prickly pear cacti, she finally spotted the square silhouette of a small building against the horizon. No lights gleamed from windows and no electricity poles rose up into the night sky, which might indicate life inside.

She aimed her bike for the dark structure, her body sagging over the gas tank, her hand barely able to push the throttle.

As she neared the building, she cut the engine and drifted to a stop, ditched the bike in the dirt and walked the remaining distance. She swung wide to check for inhabitants. Nothing stirred, nothing moved around the exterior. The building had a lean-to on the side and a pipe chimney. The place appeared deserted.

Sophia opened the door and peered inside. With the starlight shining through the doorway, she could see twin bed frames, no more than cots with thin mattresses rolled toward the head. A potbellied stove stood in one corner, and a plank table with benches on either side took up another corner.

Not the Four Seasons, but heaven in Sophia's tired eyes. She trudged back to where she'd left the bike, pushed it under the lean-to and stacked several old tires against it to hide it from view. With nothing more than what she carried in her backpack, she reentered the cabin.

The door had neither lock nor latch to secure it. Too spent to care, Sophia shook out a thin mattress, tossed her blanket over it, placed the pistol Hector had given her on the floor beside the cot and lay down.

She stared up at the dark ceiling, thinking of Hector and Anna and all they'd sacrificed to get her away from Antonio. One tear fell, followed by another. Sobs rose up her throat and she let them come, allowing her fear and sorrow a release. Tonight she could grieve. Tomorrow, before sunrise, her journey continued.

THORN DRENNAN HADN'T planned on being out this late, but he'd promised his boss, Hank Derringer, that while he awaited his first assignment as a special agent with Covert Cowboys, Inc., he'd check the Raging Bull Ranch fences for any breaks.

With the number of illegal aliens and drug runners still crossing the border from Mexico into the United States, any ranch owner this close to the border could count on mending his fences at least two or three times a week, sometimes more.

On horseback, it had taken Thorn far longer than he'd anticipated. The sun had set an hour ago, and he still hadn't completed a full inspection of the southern border of the massive ranch. He'd continued on, despite how tired he was, taking it slow so that he didn't overtax his mount.

Since the stars shone down, providing enough light to see the fence, Thorn didn't have a reason to return to the ranch sooner. He'd just climb into his truck and head to his little empty house in Wild Oak Canyon and lie awake all night anyway.

Sleep meant nightmares. The kind that wouldn't let him get on with his life—the kind that reminded him of all he'd lost.

Tonight was the second anniversary of the murder of his wife and their unborn daughter. He couldn't have gone home, even if he'd completed the inspection of the fence. And the bars didn't stay open all night.

His house was a cold, grim testament of what his career had cost him. He'd slept on the couch for the past two years, unable to sleep in the bed he'd shared with Kayla. He'd loved her since high school. They'd grown up together there in Wild Oak Canyon. She'd followed him across the country when he'd joined the FBI and back home when he'd given up the bureau to take on the role of county sheriff. He'd made the switch so that he would be home more often, and so he and Kayla could start the family they both wanted.

Their plan had gone according to schedule—until a bullet aimed at Thorn had taken Kayla's life and, with hers, that of their unborn child.

Thorn stared off into the distance. His horse, Little Joe, clumped along, probably tired and ready to head for the barn. So much had changed, and yet South Texas remained the same—big, dry and beautiful in its own way. Never had he known a place where you could see as many stars overhead. Kayla had loved lying out at night, staring up at the sky, picking out the constellations, insisting they teach their daughter all about the world and universe they lived in.

Thorn didn't know much about the cosmos other than what he'd read in magazines, but he knew how to find the Big Dipper and Orion's Belt because of Kayla. And because of Kayla, Thorn never failed to marvel at the immensity of the universe, much less the galaxies beyond their own solar system.

Tonight the vastness only made him realize just how alone he was.

Little Joe ground to a halt, jarring Thorn out of his morose thoughts, and just as well. Coiled in big, loose curls was a tangle of barbed wire where the fence had been cut.

Thorn cast a quick glance around to make sure whoever had cut the fence wasn't still lurking before he went to work mending the break. An hour later, fence mended, he stretched aching muscles. The moon had risen high above, near full, shedding enough light that it could have been daytime. The light wouldn't last long. Thunderclouds looming to the west would change that soon. He'd have to hurry if he wanted to get back to Hank's before the storm reached him.

In the dust at Thorn's feet, a single tire track, probably a motorcycle, led from the break in the fence into the ranch. At that moment, the wind wasn't blowing and the track remained intact. Thorn stowed his tools in his saddlebag and swung up into the saddle. Hank's sprawling ranch house lay in the general direction of the tracks. With the moonlight illuminating the trail, Thorn chose to follow the tracks and see where they led. Perhaps he'd catch up with the trespasser.

After thirty minutes of slow riding, dropping to the ground to double-check the direction and climbing back into the saddle, Thorn spotted what looked like an old hunting cabin ahead in the distance. The motorcycle tracks were on a collision course.

Thorn pulled his rifle out of the scabbard and checked to make sure it was loaded and ready. When he got close enough, he dropped down out of the saddle and left the reins hanging.

Thunder rumbled, and Little Joe tossed his head and whinnied.

The flash of lightning reminded Thorn that the storm would soon be on him, obliterating the moonlight and any chance of finding his way back to Hank's ranch house in the dark.

Thorn crept around the cabin, checking for any sign of life. He spotted the motorcycle buried beneath a couple of old tires. His pulse quickened.

The person who'd cut Hank's fence was inside the cabin.

Standing to the side of the door, Thorn balanced his rifle against his hip, grabbed the doorknob, shoved open the door and darted out of range.

An explosion erupted from inside the cabin and wood splintered from the door frame, bouncing off Thorn's face. He ducked low, rolled through the doorway and came up in a crouch, aiming his rifle in the direction from which the last bullet had come!

"Vaya, o disparo!" Another shot blasted a hole in the wall near Thorn's shoulder.

He threw himself forward in a somersault, coming up on his haunches. The rifle lay across the cot, pointed at the side of the shooter's head.

"Por favor, no disparar!" a shaky female voice called out. "Don't shoot!" Slim hands rose above the other side of the cot.

"¿Hablas Inglés?" Thorn asked.

"Sí. Yes. I speak English. Please, don't shoot."

"Place your weapon on the floor and push it toward the door."

The thunk of metal hitting wood was followed by the rasp of it sliding across the floor.

Thorn hooked the gun with a foot and slid it toward himself. "Now you. Stand and walk toward the door."

She hesitated. "Do you promise not to shoot?"

"I'm not going to shoot, as long as you don't do something stupid."

A slim figure emerged from the shadows, rising above the cot. Long, straight hair hung down around her shoulders, swaying slightly as she moved toward the door, picking her way carefully. For a second, she stood silhouetted in the light filtering in from the moon, the curve of her hips and breasts in sharp contrast to her narrow waist.

She glanced toward him, moonlight glinting off her eyes.

Thorn stared, transfixed.

Then, before he could guess her intentions, she flung herself outside, slamming the door shut behind her.

Thorn shot to his feet, ripped the door open and ran outside. He turned left, thinking she'd go for the motorcycle under the lean-to.

Just as he rounded the corner of the house, he realized his mistake.

Little Joe whinnied, then galloped by with the woman on him.

Thorn tore out after them, catching up before Little Joe could get up to speed.

He grabbed the woman around the waist and yanked her out of the saddle, the force of her weight sending them both to the ground.

The wind knocked out of him, Thorn held on to his prize, refusing to let go, a dozen questions spinning through his mind. Who was she? What was she doing on the Raging Bull? And why did her soft curves feel so good against his body?

Chapter Two

When Sophia landed on the man, the fall forced the air from her lungs. She lay there for a moment, gathering her wits and her breath. Then she fought to free herself of the steel vise clinched around her waist. "Let go of me." She scratched and clawed at his arm.

"No way," the deep voice said into her ear, his breath stirring the hairs at the back of her neck. "You almost killed me twice and tried to steal my horse."

She jabbed her elbow into his gut and jerked to the side.

The man grunted and refused to loosen his grip.

Lightning flickered across the sky and a crash of thunder sounded so close, Sophia stopped fighting for a second.

The horse, standing a few feet away, reared and took off, probably racing for the barn as the sky lit again, this time with a thousand fingers of lightning.

Wind whipped Sophia's hair into her eyes, and the first drops of rain peppered her skin.

The cowboy gripped her wrist and rolled her off him onto her stomach.

He came down on top of her, straddling her hips, his pressing into the small of her back. "I'll let you up if you promise to behave."

She snorted and spit to the side. "And I should trust you?"

He chuckled. "You don't have much of a choice."

Sophia squirmed beneath him, trying to free her wrist from his ironlike grasp. "Let go. I'll leave and you will never see me again."

Thunder boomed so loud it shook the ground.

"Sorry, sweetheart, you're not going anywhere in this storm."

As if to emphasize her captor's point, the water droplets grew thicker, the wind blasting them against her skin.

The dry dust kicked up, stinging her eyes and choking her breath. "Okay." She coughed. "I'll behave."

The man's weight left her body and he jerked her to her feet.

As soon as she stood, the storm unleashed its full power in a deluge so thick she couldn't see her hand in front of her face.

"Get in the cabin!" her captor yelled over the roar.

Water streamed down her face, blinding her.

A shove from behind sent her stumbling toward the open door. Her heart hammered against her ribs; fear of the storm nothing compared to fear of being trapped with this strong, dangerous stranger inside the small confines of the cabin.

He stepped around her and dragged her along behind him.

Sophia planted her heels in the mud and jerked hard.

The rain allowed her to slip free of his grip, but she hadn't accounted for how easily. She teetered backward and landed hard on the ground, mud sluicing over her clothes, soaking her all the way to her skin.

The cowboy stood in the doorway, his arms crossed over his chest. "If you're not struck by lightning, the flash floods will get you!" he yelled.

"I'll take my chances." Sophia scrambled to her feet, slipped, almost fell and steadied herself.

The cowboy's lips quirked, and he shook his head. "Stubborn woman."

Sophia's chin tipped upward. Before she could think of a scathing reply, the cowboy moved, leaving the protection of the cabin to scoop her up. He tossed her over his shoulder like a sack of onions and spun back toward the cabin.

The wind again knocked out of her, Sophia bounced along with every one of his huge steps until they entered the cabin.

The brute of a man kicked the door shut behind him and set Sophia on her feet in the dark.

The temperature had plummeted with the rainfall, cooling her body. She shook, her teeth clattering against each other. "Don't try anything or I'll...I'll..." She strained her eyes to search the room for a weapon, the darkness hampering her efforts and only flashes of lightning giving limited relief.

Finally she straightened, holding her head high, not that he could see her. She'd come too far to fall victim to yet another man who wanted to use her. Sophia dropped her tone to one she hoped sounded tough and menacing. "I'll kill you." Too bad a shiver shook her as she said the words, making them sound weak and quivery.

"Sweetheart, I have no intention of 'trying' anything with you. You look like a drowned rat and you're covered in mud. You're about as appealing as a pig. Less so. I could at least eat a pig." He shuffled around the cabin, bumping into things.

Sophia stood close to the door, debating how to make her escape. The bellow of thunder and the rain pounding the roof intensified, making her think again.

Something rattled to her left, then a scraping sound

rasped in the darkness and a match flared. The cowboy held it up and stared at the potbellied stove. "Here, make yourself useful." He handed her a box of matches. "Light one."

She took the box from him as the match he held flickered out. Hands shaking, she removed a match from the box and scraped it on the side. The blaze from the match circled her and the cowboy in an intimate glow.

He grabbed a candle from the mantel and held it to the match, then stuck it in a tin holder. "That will do for a start, but it's cold, we're wet and we'll need a fire or we'll have a really bad night of it." He lifted the lid off a box beside the stove and grunted. "Nice." Several logs lay in the bottom, along with old newspapers. "Hank knows how to stock a cabin," he muttered as he lifted the logs out and stacked them in the stove.

Sophia's heart skipped several beats. "Hank?"

The man wadded up newspaper and jammed it beneath the logs before responding. "Yeah, you're trespassing on the Raging Bull Ranch. I take it you were the one to cut the fence?" He shot a narrowed glance behind him. "Illegal alien?"

She refused to be intimidated by his glare. "I am an American citizen."

"Even American citizens don't have the right to destroy other people's property or trespass. You can take it up with the law in the morning."

Could it be she'd found her way to Hank Derringer's land? Hope rose inside her. "I'd rather take it up with this man Hank."

The cowboy shrugged. "Suit yourself, lady. I don't care." He held out his hand. "I'll take those matches now."

She handed him the box and stood back.

He got the paper burning and the dry wood caught soon

after, crackling and popping. He left the door to the stove open, the blaze lighting the interior of the tiny cabin in a soft, cozy glow.

The heat didn't extend beyond a few feet from the stove.

Still leery about the cowboy's intentions, Sophia remained outside his reach, her arms clutched around her body, her teeth chattering.

The big man stood, holding his hands to the fire. "Sure is warm over here." He cast a glance at her and shook his head. "Good grief, woman, you're freezing. Get closer before you catch your death."

"I'm f-fine," she insisted, her gaze on the flames, mesmerized by the thought of warmth.

The cowboy unbuttoned his soaked shirt and peeled it off his shoulders.

Sophia gasped and backed even farther away until the backs of her knees ran into the side of the bed and she almost fell. "What are you doing?"

"Getting out of my wet clothes. I don't plan on freezing all night." He scooped her backpack off the floor and opened it. "Do you have any dry clothes in here?"

She darted forward and snatched at the backpack. "That's mine."

He held on to the strap, his eyes narrowing. "Seeing as we have to share this cabin for a night, I'd like to know you're not hiding a knife or another gun in here that you plan on using on me in my sleep." He peeled her fingers off the other strap and dumped the contents of the backpack on the closest of the twin beds.

Foil-wrapped tortillas, a can of *frijoles pinto* and two bottles of water fell out on the bed. Enough food for two people for a single day. Beside them, a flashlight, fifty dollars of American money and one extra T-shirt was all she had to her name.

"Not much to go cross-country on."

"I was backpacking in the canyon. I didn't plan on staying," she lied.

He dug in one of the side pockets of the backpack and brought out the wire cutters. "Something you carry on hikes?"

She shrugged. "A girl never knows what tools she'll need."

"Anyone ever tell you it's not safe to travel alone in this area? Especially if you're a woman."

Sophia swallowed hard on the lump forming in her throat. She hadn't planned on traveling alone. Hector was to guide and protect her until she found Hank Derringer. Now Hector lay dead back in the canyon. With no one to help her, she had to rely on herself. She lifted her chin. "I don't need a man to protect me." Especially one who wanted to control her and keep her locked away from the world.

"Glad to know that. I didn't plan on signing up for the job." He lifted the blanket she'd tossed on the bed earlier. "Since you have a dry T-shirt, I'll use the blanket until my jeans dry." He nodded toward the bed and the pile of supplies. "Get out of your wet clothes. Getting sick will do you no good." He reached for the button on his jeans.

Sophia's eyes widened and her breath caught in her throat. "What are you doing?"

He shook his head and spoke slowly, as if to a dense child. "I told you, I'm getting out of my wet clothes. You can watch…or not." He flicked the button open and ran the zipper down in one fluid movement.

Sophia gasped and spun away from him. "I don't even know you."

"It's not like I'm going to make love to you. I prefer my women willing, dry and preferably not covered in mud."

"All the more reason to remain in my wet clothing."

"Suit yourself." He tossed the jeans over a chair beside her. "If it'll help, I'll turn my back while you strip out of those muddy things. I might even be convinced to take them out in the rain and rinse them for you so that you'll have something semiclean to wear in the morning."

She did feel gritty and cold. The dirt she could handle, but the cold couldn't be good for her baby. "Fine." She turned toward him, happy to note he'd wrapped his naked body in the blanket. "Turn around."

She'd been raised in Monterrey by her Mexican father and her American mother, but the proprieties of life in Mexico demanded she didn't strip naked in front of a stranger.

Granted, proprieties had gone by the wayside when she'd chosen to move in with Antonio, despite her parents' objections. They'd begged her to wait until she had the ring on her finger before committing to such a drastic move. But Antonio had been eager to have her to himself, and Sophia had been young and stupid in love.

"Look, I'll turn my back," the man said. "But you have to promise not to stab me in it while I do."

Sophia snorted. "I don't have a knife, and you took my gun."

Thorn kept his back to her, watching her movements through his peripheral vision and the movement of her shadow.

She eased along the wall toward the stove, wary of him and as skittish as a wild cat. If she didn't get out of the muddy clothes, they wouldn't dry by morning and she'd possibly get sick or suffer hypothermia from being cold all night.

Thorn didn't relish the idea of hauling a sick woman

back to the ranch. Especially if they were going to have to ride double on the motorcycle she'd hidden beneath the lean-to.

"Since we'll be sharing this cabin until the storm abates, it might help to know your name. I'm Thorn Drennan."

She didn't answer for a long time.

When he turned to see if she'd somehow slipped by him and left, his chest tightened.

The woman had shed her wet, dirty clothing and was slipping the dry T-shirt over her head and down her body.

Silhouetted against the fireplace, her curves were all woman and deliciously alluring.

A shock of desire ripped through him, and he closed his eyes to the image.

He hadn't felt anything for another woman since Kayla had died two years ago. Trapped in a cabin with a stranger, he wasn't prepared for the heat burning through his veins.

The woman turned toward him, her eyes narrowing. "You said you'd keep your back turned," she whispered accusingly.

"You didn't answer. I thought you might have bolted for the door."

"As you said, I'd be foolish to make a run for it in this storm."

He nodded. "You didn't answer my question."

She shrugged. "My name is not important. But you can call me…Sophia." The woman hesitated over the name, as if she wasn't used to giving it or using it.

Thorn didn't believe that it was her real name. But then, why would she keep her name from him unless she had something to hide?

Already uncomfortable with the situation, and not sure she wouldn't stab him in the back, Thorn carried her gun and his rifle to the door and laid them within reach.

"I'll take those clothes," he said.

Sophia gathered her dirty jeans and shirt and handed them to Thorn. Their fingers brushed, causing a jolt of electricity to shoot up his arm.

She must have felt it, too, because her eyes widened and her lips opened in a soft gasp.

Thorn brushed his reaction aside, blaming it on super-charged air from the lightning storm. He flung the door open, welcoming the cold rain that blew in with the fury of the storm.

With the blanket tied around his waist, he figured he'd get soaked no matter what. He held Sophia's clothes under the eaves, letting the rush of rainwater pour over the garments. When they were sufficiently free of mud, he wrung them out and closed the door.

Sophia moved another chair by the stove and hung her jeans across the back, then laid her shirt on the wooden seat. When done, she held her hands to the flames, her face pale, her jaw tight and determined.

Thorn scooped the gun she'd used to shoot at him off the floor and tucked it into the folds of the blanket around his waist. He leaned his rifle against the wall beside one of the two beds.

Sophia's gaze followed his movements, her brows knitted and her arms wrapped tightly around her middle.

Thorn liked that he made her nervous. She might be less tempted to take another stab at killing him if she was intimidated.

"Are you going to take me to the police in the morning?" she asked.

"I haven't decided." He crossed his arms over his chest, his brows raised. "Are you going to convince me not to?"

Sophia shrugged. "You have made up your mind already. Why bother trying?"

His eyes narrowed. "If you really are an American citizen, where are you from?"

She glanced to the far corner.

Thorn could almost see the cogs turning in her brain.

Finally she faced him, her brows raised. "San Antonio. *Sí,* I am from San Antonio."

"Vacationing in Big Bend, huh?" He raised a hand to his chin and stared down his nose at her. "I'm familiar with San Antonio. What section of town?"

Her eyes flared, then closed. She turned her back to him. "The north side."

"Ah, you must prefer shopping at Ingram Park Mall since it's closest to you, right?"

Her shoulders were stiff, and she remained with her back to him. "Right. Ingram."

Thorn's teeth ground together. If she really lived on the north side of San Antonio, the closest mall was not Ingram. She didn't know San Antonio any more than she knew where she was at the moment.

She dragged in a deep breath, her shoulders rising and falling with it. "What now?"

Thorn opened his mouth to call her out on her lie, but stopped when he noticed the dark shadows beneath her eyes and what appeared to be the yellowing remnants of a bruise across her cheek. He'd get the truth out of her, but it could wait until they both got a little rest. "Now we sleep."

He unfolded the second bed's mattress and stretched across it, laying the pistol beside him and lacing his hands behind his head. "You look done in. I suggest you get some shut-eye."

Her gaze swept over his naked chest, and lower. She hesitated, her tongue sweeping out across her lower lip.

The brief appearance of her pink tongue stirred a heated response low in Thorn's belly. Damn. What was wrong with him? He'd loved Kayla more than life itself. Why was his body reacting so strongly to this woman? Was it the vulnerability in her green eyes, or that she'd tried so determinedly to escape him that appealed to him on a deeper level? Whatever it was, he'd be glad when he handed her off to the authorities tomorrow. He closed his eyes to her image bathed in the glow of the fire in the stove. "I'm not going to sleep until you do, so move it."

"I'm not sleepy."

He opened his eyes. "Too bad."

Her glance darted from him to the bed beside his. "I have enough food for two people. Unfortunately, I don't have a way to open the cans. Hector—" Her lips clamped shut, and her face paled even more.

"Hector?" Thorn's eyes narrowed. He was up off the bed in a second. "You were traveling with someone else." He closed the distance between the two of them. "Weren't you?" Thorn gripped her shoulders, his fingers digging into her shirt.

Sophia, eyes wide as saucers, shook her head back and forth, tears spilling from the corners. "N-no. I was alone." She cowered, her eyes squinting, ducking her head as if expecting a blow.

"You're lying." He shook her. "Where is he?"

She gulped, the muscles in her throat working convulsively. "I don't know what you're talking about."

With her body close to his, her arms warm beneath his fingers, heat surged, followed by anger. "Damn it, woman, I'm tired of playing twenty questions. Spit it out. Where is this Hector? Do I have to stay awake all night in case he comes in and tries to kill me, too?"

"No!" Sobs shook her slight frame and her head tipped forward, her damp hair falling over her face. *"Madre de Dios."* She crossed herself. "He is dead."

The words came out in a whisper. Thorn thought he'd heard it wrong. He bent closer. "What did you say?"

A sob ripped from her throat and her head fell back, tears running like raindrops down her cheeks. "He's dead. They shot him. He tried to help me, and now he's dead! And it's my fault."

Chapter Three

Sophia swallowed hard, realizing her mistake as soon as the words left her mouth.

"Who shot him?" Thorn shook her. Not hard enough to hurt her, but enough to wrench another sob from her throat.

She looked away, the memory of Hector lying in a pool of his own blood far too fresh to erase. "I don't know." She choked back another sob, reminding herself that she couldn't cry forever. After all the time she'd spent as a captive in the compound, she'd learned one thing: crying didn't solve anything. What would it hurt to tell this man a few details? "Someone in a helicopter fired a machine gun at Hector."

His brows rose into the lock of hair drooping over his forehead. "A machine gun?"

Sophia nodded.

"Where is Hector now?" Thorn demanded.

"We were in the canyon. Hector had topped the ridge when the helicopter flew in. I h-hid beneath an over-hang." She looked at him through her tears. "I should have helped."

"Against a helicopter?" Thorn's lips pressed together. "Not much you could do on your own unless you had a rocket launcher." He tipped his head to the side. "Question is, why did a helicopter fire on you and your friend

Hector if you were only out hiking in Big Bend country?" Thorn's eyes narrowed. "Now would be a good time to tell me the truth." He dropped his hold and crossed his arms. He waited a few seconds. "Neither one of us is going any-where until you do."

She glanced toward the door. Thunder rumbled, rattling the doorknob. "I told you, we were hiking."

His lips thinned, and he shook his head. "I'm not buy-ing it. There's a motorcycle in the lean-to that wasn't there a day ago. I'm betting you rode in on it."

She stared up at him, her mouth working, but nothing came out.

"Which brings me back to my original theory. You're an illegal alien."

"I'm not. My mother *is* American and, though I was born in Mexico, I have dual citizenship."

He held out his hand. "Then you won't mind showing me your passport."

She stared at his hand, her throat muscles working at swallowing the lump lodged in her windpipe. "I don't have it on me."

"Thought so. No documents, riding a bike across the desert near the border, helicopter in pursuit." He snorted. "You are definitely an illegal and possibly dangerous."

"Think what you will." She tossed back her long light brown hair. "Tomorrow I'll be away from here, and you won't have to worry about me."

"I wouldn't count on that."

She frowned. "Count on what?"

"That you'll be gone, or that I wouldn't worry about you. I've kinda taken a liking to you. Must have been the fall." He raised his hand to the back of his head.

"I'm sorry to say I have not taken a liking to you, *señor,*" she said, tipping her chin upward.

"Really?" Thorn leaned close, his eyes narrowing even more. He stared at her long enough to make her squirm.

Then he tilted his head back and laughed out loud. "You are entirely too naive and predictable, Sophia."

She harrumphed, clasping her arms around her body. "I'm happy you find me amusing."

Lightning flashed, sending shards of light through cracks in the boarded windows, followed by a deafening clap of thunder.

Sophia jumped, bumping into Thorn's naked chest. She raised a hand to steady herself and encountered smooth, hard muscles. Heat suffused her entire body. She might not like the man, but she couldn't help admiring his physique. She told herself it was nothing more than appreciation for a fine form.

Her belly rumbled loudly, reminding her that she needed to eat or risk dry heaves. And preparing food would allow her to put distance between herself and Thorn. She nodded toward the food on the bed. "I'm hungry."

"So you said." He reached out.

Sophia flinched, raising her hand to block his as she ducked.

Thorn's frown deepened. "Did you think I'd hit you?"

Sophia straightened, her body tense. "You wouldn't be the first man."

He continued to reach past her. Plucking a metal object from a shelf on the wall, he held it up. "I was reaching for the can opener." Thorn tossed the device on the bed and turned to grip her arms. "For the record, I don't hit women."

She planted her feet wide, her eyes narrowing to slits. "No? But you grab them and hold them hostage."

"Damn it, woman. For your own good."

"And how is being a captive good?" She snorted.

"You're like most men, thinking a woman must be controlled, that she doesn't have a brain to think for herself."

"You're putting words in my mouth." His hands fell to his sides. "Given that you could have died with your friend Hector and might have been caught in a flash flood or struck by lightning, I think I can prove my case for keeping you here."

She shrugged and ducked around him. "I don't care what you prove." Sophia grabbed the can opener and set it against the lid on the can of beans. After several attempts, she gave up, her stomach twisting, the hollow feeling making her nauseous.

"Good grief, woman." Thorn took the can and opener out of her hands. "It's not rocket science."

"No? Then you do it." She backed away from him, the nausea increasing until heat radiated through her body and she knew she couldn't hold back any longer. Sophia ran for the door, her footsteps drowned out by the pounding of rain on the tin roof. Her hand closed around the knob as the first wave hit.

Before she could yank the door open, a hand closed over hers. "Going somewhere, sweetheart?" Thorn asked, staring down at her, his brows drawn together in a fierce frown. "I thought we'd settled all this running away stuff, at least until after the storm."

She clawed at his hand. "Please." Sophia swallowed again and again, trying to force the bile back. "I have to get out."

He moved to stand in front of her, his arms locked over his chest like a barroom bouncer. "No."

"So be it." She heaved. What remained of the food she'd eaten the night before rose like a projectile up her throat. She bent in time to miss Thorn's face, but anointed his bare feet.

The heaving continued until Sophia's body shook so badly she fell to her knees on the hard wooden floor.

She cowered, waiting for Thorn to curse her and call her stupid for barfing on his feet. Sophia braced her body for the beating that was sure to follow.

The harsh words and beatings never came.

When the wave of sickness abated, she lay down on the floor, pressing her heated cheek to the cool wood.

Thorn crouched beside her, brushing her hair away from her face. "I'm sorry. Had I known you were sick—"

Thorn's voice washed over Sophia like a warm blanket. She lay with her eyes closed, one hand pressed to her mouth, the other to her belly, afraid to move and set off the nausea all over again. "I'll be okay. I just need to eat."

"You can't lie there on the floor." He touched her arm. "Let me help you to the bed."

"No." She brushed away his hand. "Leave me alone. It'll pass." After several minutes, her head quit spinning and she dared to open her eyes. "I'm sorry I threw up on you."

"I'll live." His frown had softened to an expression of concern. "Think you can move now?"

She nodded, lying there for a moment longer before attempting the simple task.

"I'm going to clean up this mess." Thorn moved about the cabin, the soft rustles giving away his location and negating the need for Sophia to look.

Before she could brace her hands on the floor and push herself to a sitting position, Thorn's strong fingers scooped beneath her legs and back, and he lifted her up in his arms in one smooth, easy motion.

Sophia closed her eyes, praying her stomach wouldn't churn and release again. "Please, put me down."

"I will." He crossed to the mattress he'd unfolded for

himself and laid her out on a blanket. "I found another blanket in a box."

With the back of her hand resting over her eyes, she breathed in and out several times, her mouth tasting so bad she feared she'd lose it again.

The snap of metal on metal made her glance across at Thorn.

With deft fingers, he had the can of beans open in a few quick twists of the can-opener key.

Sophia's lips tipped upward. "How is it you say…show-off."

"I never learned how to cook, so I had to get good at eating canned food or starve."

She smiled.

THORN'S HEART TUMBLED and came to a crashing stop.

Despite her pale face and slightly green complexion, her smile managed to light up the room, chasing away Thorn's natural distrust of the woman who'd done nothing but lie to him the entire time they'd been together. Something about her sad eyes and her inherent vulnerability called to his protective instincts. He still held the can, and his heart pounded against his ribs.

Sophia's smile faded. "You're staring at me."

He spun away, wondering what the hell had come over him. He rummaged in the wooden box where he'd found the blanket and emerged with a pot. He emptied the can of beans into the pot and set it on the potbellied stove. Then, using a stick from the box of wood, he stirred the embers inside the stove, making them glow brighter. Heat warmed his cheeks.

The bedsprings creaked behind him.

Sophia had pushed to a sitting position and was reaching for the foil-wrapped package on the other bed.

Thorn got to it before she did and unwrapped several soft tortillas. "Is this what you were going for?"

She nodded and peeled one off the top. Sitting with her legs pulled up beneath her, she nibbled on the corn tortilla, color slowly returning to her cheeks.

"How long has it been since you've eaten?" he asked.

She refused to meet his gaze. "I don't remember."

"And you were out for a hike on motorbikes." Thorn stared at her for a long time. "Still not talking?"

She finished the tortilla and nodded toward the stove. "You're burning the beans."

Thorn spun back to the stove and rescued the boiling beans. He scrounged up two tin plates and spoons from the storage box, held them under the eaves by the door to rinse them off and scooped beans onto each damp plate.

Sophia accepted the plate without complaint and dug her spoon into the fragrant beans, eating every bite.

Thorn sat back, his own plate forgotten. "How can you eat like that after being sick?"

She accepted another tortilla and sopped up the remaining juices from her plate. She finished the tortilla before answering. "I get sick if I don't eat."

"Are you anemic or something?"

"Something." Sophia set the plate on the floor, stretched out on the mattress and pulled the blanket over herself, closing her eyes.

"That's it?" Thorn asked.

"I'm working on, what did you call it? Shut-eye." Her eyes remained closed.

The fire burned down into glowing coals, heat from the stove filling the small space, making it cozy and comfortable despite the storm outside.

Thorn ate the beans on his plate, and then rinsed the pot and both plates and spoons in rainwater. Once he'd returned the eating utensils to the box, he cleared her back-pack off the remaining bed, gathered the handgun and rifle beside him and settled on his side, facing Sophia. In the fading light from the fire, he studied the stranger. Her Spanish accent led him to believe she'd spent the majority of her life south of the United States border, but her grasp of English made him want to believe her story that her mother was American.

Her dark blond hair and pale skin could mean either her mother was American, as she'd insisted, or she could be Mexican of Spanish decent.

Sophia's chest rose and fell in a deep, steady rhythm, her eyelids twitching as if her dreams were not all that pleasant.

What was she afraid of? Why wasn't she telling him the truth about her presence on the Raging Bull? Who had hit her to make her so skittish?

The more he reflected on Sophia and her possible reasons for being in the cabin, the more questions Thorn came up with. Finally, exhaustion pulled at his own eyelids, dragging them downward.

His final thought of the woman beside him was one that left him frowning into his dreams. She'd stirred in him a spark of awareness he hadn't felt since Kayla had died in his arms. And worse, he didn't understand the desire he felt inside to protect her from whatever she was running from.

Hiking in the mountains. *Not likely.*

With one hand on the rifle, the pistol tucked beneath him, he drifted into a fitful sleep, the storm outside raging well into the early hours of the morning. His dreams were filled with the horror of the shooting that had taken his wife and unborn child, the nightmare of holding Kayla in his arms as she bled out. He'd held her so long that the

EMTs had to remind him where he was and that he couldn't stay in the middle of the street. He had to let go and get up.

"Get up!" a voice said into his ear. A hand grabbed his arm and shook him.

At first Thorn thought it was the EMT telling him they had to load his wife's body. As he swam to the surface of consciousness, he remembered his wife had been dead for two years. The hand moved from his shoulder, and something tugged in his fingers.

Thorn sat up and grabbed the hand trying to pry the rifle from his fingers. "Let go, or I'll shoot you," he said, pointing the pistol at his attacker.

Sophia raised her hands and backed up a step. She wore the jeans and shirt she'd spread out earlier to dry, and her gaze flicked to the door of the cabin, her eyes wide and filled with terror. "Please, don't let them take me back."

Thorn frowned. "What are you talking about?"

"Someone is outside. It might be the men who shot Hector." Sophia tugged at his arm. "Get up. Hurry."

As the fog of sleep cleared, Thorn realized the rain had stopped and, with it, the lightning. But what he'd thought was thunder was the rumble of an engine, like that of a heavy-duty diesel truck.

He jammed his legs into his jeans and boots, grabbed his rifle and reached for the doorknob. Before he could open the door, it was flung wide, slamming against the wall.

A towering figure filled the frame, backlit by the headlights of a truck standing a few feet behind him, engine running. From his silhouette, he appeared to hold an assault rifle.

His heart racing, Thorn raised his weapon and aimed for the middle of the man's chest. "Not a step farther."

The man froze in the doorway.

A voice behind the man in the door called out, "Thorn? Is that you?"

Thorn stared past the man with the assault rifle, his hand steady on his own gun. "Hank?"

The older man pushed past his bodyguard and held up his hands. "You gonna put that rifle down or shoot me?"

Thorn lowered the weapon, ran a hand through his hair and stared out into the darkness. "What are you doing here at this hour?"

"Thought you might need rescuing. When your horse came back without you on it, I sent out a search party, figuring you got thrown or bushwhacked." His gaze swung to the woman cowering in the corner by the potbellied stove. "Ah, you have company."

"Sorry to get you and your men out in that weather. The storm scared my mount, and he took off without me." Thorn turned toward Sophia. "I took shelter in this cabin, only to discover a squatter beat me to it." He waved toward Sophia. "Hank, this is Sophia. Sophia, this is Hank Derringer, the owner of the property you're trespassing on."

Before Thorn's last word left his lips, Sophia flung herself at Hank.

Hank staggered backward, his arms going around Sophia to steady them both.

The bodyguard reached for Sophia's arm.

"It's okay," Hank said. "She's not hurting me. Sophia, this is Max. Max, Sophia. There. You've been properly introduced."

Sophia buried her face in Hank's shirt, silent sobs shaking her body. "It is a miracle," she whispered, then her body went limp and she would have fallen to the floor if Hank hadn't had his arms around her.

Thorn stood by, his hands aching to go to Sophia's rescue, but he forced himself to stand back.

Hank stared over the top of the unconscious woman's head. "What the devil is going on here?"

Chapter Four

Thorn shook his head. "It's like I said, she was here when I got here." He explained about the damaged fence, the tracks leading toward the cabin, Sophia's wild story about hiking in the canyon and her guide being gunned down by a helicopter.

The whole time he'd been talking, Sophia lay limp in Hank's arms.

"Here, let me get her." Finally Thorn could stand it no longer and stepped forward, gathered Sophia into his arms and carried her to the bed. He stretched her across the blanket and tucked the ends around her. Her face was very pale in the light from the truck slanting through the door frame.

"If someone shot her guide, it might not be safe for her to stay out here," Hank said. "They might come back to take care of witnesses. We should get her back to the ranch house as soon as possible."

"Agreed."

"Max," Hank called out. "Check the perimeter."

Max nodded wordlessly and ducked out of the beams of the headlights.

Hank unclipped a radio hanging on his belt. "I'll let my foreman and security team know we've found you and to head back to base."

Thorn lifted his still-damp shirt from the back of the chair and shoved his arms into the sleeves.

Hank keyed the button on his handheld radio. "Scott."

Scott Walden, Hank's foreman, responded immediately. "Walden here."

"Found him. Notify the team, and let them know to head back to base."

"Will do," the voice crackled along with static over the radio.

"And be on the lookout for gunmen," Hank warned.

"Run into trouble?" Scott asked.

"Not yet." Hank stared at the woman lying unconscious in the bed. "But we could." When he'd finished, Hank nodded his head toward Sophia. "You got her?"

Thorn nodded. "If you can get the truck door."

"Got it." Hank exited, hurrying toward the passenger side of the waiting truck.

Outside the cabin, the air had a damp, rain-washed scent that stirred up all the differing aromas from the vegetation surrounding them. The dark sky of early morning sported an array of stars like a blanket of diamonds on black velvet from horizon to horizon.

Hank held the back door to the four-door pickup open while Thorn settled Sophia across the leather seat and climbed in beside her. He rested her head on his lap and buckled the seat belt around her middle.

Hank took the wheel while Max climbed into the front passenger seat, his M4A1 carbine assault rifle across his lap, his gaze scanning the horizon on all sides.

As Hank pulled away from the cabin, Sophia stirred, her head pressing against Thorn's jean-clad thigh. "Where… What happened?" She blinked up at him. "Hank." She tried to sit up but the vehicle bounced at that moment, keeping her from rising.

Thorn looped his arm around her to keep her from tipping forward. "You're in Hank's truck, headed for his ranch."

"Madre de Dios." She made the sign of the cross over her chest.

"Now that you're awake, you can tell me why you threw yourself at my boss." Thorn's lips pressed into a tight line. Sophia had given him so little information, he felt he was missing a big part of her story that could cause potential danger to all those around him.

"I was told he could help me." She laid her hand over her eyes, a sigh escaping her lips. "He is my only hope."

Hank glanced at Thorn in the rearview mirror. "Only hope for what?"

Sophia attempted to sit up again, this time succeeding. "To protect me from the man who would take me back to Mexico and imprison me."

"Why would someone imprison you? Have you committed a crime?" Hank asked.

"Only the crime of stupidity," Sophia responded. "Of trusting someone who promised to love me."

"And that would be?" Thorn asked.

"My fiancé."

Max snorted. "Nice guy."

Thorn's fingers tightened into fists. "What kind of man would imprison his fiancée?"

Sophia's face was pale and grave in the light from the dash. "Mine."

A loud metal pop sounded against the side of the truck.

"Gunshot!" Thorn shouted, and pushed Sophia's head back into his lap. "Stay down."

Hank punched the accelerator, shooting the truck forward. He swerved to miss a dwarf mesquite tree, ran over a clump of prickly pear cactus and raced on across the dark terrain at breakneck speed.

Max flicked the safety off his rifle, hit the down button on the window and swiveled in his seat. "They're coming at us from both sides." He fired off a burst of rounds.

Thorn ducked his head and turned right and left. "Two motorcycles on the near left. Three on the right from what I can see."

Max swung around, rising to his knees on the seat to get a better shot out the window, and sent another burst of rounds into the darkness.

Thorn struggled with Sophia to keep her low while trying to swivel against the restraint of his seat belt.

The windshield behind him exploded, showering him and Sophia with splinters of glass. "Don't move!" he shouted to Sophia.

Thorn punched the release on his seat belt and rotated in his seat, bringing his weapon to his shoulder. With the barrel of the rifle, he cleared the jagged edges of the fractured glass out of the way and aimed out the window. Without the headlights from the truck, he had to let his vision adjust to the near inky blackness before he could see the gang of dirt bikers closing in on the truck. He lined up his sights the best he could with the truck bouncing over every dip, rock and clump of vegetation. With a cyclist caught in the crosshairs, he squeezed the trigger.

The dirt bike swerved and flipped, sending its rider over the handlebars.

One down, nineteen to go.

A bullet winged past his ear. The bodyguard cursed behind him.

"Max," Hank called out. "You hit?"

"No, but it was close," the man said, his voice strained. "Punch it, they're gaining on us."

Another bullet nicked the broken glass of the windshield and scraped Thorn's shoulder before lodging in the back of Max's seat.

Thorn hissed, biting down hard on his tongue to keep from saying anything. For a moment, his rifle wobbled and almost fell from its position. Forcing the burning pain of the wound to the back of his mind, he focused on his targets.

Hank hit the gas and the truck leaped forward, pushing past their attackers.

Thorn prayed they'd get to the ranch compound before the bikers made Swiss cheese out of the truck and bullets started penetrating the thick metal sides.

"They're after me," Sophia said.

"Why?" Thorn aimed and fired off another round. The biker he'd been aiming for swerved to avoid a cactus at the last minute, and the bullet missed him completely.

"My fiancé doesn't let go of what he considers his. He won't stop until he has me or I'm dead."

"Well, he'll have to go through us first." Thorn's jaw tightened and he fired again, hitting the biker nearing the back of the truck. The biker's arm jerked backward, and he spun off the back of the dirt bike, hitting the ground hard.

Each time Thorn pulled the trigger, the pain in his right shoulder ripped through his arm. Warm liquid spread across his shirt and dripped down his arm to his elbow.

Two pairs of twin headlights shone across the landscape, headed straight for them.

"Don't shoot at the trucks!" Hank yelled over his shoulder. "I think they're ours."

The cavalry arrived, bearing arms, plowing through the fleet of bikes, chasing them back.

Thorn held his rifle propped on the backseat, aimed out the shattered window in case the cyclists got close enough to be a danger. His blood hammered through his veins, pulsing through the open wound and sending shards of pain across his nerve endings, but he held steady and at the ready.

The assailants split up and scattered, dropping off to the east and west as the trucks closed ranks with the one Hank drove. Bullets continued to fly until the last motorcycle disappeared into the darkness.

Thorn settled back in the seat and brushed glass out of Sophia's silky hair.

She sat up and glanced behind them. "They're gone?"

"For now," Hank said.

Sophia glanced down at her arm, her eyes widening. "Blood," she whispered, checking her own skin for lesions. When she found none, she leaned away from Thorn, her gaze skimming over his body until it zeroed in on his shoulder. "You're bleeding." She ripped the hem of her T-shirt and wadded it up, pressing it to Thorn's shoulder.

"I'm fine. It just nicked me." Even as he played down the wound, he accepted the wad of fabric, covering it with his big hand. "Nothing major."

"I'll have Scott check it out." Hank shot a glance at Thorn in the rearview mirror. "We might want to take you into the clinic in Wild Oak Canyon and have them look it over, as well. Make sure the bullet didn't lodge inside the flesh."

"Walden can handle it," Thorn insisted.

"He's better with animals," Hank parried.

Thorn settled his weapon in his lap and winced. "What's a human but a glorified ape? Walden can do it. Besides, the bullet just nicked me." If he went to the hospital, Sophia would be exposed. He didn't want to leave her, not after killers had attacked them, possibly trying to get to her, like she'd said. He didn't know her and was under no obligation to protect her, but, somehow, he couldn't stop himself.

STILL SHAKING FROM the torturous ride and the anticipation of a bullet taking out one of the men trying to help her, Sophia reined in her fear and focused on the man bleeding on the seat beside her. She recognized the posturing of a male used to being shot at and shook her head. She'd witnessed too many of Antonio's men who remained doggedly at his side as they bled to death from rival gunshot wounds.

Hank's gunman had been harmed because of her, and Sophia felt responsible. He could have died. Despite the way he'd strong-armed her at the beginning, he'd done everything in his power to protect her since. She couldn't let Thorn die because of her.

Having lived in *la Fuerte del Diablo,* the desert hideout of *la Familia Diablos,* for over a year, she'd fished bullets out of open wounds, cleaned and dressed gashes caused by knife stabbings and even cauterized bleeders with a hot poker to save the lives of Antonio's servants and men. Some of the wounds Antonio had inflicted himself.

Sophia's back teeth ground together. Her fiancé had been anything but the charming, benevolent man he'd led her to believe he was during their brief courtship in Monterrey.

In front of her family, he'd been the perfect gentleman, catering to her every need, respectful of her, her family and her friends.

Once he had convinced her to leave her parents and join him at his home, he'd whisked her to the hidden desert compound and kept her prisoner. When she'd asked to leave, he'd flown into a rage and beaten her again and again until he finally wore himself out.

She'd barely survived that first incident and vowed to

never let it happen again. José, his second in command, had the audacity to tell her she was lucky he'd only broken her nose and ribs.

From that point on, she'd walked and spoken quietly, careful not to ignite the tempest of his full wrath. Her desire to remain quietly in the background had backfired. The more subdued she acted, the angrier Antonio became. Even the most insignificant of slights set him off.

Making love had settled into something more akin to rape.

Soon her own life seemed unimportant, but when Sophia discovered she was pregnant, she knew a baby wouldn't survive the hell she'd lived in for the past year.

That's when she'd vowed to escape or die, and take her baby with her rather than subject it to the terror that was its father.

An oasis of lights glowed in the distance.

"Is that your home?" Sophia leaned forward, her pulse quickening.

"That's it," Hank replied. "You'll be okay once we get you inside the perimeter of the security system."

A safe harbor sounded as near to heaven as she'd dreamed for months. Tears welled in her eyes. But she knew it wouldn't last long. Antonio would be after her, and he wouldn't stop until he had her back. She sat against the leather seats of the pickup, concerned for her rescuers and unwilling to see another wounded on her behalf. "Maybe you should leave me here."

Thorn's hand clasped her arm. "What are you talking about?"

"Those men shooting at us came for me." Sophia glanced behind them as if the bikers would appear again. "They'll be back to collect me."

Thorn's fingers tightened on her arm. "You're not going anywhere."

"You've already been shot because of me. No telling how many others have been injured. I couldn't live with myself if someone else died. My life is not worth that much. Stop the truck." She leaned forward, placing her hand on the back of Hank's seat. "Let me out."

Hank shook his head, his lips pressed into a tight line. "I'm not turning you over to those killers."

Sophia squared her shoulders. "Better one than many deaths."

"No one's dying on my watch," Thorn gritted out. "We'll get to the bottom of this. Until we do, you'll be safe in Hank's home."

Sophia sat back in her seat, biting her lip. As soon as she could, she'd leave the Raging Bull Ranch. Despite Anna's reassurances that Hank could help her, Sophia refused to let these good people die protecting her.

As they neared the large ranch house and its surrounding fences, Sophia's heart fluttered. The lights looked welcoming, comforting, not harsh and dangerous like those located around the outskirts of *la Fuerte del Diablo* in Mexico.

The closer they moved, the faster her pulse pounded in her veins, like racing for the finish line with an overpowering urge to shout, "I've won! I've won!"

For a long moment Sophia closed her eyes, her hand going to her still-flat belly. *It's going to be okay. I swear to you, baby, we're going to be okay.*

A hand on her arm made her open her eyes, and she stared up into the clear gaze of the man who'd saved her life.

"Are you feeling ill again?" Thorn asked.

She smiled and shook her head. "No. Just glad to be

safe for the moment." As soon as she got her bearings, she'd strike out on her own and find a safe place to hide. Maybe in Arkansas or Iowa. Someplace Antonio would never think to look for her. She'd change her name and start over.

A man carrying an assault weapon swung open a gate as they neared.

Hank barreled through and came to a halt in front of a huge barn. Two more men, dressed completely in black, surrounded the truck, also carrying assault weapons.

Sophia frowned, her confidence shaken at the militaristic stance of the gunmen. "Are you with the American military?" she asked.

Hank snorted. "No. I've made a few enemies through my business dealings that have cost me dearly." Hank's expression in the rearview mirror hardened. "These men help me keep that from happening again." The older man climbed down.

Thorn helped Sophia unbuckle her belt, brushing aside the fractured glass. He leaned close and spoke softly. "From what I've heard and read, Hank lost his family to intruders."

Sophia gasped and crossed herself. *"Madre de Dios."*

As Thorn helped her from the truck, Sophia's gaze followed the man Anna had asked her to contact, her hand going to her belly. How would she feel about losing her child to killers? The infant had yet to make its appearance, yet she already had an unbreakable bond with the tiny being growing inside her.

The other two trucks pulled up beside Hank's, and men piled out and gathered around their leader.

Sophia slipped toward the barn, hiding in the shadows. The fewer people who knew she was here, the better.

While Hank briefed them on what had happened, Thorn

stood back from the group, holding his arm. He glanced around as if searching for someone. When he spotted her, he closed the distance between them. "Why are you hiding?"

She shrugged, her heart squeezing in her chest at the amount of blood staining his shirt. "We should get you inside and treat your wound."

Thorn frowned. "I'm fine."

She shook her head. "Stubborn man." She reached out from the shadows and snagged Max's sleeve, dragging him back into the darkness with her. "Which man is Scott Walden?"

Max nodded toward a man standing close to Hank. "I'll get him." The bodyguard stepped toward the foreman and spoke to him quietly.

Scott Walden broke away from Hank and hurried toward Thorn. "Let's see to that wound." He hooked Thorn's arm and marched him toward the house.

Sophia hung back, lurking in the shadows of the barn, debating whether or not now was a good time to make her move to leave these people. Before she could make a move, Thorn dug his heels into the ground and came to a halt. "Not without her." He shot a glance back at her.

Why did the man have to be so stubborn? Sophia sighed. She'd have to follow, but she didn't want the other men to see her. The more people who knew she was there, the harder it would be to keep her presence low-key.

Thorn stepped back into the darkness beside her. "Why are you hiding?" he asked again.

"The fewer people who see me, the better."

Thorn waved Max and Scott toward him. They formed a force field of strength around her, shielding her from the lights shining overhead from the corners of the barn and house.

Once through a side door, Max disappeared back outside, leaving her with the foreman and Thorn.

Sophia wanted to make sure the man got proper medical care for the gunshot wound. It was the least she could do before she left. The man had saved her life.

Hank entered the house behind them. "I'll get on the horn with the local authorities. Let them get out there and clean up any bodies that might be lying around."

Thorn's lips pressed together. "You might want to put a bug in the Customs and Border Protection's ear. They might be more help than the local sheriff's department."

Sophia stopped in the middle of a hallway, her eyes widening, her pulse pounding. "Are you going to turn me over to them?"

Clutching his bleeding arm, Thorn stopped as well and gave her a half smile. "It's up to Hank. You're a trespasser on his property."

Hank patted her arm. "No, I won't turn you in to the authorities." His mouth turned down on the corners. "But I'll need to know everything. No lies, no holding anything back."

Sophia sucked in a deep breath and let it out slowly. "I'll tell you the truth if you promise not to tell the authorities I'm here." She'd tell him almost everything, but the most important piece of information she wouldn't tell anyone until she was safely hidden away in a new life as far away from *la Fuerte del Diablo* and Antonio as she could get.

"My men know you're here, and the men who chased us may have figured it out, as well."

Sophia twisted the torn hem of her shirt. "I won't go back."

"We won't let them take you back." Hank touched her arm. "You can trust me."

Scott cleared his throat. "We need to patch up Thorn

before we do anything. He's bleeding like a stuck pig, and I'm sure the housekeeper won't be happy about cleaning up the mess in the morning."

Hank nodded. "You're right. Let's get him into the kitchen. The first-aid kit is in the pantry."

Scott led the way, followed by Thorn and Sophia.

As they entered the kitchen, a younger man came hurrying down the hallway toward them. "Hank, got the sheriff's deputy on the phone wantin' to know what the hell's going on out here. Says he's on his way out."

Sophia's heart clenched, the blood leaving her head, her vision blurring.

"Brandon, get her to the basement," Hank said. "I'll handle the local law."

"You're not going to turn me over?" Sophia asked.

"Not yet," Hank promised. "I want to get to the bottom of this."

"Scott, get the first-aid kit." Thorn slipped his uninjured arm around Sophia. "I'm going with Sophia. We can do what needs to be done in the bunker."

Chapter Five

Hank guided them through the maze of secret doors and security locks to the hidden facility below his house with thick concrete walls and video cameras everywhere.

Thorn had been down there only twice since he'd started working for Hank. The place was built like a bomb shelter or fortress, capable of withstanding the impact of high explosives. It also had its own generators and satellite receivers should the electricity be cut off.

Hank had the money; he could afford every modern convenience and protective gadget a man could want, and his computer genius, Brandon, was tapped, or hacked, into just about every government database there was.

Having been the sheriff of Wild Oak Canyon, Thorn wasn't keen on the idea that Hank was breaking the law to get information. But from what he'd seen of Hank's operation, the man was really out for truth and justice, using whatever means he could to get there.

"Can you get out of that shirt while I wash up?" Scott asked.

"Sure." Thorn fumbled with the buttons down the front of his shirt.

Sophia stepped in front of him and brushed his fingers aside, making quick work of the buttons all the way down to where the shirt disappeared into his trousers.

Every time her knuckles brushed against his skin, an electric current zinged through him, setting his pulse pounding faster.

She tugged the shirt out of his waistband and shoved it over his good shoulder, then peeled it off his wounded shoulder. Some of the blood had dried, gluing the shirt to his skin.

Sophia's brows wrinkled, and she glanced up into his eyes with her own deep green ones. "This might hurt a little," she warned, capturing her teeth between her full, sensuous lower lip.

Thorn found himself wanting to bite her lip. Her fingers pressed against his skin, easing the fabric free of the caked-on blood. She stood so close that her breast brushed against his chest, the warmth of her body radiating through him.

His breath hitched in his throat and he fought to keep from grabbing her around the waist and crushing her against him, shocked as the urge washed over him.

He reached out, gripped her arms and set her away from him.

"But I'm not finished," she protested.

"Yes—you—are," he said through gritted teeth, and ripped the shirt from his shoulder, wincing at the pain, but glad for it because it helped take his mind off the way Sophia's hair slipped across her face, and the scent of her skin wafting over him.

Sophia glared at him. "You've started it bleeding again."

"I don't need you to fix it. Scott's the horse doctor."

"I've had experience treating wounds."

"Really?" Thorn shot back. "Where? What hospital?"

She glanced away, a shadow darkening her green eyes. "Not at a hospital. At *la Fuerte del Diablo,* where I was kept prisoner."

Thorn's chest tightened and he regretted his sharpness, wondering what Sophia had endured at the hands of her abusive fiancé.

Brandon entered the room, carrying a towel and a bottle of water. "Thought you could use this."

"Brandon, with all the gizmos you have down here, do you have a police scanner that picks up out here?" Thorn asked.

The younger man grinned. "As a matter of fact, I do."

"See if you can pick up anything about what's going on."

"All I've gotten is that the sheriff's department is sending a couple of units out this way to investigate gunshots fired." Brandon half turned toward the door. "I'll get back on it, if you think it's important."

"Do it. I'd like to know how the incident is being handled and what's being reported back."

"On it." Brandon left the room.

While Scott cleaned and examined his wound, Thorn studied the woman standing in the corner, gazing down at her fingers as she twisted the edge of her tattered T-shirt. She stood as far away from him as she could get without leaving altogether.

A twinge of guilt hit Thorn's gut at his shortness with her. He figured better short than act on impulses he'd thought long buried with his dead wife.

His instinctive reaction to her was a reminder of his need to keep his distance. Thorn pulled his thoughts together and winced as Scott applied a good dose of alcohol to the gash in his arm. "Sophia, do you have family here in the States?"

She glanced up, her eyes widening. "No."

"In Mexico?"

Her gaze lingered on him, and she chewed on that confounded lower lip again.

Damn.

Thorn dragged his attention back to her green eyes.

After a moment's hesitation, she answered, "In Monterrey."

"Why didn't you go back to them?"

She shook her head. "I had to get as far away from my fiancé as possible. I need to disappear completely to keep him from finding me." Her voice caught on the hint of a sob. "I'm not safe in Mexico."

She had family in Monterrey. Thorn understood how unstable the government was and how dangerous it could be if a cartel was after you.

"How will you get by here in the States without family? Do you have your own money?"

She shook her head. "No. I have a little, not much. Everything I own is in that backpack. I wasn't able to bring anything with me when I escaped."

Which meant she had a total of fifty dollars, and now, not even a change of clothes to start a new life in the States. Thorn tried to tell himself that it wasn't his problem. Sophia was not his responsibility.

Her gaze captured his, her eyes narrowing as if she could read his thoughts. "I don't need your help."

Her words stung as much as the antibiotic ointment Scott slathered onto Thorn's open wound. He winced and shot back, "I wasn't offering."

"Good." The sharp comeback was watered down by the shiver that shook her body. The hollows beneath her eyes made her appear tired, waiflike, in need of someone to protect her.

Brandon came back with a handheld scanner.

"What are they saying?"

"So far there've been a few communications warning the deputies to be ready for possible gunfire and to be on the lookout for a man and a woman, possible illegal aliens wanted for murder on the other side of the border."

Thorn's gaze shot to Sophia.

She shook her head. "That's not me. I've never killed a man in my life."

"And the man who helped you escape?" Thorn asked.

"I can't vouch for his record. All I know is that I owe him my life. He got me away from my fiancé and across the border into the States." Her head dipped as silent tears slid down her cheeks. "In my heart, he died a saint."

"Thanks, Brandon." After the foreman applied a wad of gauze and adhesive tape to his arm, Thorn stood. "I'm going up. I want to be topside when the sheriff gets here."

Sophia's eyes widened. "What about me?"

"Stay here until we give you the all clear." Thorn glanced from Brandon to Scott.

They nodded.

"We'll keep an eye on her." Scott started to pull his shirt off his back. "You might want a shirt."

"Thanks." He held up a hand, stopping the guy. "I'll get one from my room upstairs." The foreman was wiry thin. The shirt wouldn't go over his arms, much less his shoulders. Thorn cast a last glance at Sophia. "When the sheriff leaves, we're gonna have us a talk."

She nodded.

Thorn left, climbing the stairs out of the bunker and closing the hidden door behind him softly.

Voices sounded in the front foyer.

He hurried to the room Hank had assigned him and yanked a shirt on over the bandage, thankful the blood hadn't dripped onto his dirty jeans. Still buttoning the front, he strode down the hallway toward the voices.

Hank stood in the middle of the foyer with Max and three deputies dressed in the uniform of the local sheriff's department.

A twinge of regret rippled across Thorn. He'd worn just such a uniform not long ago and had been sworn in as the sheriff to protect the people of the county from crime.

Hell, he hadn't been able to protect his own family from a shooting that had taken the lives of his wife and unborn daughter. What made him think he could help protect a stranger?

"Drennan, good to see you." Deputy Sanders held out his hand and shook Thorn's as he came to a halt beside Hank.

"Sanders, how's the family?"

The deputy grinned. "Jordan turned two a week ago, and Brianna will be five next month. Can't believe they're that old already. Seems like yesterday Jessica and Kayla were pregnant—" The other man stopped in midsentence, his smile dying. "Sorry."

Thorn's chest tightened, and he glanced away for a moment before returning his attention to Sanders. "What brings you out here?"

"As we were tellin' Mr. Derringer, we had a report of gunfire out this way."

"Really?" Thorn asked. "Who called it in?"

"It came in on a blocked cell-phone ID. Anonymous." Sanders's lips twisted. "Since there was nothin' else goin' on, we decided to investigate. On the way out here, we got a report from the CBP that a man and woman wanted for murder had slipped across the border from Mexico."

"Who'd they kill?" Thorn asked.

"Two undercover DEA agents."

"Did they give you a name or description of them?" Thorn asked.

Sanders glanced at his notepad. "Antonio Martinez, five feet eleven inches tall, dark hair, dark eyes, slim and athletic. Elena Carranza, five feet four inches tall, dark blond hair, green eyes."

Thorn's gut twisted. "Murder?"

"That's what the CBP is reporting."

Hank tipped his head. "What about a photo?"

"They're working on it. We're supposed to get a photo or composite back at the station within the next couple of hours."

"I'd like to see that when you do." Hank glanced at Thorn. "My men and I will keep an eye out for them."

"In the meantime, we'll check into the incident you had earlier, although we won't be able to do much until daylight. At least we can check for bodies or any injured left behind. The CBP has representatives on their way, should be here momentarily."

"If you want to wait outside," Hank offered, "I'll send my foreman out to show you and the border patrol where we were ambushed."

"Any idea why they'd shoot at you?" Sanders asked.

Thorn held his breath, waiting for Hank's answer. "None."

"Why were you out that late?"

"One of my men was working the fences when that storm blew in. When his horse came back without him, I sent a search party out looking for him."

Sanders made notes on his pad. "Mind if we question him?"

Thorn raised a hand. "That would be me."

Sanders grinned. "Why were you out there working so late?"

"I was almost finished checking the entire southern fence line. Didn't see a need to head in until I got it done."

Thorn shrugged. "The storm moved in before I got back. To make matters worse, lightning struck, my horse threw me and took off."

"You're lucky you didn't break your neck."

Thorn touched his shoulder. "Just bummed my shoulder. Fortunately there was a hunting cabin close by. I holed up there until Mr. Derringer showed up to give me a lift."

"No sign of the woman or man?" Sanders asked.

"Never heard of this Antonio or Elena," Thorn replied, not exactly lying, but not telling the whole truth.

"Well, if you see them, call us, the CBP or the FBI." Sanders folded his pad and tucked it into his front pocket. "Don't try to capture them yourselves. They're supposed to be armed and dangerous."

"We appreciate the warning," Hank said. "Now, if you'll wait outside, I'll have my foreman meet you in front of the barn."

"Thank you, Mr. Derringer." Deputy Sanders shook Hank's hand, then held his out to Thorn. "When are you reclaiming your role as sheriff?"

Thorn shook his head. "Don't count on it. I've got a job with Mr. Derringer."

"Sorry, I didn't realize that. We don't have a sheriff right now. I'm sure if you wanted the job, you could get it back pretty easily."

"No, thanks." Thorn strode to the door and held it open. "Scott Walden will be out in a few minutes. He can show you where we were attacked."

Sanders gave Thorn another long look. "Kayla was my friend, too, you know."

Thorn's lips pressed into a thin line. The three of them had been inseparable in high school.

"She knew how much you loved being a cop. She

wouldn't have wanted you to give it up because of what happened."

Thorn held up his hand. "Don't."

Sanders nodded. "Just saying. We could use a good sheriff. And you were the best we've ever had."

"Why don't *you* run for the position?" Thorn asked.

Sanders shook his head. "I've only been at this job for a couple years. You're the one with all the experience."

"Not interested." Thorn held the door, his fingers so tight around the knob he thought he might crush it.

Sanders sighed. "Hasn't been the same since you left."

"Change is good," Thorn responded.

When the deputy finally walked through the door, Thorn let go of the breath he'd been holding and carefully closed the door behind his former employee. They'd been through a rough time with the previous sheriff being arrested for human trafficking. The lowlife had been responsible for allowing truckloads of women to cross into Texas and beyond, for sale into the sex-slave market.

After Kayla died, Thorn had quit the department, and a new, corrupt sheriff had been hired.

Too deep in his own misery and loss after quitting, Thorn hadn't brought his head up long enough to know what was going on. Another wave of guilt washed over him. He should have taken an interest in the town and county he'd loved. But he hadn't. How many people had suffered under the new sheriff's administration?

What Hank saw in this broken-down cowboy, Thorn didn't know. He was just thankful for a job at this point, wondering what assignment Hank would give him.

"Scott still in the bunker?" Hank walked toward a phone in the hallway.

Thorn nodded. "I asked him to keep an eye on Sophia while I came up."

As the two men headed for the secret doorway, Scott Walden blasted around a corner in the hallway. "Did she come this way?"

Thorn's brows knit. "Sophia?"

"Yeah. Said she had to use *el baño*." He shook his head. "Showed her where it was and spent a minute or two talking to Brandon. About the time I thought she'd been in there too long, I knocked. Got no response, opened the door to find she'd flown the coop."

Thorn raced around the corner, ripped the hidden door open and had to wait for Hank to press his thumb to the scanner.

When the heavy metal door opened, Thorn charged into the bunker, tearing through every room, startling Brandon at his desk.

"Did you see her?"

"No. I checked all the rooms, no sign. I was just backing through the security footage." Brandon sat back at his desk and clicked the mouse through several screens. "She might have overheard them talking on the scanner about the BOLO for the two murderers coming up from Mexico. She seemed to get really quiet after that. That's when she asked to use the facilities."

"How did she get out of the bunker?"

"I thought she'd take longer and wasn't keeping a close eye on the bathroom door. Then an alarm went off on my computer, so I was checking it. Guess that's when she made a run for it." Brandon shifted. "And, well, though you have to have clearance to get in, it's easy to get out."

Thorn leaned over his shoulder and stared at a dozen different views on the bank of computer screens. For the most part, nothing moved. Then a figure appeared in one of them, sneaking along a hallway toward a door.

"There!" Brandon pointed at the screen.

"Where is that?" Thorn asked.

"Near the back door by the kitchen," Brandon said.

Before Brandon had the last word out of his mouth, Thorn was halfway up the stairs leading out of the bunker.

Hank was waiting at the top. "Find her?"

"Back door." Thorn pushed past his boss and sprinted toward the back of the house.

As quiet as he could be in cowboy boots, he raced the length of the hall and skidded around the corner into the kitchen as Sophia reached for the doorknob to the back exit.

She gasped and turned to see who'd run in behind her. "You!"

"Going somewhere?" Thorn demanded.

She whipped the door open and would have run out, but Thorn got there first, his arm blocking her exit. And just in time.

Beyond the back door was the barnyard where the sheriff's deputies awaited the foreman's guide services to find the location of their earlier attack.

Thorn grabbed Sophia's wrist and tore it from the knob. Then he eased the door to the kitchen closed before anyone glanced their way. Once the door blocked their view to the barnyard and subsequently the view of them *from* the barnyard, Thorn crossed his arms and glared down at Sophia.

"Start talking now, or I'll let you walk right out there and turn yourself in to the deputies."

SOPHIA'S BREATH CAUGHT in her throat. The anger in Thorn's eyes seared a path to her heart. She'd been too damned close to being discovered by the authorities. Even if the big cowboy with the iron clamp around her wrist had been gruff about her escape, he had kept her from getting caught once again.

"Why did you try to run?" Thorn asked. "Who did you kill?"

Her chin dropped and she stared straight ahead, directly into Thorn's chest. "I'm not a murderer. I didn't kill anyone."

"Then why are you running? Why is it being reported that a woman named Elena Carranza and some guy named Antonio Martinez killed two DEA agents and fled Mexico?" Thorn stepped closer until he stood toe-to-toe with her. "What is your real name?"

She inhaled and let it out slowly. "My name is Sophia. I didn't lie. It's *Elena* Sophia Carranza. And I didn't kill anyone. I was running because I can't be caught. The authorities might send me back, and I refuse to go back. They'll kill me. Now it's even worse." Sophia closed her eyes and willed the headache building across her forehead to go away. "If they are looking for me as a murder suspect, who's going to believe my word against the border patrol who reported me as a criminal fugitive?"

"How can anyone trust you if you don't tell us the truth?" His hand tightened around her wrist, and a muscle twitched in his jaw as Thorn stared at her for a long, painful moment.

"What do you care if I stay or leave? You wanted to turn me over to the police. What's stopping you?"

"You know, you're right. I don't know why I should believe you. You've done nothing but lie and give me half-truths." He dropped her hand and stepped away from her. "Leave."

Sophia rubbed the red mark around her wrist, her pulse beating rapidly at the base of her throat. She'd pushed him too far because of her anger, and where would that get her? "I would leave," she said, then added on a whisper, "if I had somewhere to go."

"You seem to know what's best for you, and you claim you have it all figured out." He waved his hand toward the closed back door. "Go."

Sophia chewed on her lip. "But the police, the border patrol—"

"Will be gone in a few minutes. You'll be able to sneak out of here without disturbing a soul. Hank doesn't even have to know. I'll cover for you."

Her breath caught and she stared up at him, searching his face for some element of empathy but finding none. She straightened her shoulders and tipped her chin up. "Thank you. I will." She took a step toward the door and stopped, fear making her hands clammy and her feet drag.

As she reached for the doorknob, a sense of doom settled over her. Hector had given his life, for what? For her to get caught and sent back to face the cartel and Antonio's anger?

A hand caught her arm and spun her around. "Don't."

"But you want me to go."

"Yes, you make me crazy and I want you the hell out of my life." His lips thinned and the muscle in his jaw ticked. "But I can't let you go."

Sophia pressed her hands against the solid wall of his chest, her gaze finding and locking with his. "I didn't come here to mess up your life."

"Somehow, I think you did."

"Not intentionally. I can make it on my own. You aren't responsible for me." She couldn't let this man see how scared she was after coming this far. "I'm not afraid of anything," she said, biting down on her lip.

"Don't do that," he said, brushing his thumb across her bottom lip, forcing her to release her hold on it.

"Why?"

"Because it makes me want to do this." He bent and

claimed her mouth, crushing her against him, his arms tightening around her.

Her hands lay flat against his chest, pressing into him for the first few seconds. Then she curled her fingers into his shirt, her nails digging into the skin beneath. Despite the voices in her head telling her she was being stupid, she couldn't stop. He'd crashed into her world like a thunderous storm but kept her alive, protecting her when he didn't have to. He was a man of honor, unlike Antonio.

Sophia wanted to remain in the safety of his arms, to forget where she was and who was after her and just feel the warmth and security she knew in Thorn's embrace.

THORN PULLED HER closer, smoothing her hair back from her face. He eased up on the kiss, ending it with a feathery brush of his lips.

For a moment, he rested his cheek against the softness of her hair while he gathered his senses and wits about him. At long last, he pushed her away, letting his hands drop to his sides.

She stood for a long moment, her lips swollen from his kiss, her eyes rounded, glazed with a wash of unshed tears. "Why did you do that?"

Guilt hit him with the force of an F5 tornado, and he stepped farther back. "I don't know."

She pressed her hand to her mouth and turned to yank the door open.

Thorn's heart tripped over itself and fell into his belly with the weight of a lead bowling ball. More than anything, he wanted this woman out of his life so that he could think about what he'd just done.

But when she stepped out the door, he couldn't let her go. She was in danger and needed him, whether or not he liked it.

"Wait."

She sucked in a breath and huffed it out. "What do you want?"

You.

The thought popped into Thorn's head before he could brace himself for the full impact. His breath caught and held in his chest, and he stared at her. "Stay."

Sophia paused. "Why? I thought you wanted me to go."

"I do. But you won't last two minutes against whoever is trying to kill you."

"You and I both know that by staying, I put you all at risk." She nodded toward his arm. "You got shot because of me."

"I'm willing to take the risk."

"And the rest of Hank's men? Are you speaking for them?"

"No. But they'd do anything for Hank." His lips quirked on the sides. "Even take a bullet for him."

"Well, I don't want anyone taking a bullet for me." She stepped through the door and out into the now-empty barnyard.

"Drennan, did you find her?" Hank stepped up behind Thorn.

"Yes," Thorn answered, without taking his gaze off the woman walking away from him.

"Where is she?" Hank asked.

He nodded to where Sophia was stepping off the porch onto the ground. "Leaving."

"Hell, no, she's not. I just lied to the deputies for that woman." Hank gave Thorn a push. "Get her back. I want answers."

His pulse quickening and a smile curling the corners

of his lips, Thorn stepped off the porch and caught Sophia's arm before she could take off. "Sorry, you'll have to leave later."

Chapter Six

Sophia sat in a wingback chair on the other side of Hank's desk in his study, her head drooping, the gray of predawn peeking through the blinds covering the windows in Hank's office.

"I didn't kill anyone," she said for the hundredth time. "I left my fiancé because he was cruel and part of the cartel. I knew if I wanted to live to be twenty-six, I had to get out."

"The CBP is searching for you and a man called Antonio Martinez."

Sophia gasped.

Hank pinned her with his stare. "Who is he?"

"My ex-fiancé." She frowned and sat up straighter, at a disadvantage with the cowboy towering over her. "He didn't come with me." Had he discovered her missing so soon and crossed the border looking for her?

"Thorn said you came across with a man named Hector. How does he fit in this picture?"

She swallowed hard on the lump rising up her throat. "Hector didn't kill anyone, either. He got me out. That man risked his life to get me across the border."

"Are you sure that's how it went? The CBP has an entirely different story. They say you and Antonio killed a couple undercover DEA agents."

"I swear, I am not with Antonio." Sophia shook her

head, fear making her breathing difficult. What if these men didn't believe her? Would they turn her over to the CBP? A sob rose up her throat, and she swallowed hard. "I left to escape him. Another captive told me to contact Hank Derringer, and Hector volunteered to get me out."

"How much did you pay him?" Hank fired off one question after another.

She snorted. "I didn't have any money. He told me he did it because I reminded him of his daughter." Her voice caught on a sob. "He gave his life for me, and for what?" She waved a hand. "I'm trapped here as if I traded one prison for another."

"You don't have to stay." Hank stood before her. "But if you want to live to be twenty-six, as you say, you might want to consider taking me up on my offer to provide your protection."

"How will you do that? Antonio has a network of people on both sides of the border willing to kill anyone who gets in the way of what he wants."

"You want to live?" Thorn asked.

Sophia touched her belly, reminding herself she wasn't alone. She had to consider the child growing inside her. "I can't pay you."

Hank chuckled. "I don't need your money. I have enough."

By the appearance of his house and the fully equipped bunker hidden beneath, he had more than enough. "What can you do to guarantee my safety?" Sophia asked.

"I'd start by assigning a bodyguard to watch over you."

Sophia's gaze darted to Thorn. "Him?"

Thorn snorted. "Please, don't look so enthusiastic."

Hank laughed. "Thorn was trained as a police officer and has served in the local sheriff's department before he came to work for me. He knows what it means to be under fire."

"What if he doesn't want the job?" Sophia's gaze swept over Thorn, challenging him.

"I'll do it," Thorn responded. "Whether or not I *want* to is beside the point. You need a keeper."

Sophia snorted. "I'm better off by myself."

Hank frowned. "Is there something going on between the two of you I should know about?"

Thorn shook his head. "Absolutely nothing." The look he pinned on Sophia dared her to refute that.

"Nothing."

"Then it's done." Hank crossed to his desk and sat behind it. "Thorn will be your bodyguard while we sort this mess out."

Sophia wasn't sure how she felt about Thorn being her bodyguard. Not after that kiss. What if he kissed her again? Her pulse fluttered and her cheeks warmed. She pushed aside the unwanted longing and focused on what Hank had said. "I don't know what you think you can sort out. I told you, my ex-fiancé will not stop until I'm either dead or back in his prison of a compound."

"This Antonio Martinez…he was your fiancé?" Thorn's eyes narrowed. "The name sounds familiar."

Sophia sat back in her chair, the fight gone out of her, exhaustion taking hold. "If you know anything about *la Familia Diablos,* you know that he's one of their leaders. Still want to protect me? Think you can?"

Thorn's brows dipped, and a snarl curled his lips. "I'm not afraid of the cartel."

She stared back at him. "You should be."

"I'll have Brandon do research on Martinez and *la Familia Diablos.*" Hank rose from behind his desk and stretched. "Once we've all had a little sleep, we can reconvene and figure out where we go from here."

Thorn nodded.

"Drennan, you can show Miss Carranza to the room next to yours. Security is pretty tight around here, but it doesn't hurt to have your bodyguard close."

Sophia opened her mouth to tell Hank she didn't want to be that close to Thorn but closed it again, knowing it would be a lie. The man might be stubborn and hardheaded, and kissed like the devil, but he'd come through more than once to save her life. Instead of arguing, she nodded. "Thank you, Señor Derringer."

Hank left the room without another word, leaving Thorn and Sophia alone.

Thorn glanced at her and sighed. "Lack of sleep leads to poor decisions. What say we get some rest?"

Sophia could have bet he was talking about the kiss, blaming his lapse in judgment on a sleepless night. A flutter of disappointment rippled through her. Having been awake for close to thirty-six hours, crossing rough terrain and dodging bullets had taken their toll. She trudged along behind Thorn. "Is there a possibility of getting a shower somewhere in this huge house?" The idea of scrubbing the dirt off her skin sounded like heaven.

"You're in luck. There's a bathroom in the suite." He led her along a hallway and stopped in front of a door. He twisted the knob and pushed the door inward.

Sophia stepped inside, her gaze going to the big bed with an off-white comforter spread across it. Exhaustion pulled her toward it. If she wasn't so dirty, she'd fall onto the covers and sleep like the dead.

"I'll be in the room beside this one." He nodded to a door on the wall inside her room. "There's a connecting door if you need anything."

Sophia's heartbeat fluttered. The thought of Thorn's bedroom being down the hall was quite different from a connecting door between the two rooms.

"Don't worry, I won't disturb you." His mouth slipped into a sexy smile. "Unless you want me to."

"I don't want you to," she was quick to say.

"Good." He stretched his arms over his head, winced and let them drop to his side. "I'm tired."

A twinge of guilt tugged at Sophia. "The wound?"

"Just a little sore. No more bleeding."

She nodded and stepped into the room.

Thorn turned to go.

Sophia paused in closing the door between the rooms. "Thorn?"

He glanced back.

"Thank you." Sophia shut the door and leaned her back against it.

The room was bigger than the living room of the apartment she'd shared with Antonio in the compound. The bathroom was on the opposite side of the room from the connecting door to Thorn's room. Sophia crossed to the connecting door and twisted the knob. It turned easily; it was not locked, and there wasn't a lock on her side.

A little uncomfortable with the idea of an unlocked door between them, she scooted off to the opposite end of the room and into the bathroom, where the lock worked perfectly fine. She twisted it and took a moment to appreciate her surroundings.

The bathroom had large pale cream ceramic tiles, granite countertops and a glass-brick wall surrounding the walk-in shower, large enough for six people, with two showerheads.

A two-person tub filled one corner of the room, with large fluffy towels draped over its side.

The grime of her trek across the Rio Grande and through the canyons of the Big Bend National Park prodded Sophia to strip her dirty clothes and step into the shower.

The water started out cold but quickly warmed, washing away the dirt, glass and blood that had been splattered across her over the past thirty-six hours. When her skin felt clean and her eyes drooped low, she shut off the water and dried off with one of the luxurious towels.

Then she remembered she didn't have clean clothes to wear. Too tired to care, she wrapped a dry towel around her and crawled into the big bed, pulling the comforter up over her body.

She lay still for several minutes, breathing in and out, trying to calm her racing heart. Light shone around the blinds covering the windows. The early-morning sun edged through every crack, but not quite enough to light the entire room. Shadows darkened each corner of the unfamiliar room. Every little sound—the crack of timbers as the house settled, a bird chirping outside the window, the lonely howl of the wind pushing against the glass—made Sophia's heart skip beats and her body tense. No matter how much she tried to relax, she couldn't.

The door on the other side of the room creaked open, and a head slipped around the panel.

Sophia squealed, pulling the comforter up to her chin. When the dim light touched his face, she realized it was Thorn.

"Sorry, didn't mean to startle you," he said.

"What are you doing in here?" she asked, her voice high and tight.

"Why aren't you asleep?" he countered.

She shook her head. "I don't know."

"New place make you nervous?"

She nodded. "That and the fact Antonio has his men looking for me."

He stepped into the room and glanced around. "Want me to check the closets and beneath the bed for monsters?"

She stared across at him, gauging whether or not he was being sarcastic. Thankfully, he wasn't sneering. *"Sí, por favor."*

Thorn moved about the room, padding softly in bare feet. He wiggled the doorknob to test the lock, tried the windows, which all remained securely closed, and opened the closet and inspected it thoroughly before crossing to where she lay in the bed.

Sophia's eyes rounded as he came closer, her hands clenching the comforter pulled up to her chin. "You don't have to look beneath the bed."

"How are you going to sleep if I don't make sure there's nothing or no one hiding beneath you?" His smile was no more than a gentle lift of the corners of his mouth, but the gesture was more calming than words. Thorn dropped to his haunches and ducked his head low, peering beneath the bed. "Dark but empty. Not even a single dust bunny to attack you."

Sophia laughed softly. "I know it's silly, but thanks for checking."

"You really should get some sleep. We could have a tough day ahead of us. You'll need your strength."

"I shouldn't have come here," she whispered.

"Based on all you said, you did the only thing you could."

"I didn't want to bring others down with me. My life is the way it is because of my own poor choices. No need for anyone else to suffer."

"You're here now, so stop worrying about it. Let Hank's team figure a way out of this mess for you."

"It's not easy turning over the reins to someone else. Not when your life depends on it." *Or the life of your unborn child.*

Thorn straightened beside her bed, so close he could touch her.

Sophia's blood heated, sliding through her veins like liquid lava, her skin twitching, aching for something.

When Thorn reached out and smoothed back a strand of hair from her forehead, Sophia's breath caught in her throat and she stared up into the most incredible blue eyes she could have imagined. As his fingers left her forehead, the warmth left with them. She'd never felt so safe as she did when she was with Thorn, and it scared her while simultaneously helping her relax. "Wh-why did you do that?"

His lips twisted upward on one side. "I don't know. It just seemed like the right thing to do."

She could get lost in his eyes. Her gaze remained on his for a long moment, all her muscles relaxing until a yawn rose up in her chest and nearly made her split her jaw. She covered her mouth and blinked, her eyelids drifting downward. She let them close for just a second. "Must have been sleepier than I'd thought."

Movement made her eyes flutter open.

Thorn no longer stood beside her bed. In the short time Sophia had closed her eyes, he'd slipped halfway across the room.

"Where are you going?" she whispered, hardly able to keep her eyes open.

"To my room. If you want, I'll leave the door open between us."

Her eyelids felt as if they had lead weights resting on them, driving them downward. *"Por favor."*

"Please, what?" he asked.

"Please stay until I go to sleep. It won't be long." She lay for a long time with her eyes shut.

The crackle of leather made her glance up.

Thorn had settled into the sturdy brown leather chair beside the bed. Sophia smiled.

"I'll stay until you fall asleep," he said, his voice low, caressing. Incredibly sexy.

A shiver rippled across Sophia's skin, and she closed her eyes to the alluring cowboy sitting so near.

"Sleep," he urged.

It felt more like a lifetime ago since she'd felt safe. Having grown up in a loving family, with an overprotective father and mother, she thought of violence and death as things that happened to other people. Not her. Until she'd made the mistake of trusting Antonio.

Sophia turned on her side, facing him, snuggled deeper into the comforter and drifted into the first deep sleep she'd had since she left her parents' home over a year ago.

THORN SAT FOR the longest time in the chair beside Sophia's bed, wondering what the hell he'd done. This woman had trouble written all over her. If he took the job of protecting her from whoever it was she was running from, there was a strong possibility he'd get shot at again, maybe killed.

As she lay with her palms pressed together and tucked beneath her cheek, she looked like a child, her thin cheeks and silky light brown hair fanned out on the pillow behind her. Gone was the little hellcat he'd fought in the cabin. In her place was an angel, with lips so soft, velvet didn't even describe them. Her hair feathered out to each side of her head in a spread of light brown strands. Though her eyes were closed, Thorn could envision the deep green of them boring into him as if he had the answers to all her problems. Trouble was, he had no answers. And if he didn't find some soon, she might not make it another day.

When her breathing became slow and regular, Thorn stood and stretched, ready to embark on a bit of intelligence gathering to discover just who Elena Sophia Carranza was. He'd asked Brandon to do some digging to see if she showed up on any wanted or missing persons lists in Mexico, the United States or Canada.

A soft moan rose from her throat.

Thorn leaned over her and stroked her hair. "Sleep. You'll be okay."

Her eyelids twitched but didn't open.

He bent and pressed a kiss to her temple, her soft skin making his lips tingle.

She smelled of honeysuckle, her hair still slightly damp from her shower. Sophia rolled to her back, the comforter sliding down to reveal the tops of her gently rounded breasts, the towel she'd wrapped around herself loosening.

Thorn made a mental note to ask Hank if he had some clothes she could borrow until they could get her to a store for something that fit. The woman had sacrificed her last T-shirt to use as a compress to stop Thorn from bleeding to death. It clearly was not the act of a murderer.

He brushed a strand of hair out of her face and straightened. If he stayed he'd be tempted to crawl into the bed beside her, something he hadn't been tempted to do since Kayla died.

Guilt swelled in his chest, driving Thorn out of the room and back into his own. He pushed aside the blinds and stared out at the South Texas morning sky, filled with purple, blue, mauve and orange. Steam rose from the ground from the rain they'd received during the night. Before long, the sun would soak up the moisture and the storm would be nothing more than a memory.

He lay on top of his bed, clothed in clean jeans and a T-shirt, and stared up at the ceiling. As soon as Hank was up and about, Thorn would ask him to find someone else to play bodyguard to the pretty fugitive. Already Thorn could feel himself getting too close to his client, a dangerous place to be should something happen to her. She stirred feelings in him he didn't want to face. He couldn't handle any more guilt and sorrow than he already lived with.

Fifteen minutes passed, and he still couldn't fall asleep.

Thorn rolled out of bed, checked on Sophia through the open doorway then slipped out into the hallway.

Noises drifted to him from the area of the kitchen. He headed that way, hoping for a piece of toast or cup of coffee.

Hank stood with his back to the doorway, pouring a cup of coffee from a glass carafe. "Want one?" he asked without turning.

"Please." Thorn hooked a chair with his bare foot, swung it away from the kitchen table and sat.

"How's our guest?" Hank set a cup of coffee on the table in front of Thorn.

"Sleeping." Thorn lifted the steaming cup and sipped. "I don't think she's slept in days."

Hank retrieved his cup and settled in the seat across from Thorn. Judging by Hank's well-worn jeans, button-up denim shirt and scuffed cowboy boots, no one would know the man was worth millions. "Scott should be back any minute from taking the border-patrol agents out to the shooting site. I hope to get an update then. In the meantime, we wait."

"Think they'll ask to search your house?"

Hank shook his head. "They'd have to show up with a warrant to do that." He glanced across his mug at Thorn.

"Don't worry—I won't let them know about Ms. Carranza."

"That puts you at risk for harboring a fugitive."

"I can handle it."

"Do you think the biker gang was after Sophia?"

"She seems to think they were."

"But do you?"

Hank sighed and set his mug on the table. "If they think I have her, they'll come after her here."

Thorn nodded. "Exactly my thoughts. Despite the amount of security you have, I don't think she's safe here."

"The sheriff said the CBP was setting up roadblocks on the highways leading out of this area. She'll never make it out by road."

"What about flying her out?"

"My helicopter is in the hanger in El Paso for annual maintenance and inspections." Hank shoved a hand through his graying hair and leaned back in his chair. "I could hire another one and move her, but that might draw attention she doesn't need."

"What can we do to keep her safe?"

Hank drummed his fingers on the table as the silence between the two men lengthened. "We need to hide her."

"Difficult when you have so many people around you. Any one of them could slip, whether on purpose or accidentally."

"Then we need to hide her in plain sight." Hank leaned forward, a light twinkling in his eyes. "Elena Sophia Carranza can disappear completely."

Thorn frowned, pushed his coffee aside and leaned toward his new boss. "What do you mean?"

"Right now, the only people who know she's here are you, me, Max and Brandon. She did a good job staying in the shadows when we brought her in."

"Right. So?"

"So we change her appearance and introduce her to the biggest gossips in town as your long-lost college sweetheart. Before you know it, the entire town will know her as…"

"Sally Freeman." Thorn smiled. "All we have to do is change her hair color and get her some clothes and a new driver's license, and we're good to go."

Hank stood. "I'll get my daughter PJ working on Sophia's transformation. She comes out often enough that they won't question why she's here. Once Sophia looks different enough to fool the sheriff's deputies and the CBP, she can move about Wild Oak Canyon without worrying."

"I don't know about that, but at least the authorities won't be looking at her as a murderer."

"I'll be back. I need to call PJ."

Thorn held up his hand. "Hank."

Hank paused.

"PJ needs to know not to leak any information about Sophia."

"She's good about keeping secrets. After all, she's her father's daughter." Hank's chuckle followed him down the hall until he disappeared around a corner.

Thorn collected his coffee mug and returned to his room.

He set his mug on the nightstand and strode for Sophia's room, a nagging feeling that something was wrong pulling him through the doorway. One glance across the room and his pulse ricocheted through his veins.

The bed was empty. Sophia was gone.

Chapter Seven

The compound lights blinked out yet again, as they did quite often, plunging her little room into complete darkness. Sophia swallowed a sob of terror, the sound of a little boy's cries cutting through her own fear, making her realize just how selfish she was to worry about how much she hated the darkness when a little boy cried in the night, unable to understand the instability inherent in a desert compound out in the middle of nowhere, dependent on generators and fuel. They were lucky to have any kind of electricity at all.

Though when the lights went out, Antonio usually returned to their room, intent on making love and further proving his power over her. She waited in the darkness, clutching the bedsheets around her, praying he wouldn't break one of her bones.

A woman's scream ripped through the night, penetrating the concrete-block walls and stucco.

Anna.

Sophia flung aside the covers and leaped out of the bed. The little boy's cries joined the woman's scream, galvanizing Sophia into action. She tore open her door and raced down the hallway to the rooms at the end where Anna and her son lived.

The door stood open, a flickering light illuminating the room within.

When Sophia barreled through the doorway, she smacked into Antonio, knocking him forward into a low table. He tripped and fell, landing with a grunt, the air around him reeking of cigarette smoke and stale alcohol.

"Pendejo!" he grumbled, pushing to his feet. More curses flowed from his lips as he closed the distance between them. "I'm going to kill you for that."

Sophia backed up and spun to race down the hallway and away from the fury etched in the man's eyes. Before she could take the first step, Antonio grabbed her hair and yanked her back.

She fell against him, pushing hard to throw him off balance. Her only hope was to get away and hide from him. Sophia fought, twisted and kicked, but his grip tightened, his fingers tangling in her hair like a knot.

"Leave her alone!" Anna screamed, pounding against the man's back with her fists. She tripped and fell to her knees.

Sophia planted her bare feet on the floor, tucked her shoulder and plowed into the man, sending him flying over Anna's body to land on his back on the hard Saltillo tile.

His hand, still tangled in her hair, dragged her backward and on top of him.

While Antonio caught his breath, Sophia scrambled free and shot to her feet. She gathered Anna and Jake and shoved them out the door in front of her, herding them down the hallway as fast as she could go. Their only hope was to find a place to hide until Antonio slept off the effects of the alcohol and drugs he'd been taking.

She stashed Anna and Jake in a storage room filled with sacks of pinto beans, flour and cornmeal. She piled the sacks in front of the two until no one would see them on a quick inspection of the tiny storeroom. There was only room for the two of them. Sophia backed toward the door.

Anna held out her hand. "Don't go. He'll kill you."

"Don't worry. I'll find a place to hide until he's sober." With a quick glance at the empty hallway, Sophia left the storeroom and ran down the corridor.

Antonio's roar echoed off the walls, and his footsteps thundered through the building.

She didn't have time to find another room. Once Antonio rounded the corner, he'd see her. And if he saw her, she was doomed to suffer another beating.

Sophia dove into their room, praying he wouldn't see her going there, hoping he'd think she'd left the main building to hide in one of the outlying structures.

With nothing more than a small cabinet that held her clothes, her only hiding place was beneath the bed she shared with her fiancé. With the footsteps closing in fast, Sophia dropped to the cold ceramic tile floors and rolled beneath the bed, pulling the blanket down to hide her in the shadows.

The door slammed open and Antonio bellowed, "Elena Sophia Carranza!"

She pushed herself as far back as she could go until her back hit the cool stucco wall. For several long minutes she lay as still as possible, afraid to move and even more afraid to breathe lest he hear her.

The man she'd been stupid enough to fall in love with tossed pillows, then flung the candlestick holder and her books across the room in his rage.

Sophia closed her eyes, as if that would help to hide her from Antonio's wrath.

Silence fell over the room. For a moment, Sophia thought Antonio had left, until she heard the sound of his breathing and the light scuffle of his shoes across the tiles.

With her breath lodged in her throat, Sophia waited.

A hand shot beneath the bed, grasped her ankle and yanked her hard, dragging her from her hiding place.

Sophia kicked and screamed, blinking back tears of fear and choking back sobs as she fought for her life, positive Antonio would make good his threat and kill her this time. His fingers closed around her throat and squeezed until she couldn't breathe. She tried to cry out, but nothing made it past her vocal cords. A gray shroud descended on her as her life slipped from her body.

"Sophia!" a deep voice called out.

Sophia strained to hear it again.

"Sophia, wake up!" A hand shook her shoulder. The one holding her arm was gentle, not the torture of Antonio's grip. She struggled to break free.

"Sophia," the voice said again, and strong arms wrapped around her, crushing her against a hard wall.

Sophia bucked and kicked, straining against the vise-like clamps around her body.

"Open your eyes, Sophia." The voice softened, and a hand smoothed the hair back from her forehead. "It's Thorn. Wake up."

She blinked, her eyes opening to the soft gray light of the shadowed room. A room far different from the one she'd shared with Antonio at *la Fuerte del Diablo* in Chihuahua.

A sob rose up her throat and shook her frame as tears slipped down her cheeks. *"¿Dónde estoy?"*

THOUGH SHE ASKED where she was in Spanish, Thorn replied in English. "At the Raging Bull Ranch. You're safe." He loosened his arms, allowing her to move and breathe more comfortably. Then he turned her to face him.

Her eyes were wide, her lips parted as she dragged air into her lungs as if she'd been running a marathon.

"You were havin' one heck of a dream." He kept his voice smooth, the same way he spoke when he worked with a frightened horse. "Must have been pretty bad for you to hide under the bed."

For a moment Sophia stared into his eyes, then she blinked and melted against his chest, burying her face in his T-shirt.

Her warm body shook against him. What kind of horrors had she endured to bring on such a terrible nightmare? The protector inside him wanted to find her nemesis and grind him into a pulp.

For several minutes, Thorn sat on the floor with Sophia nestled against him, trying not to think about the towel wrapped loosely around her, or the fact that it had inched up, exposing a significant amount of her thighs. He cleared his throat to break the silence. "Wanna talk about it?"

She shook her head and curled her fingers into the soft jersey, her fingernails scraping his skin through the fabric.

Okay, she didn't want to talk. Unfortunately, the longer she lay across his lap, the more his body responded to hers.

His pulse hummed along, driving blood to his lower extremities, making his jeans uncomfortably tight. He shifted her, easing her away from his growing erection.

Now was not the time to scare the poor woman. What if she'd been reliving the nightmare of rape?

Thorn tried to tell himself he'd been in love with his wife, and her memory could not be so easily set aside for a woman he barely knew.

The thought of Kayla usually had the effect of bringing Thorn back to the reality of his life and loss. Not so much at that moment. With Sophia so real and immediate stretched across his thighs, he could barely recall Kayla's pretty face. That bothered him enough to move.

He pushed Sophia off his lap onto the cool tile floor, stood and bent to gather her into his arms.

"I can get up on my own," she said, pressing her hands against his chest as he straightened.

"I know you can." He set her on the bed and pulled the sheet up over her gorgeous legs, as if hiding them would erase their image from his mind.

It didn't.

Sophia's cheeks reddened, and she tugged the towel over her breasts. "Do you suppose Señor Derringer would have some clothing I could borrow?"

"He sent for some. They should be here shortly."

"Has he heard anything else from the authorities?"

"Not yet. He expects them anytime, though." Thorn turned his back to her and walked toward the window. If he stared at her much longer, he'd be in a world of hurt. Why now, of all times, was he attracted to a female? Since his wife had died, he hadn't even looked at another woman.

Then Sophia had blown into his life and almost killed him. Why would he be attracted to her? She'd lied to him, shot at him and, if the CBP reports were accurate, could be a murderer running from Mexico to escape prison or a firing squad.

He glanced back at the woman lying in the bed, tugging at the towel across her chest, her cheeks a soft shade of pink.

No, he couldn't see her as a killer.

Movement out of the corner of his vision drew his attention back to the barnyard. "Looks like the CBP and the foreman are back."

Sophia's eyes widened, and she clutched the sheet in her hands.

He shot a frown her way. "Can I trust you to stay put while I go see what they found?"

Her lips twisted. "I have no clothes. I wouldn't get far in a towel."

Thorn's mouth twitched at the image of Sophia's escape in nothing but the fluffy white towel she could barely keep around her. He fought back a smile. "You didn't answer me. Do I have your word?"

Sophia's eyes narrowed and she studied him before she answered on a sigh. "Yes."

Thorn nodded. "I'll see about those clothes while I'm out." He left the house through the French doors in his room and hurried out to the barnyard.

Hank was there, standing beside Scott Walden. Max flanked his other side.

The sheriff's deputies and CBP men were gathered a few steps away around a topographical map laid out over their vehicle, pointing and discussing specific coordinates.

Thorn stepped up to Hank and Scott. "What did they find?"

Scott shook his head. "Not much. The bikers must have policed up their own. The only thing we found was a bike they couldn't haul out of there. The CBP took pictures and marked the spot on their maps. They'll send a truck out to collect evidence."

"Did they pull any slugs out of my truck?" Hank asked.

Scott shook his head. "They want to wait until the state crime-scene investigation team can get out here to process the evidence, since it's not certain the attackers were illegal aliens. Could be a local gang."

"Did you tell them about the man who helped Sophia escape?" Thorn asked, keeping his voice low enough that the CBP wouldn't hear.

Hank shook his head. "I thought we'd go find him first, so that they don't question how we knew he was out there."

"Good idea," Thorn agreed. The less the authorities knew about Sophia, the better. "If you think the woman is safe here with your bodyguards, I'd like to be in on that search party."

Hank glanced at him, his eyes narrowed. "We can hold her in the bunker." The ranch owner held up his hand. "And we'll keep a better eye on her this time. Plus, my daughter, PJ, is on her way out with some items I think will help us in our effort to camouflage our guest."

The leader of the CBP team broke away from those gathered around the map. "We had a call from the FBI. They want in on this investigation since it could be that the men who attacked you might have something to do with cartel members and the murder suspects." The man sighed. "I'd rather we handled it on our own, but I'm getting pressure from my supervisor. A regional director will be out here in the next couple of hours, along with the state crime-scene lab technicians. You'll need to be available to talk to them."

Hank's lips pressed into a line, then he shrugged. "We'll cooperate fully."

"In the meantime, keep your men clear of the attack site until the crime lab has a chance to gather more evidence."

"Can't keep the cattle from wandering," Hank warned.

The CBP officer shook his head. "Do the best you can."

"Will do." Hank stuck out his hand.

The CBP team lead grasped it and shook it briefly, then let go. "We'll be working out of Wild Oak Canyon for the short term until we get a handle on the murder suspects and where they might be headed." He directed his glance from Hank to Scott, then to Thorn. "If any of you see or hear anything, let us know immediately."

Thorn gave a single nod of acknowledgment, refusing to promise anything.

The CBP team folded the map, climbed into the government-issue SUV and drove down the gravel drive to the highway outside the gates of the Raging Bull Ranch.

Deputy Sanders stepped up to Hank. "Looks like the feds will be taking over. If they set up a task force, we'll assign a deputy liaison. In the meantime, call us if you have any more trouble. We're here for you." Sanders and his men climbed into their SUVs and followed the CBP off the ranch.

Hank sighed. "Let's get out to the canyon and find that body before the rest of the party shows. Maybe it will give us more of a clue as to the real identity of our guest."

"Will you report the body?" Having been an officer of the law, Thorn didn't like withholding information in an ongoing investigation. Then again, he'd have to explain how he knew about the body in the first place.

Though Sophia hadn't been completely up-front with him in the beginning and she could still be hiding something, Thorn wasn't ready to hand her over to the authorities. The nightmare that had caused her to crawl beneath the bed had to be rooted in some pretty bad stuff. There was more to her story, and he wanted to know what it was before he gave her to the sheriff, CBP or FBI.

The handheld radio clipped to Max's black utility belt chirped. He stepped away from the others and listened to the staticky call, answering with, "Let her in." When he rejoined the group, he leaned into Hank and said quietly, "Your daughter has arrived with Bolton."

"Good." Hank's mouth turned up in a smile at the mention of his daughter and her fiancé-bodyguard. "While PJ and Chuck keep Sophia company, we'll see about finding a body." He turned to Thorn. "It's rained pretty hard since she crossed the border, so we'll have our work cut out for us finding her trail."

Thorn stared out over the landscape, visualizing what he'd seen the previous evening before the sun had completely set. "We'll start from the point where she cut the fence and work our way into the canyon from there."

"Regroup in ten minutes?" Hank stared around at the men.

The foreman nodded. "I take it we'll be on four-wheelers?"

Hank nodded. "I think we'll get there and back faster."

"I'll get them ready." Though Scott hadn't slept in over twenty-four hours, the man sprinted toward the barn.

Thorn hurried back to the house and entered his room. The connecting door to Sophia's room was closed. He frowned and hurried toward it, his heart thudding against his chest. Had Sophia made another run for it?

He flung the door open and charged in.

Sophia stood naked in the middle of the room, her towel clutched to her chest, eyes wide and wary. "Don't you ever knock?"

Heat climbed up Thorn's neck to his cheeks and spread low into his groin at the sight of her slender legs, softly flared hips and narrow waistline. "Pardon me. I thought…"

"You thought I tried to run?" She turned her back, exposing the full length of her naked body to him while she dropped the edges of the towel in order to wrap it around her middle. "Kind of hard to do when you have no clothes." When she spun back to face him, tucking the corner of the towel in at her breasts, she glared at him. "A gentleman would look away."

More heat poured into his cheeks, and his lips tightened. He hadn't expected to see her naked and he certainly hadn't counted on his body's immediate reaction.

He summoned anger to push aside the lust threatening to steal his last brain cells. "You're covered now, and I'm in a hurry."

Her frown straightened, and she stepped forward. "What's happening?"

"Hank's daughter is here. You're to cooperate with her and stay in the bunker while we head out to find your dead accomplice."

Sophia tensed and bit down on her bottom lip. "You didn't inform the border patrol about Hector?"

"No. And we didn't tell them about the helicopter. All they know is that Hank was attacked by a group of dirt bikers on his property. That and what they'd been told about a couple of murderers possibly crossing the border near here."

The woman let out a long breath. "Thank you for believing me."

Thorn stared at her long and hard. "I wouldn't go that far. Until we find the body of your man Hector and determine his cause of death, I'm withholding my judgment."

Sophia frowned but nodded. "Understandable. You don't know me. I wouldn't trust me if I was in your boots."

"In the meantime, you'll stay in the bunker. The fewer people who know you're here, the better for all involved. I don't want Hank to be arrested for harboring a fugitive."

"I didn't kill anyone."

"So you say." Thorn hooked her arm and led her toward the door to the room. "Hank's daughter and bodyguard will be in charge of you today. If you want Hank's help, I suggest you cooperate fully."

Sophia shook off his hand and glared up at him. "Don't push me."

"Then move."

She tossed her long light brown hair back over her shoulder and reached for the doorknob, flicking the lock free.

After a quick glance down the hallway to ensure it was clear, she stepped out with as much pride and bearing as she could muster dressed in nothing but a towel, her hair uncombed and her face free of all cosmetics.

Sophia refused to let his autocratic ways cow her. She'd been beaten, cursed and held prisoner by a madman. Thorn Drennan didn't scare her one bit.

But when his hand cupped her elbow or pushed the hair out of her face, or when he pressed his body against hers...

Warmth sizzled across her skin and rippled through her nerve endings.

After all she'd been through with Antonio, Sophia couldn't understand the knot of desire building low in her belly for this taciturn cowboy marching her along the corridor.

He led her to the hidden doorway, pressed his thumb to the thumb pad and entered a combination. The door opened to the staircase leading downward into the basement beneath the ranch house.

He guided her down a long corridor and into a room with a large solid-oak table at the center. White dry-erase boards lined two walls, and a large white screen dominated the end of the room.

"Have a seat," Thorn ordered.

"Can't you say please? Or *por favor?*" When he didn't respond, Sophia tucked the towel closer and held her ground. "I prefer to stand."

He shrugged and left the room.

A moment later he returned with a lovely young woman with sandy-blond hair and soft gray eyes. A big man followed her through the doorway, his shoulders filling the frame.

Thorn turned to the two. "Sophia, meet PJ Franks and Chuck Bolton. They're going to stay with you until we get back."

Sophia gasped. "Get back?"

"I'm going with Hank and his men to find Hector's body."

"Oh." Her heart sank into her belly like a ton of bricks. Though Chuck and PJ looked fully capable, Thorn had been there for her from the moment she'd landed in his arms in the cabin. He'd kept her alive during the shootout with the biker gang and had held her through a nasty nightmare, soothing her brow and holding her until she'd stopped shaking.

His gaze captured hers, his eyes narrowing. "You'll be fine with PJ and Chuck until I get back."

Sophia swallowed the knot in her throat, turned away from Thorn and held out her hand to PJ. "Nice to meet you."

Thorn stood for a moment longer, and then left the room.

PJ took Sophia's hand in a firm but gentle grip. "Don't worry, he'll be back. Hank takes care of his own." PJ let go of her hand and turned to the man behind her. "We brought some things we thought you might need." To Chuck she said, "You can set the bag down and get out of here."

"Yes, ma'am." The big man grinned and set a couple of bulging plastic bags on the table. When he turned to leave, he captured PJ in a hold around her waist and kissed her soundly on the lips.

She slapped his shoulder, a smile spreading across her face. "Save it for later, cowboy."

Chuck stepped through the door and PJ closed it behind him, her smile still in place.

A pang of envy tightened Sophia's chest. "I take it you know each other."

PJ blinked as if she realized there was another person in the room. "Chuck's my fiancé and the father of our baby girl." She laughed. "Long story. If you plan on sticking around, I'll tell you all about it. In the meantime, I understand we have work to do."

Sophia frowned. "I don't understand."

"My father, Hank Derringer, told me you have a BOLO issued on you."

"BOLO?" Sophia shook her head, wondering if she had stepped into another world.

"Be on the lookout. It's a term law enforcement uses when they want all personnel to be on the alert for certain people they want to bring in for a crime or questioning." PJ's brows wrinkled. "He said the word is out that an Elena Carranza is wanted for murder in Mexico."

"I didn't kill anyone."

"So Hank said." PJ smiled. "You don't look like a killer to me, if that makes you feel better."

"Thank you." Sophia liked this woman with the open smile and the pretty eyes.

"The point is, Hank showed me the picture going around with your face on it. The features are a bit fuzzy, and your hair is really dark in the picture. If we make a few changes, you could pass for someone else."

"How will this help?"

"The roads in and out of this area have been set up with roadblocks. Until the dust settles, you'll be here awhile. We need to come up with a cover story for you."

Her pulse leaped and thundered through her veins. "I can't leave?" All the terror of leaving the compound in

Mexico returned, and her hands shook. "He'll find me," she whispered. "He'll find me and kill me."

PJ's brows knit. "Who will find you?"

"My ex-fiancé." Sophia shook her head. "I cannot stay here. I have to leave."

"Sorry, sweetie, it's not possible. There are cops, border patrol and FBI descending on this place. If you want to hide, you have to change your appearance and lie low."

"You don't understand." Sophia grabbed PJ's arm. "Everyone around me will suffer. No one is safe until he gets me back."

PJ held Sophia's hands steady. "My father won't let anything happen to you. That's why he's assigned Thorn to protect you outside these walls."

"Antonio has eyes and ears on both sides of the border." Sophia swallowed a sob. "It's only a matter of time before he gets word of where I'm hiding. I have to get away."

"And you will," PJ said. "When the hoopla dies down. And giving you a new identity will help keep the authorities out of your business should they see you."

Sophia breathed in and out several times to tamp down the rising panic. PJ was right. With so many people converging on the area, she wouldn't get out without running the gauntlet. If changing her appearance helped to hide her, so be it. It might also help her in her new life away from Mexico. "Okay, how do you propose to change me?"

PJ grinned. "Since Thorn has been assigned as your bodyguard, you'll be Thorn's old girlfriend from college come back to town to rekindle the romance." She held up a box with the face of a beautiful woman with flowing golden hair. "And you're going blond."

Chapter Eight

Thorn led the way out to the cabin where he'd first found Sophia. As he bumped along on the four-wheeler, his thoughts strayed to the woman, wondering if she'd try to escape again, and, if she succeeded, whether or not she'd make it on her own evading the men trying to kill her.

They skirted the area marked off by flags poking out of the ground, swinging wide to avoid disturbing potential evidence the state crime-scene investigators, CBP or FBI might use in their investigation of the biker gang and their possible connection with Mexican cartel members and the two reported murderers the Mexican government wanted extradited to face their crimes.

A small plume of smoke rose from the direction the cabin had stood the night before, providing shelter from the raging storm. Even before he reached the site, Thorn could smell smoldering wood.

His gut tightened. Had he not been the one to find Sophia first, she might have been burned to death in the rubble of the tiny hunter's shelter or dragged back to Mexico to a man who had abused her.

Thorn's fingers clenched around the four-wheeler's handles as he pulled to a halt in front of the charred remains of the shack.

Hank pulled in beside him. "Damn."

Without a word, Thorn dismounted and circled the blackened studs rising three or four feet from the ground. The roof had collapsed, and the corrugated tin twisted from the heat of the fire.

At the back of what was left of the building, Thorn kicked through part of the fallen roof to find the shabby dirt bike buried beneath, the tires and seat nothing more than melted black goo.

"Think Sophia was right and they were after her?" Hank stepped up beside Thorn.

"Looks like it. But we won't be certain unless they target her alone."

Hank's lips pressed into a thin line. "I hope the job PJ's doing on her will throw them off her trail a little longer until we can find the source of her troubles."

"Whoever's responsible has contacts on this side of the border."

"Stands to reason. Cartels wouldn't operate very well unless they had contacts on both sides of the border." Hank stared at the burned remains. "Most of the drugs they traffic end up in the States. The demand ensures the supply continues to flow."

Thorn nodded. He knew that. He'd busted his share of junkies and pushers in his job as the county sheriff before he'd quit. He'd even upset a few major drug runs on the highways headed north. Sadly, the drugs never stopped coming. In the losing battle to clean up the drug problem in his county, the price had been greater than the reward. His efforts had cost him the lives of his wife and unborn child, and his career.

For every bust, for every man taken out of the drug-running business, he could count on two more thugs filling that doper's shoes. When trafficking drugs exceeded anything an uneducated man could make in the States, and greatly exceeded the pathetic wages of an honest man in Mexico, the choice was easy.

"Come on. I'll show you where she cut the fence." Thorn straddled his ATV, swung wide of what was left of the cabin and sped toward the fence on the southern border of the Raging Bull Ranch.

The fence was still intact for as far as he could see in either direction.

While Thorn struggled with the barbed wire, Hank sent Max in one direction while he sped off in the other.

It took Thorn and Scott a few minutes to locate the spot he'd patched, and a few minutes more to unwrap the wire he'd used to pull the fence together. They were minutes he had the feeling he couldn't spare. Finding the body of Sophia's escort would prove time-consuming with her tracks effectively washed away by the previous night's storm.

By the time Thorn had the fence down, Hank and Max had returned.

"No breaks in the fence for at least a half mile to the west," Hank reported.

"None that far to the east," Max said.

"It appears the bikers didn't come from this end of the property."

"Which begs the question, were they really after the woman, or were they after Hank?" Thorn didn't expect an answer. He mounted his ride and gunned the throttle.

The group of men crossed the property line and entered Big Bend National Park, speeding toward the rugged hills and canyons heading directly south.

Thorn prayed they'd catch a break and stumble across the man's body soon, rather than spending hours combing over potentially thousands of acres.

He headed toward the pass leading down into a canyon, rationalizing Sophia's guide would stay low as long as possible before climbing out of the quasi protection of the canyon walls.

The path led downward, narrowing so much that their four-wheelers clung to the edges.

A sharp bend in the trail led to a straight stretch that climbed back up toward the top of a ridge. The roar of the four-wheeler engines echoed off the canyon walls, and buzzards lifted off the ground from the top of the ridge, spreading their wings to catch the thermals. They hovered above the approaching machines, watching, awaiting their turn to scavenge flesh from a dead animal.

Or in this case, the dead human.

Thorn reached the body first, skidding to a halt, thankful for the night's rain keeping the dust from rising and coating the man's body.

He lay sprawled across the trail. A motorcycle leaned against a boulder halfway down the steep hillside below, and the rocks between had a scraped or raked appearance as if the bike had slid on its side down the incline.

The ground around the man's body and what was left of his face was stained dark brown. Even the rain hadn't washed away the evidence of his demise.

"Jesus." Scott backed away from the gore and turned to purge his breakfast.

"Probably died instantly." Thorn's belly roiled, but he kept his composure, studying the ground around him a moment longer before he glanced around at the others. "See all we needed to see?"

Hank stood over the dead man. "How did she survive this attack?"

"Sophia said she was down the hill, in the shadow of an overhang when the helicopter flew over." Thorn stepped to the edge of the ridge and peered down another trail on the other side. As Sophia had indicated, a giant bluff leaned over the trail, providing a deep shadow beneath.

So far, Sophia's story checked out. Thorn turned around. "Let's get back. We can report this to the CBP, now that we know where he is. We can tell them a bull breached the fence and we went after him."

"Sounds good." Hank's face was pale and a little grayer than when they'd started out. "No man deserves to die like that."

And Hector had been helping Sophia escape.

Thorn leaped onto his four-wheeler, hit the starter and executed a tight turn on the narrow trail, heading back the way they'd come. Images of Kayla lying in a pool of her own blood stormed through Thorn's memory, spurring him on. He couldn't let the same thing happen to Sophia.

PJ switched off the hair dryer and laid her brush aside.

After an hour and a half of sitting in a chair, Sophia prayed the woman was done.

"What do you think?" PJ handed Sophia a mirror.

Sophia stared at the stranger in the reflection. Naturally a light brunette, the pale, golden blond strands fit her complexion and complemented her green eyes. She cupped the shorter ends falling only to her shoulders, liking the way it bounced. After one year in the compound, without a decent stylist, Sophia's hair had grown long and shaggy, down to the middle of her back. This shorter, lighter hair gave her an entirely different look.

"With the hair and those clothes, you won't look anything like the woman we started out with." PJ grinned. "You look fabulous."

Hope swelled in Sophia's chest and tears filled her eyes. "Thank you." She might have a chance of fooling people.

Maybe even starting over somewhere Antonio couldn't find her.

PJ turned to Max. "What do you think?"

Max had been leaning against the wall, his back to the women as PJ worked her magic on Sophia.

He turned to face them, his narrowed gaze widening when he saw Sophia. After a moment, he grunted.

PJ laughed. "I'll take that as approval." She turned back to Sophia and helped her out of the chair. "And I bet Hank knows someone who can fix you up with personal identification—a driver's license, social-security number, the works."

"He's already on it," Max confirmed.

Sophia straightened, her legs stiff from sitting so long, staring at a picture of the Grand Canyon on an otherwise-empty white wall in the cavernous conference room.

She smoothed the wrinkles out of the pressed khaki trousers and white short-sleeved ribbed-knit top PJ had provided for her. Sophia hoped the outfit gave her a casual, carefree, I'm-on-vacation look that would fool others enough they wouldn't think she was a cartel fugitive or illegal alien who'd slipped across the border in the middle of the night.

Her stomach rumbled, reminding her she'd better eat or risk being sick again.

PJ laughed. "I take it you're hungry."

Sophia's lips twisted. "I guess I am."

"Think it would be all right to go topside to the kitchen?" PJ asked Max.

The bodyguard's brows dipped. "Mr. Derringer gave specific instructions not to let Ms. Carranza out of the bunker until they returned."

"Then could you send Brandon up for something to eat?" PJ asked. "We could all stand a bite of lunch."

Max nodded, then frowned at them. "Don't go any-where."

Sophia gave the big guard a tentative smile. "I promise."

A moment later, Brandon entered the room. "Max asked me to keep an eye on you while he went to the kitchen. I thought you might be more entertained in the computer room, if you'd like to join me."

Sophia followed the young gadgets wizard, and PJ brought up the rear.

They entered the computer room, which was equipped with several workstations and a bank of a dozen monitors depicting alternating views of Hank's ranch from the corners of the house to what looked like the front gate.

Sophia was familiar with this kind of technology at *la Fuerte del Diablo.* Drug running was big business and the elusive *El Martillo,* the kingpin of the cartel, spared no expense to protect his investment. Though Antonio was one of *El Martillo*'s top men, he wasn't in charge. *El Martillo* slipped in and out of *la Fuerte del Diablo* under the cover of darkness to mete out his brand of justice to those who went against his wishes, serving as a reminder that he wasn't called The Hammer for nothing.

Sophia had never actually met *El Martillo.* She wasn't sure what his real name was or what he looked like. She'd only seen him in profile once. A tall man, he'd carried himself straight, almost like a businessman. But he was known for some unspeakable acts that kept his people in line when he wasn't around.

Her and Hector's escape from the compound would probably anger *El Martillo* and put Antonio under scrutiny, if not on notice, or even get him killed.

After all the abuse Antonio had heaped on her, she couldn't feel sorry for the man. He deserved whatever *El Martillo* did to him. If The Hammer allowed Antonio to live, he'd seek revenge on her for betraying him and putting him in danger of *El Martillo*'s wrath.

Sophia studied the monitors, searching for any signs of Antonio or the biker gang who'd attacked them the night before. "Do you also have some sort of radar to detect aircraft?" Images of the helicopter hovering over the top of the ridge strafing the ground with bullets sent a shiver over Sophia's skin.

Brandon shook his head. "No, not yet, but Hank has mentioned installing one. I'm in the process of evaluating what's available to come up with the best for the cost."

Movement on the screen overlooking the front gate drew Sophia's attention. "Are you expecting visitors?"

A large black SUV pulled up to the gate, and a man dressed in an olive drab shirt and dark sunglasses leaned out the window to press the button on the keypad. A beeping sound alerted them to the caller.

Brandon frowned at the monitor. "Hank mentioned the FBI would be checking in, but he said it would be later today." He leaned over a microphone and hit the talk button. "May I help you?"

"FBI," a disembodied voice crackled over the speaker.

Sophia's heart skipped a beat, and she clenched her fists to keep her hands from shaking. Though the man at the gate couldn't see her, she felt exposed. Did he know Hank was harboring their suspected murderer? Had the ranch owner lied and sent them to collect her and ship her back to Mexico?

"We're here to speak with Hank Derringer," the FBI agent continued.

PJ stepped up beside her and slipped an arm around her shoulders. "You'll be okay," she whispered.

The woman's reassuring words helped, but Sophia knew what would happen if she was sent back to Mexico. Antonio would kill her and her baby. "I can't go back," she murmured beneath her breath.

PJ's arm tightened around her. "And Hank won't let them take you back."

Brandon shrugged. "I'm sorry, Mr. Derringer is not available at this time."

"Do you know when he'll be back?"

"He should be back after lunch," Brandon said.

"We'll wait." In the view screen, the agent's head ducked back into the vehicle. From the angle of the camera, Sophia could see him lean back and say something to the man in the backseat.

The window went up, the dark tint on the glass blocking the view of the driver and the interior of the SUV.

Brandon lifted a radio and hit the transmitter key. "Max, we have company at the gate. FBI. They're waiting there until Hank gets back."

Max responded. "Roger."

For a long moment, Sophia stared at the screen. The SUV didn't move. Good at their word, the FBI wasn't leaving until they spoke with Hank. After five minutes, the doors to the SUV opened and the men got out, stretching. Four of the five men wore jumpsuits with *FBI* emblazoned on their arms. The fifth man emerged, an imposing figure in khaki slacks and a polo shirt with *FBI* embroidered on the front.

Sophia didn't recognize his face, but something about his size, the way he stood and his movements struck a chord of memory she couldn't place.

The leader of the agents spoke with one of his men, a tall, slender, light-haired man with narrow eyes and an angular face. He didn't speak with any of the others, only the leader, and he held a military-looking weapon as if it were an extension of his body.

A chill slithered down Sophia's spine, but she put it off as paranoia because these men were with the FBI, and they had the power to take her to jail for a crime she hadn't committed.

Sophia's pulse hammered through her veins. Like an animal trapped in a cage, she paced across the floor several times, always ending up back at the monitors to view the men determined to wait as long as it took until Derringer got back.

When would Hank and Thorn return? And how would they get her out of there without the FBI noticing her?

Movement on another monitor drew her attention away from the front gate and the FBI. A line of four-wheelers approached a camera. Leading the pack was a tall, sandy-haired man with broad shoulders and a determined set to his brow.

Thorn.

Sophia let out a breath she felt she'd been holding since he left. The man might not be able to protect her from the FBI or the CBP, but having him around made her feel better, like someone was looking out for her, whether she'd asked for his help or not.

"They're back," Brandon stated.

The four-wheelers slipped past the camera at the rear of the barn and appeared in the view screen in the barnyard.

Max strode into view.

Thorn, Hank, the foreman and the two bodyguards who'd gone with them dismounted and converged on Max, all eyes turning toward the driveway leading into the ranch compound.

Hank nodded at Max.

Max unclipped the radio from his belt and lifted it to his lips. His words crackled over the radio in front of Brandon. "Let the FBI through the gate."

The young computer guru responded, "Roger." He hit a button on a control panel.

Sophia's gaze returned to the monitor with the FBI SUV view. The gate swung open, the men piled into the vehicle and the SUV pulled through. Her pulse quickened, and she had the intense urge to run.

"Don't worry. My father wouldn't turn you over to them." PJ's arm squeezed her shoulders. "Just keep calm and stay here until Hank has a chance to talk to them and we know what they want."

Though she appreciated PJ's encouragement, Sophia wished Thorn was there with her. After his actions to ensure her safety from the biker gang attack, she trusted his strength and fighting ability to keep her alive. For a moment she wished he'd stay with her all the way to her new life. Too soon she'd be on her own again, as soon as she could get safe passage out of the area.

When Max met them at the barn, Thorn's first thought was that Sophia had escaped. His breath caught and held until he heard the bodyguard out.

He'd barely released his breath when Max assured them Sophia was still safe in the bunker, but the FBI had arrived and wanted to be let in.

Hank gave the approval.

"Are you sure that's a good idea?" Thorn asked.

"Sophia is to remain in the bunker. If you'd like to join her, please do. Max can stay with me."

"If you're sure she's okay…" Thorn turned to Max.

The other man's lips twitched on the corner. "She's fine, but you won't recognize her."

Hank grinned. "I knew PJ would come through." He tipped his head toward Max. "Resume your watch on our guest. I'll send Thorn down to relieve you as soon as we figure out what the FBI is up to."

Anxious to see Sophia and prove to himself she was still there and okay, Thorn waited impatiently for the FBI SUV to stop in the barnyard.

Four men climbed out, all wearing the green jumpsuits of a tactical team, with *FBI* emblazoned across one arm and Glocks strapped to their black utility belts. One man held the door for a fifth man to emerge from the middle of the backseat.

It was Grant Lehmann, a regional director for the FBI and an old friend of Hank's.

Hank stepped forward. "Grant, good to see you."

The man wore khaki slacks and a black polo shirt with *FBI* embroidered on the upper-left front. He wore sunglasses, which he removed as he stuck out a hand to shake Hank's. "Hank, you seem to keep this part of the country busy."

Hank dipped his head, his lips firming. "Just trying to clean up a little riffraff. Make this part of Texas a safer place to live."

Lehmann chuckled. "So how's that working for you?"

Hank shrugged. "One bad guy at a time."

"Sure you're not setting yourself up as a target by taking on the drug cartels?"

"Someone's gotta do it if the U.S. government isn't willing to engage." Hank's jaw tightened.

If Thorn hadn't been watching the exchange closely, he wouldn't have caught the slight narrowing of Lehmann's eyes before he laughed.

"You know how to call a spade a spade, Hank."

"And the drug running doesn't seem to end."

"Well, we're here to help." Grant glanced around the

barnyard. "We need a place to set up operations to bring in some of those bad guys you were talking about."

"Care to share what you know?" Hank brushed his cowboy hat against his leg, stirring up a cloud of dust.

"There's a BOLO out on Elena Carranza and Antonio Martinez. They were thought to have crossed the border from Mexico headed this way."

"What makes you think they're in this area?"

"Undercover contacts on the other side got wind they'd left a cartel compound headed north."

"They could have crossed anywhere."

"Eyewitnesses saw them on motorcycles at a low-water crossing of the Rio Grande yesterday morning, directly south of the Raging Bull. They should have come across the river and entered the Big Bend National Park canyons in the afternoon."

"Just two?" Hank waved a hand at the four men in tactical jumpsuits. "They must be special."

"They are. We've already briefed the CBP that these two are armed and extremely dangerous. They've been instructed to shoot on sight."

Thorn was shocked by the man's words. Shoot on sight? Pretty harsh command for an FBI regional director. Something about the man didn't feel right.

Hank placed his hat on his head, shadowing his expression. "From what the CBP said, the Mexican government was interested in extraditing them."

"If it comes down to your life or theirs…" Lehmann's eyes narrowed "…don't hesitate. Shoot."

"That bad?" Hank asked.

"The worst," the regional director confirmed. "I wouldn't be here if it wasn't that important."

"Does seem strange for them to pull in a regional director for a couple of Mexican fugitives." Hank scratched his chin. "Guess they wanted the best on the case."

Grant snorted. "They'd have thrown the entire department at them if they'd had the funding."

Thorn stepped forward. "Do you have photos of the two?"

Grant's brows rose.

Hank turned to Thorn. "Grant, this is Thorn Drennan, one of the men I've hired on as ranch security. Thorn, Grant Lehmann, FBI regional director."

"And old friend." Grant shook hands with Thorn. "Hank and I have known each other for years. Been through rough times together. Isn't that right?"

Hank nodded. "Grant led the search effort when my wife and son were kidnapped."

"Unfortunately, we never found them or any clues as to who took them and where." Grant shook his head. "Lilianna was a beautiful woman and Jake was a smart little boy, just like his father."

"Photos?" Thorn prompted.

Grant frowned and turned to the man nearest the vehicle. "Hand me the case file."

Without a word, the agent reached into the SUV and retrieved a folder filled with documents.

Grant flipped it open and pulled out two grainy photos. The woman in the first was smiling, and she wore her hair up with long dangling earrings swinging beside her cheeks. She held a margarita glass in one hand. The photo appeared to be a scanned and enlarged photograph of a young lady partying at a bar.

Despite the graininess, Thorn could tell this woman was the one they had hidden in Hank's bunker.

"She looks about as dangerous as a college coed." Thorn handed the photo back to Lehmann.

"Looks are deceiving. She and her boyfriend, Antonio Martinez, killed two undercover DEA agents."

"Why would they kill agents then run to the States?" Thorn asked. "It doesn't make sense."

"They skipped out of Mexico with a suitcase full of drug money. They'd be more afraid of cartel retaliation than being caught by the U.S. government." Grant's voice dropped to a low, dangerous tone. "They have a million reasons in that suitcase to run."

Chapter Nine

Grant Lehmann and his team stayed another ten minutes before they loaded up and left the Raging Bull Ranch with a promise to return to set up operations.

"Are you sure you want them here?" Thorn asked.

Hank nodded. "As long as they're here, I get information about their operation. Even if they don't feed it to me, I'll have Brandon bug them. We'll know what's going on."

"Why didn't you tell them about the body we found in the canyon?"

"I'm going to let the CBP find it." Hank smiled. "I'm also going to let the CBP set up operations co-located with the FBI—joint operations forcing the agencies to work together. The more people they have on this operation, the more confused it'll be." His smile faded, and his gaze captured Thorn's. "We need to get Sophia out of here before they return."

"What if what Lehmann said was true? What if she's in on the murders and the theft of the drug money?"

"What do you think? What do you believe?" Hank fired back.

Thorn usually trusted his gut. And his gut told him Sophia had told him the truth. He ran a hand through his hair. "I think she's telling the truth."

"I have a hunch she is, too." Hank turned toward the

house. "And if she's telling the truth, who's feeding the FBI a load of hooey?"

"Lies that could get Sophia killed on sight." Thorn didn't like it. That the FBI would fall into it so solidly had him scared for Sophia.

"First of all, I don't trust that the FBI is getting the right information. I still think there's some bad blood floating around in the bureau. Someone knows something about Elena and Antonio. And call me a fool, but I still like to think, though it's probably wishful thinking, that someone might even have information on the whereabouts of Lilianna and Jake."

"Then, yes, it's a good idea to keep the FBI close."

Hank waved a hand toward the hallway. "Let's see how it went with PJ. We'll need someplace to hide her away from here, and a believable story in case someone does spot her."

Thorn followed Hank to the bunker and waited while Hank pressed his thumb to the scanner. When the door opened, Thorn stepped past his boss and practically ran down the steps into the concrete-walled basement.

Hank chuckled behind him. "Afraid she's gone?"

Hell, yeah.

Thorn entered the conference room where they'd left Sophia with PJ. It was empty except for the cape, empty bottles of hair color and lingering acrid stench of chemicals.

Voices carried to them from the computer room.

"I bet they're with Brandon." Hank moved past the conference room and down the long hallway to the computer bay.

Brandon sat at his desk while the two women gazed at the bank of display screens.

As Hank and Thorn entered, a beautiful blonde with

deep green eyes turned toward them, her eyes widening. Her lips parted on a silent gasp, and she flew across the room into Thorn's arms. "Thank God you're back."

Thorn held her for a long moment, dumbstruck by the transformation. "Sophia?" He pushed her to arm's length and gazed down at her face.

Despite the change in hair color and style, the same green eyes stared back at him, misted in a film of tears. "You were away for a long time. Then the FBI came…"

"They're gone for now," Hank said. "You can't stay at the Raging Bull. They're coming back to set up operations here on the ranch."

Sophia's gaze bounced from Hank to Thorn. "Is it safe to leave the area?"

"No," Hank replied. "There are roadblocks everywhere. If you try to leave, even with the new hair, they might figure it out. Especially since I don't have your identification documents yet."

PJ touched her finger to her chin. "I'd offer to let her stay in my apartment, but there's barely enough room for me, Chuck and the baby. Plus, it's smack-dab in the middle of town. She needs to stay where no one really goes."

"Thorn, don't you live on the edge of Wild Oak Canyon?" Hank asked.

"Yes." Thorn tensed.

Brandon pulled up a map of the area on the computer and keyed in Thorn's address. He switched the view to satellite. "The house sits on the edge of town. I believe the house next to yours is empty?"

His gut knotting, Thorn didn't like where this was going. "The house next door is for sale." And had been for over a year with no prospects.

"The road leading out of town is a farm-to-market road, not a major highway. Traffic will be minimal." Brandon spun in his chair to face Thorn. "I can set you up with some cameras, but it'll take time. Maybe tomorrow?"

A heavy feeling pinching his lungs, Thorn wanted to tell them no. The last woman in his house had been Kayla, before she'd been shot to death. Going home was his own self-torture, which he preferred to do alone. He hadn't emptied her closet of clothes, and he hadn't painted over the half-finished wall in the nursery.

Kayla had asked him to paint it pale yellow, a neutral color that would suit a boy or a girl. She'd insisted on being surprised by the sex of their child. No matter whether a boy or a girl, she'd love that baby with all her heart.

She'd been killed the day of her monthly appointment. Thorn had picked her up from the house, the proud daddy going to every obstetrician appointment throughout her pregnancy.

Thorn hadn't known that the previous day, a drug addict he'd put away for peddling drugs to the teens in town had been released from Huntsville prison after serving only two years of a five-year sentence. Marcus Falkner was met by his girlfriend and driven all the way from the prison north of Houston to Fort Stockton. There he'd met up with one of his old gang members who supplied him with a 9 mm Beretta and a fully loaded ten-round clip.

He'd made the trip from Fort Stockton to Wild Oak Canyon, flying low in his girlfriend's black, souped-up Camaro, strung out on a fresh batch of crystal meth, arriving just in time for Thorn to help his wife from their truck in the parking lot of the clinic.

He'd fired off two rounds before Thorn had known what was coming.

Thorn had thrown himself at Kayla, knocking her to the pavement, covering her body with his.

Too hyped up on meth to shoot straight, Marcus emptied the rest of the clip and squealed out of the parking lot, fishtailing on loose gravel. He drove straight into a telephone pole, snapping his neck. Marcus had died instantly.

When Thorn had risen from the ground, he'd known something was terribly wrong with Kayla. She'd been lying facedown, moaning, her skin pale, a pool of blood spreading out from beneath her.

"You okay, Drennan?" Hank waved a hand in front of Thorn's face.

Thorn shook himself out of the memory and focused on his boss. "Yes."

"Then you'll take her to your house, and if anyone asks, she's an old girlfriend from your college days."

Thorn gritted his teeth, the thought of bringing any woman back to the house he'd shared with Kayla grating against his nerves. He glanced at Sophia's deep green eyes, noting the shadows beneath them and the yellowish-green bruise on her cheekbone that her long light brown hair had covered. He reached out and brushed his hand against the spot. "Did Antonio do this to you?"

She nodded, her face turning into his palm.

Thorn couldn't tell her no. He had a duty to protect her. If taking her to his house and pretending she was his old girlfriend was how he did it, then so be it. "Let's go before the FBI and border patrol make camp here." He turned to leave.

Sophia touched his arm. "You don't have to do this."

Thorn stared at where her hand touched his arm for a long moment, every emotion he'd ever felt for Kayla and her loss warring with the need to protect this woman the law was after for murder. For all he knew, she could be a killer.

Maybe he was an idiot, but he believed her story.

SOPHIA FIDGETED IN the passenger seat of Thorn's truck, carefully studying the road as they neared the town of Wild Oak Canyon, watching for any signs of police, FBI, CBP and cartel thugs carrying automatic weapons. Every time they passed a vehicle, she had to remind herself not to duck or act as if she was hiding. For this disguise to work, she had to look like a happy, carefree young woman on vacation visiting an old boyfriend. She forced a smile on her face that she didn't feel, and her cheeks hurt as they drove through town.

"Relax." Thorn glanced her way. "Your hair color and haircut will make it hard for the FBI to match you to the photo they have. Let it hang across your cheeks a little to break up the lines of your facial structure, and you'll be good to go."

"Won't you and Hank be in big trouble if the FBI finds out you are harboring a Mexican fugitive accused of murder?"

"Only if they catch us." His hands tightened on the steering wheel, his knuckles turning white. "First test coming up." He nodded toward the black SUV sitting in front of the sheriff's office. Beside it was a green-and-white Customs and Border Protection vehicle. Grant Lehmann was talking with a CBP officer, looking none too happy.

Another man wearing a green jumpsuit, with *FBI* written in bold letters on one sleeve, stood with a wicked-looking weapon slung over his shoulder, his gaze scanning the road. When it locked on Thorn's truck, Sophia shivered.

"Just look toward me." Thorn draped an arm over the back of the seat and smiled her way, his blue eyes twinkling at her from beneath the brim of his cowboy hat.

Sophia's heart fluttered. She blamed it on nerves at having to pass the very agents she was trying to avoid, but she knew it was Thorn's smile that gave her a thrill. She could almost forget she was a fugitive.

She didn't have to force her answering smile. "You look so much younger when you smile."

"And you look beautiful when you smile."

The tingling sensation spreading through Sophia's body had everything to do with Thorn's compliment, given in that deep, rich voice. Too bad it was all for show. Not that it mattered. Sophia had no intention of starting a relationship with the man anytime soon, if ever. Her stay in Wild Oak Canyon was temporary, to be ended when she could get out safely. Then she'd start a life somewhere no one could find her. The thrill of the moment before faded into intense sadness. Her baby would never know her grandparents. As long as Antonio was alive, Sophia could never go back to Monterrey.

The cowboy returned his attention to the road ahead and made a left turn at the next street. "Other than the one man, the rest of them didn't look our way. So far, so good."

They drove to the western edge of town, where the road disappeared out into the desertlike landscape. A soft, cream-colored clapboard house sat back from the road, its antique-blue shutters giving the building a splash of color. In the front yard, a scrub oak tree shaded the swing on the wraparound porch. The structure had charm and a feeling of home, making Sophia want to sit on that porch and sip lemonade.

Thorn slowed as they approached the driveway.

"This is your home?" Sophia asked.

The cowboy's hands gripped the steering wheel, his knuckles white. "Yes." He dragged in a deep breath and turned down the driveway, pulling up beside the house. He stared at the house for a long moment before he got out of the truck.

Sophia scrambled out and grabbed the suitcase Hank had given her, filled with toiletries and a change of clothing PJ had provided. For a moment she almost felt like a woman on vacation. If not for the overwhelming sense of dread hanging over her head and a sad feeling that she was trespassing on Thorn's privacy, she would have enjoyed exploring this quaint little house.

Thorn started up the steps without offering to let her go first. He stuck the key in the lock and twisted, then stepped back, his jaw tight, his face set, inscrutable.

Sophia entered the house, curious about the way Thorn lived. Mail was stacked on a table by the door. Some of it had slipped to the floor unopened, as if Thorn hadn't been home for a while.

All the windows in the living room to the right had the blinds drawn, blocking out the sun. In the corner, a small upright piano stood with music leaning on the stand as if waiting for the player to return.

"Do you play?" Sophia nodded toward the piano.

Thorn's lips tightened, and he said curtly, "No." He took the suitcase from her and climbed the stairs to the second floor.

When she didn't follow, he turned back, frowning. "Your room is up here."

Sophia followed slowly, wondering what had Thorn so tense. She stepped onto the upper landing, a few steps behind him. "If you're worried about getting caught hiding me, I can make it on my own. You don't have to do this."

"I'm not worried about being caught." Thorn entered the first bedroom on the right. Though small, the room had all the charm of the early twentieth century. A full-size white iron bed was centered on one wall, the mattress covered in an old-fashioned quilt in beautiful shades of pastel blue, violet and green. Light, white eyelet curtains framed the window, and sunshine shone through, welcoming her.

He set her case on the floor. "Bathroom is down the hall. You'll find towels and soap in the cupboard." He performed an about-face and inched past her as if trying not to brush against her.

Before he could leave her, Sophia touched a hand to his arm. "Did I do something to make you mad?"

Thorn stared down at the hand on his arm for so long that Sophia let go. Then his gaze shifted to hers.

"I haven't had another woman in the house since…" His lips thinned, and he turned to leave.

"Since when?" Sophia asked. "Since your wife died?"

Thorn spun to face her, his eyebrows drawn down. "How do you know about her?"

Sophia's lips quirked upward. "PJ mentioned you'd been married but that your wife died a couple years ago." Sophia sighed. "I am sorry for your loss." She stared up into his eyes, noting the deep creases at the sides and how gray his blue eyes had become.

"It was a long time ago."

"Not long enough for the pain to pass." Sophia nodded. "I'll try not to be too intrusive."

Thorn closed his eyes. "You're not. It's my problem. I'll deal with it. In the meantime, make yourself at home. Kayla would have wanted you to." He left her in the room and returned to the first floor.

Kayla—his dead wife's name.

Now that Sophia had a name to go with Thorn's grief, she understood the glimpses of the woman's presence in the house. Many of the decorations were far more feminine than what she'd associate with the stern, often sad Thorn. The piano in the corner of the living room, the colorful pillows on the sofa all spoke of someone who had loved this home and wanted it to be a haven of happiness for those who lived there.

Sophia swallowed hard on the lump building in her throat. Thorn must have loved her so much that it hurt to bring another woman into the same house he had shared with Kayla.

A sense of yearning seeped into her consciousness. What would it feel like to be loved like that? Other than their first encounter, when she'd tried to shoot Thorn and he'd threatened to shoot back, he'd been a gentleman and surprisingly concerned for her safety. The night before, when Sophia had stayed in Hank's house and had the horrible nightmare, Thorn had held her until she quit trembling. He'd even stayed near the bed until she'd fallen back to sleep. From what she'd seen, he'd been kind, caring and gentle. A far cry from the man she'd almost married.

A shiver reverberated down her spine. Even had she married Antonio, she'd have left him, given the same opportunity. He was a monster without a heart. Sophia wouldn't subject her child to his bouts of rage or the life they'd lived in the cartel compound.

Her best bet was to be prepared for her next move. It wouldn't hurt to study the layout of the house and surrounding properties in case she had to make a run for it.

Sophia left the clothes in the suitcase and wandered down the hallway, trying to remember which door led to the bathroom. She opened the first door past hers and gasped.

The room appeared to be a work in progress, one wall painted part of the way in a pale yellow while the rest remained a light beige. What caught her attention was the white crib standing in the corner beside a white dresser covered in a pad that would serve as a baby's changing table.

Sophia's heart squeezed so hard in her chest that she pressed a hand to the pain, her eyes filling with tears. Had they been expecting a baby when Thorn's wife died? Not only had he lost his wife, he'd lost his unborn child, too.

She stepped into the room, drawn by the baby bed. A thick layer of dust covered the railing, which indicated it had not been disturbed for a while. Two cans of paint stood on the corner of a painter's drop cloth, as if whoever had been doing the work had stopped in the middle with the intention of finishing the job later.

As she stared down at the empty crib, a sob rose up Sophia's throat. She backed out of the room and closed the door softly, her hand hesitating before she let go and moved on to the next door. Her heart ached for the man who had to come home every day to an empty house and reminders of what should have been.

The next door revealed the master bedroom. Sophia could see a king-size bed standing in the center of the room and a cherry dresser with a silver hairbrush and picture frame in the center. His closet stood open. From where she stood, she could see both men's and ladies' clothing hanging inside. No wonder Thorn hadn't wanted another woman in his house. He'd kept his pain trapped inside the walls. He had yet to let go of his memories.

A noise below made her jump and scurry toward the bathroom, where she washed her hands and splashed water on her face, rinsing the tears from her eyes. She stared at the woman in the mirror, barely recognizing herself. With blond hair falling just to her shoulders, she could be that girl on vacation. Only she knew she wasn't.

She ran her fingers through the strands, liking the look and feeling more hopeful that she stood a chance of making good her escape to a better life.

When she left the bathroom, she followed the sounds of pots and pans clattering in the kitchen on the first floor.

Thorn had a pan on the gas stove frying hamburger meat, and he was filling another with water. "I hope you like spaghetti. It's all I know how to cook."

"I love spaghetti. My mother used to cook it for us. May I?" She took the pot of water from him, set it on the stove and lit the element. "Do you have tomatoes, bell peppers and onion for the sauce?"

"Sorry." He gave her a crooked smile. "But I do have ready-made sauce." Thorn reached over her head, his body pressing against hers as he retrieved a jar from the cabinet.

When he set it on the counter beside her, he didn't move away at first. "You smell good."

She laughed, the sound shaky even to her own ears. "It's the cooking food. You must be hungry."

He turned her to face him. "It's not the food, unless you're cooking honeysuckle and roses."

She stared up into his eyes and her breath caught in her lungs, refusing to move into or out of her chest. Her gaze shifted to his lips.

For once, they weren't set in a thin, tight line. His lips were full, sensitive and very kissable.

Sophia swiped her tongue across her own suddenly dry lips. "Thank you."

He cupped her cheek with his palm and thumbed the fading bruise. "No man should ever hit a woman."

"I agree. That's why I left." She reached up and captured his hand against her face. "Don't."

"Don't what? Do this?" His mouth descended and claimed hers in a soul-shattering kiss.

Her breath escaped her on a sigh and she leaned into him, craving more, wanting to feel his strong arms around her. Not holding her captive but holding her safe and warm, making her forget everything else around her. The fear of escape and crossing the border, the horror of the helicopter gunning Hector down and her dread of being caught and deported back to Mexico where the cartel ruled all melted away.

For the moment, she was just a woman kissing a man who wasn't going to hurt her.

Thorn's hands slipped to her shoulders and he set her away from him, his face tight, a muscle ticking in his jaw. "That was a mistake. It shouldn't have happened." He wiped the back of his hand across his mouth, his gaze still on her face, his blue eyes gray and distant.

"Do not worry." Sophia fought to keep from wincing at the pain spreading through her chest as reality set in and reminded her where she was. In the house Thorn had shared with his wife. "It will not happen again." She turned toward the stove and the sizzling meat, letting the heat of the cooking food warm her cold cheeks. "You belong here, and I'm leaving as soon as I can get out of here safely."

The sound of an electronic chirp made Sophia spin around.

Thorn pulled a cell phone from his pocket and hit the talk button. "Drennan." He listened for a moment, his face inscrutable. Then he looked across at Sophia.

Her pulse leaped and her hands trembled, dread building with each passing moment. What now?

"We'll be on the alert." Thorn clicked the phone off, slipping it into his jeans pocket.

Sophia pressed her hands together to keep them from shaking. "What happened?"

"The CBP and FBI have started setting up camp on Hank's property. Brandon tapped into their radio communications and got word they'd found an ultralight aircraft on a neighboring ranch with tire tracks leading away. Do you know anyone who flies an ultralight?"

Sophia's gut clenched and burbled. "I only know one person who owns such a craft." He'd followed her. Her vision blurred, and she would have fallen if Thorn hadn't reached out to catch her before she hit the ground.

"Who is it?"

"The man I was running from, Antonio Martinez, my former fiancé." Thankful for the steely arms around her, Sophia fainted away into blessed darkness.

Chapter Ten

Thorn lifted Sophia into his arms and carried her into the living room, laying her across the sofa. He smoothed the blond hair out of her face, pulled his phone from his pocket and speed-dialed Hank.

"What's up, Drennan?"

"Sophia says the ultralight could belong to her ex-fiancé, Antonio Martinez."

"The man the FBI says murdered two DEA agents?"

"That's the one."

"Poor kid. Not only does she have the feds after her, now she has to worry about her ex finding her."

"I'm betting her welcoming committee last night was some of his doing."

"I had Brandon look up Antonio Martinez. If he's the guy we're thinking he is, he's second in command to the head of the *la Familia Diablos* cartel. He could have been the one to send out the helicopter that killed her escort."

Thorn had thought about that. "If he had the access and authority to send the helicopter, why did he land an ultralight nearby? Seems like he would have had the helicopter set him down and then bug out."

Hank was silent for a moment. "Antonio is only second in command. Maybe his boss sent the helicopter."

"That's my bet. And I'd also bet that his boss isn't too

happy he couldn't keep his woman in line. She could lead people back to their hideout."

"Could be," Hank said. "Which would explain the leak to the FBI combining Martinez with Sophia and telling them that they were dangerous. What better way to get rid of two traitors?"

"Right. Shoot first, ask questions later." Thorn didn't like it.

"Do we need to change our plans? With the FBI and CBP here, I'm not certain she'd be any safer here."

"For now, she can stay with me." Much as he didn't like another woman in the house he'd shared with Kayla, he couldn't let Sophia roam the streets with so many factions after her. "If you could put feelers out to your local informants to be on the lookout for Martinez, that might help. The FBI and CBP might not see past Sophia's disguise, but Martinez would."

"Right. I'll circulate a copy of Martinez's photo to my contacts. In the meantime, keep a low profile."

"Will do." When Thorn ended the call, he found himself standing in front of the piano Kayla had loved playing. A photograph in a wooden frame stared back at him. He lifted it from the piano, memories flooding over him. They'd taken the picture on their honeymoon to South Padre Island. He and Kayla were smiling in the photo— two young people with their whole lives in front of them. They'd dreamed of owning a house, raising children and growing old together. His fingers gripped the frame, and his heart hurt. Kayla shouldn't have died.

"She was beautiful."

Thorn spun toward the voice.

Sophia sat up on the sofa, her gaze on the photograph in his hand. "That's Kayla, isn't it?"

Thorn nodded, afraid to speak around thickened vocal cords.

"You two look good together. You must have loved her very much."

"I did."

"How did she die?"

For a long moment he hesitated, not wanting to talk about Kayla and that horrible moment when he'd held her in his arms as she'd bled out.

Sophia rose and touched his arm. "I'm sorry. You don't have to tell me if it's too painful."

The warmth of her hand on his arm loosened his tongue. "Drug addict aiming for me, got her instead."

"I'm sorry."

"Why? You didn't do it."

"I'm sorry for your loss." She squeezed his arm. "I've been thinking about Antonio."

Thorn's brows descended. "What about him?"

"He's coming for me." Sophia stepped away from Thorn. "He'll kill anyone who gets in his way of taking me back. I should leave now, before anyone else gets hurt."

"You can't go. They'll be looking for you at the checkpoints."

"Then I'll get out on foot."

"It's a long way between towns. There's little vegetation to hide behind, and if the heat doesn't get you, the coyotes might."

Sophia shrugged. "I'd rather face the coyotes than Antonio."

"We've been through this. You're staying. No arguments." He turned at the sound of something hissing in the next room. "We'd better save the spaghetti before it burns the house down." Thorn placed the photo facedown on the piano, hurried into the kitchen and switched on his own police scanner, which he'd kept from his days as sheriff. As he salvaged the charred hamburger meat and poured sauce over it, he listened to the chatter between the deployed units and dispatch.

Sophia joined him and poured a handful of noodles into the pan of boiling water, stirring to keep them from sticking together. For the next ten minutes they worked side by side at the stove, preparing a meal like any married couple.

Kayla had always had supper ready when he got home from work. She'd never invited him to help, always letting him relax.

Despite himself, he couldn't help that he liked having Sophia there. He'd gone too long without company.

As Sophia drained the water from the cooked noodles, the scanner erupted with an excited deputy announcing, "Checked out that report of trespassers at the old Fenton place and found something interesting. You might want to send the FBI this way."

Thorn took the pan from Sophia and laid it on the stove quietly as he listened to the exchange.

Dispatch responded, "What did you find?"

"Empty cartridge boxes, wooden crates that could have held weapons and a few blasting caps scattered on the ground. The kind they use with C-4 explosives."

"I'll notify the FBI."

Thorn removed his phone from his pocket and hit redial. Before the call went through, a loud explosion rocked the house.

Sophia screamed, dropped to her knees and pressed her hands to her ears. "What was that?"

"I think someone found the explosives." Thorn ran out the front door onto the porch.

A truck skidded to a stop in front of the house, and PJ

flung the door open and stepped out on her running board, looking back over her shoulder. "Did you hear that?"

A thought struck Thorn. "Where's Charlie?"

"Thankfully, I left her with Hank's housekeeper at the Raging Bull. I was just coming by with a few more things your guest might find useful."

Thorn shaded his eyes and studied the plume of black smoke rising above the rooftops, his sense of duty toward the city and its inhabitants urging him to check it out. He couldn't stand back and let the town burn down and do nothing to stop it. "I need to see if anyone was hurt."

"Go." Sophia opened the screen door and peered out. "I can take care of myself."

Thorn frowned, knowing he should stay. Even with her changed appearance, she could still be in danger.

Sophia smiled. "You probably know everyone in town. You can't stay with me when someone you care about could have been injured." She touched his arm. "Go. I'll be okay."

"Are you sure?"

"I'm sure."

Thorn ran out to PJ. "Can you stay here with S—my guest while I check it out and see if anyone was hurt?"

"Sure, take Chuck's truck." PJ grabbed a canvas tote bag from the backseat and hopped out.

Thorn jumped in and turned the truck around, leaving a trail of black tire marks.

An explosion big enough to rock his house on the edge of town had to have done some major damage downtown. God, he hoped everyone was all right and that Sophia stayed safe while he checked it out.

Sophia backed behind the screen door as Thorn drove away.

PJ stood in the middle of the street for a few moments

longer before she sauntered across the yard and climbed the stairs. "God, I hope no one got hurt."

"Me, too."

PJ closed the door behind her and handed Sophia the bag. "More clothes. Hope they fit."

"Thank you. I'm sure they'll be fine." Sophia set the bag on the sofa and stepped to the window, lifting one slat on the wooden blinds to peer out at the empty street. "I wish I knew what was going on."

"You and me both."

Sophia frowned. She left PJ standing in the living room and hurried to the kitchen, where the police scanner was blaring with reports from the deputies responding to the explosion.

A loud blast of static was followed by a man's voice. "A woman reported an explosion at Cara Jo's Diner on Main."

PJ gasped. "Cara Jo's. Oh, dear God."

"Sanders here. I'm almost there—holy hell."

"What's going on?" Sophia assumed the voice was the dispatcher.

"The diner's nothing but rubble," Sanders said. "We'll need the fire department and ambulance ASAP."

"On their way."

"Oh, my God." PJ's face paled, and she pressed her hand to her lips. "I work there. Today was my day off." She paced the kitchen floor, stopping to stare out the window toward the smoke now billowing toward the sky. "I hope Cara Jo and Mrs. K are okay."

"Don't stay on my account." Sophia waved PJ toward the front door. "Go. Check on your friend."

"I shouldn't. You need someone—"

"No. I don't. I can look out for myself." Sophia walked her to the door and opened it.

PJ reached for the screen door and stopped so fast

Sophia bumped into her. "Uh, Sophia, we might have a problem."

"What do you mean?" Sophia stood on her tiptoes and glanced over the taller woman's shoulder. A black truck with dark tinted windows and four motorcycles were headed their way.

PJ backed away from the door, then closed and locked it. "I'm not sure they're coming here, but we don't want to take the chance. Let's head out the back door. Go!"

Sophia ran through the house to the door leading away from the street into the backyard.

Since the house was on the end of the street, there was only one direction they could go to escape being seen. Back toward town.

Sophia ducked behind a scraggly holly hedge in back of the house next to Thorn's and crawled to the edge of the property. A ten-foot gap stretched between the bush and a storage shed at the back of the house next door. From where she stood, she could see the black truck getting closer.

"Holy cow," PJ whispered.

"If we're going, it better be now." Sophia grabbed PJ's arm and hustled her across the expanse to the back of the shed. The truck passed by and pulled into the yard in front of Thorn's cute little cottage.

The four motorcycles spun out in the front yard. Men piled out of the truck carrying wicked-looking guns aimed at the house. Another man stepped from the truck.

The air whooshed out of Sophia's lungs and blood rushed from her head, leaving her dizzy.

"What?" PJ whispered.

"He found me."

"Who? Your ex-fiancé?" PJ peered around Sophia.

"Antonio." Her world seemed to crash in around her and her feet felt leaden, glued to the ground. He'd found her and he'd take her back to Mexico, beat her until she bled and then kill her and the baby she carried. "I can't let him take me back."

PJ pulled her back from the edge of the shed. "I won't let him take you. We'll watch and wait for our chance to run."

Sophia stared out at the landscape, her heart slowing, her breathing becoming more labored. "He'll kill you, me and—" She clamped her lips shut before she blurted the word *baby.*

PJ grabbed Sophia and shook her. "Look, I'm not letting him kill anyone. I have a little girl waiting for me at Hank's. I'll be damned if anyone takes away my chance to see her grow up." PJ shook her again. "Snap out of it." Then PJ peeked around the corner of the shed. "We have to wait for our chance."

"Elena!" Antonio yelled.

Sophia flinched and eased forward, hate welling up inside. This man had claimed to love her and instead had beaten her until she lost her will to live. The only thing keeping her going was the baby growing inside her. Her child would live without fear, damn it.

"Elena, mi amor, salir." Antonio waited a moment, then waved forward his men with the ugly guns. They broke through the front door and disappeared inside. Footsteps could be heard pounding on the wooden floors, going up the stairs and back down. Then the men reappeared, shaking their heads. One shouted, *"Nadie aquí!"*

Antonio jerked his head and the four men crossed the yard to where he stood. He said something that sounded low and angry, but Sophia couldn't make out the words.

The four men faced the house, stood with their feet braced and fired their weapons, unloading their clips into the building. Glass shattered and wood splinters flew.

Sophia half rose, horrified at the damage they were

leveling onto Thorn's home. The home he'd shared with the only woman he'd ever loved. A woman who'd been pregnant just like Sophia when her life had been cut short.

When the gunmen stopped shooting, Antonio spoke lowly again, following his words with a sharp, *"Rápidamente!"*

The men raced to the truck and lifted out plastic jugs. They ran back to the house and doused the walls with liquid.

"Gasoline," PJ whispered. "They're going to burn it."

"No." Sophia lunged for the house.

PJ grabbed her and forced her back behind the shed. "Thorn can build another. Your life is more important."

Antonio pulled a matchbox from his pocket, kissed it then struck one against the side. *"Para ti, mi amor."* He threw the match, igniting the gasoline. Flames leaped into the air, and black smoke rose.

Sophia's heart broke as the house went up in flames, everything Thorn held dear burning within.

If she wanted to stay alive for her baby, they had to move before the fire spread or Antonio and his men saw them. Sophia waited for the moment when all the men turned toward Antonio, awaiting his next instruction. Meanwhile the fire flared, blocking her view of them and theirs of her and PJ. "Now!" Sophia hooked PJ's arm and ran as fast as her feet could carry her.

She didn't look back to see if they were being followed, instead running as if her life depended on it. She refused to be a victim ever again.

THORN SKIDDED CHUCK'S truck to a stop a couple of blocks from what used to be Cara Jo's Diner on the corner of the Wild Oak Canyon Resort on Main Street. A fire truck from the all-volunteer firefighting department was there, along with half a dozen firefighters still pulling their suits up over their street clothing. Pickup trucks with rotating red lights on top of them lined the street, and more were coming. Deputy Sanders was talking with Raymond Rausch, the Wild Oak Canyon fire chief, who was pointing at the gutted structure.

Cara Jo was one of Thorn's friends. He'd had coffee at the diner every morning for the years he'd been sheriff of Wild Oak Canyon and at least once a week since he'd quit his job on the force.

Thorn dropped down out of the truck and ran toward Sanders and Rausch, his heart thumping against his ribs as he scanned the faces, searching for Cara Jo and Mrs. Kinsley, the cook. It was late afternoon, before the typical evening dinner crowd converged on the diner. Hopefully there weren't many injured, or injured seriously.

Thorn stopped next to the fire chief. "Sanders, Raymond, what happened?"

Sanders frowned. "An explosion in the rear of the diner. We're not certain yet as to the cause."

"Cara Jo and Mrs. Kinsley?"

"Mrs. Kinsley was off this afternoon. We found Cara Jo in the dining room. The paramedics are loading her up now into the ambulance." Chief Rausch pointed toward the waiting ambulance. "She's pretty banged up, but the EMTs think she'll be okay. They're taking her to the hospital for further evaluation by a doctor."

Thorn ran to the paramedics wheeling the gurney toward the back of the waiting ambulance. He caught up with them and touched the shoulder of one of the paramedics. "What's the verdict?" he asked.

"Hey, Sheriff." Fred White, a man Thorn had known since high school, knew Thorn was no longer sheriff, but old habits died hard and Thorn didn't want to waste time arguing.

Fred nodded toward Cara. "Several lacerations on her arms, legs and face. Nothing life threatening, possible cracked ribs and a concussion. We're taking her in for X-rays and to give docs a crack at her." Fred leaned over Cara Jo. "Pun intended."

"Ha. Ha." Cara Jo wore a neck brace and was strapped down, completely immobile. "Thorn? That you?" Her voice was gravelly and weak.

Thorn leaned over her face so that she could see him without straining. "Hey, Cara Jo, going all dramatic on us?"

"Darned tootin'." She attempted a smile through her split lip. "Always aimed to go out with a big bang."

"Fortunately, you're not going out yet. Do you know what happened?" Thorn looked before he touched her hand to make sure he wasn't going to hurt her.

"I heard someone in the back. Thought for moment Mrs. K had returned, then all hell broke loose and everything went black for me." She snorted and grimaced. "Woke up lying in the street, with Fred shining a light in my eyes."

"A little unnerving?" Thorn shook his head. "They say you'll be okay."

"Then why do they have me strapped down? It's not like I'm gonna run anywhere anytime soon."

"Just a precaution," he reassured her.

"Yeah, yeah." Cara Jo's eyes closed for a moment. "Thorn?"

"Yeah, Cara Jo?"

"Heard you had a girlfriend in town. Sally Freeman, huh?"

News traveled fast in Wild Oak Canyon. Thorn hated

lying, but in this case, Cara Jo would understand. "Sally's a friend from college."

Cara Jo opened her eyes and raised her hand to clasp his. "Don't sell yourself short, hon. You deserve to be happy."

Thorn's heart contracted at Cara Jo's words. She was thinking of him when she was the one lying on a gurney with injuries from an explosion.

"Sorry, Sheriff." Fred nudged his arm. "I need to get Cara Jo to the hospital."

Thorn squeezed his injured friend's hand carefully and let go. "I'll be by to see you later."

"Countin' on it," Cara Jo whispered.

Fred and his partner loaded the gurney into the back of the ambulance and drove away.

Seeing Cara Jo covered in blood, cuts and bruises, lying strapped to the gurney, brought back memories of Kayla and the ambulance that had taken her to the hospital, where the doctor had pronounced her dead on arrival.

Anger slammed through his veins. This was his town, the town he'd grown up in, the place he'd played football, fell in love and got married in. He'd be damned if he lost another one of his people to senseless violence.

Thorn stalked back to the fire chief, ready for answers, and he wasn't going anywhere until he had some.

Chief Rausch leaned toward Deputy Sanders, his brows furrowed.

Sanders was on his radio, a frown creasing his forehead. He spun toward the west, his gaze scanning the rooftops.

Thorn turned, too, and his heart sank to his feet. More smoke rose over the roofline, from the direction he'd just come.

Holy hell.

He ran for his truck as other vehicles turned in the middle of the street. Sirens blared from the direction of the firehouse as another truck left the station.

As Thorn climbed into his pickup, he sent a fervent prayer to the heavens. *Please don't be my house. Please spare PJ and Sophia.*

Chapter Eleven

Sophia kept running until she was within a couple blocks of the center of town. Her sides ached and her lungs burned, but she refused to stop until she was certain they hadn't been followed.

When she looked back, no one was behind her and PJ. No black truck, motorcycles or Antonio. When she finally slowed, Sophia staggered to the corner of a house and leaned against it, heaving air into and out of her lungs. Then she bent double and lost what remained of the contents of her belly.

"Are you all right?" PJ pulled Sophia's hair away from her face and ran her hand over her back like a mother soothing her child.

Sobs rose up Sophia's burning throat. She moved away from PJ, stumbling toward the next house, determined to get as far away from Antonio as possible.

PJ caught up with her and grabbed her arm. "You can't keep going."

The wail of sirens cleaved the air, and Sophia watched through the gaps between the houses as vehicles raced by on the main roads, two blocks away.

Not knowing whether Antonio and his gang were still looking for her, she wasn't willing to step out of hiding onto Main Street to flag someone down.

"We need to make a call, but I left my purse and cell phone in Thorn's house. We have to get to a phone." PJ stared at the house across the street. "I think I know how."

"How?" Sophia asked.

PJ pointed at a small white clapboard cottage with a splash of bright gold lantana and marigolds growing in the front garden. "Mrs. Henderson and her husband live in that house. She works for Kate Langsdon. Mr. Henderson is retired. Hopefully he'll let us hide there until we can get in touch with Thorn or Hank." PJ patted Sophia's arm. "Stay here until I wave you over."

Sophia sagged against the wall. "I don't think I could run another step even with a gun pointed at me."

"Fatigue is hard to battle in your first trimester. Let me handle this." With a reassuring smile, PJ scanned the street before leaving the shadows and stepping out into full sunlight.

Sophia's belly tightened. *She knows I'm pregnant.* But how? She'd told no one. And throwing up once in front of the other woman wasn't necessarily a clue. She couldn't tell anyone. If Antonio learned the truth, there'd be no stopping him.

Too drained to consider running again, Sophia propped herself against the wall of the house she stood beside, half-hidden by a bushy crepe myrtle, whose bright fuchsia blooms spoke of carefree summer days.

Sophia would have laughed at the irony of her thoughts of the pretty pink flowers if two fires weren't still burning and she had enough lung power to summon humor.

PJ stepped out into the street, hands in her pockets, looking like anyone out for a stroll. She looked both ways before she crossed the road to the Hendersons' house and knocked on the door.

Her head jerked back and forth, and she turned completely around once before the door cracked open and an older man peered out.

PJ spoke to the man, turned and scanned both ends of the street, then waved Sophia forward.

Sophia's pulse raced as she left the security of the shadows and ventured out into the wide-open street. She tried to look natural, but by the time she was halfway across the pavement she was running again, fear driving her feet faster.

PJ and Mr. Henderson stepped to the side as Sophia fell through the open doorway, landing on her knees.

PJ slammed the door behind her. "I'm calling Thorn and Hank." She pointed at Sophia and gave her a stern look. "You stay there until you catch your breath."

Too exhausted to argue, Sophia rolled onto her back and sucked in air, filling her starving lungs.

Mr. Henderson leaned over her. "Are you okay? Want me to call nine-one-one?"

Sophia and PJ answered as one. "No!"

The old man's eyes widened, and he held up his hands in surrender. "Just tryin' to help."

"I'm sorry, Mr. Henderson." PJ touched the man's arm. "It's a long story, and someday I'll tell you all about it, but right now we need a telephone."

"It's on the counter in the kitchen." Mr. Henderson pointed to a doorway down the hall. "Help yourself."

PJ disappeared through it and Sophia sat up, her breathing slowly returning to normal.

Mr. Henderson held out his hand and helped her to her feet. "You could sit in the living room and rest while you're waiting. Mrs. Henderson should be home soon."

"No, thank you. I'd like to join PJ." She headed for the sound of PJ's voice. When she reached the kitchen, PJ was replacing the phone in the charger. "Hank's already halfway to town. He's going to take us out to the ranch. Apparently the explosion in town was at Cara Jo's Diner. Cara Jo was sent to the hospital. It destroyed the diner and part of the Wild Oak Canyon Resort." PJ sighed. "I wonder how my apartment fared. It's at the back of the resort, close to the diner."

A lead weight settled in Sophia's empty stomach. She couldn't help feeling as if it was all her fault. She'd brought disaster to this nice little town. "What about Thorn?"

"I couldn't reach him on the phone. I left a message on his voice mail that he could find us at Hank's."

"Is it safe for me to go out there? The FBI and border patrol have set up operations there."

"I asked him the same question." PJ smiled. "Hank seems to think he can sneak you past them." She hooked Sophia's arm and steered her back down the hall to the living room. "Sit. You look all in. If you're not careful, you'll lose that baby."

Sophia halted, bringing PJ to a standstill, as well. "How did you know?"

PJ smiled. "Honey, you've got pregnant written all over you."

Tears welled in Sophia's eyes. "You can't tell anyone. If word gets back to Antonio, I'll never be free of him."

The other woman's eyebrows dipped. "That bastard is not going to get his hands on you. Not if Hank, Thorn or I have anything to say about it."

Sophia's heart warmed at PJ's passion, even as she shook her head. "My being here has already caused too much damage. I need to leave."

"Sophia, you're carrying a child. You can't do this on your own. I won't let you." PJ hugged her. "I know what it's like to lie in a hospital without anyone by your side. It's hard enough to give birth. It's even harder to do it alone."

For a long time Sophia hugged PJ back. After suffering so long at Antonio's hands, the warmth of a hug was more than she could have hoped for. "Thank you."

"Can I get you ladies a drink?" Mr. Henderson hovered in the hallway. "The missus would be mad if I didn't offer."

"That would be nice." PJ stared at Sophia. "And if you have a few saltine crackers, we'd be appreciative."

Sophia smiled, touched by PJ's concern.

"Got those. I'll be right back." The man shuffled off with a purpose, and soon the sound of cabinet doors opening and closing and the beep of a microwave oven drifted into the hallway.

"You need to sit for a few minutes." PJ led Sophia into the living room and eased her into a chair. "Hank should be here any moment."

"Why do you call him Hank?" Sophia asked. "Isn't he your father?"

"That's a long story. I'll tell you about it someday over a cup of coffee." PJ laughed. "I guess we all have long stories to tell. Right now, what's important is that you rest. You're so tense—it can't be good for you."

Sophia breathed in and out, willing her muscles to relax after the terrifying race across the town. "I'm fine. Really."

Mr. Henderson entered the living room carrying a tray with two teacups and a plate of plain saltines. "I'm sorry, but we're fresh out of cheese to go with the crackers."

Sophia smiled at the old man. "They're perfect just as they are." She accepted a cup of tea and bit into a cracker, thankful that it absorbed the churning acid in her stomach.

"Mrs. Henderson just drove up with groceries. I have to help her unload."

"Don't worry about us." PJ waved him out the door. "We'll be fine."

After Mr. Henderson left the room, PJ leaned forward

in her chair, her eyes sparkling. "Do you know how far along you are?"

The excitement in PJ's eyes made Sophia's heart flutter. She'd dreamed about having a baby ever since she was a little girl. It was supposed to be a happy time, filled with anticipation, not fear. "If I'm right, I'm about two and a half months along."

"Does Thorn know?" PJ asked.

Sophia shook her head, sadness creeping in on her. "No. And the fewer people who know, the better."

"You really should tell him. He's responsible for your protection. How can he take care of you if he doesn't have the full picture?"

"I can't." An image of a half-painted baby room in Thorn's house rose up in Sophia's mind. "What happened to Thorn's wife?"

PJ's eyes misted. "It was so sad. He was working as the sheriff of Wild Oak Canyon. One of the drug dealers he put away was released from prison. He came back after Thorn."

Sophia's hands clenched around the teacup as she listened to PJ's words, pain radiating through her for the big cowboy who'd lost everything.

"Somehow the guy got a gun and went after Thorn, but got Kayla instead. She died instantly."

"And she was expecting a baby." Sophia didn't ask. She knew.

PJ nodded. "She was four months along. I'd never seen such a happy couple. Thorn was over the moon about it all. Until…"

"Kayla and the baby died."

"Yeah, he hasn't been the same since. He quit his job as sheriff shortly after and has been doing odd jobs, kinda aimlessly, until Hank hired him."

Sophia stared across at PJ. "You see why I can't tell him?"

"I guess I get your point." PJ sighed. "I still think he needs to know."

"I'm not going to be here forever." Sophia set her cup on the tray. "Why cause him more pain?"

Mr. Henderson's voice carried through to them from the kitchen, along with a woman's voice and the sounds of plastic bags being settled on the counter.

A moment later Mrs. Henderson entered the room, her face creased in a frown. "Are you two ladies okay? What a nightmare. Cara Jo is in the hospital, and it looks like half the town is on fire." She flapped a hand in front of her face. "I was leaving the grocery store when the explosion went off."

"We're okay, Mrs. Henderson." PJ rose from her seat. "We're just waiting for my father to come pick us up." She hugged the older woman. "I'm glad you're okay, as well."

"I don't know what this world is comin' to." Mrs. Henderson held out her hand to her husband, who took it. "My husband tells me you two were running from someone when you showed up on our doorstep." She glanced toward the front window. "Do you need to borrow a gun?"

PJ smiled. "Thanks, but I think Hank and his bodyguards will be able to handle things for us."

Mrs. Henderson looked around the room. "Where's that sweet baby of yours?"

PJ chuckled. "Charlie's safe at Hank's house. I wouldn't be nearly as calm if she wasn't." She glanced toward the window. "There's Hank now."

Sophia rose from the couch, her gaze following PJ's.

A big, black, four-wheel-drive truck rolled to a stop on the street. Three bodyguards dressed in black jeans, black T-shirts, sunglasses and shoulder holsters piled out, pistols drawn, setting up a perimeter around the truck. Hank climbed out and spoke to the bodyguard closest to him. That man disappeared around the side of the house while the others closed in around their boss.

Hank Derringer wore cowboy boots, pressed blue jeans and an equally pressed blue chambray shirt. On his head he wore a straw cowboy hat. If not for the bodyguards in defensive position around him, he could have been any Texas cowboy instead of the millionaire he was.

"I thought his truck was ruined in the shoot-out last night," Sophia noted.

"Honey, Hank has more than one truck. It takes a lot of people and equipment to run a ranch the size of the Raging Bull." PJ met Hank at the door. "Glad you came. We need to get Sophia somewhere safe."

"Where's Thorn?" Hank removed his hat and entered the house, leaving his two bodyguards out front.

"He headed for the explosion," PJ said. "We haven't seen him since."

"I tried to reach him on his cell with no luck." Hank glanced at Sophia. "I headed into town as soon as I heard dispatch on the scanner announce an explosion on Main. Thought you might be the target."

Guilt twisted like a knife in Sophia's gut. She almost wished she *had* been the target instead of the woman who'd been taken to the hospital. But she had her defenseless baby to consider. "No, Señor Derringer, we weren't anywhere close. I think it might have been a diversion to give my ex-fiancé a chance to find me."

The lines in Hank's forehead deepened with his frown. "In which case, it was effective."

"Unfortunately, our attempt to hide Sophia in plain sight didn't work." PJ's shoulders sank. "I'm sorry."

Mrs. Henderson waved them farther into the house. "Come in and have a seat. I'll make some coffee."

With a hand held up, Hank smiled politely at the older woman. "No need, Marge. We're headed back to the ranch. With all that's goin' on in town, we need to get Sophia somewhere safe. And I'm sure PJ will want to see Charlie."

Mrs. Henderson nodded. "You're right. I'd want to get to my baby, as well."

Sophia thanked the Hendersons and allowed Hank to hustle her out the door and into the backseat of the waiting truck. Two of the three bodyguards who'd arrived with Hank got in on either side of Sophia. PJ settled into the front passenger seat.

Hank took off, bypassing the circus responding to the aftermath of the explosion on Main Street, and headed out of town toward the Raging Bull Ranch.

Sophia craned her neck to look back at the trucks and vehicles crowded around the small town, hoping to catch a glimpse of Thorn. The farther away they got from town, the more alone she felt, even surrounded by PJ, Hank and his bodyguards. She hoped Thorn was okay.

As if reading her thoughts, Hank announced, "I left a message on Thorn's cell phone that I would be taking you two out to the ranch. Hopefully he'll get it."

Sophia wanted to see him and tell him she was sorry about his house. Her stomach roiled at the thought of all his photos and memories turned to ashes. It was hard enough to lose the one you loved, but to lose everything from your life with that person would be devastating. Knowing she was responsible for bringing this wave of destruction to the good people of Wild Oak Canyon, Sophia knew it was time to leave. To take the dark cloud of death that followed her and get out of the area.

As soon as she could figure out an exit strategy, she'd do it.

THORN JAMMED HIS foot on the brake and skidded to a stop a block away from the flaming inferno of his house.

Firemen had just arrived, jumping down from their seats and going straight to work, unrolling hoses and shrugging into their fireproof jackets.

Flames consumed the old porch and rose up the curtains inside the shattered glass of the front window. All along the front of the house, it appeared as if someone had fired a machine gun into the exterior.

Thorn's pulse pounded against his eardrums as he dropped down from his truck and ran toward the building. He scanned the yard and the vehicles parked nearby but didn't see Sophia or PJ. Had they gotten out? Or were they lying on the floor having been shot, maybe alive but too injured to move? He should never have left them alone.

"Anyone inside?" he asked as he ran past Cody West, a volunteer fireman he'd had drinks with on occasion.

"Don't know. We just got here."

Another fireman called out after him, "Hey, don't go in there. It's too dangerous!"

Thorn ignored the fireman, ran up the porch and grabbed the front doorknob, the heated metal burning his palm as he shoved open the door.

A black cloud billowed out, forcing him to crouch as he entered. Before he'd taken two steps, his lungs took a hit of smoke and his eyes stung and watered. Thorn pulled his shirt up over his mouth and ducked as low as he could get, blinking as he moved through the house. The living room and kitchen were empty, leaving the upstairs, where all the smoke rose. He ran back to the staircase and would have raced up to the burning second floor if hands hadn't grabbed him from behind and dragged him back out the front door.

Thorn fought to get loose, coughing the smoke out of his lungs. "Have to find them."

"They're not there." Chuck Bolton spun him around, maintaining a viselike grip on his arm.

"Then where are they?" Thorn reached for Chuck's shirt collar, ready to shake the man, his mind in a panicked haze of possibilities, all equally bad. "Did the cartel get them?"

Chuck shook his head. "No. They're okay. Get hold of yourself, man." He pulled his cell phone out of his pocket and held it up. "I got a text from Hank. He has Sophia and PJ and is taking them out to the Raging Bull Ranch."

All the tension left Thorn. He released Chuck's shirt and nearly dropped to his knees. "You're sure?"

"Read it yourself."

His eyes still burning, Thorn blinked several times before he could focus on the words in the text message.

"Man, Hank's been trying to get hold of you on your cell phone for the past twenty minutes."

Thorn reached into his back pocket for his cell phone. It wasn't there. He stared at the burning house. He must have left it in there.

"Come on, I'm in one of Hank's trucks and I've got a bodyguard with me. I need to get back to the Raging Bull. You can ride with us or follow me out there." Chuck frowned at the truck parked on the curb behind the fire truck. "Is that mine?"

"Yup." Thorn glanced at the side of the house where he'd parked his vehicle. His own truck had been hit with the same gunfire the house had suffered. Even if it wasn't covered in smoke, ash and debris from the fire, he doubted it would run. "Guess I'll follow you out to the ranch in your truck."

As Thorn pulled away from the burning house, he was hit afresh with a wave of grief so strong he had a tough time breathing. Everything from his life with Kayla had gone up in flames. The pictures, her jewelry and clothing, their wedding album and the quilt her grandmother had given her.

Tears trickled down his cheeks. Thorn rubbed his sleeve over them, smearing soot on his arm.

He was no better off than Sophia. No clothes but the ones on his back, no home to go to, no one waiting for him there.

But Sophia wasn't wallowing in her loss. She was fiercely determined to move on with her life, start over somewhere away from the tragedy of her past.

The woman was not only beautiful, she had spunk and grit. She'd been through hell and come out a survivor.

It hit Thorn, then—he hadn't been living his life. He'd been going through the motions, more of a spectator than a participant, letting everything pass by and refusing to engage.

How had he let himself sink so low?

He hadn't been raised a self-indulgent man, prone to pity. His father had raised a cowboy, rough, ready and willing to tackle any challenge.

It had taken a woman to remind him of that. A woman who was being chased by an abusive cartel thug. Whether or not Thorn had a life to go back to, he had one to protect. And he'd be damned if he let any more harm befall her.

With renewed purpose, he pressed his boot to the accelerator and spun Chuck's truck around, headed toward the Raging Bull and Sophia.

Chapter Twelve

Hank's housekeeper and PJ ganged on up on Sophia, insisting she eat a sandwich and drink a glass of milk. The food helped to settle her stomach and replenish the energy she'd been lacking earlier.

PJ had urged her to take a nap while she waited for Thorn to return from town. Sophia had refused, preferring to sit on the floor of the living room with PJ and Charlie as the baby played with her toys and made many attempts to roll over.

Sophia's chest swelled and her hand drifted to her belly, wondering what her baby would be like. Would it be a boy or a girl? Would she have green eyes like her mother or the dark, angry eyes of his father?

Too twitchy to lie down, Sophia rose from the floor and wandered through the house, careful not to stand too close to the windows should the FBI or border patrol wander by and see her. They'd been lucky the fire in town had drawn most of the agents that direction on the off chance their assailants were involved. Hank had no problem sneaking Sophia through the side door of his spacious home.

The one-story ranch-style house, with its cathedral ceilings and hardwood floors, had an open, airy floor plan with lots of thick, double-paned windows letting in the Texas sunshine but not the oppressive heat. The living room was bigger than the entire apartment Sophia had rented in Monterrey. A huge stone fireplace took up the majority of one wall, gray stone rising to the peaked ceiling.

The couch was bomber-jacket brown leather and as soft as a woman's skin. Tables scattered around the room were solid wood, possibly mesquite and beautifully handcrafted.

Sophia wandered from the living room into a foyer and across to an open door that led into a study. A massive desk made of the same mesquite sat squarely in the center of the room. On three of the four walls, bookcases rose to the ceiling, filled with books. Some were bound in leather; others were paperbacks with well-worn bindings.

The room smelled of leather, wood and the aftershave Hank used.

With nothing to do, Sophia continued her self-guided tour of Hank's abode, glancing toward the foyer every few minutes to see if Thorn had arrived.

Another door farther down the hall was mostly closed, the shadowy interior teasing, beckoning Sophia to glance inside.

As if drawn by an invisible string, Sophia entered, pushing the door wide. The curtains in this room had been drawn over the windows. Sophia found the light switch, flipped it and let out a soft gasp.

Light from a delicate crystal chandelier that hung from the center of the ceiling filled a room that looked to be straight out of a Victorian storybook. The soft, ivory walls were the background for deep red curtains and a red patterned settee with a carved wooden back and arms. Against one wall, an antique cherry secretary desk stood with the desk folded down and stationery spread across the wooden surface, as if whoever had started writing a letter had been interrupted but was expected to return.

Sophia entered the room, enchanted by the difference between the warm masculinity of the other rooms and the delicate beauty of this one. It felt like she'd walked into the room of a princess in a fairytale.

Though her family in Monterrey had been considered well-to-do, Sophia had never seen such beauty and luxury in one place.

She'd lived in the best part of Monterrey, attended private schools and partied with the same families growing up. But this little piece of antiquated heaven was like something straight out of a Victorian countess's home.

"Lilianna loved this room." Hank's deep voice filled the space.

Sophia jumped and turned toward the door, her face heating. "I'm sorry. I should have asked if it was all right to look around."

The older man smiled softly. "You're welcome to look wherever you like on this level."

She returned her attention to the beauty of the antiques and decor. "This room *es muy bonito.*"

Hank stared across the room at a portrait over the fireplace. "My wife inherited much of the furniture. It was passed down through her family for centuries. She treasured it all, and could tell you a story about every piece."

For a moment Sophia studied the wealthy man, the sadness in Hank's voice and expression ultimately making her turn away. It hurt to witness his pain. The loss of his family reminded her too much of her own. "You loved her very much, didn't you?"

"Family is everything," he said quietly.

Sophia's chest ached. "I miss my family, too."

"Why don't you go back to them?"

"I will never be safe in Mexico." She pressed a hand

to her belly and the baby growing inside. "As long as Antonio is looking for me, I cannot go back to my family."

"Do they know you're alive?" Hank asked.

Sophia shook her head. "I haven't been allowed to contact them since Antonio imprisoned me. They must think I'm dead." Her voice caught on a sob.

"You should let them know that you're alive and well."

"I don't wish to give them hope." Sophia's gaze shifted away from Hank. "I don't know how this will end."

"Think about it, Sophia." Hank touched her arm. "I'd give anything to know whether my wife and son were still alive." His gaze drifted again to a large portrait over the mantel.

Sophia glanced at the image, her throat tightening. Her family had a portrait similar to this hanging over the mantel in her home back in Monterrey. She had been eight; her brother had been a baby. A young family, full of hope and promise.

Unlike the other things in the room, the picture, though encased in an antique oval frame, wasn't old and it wasn't painted. It was a professional photograph printed on canvas of a family—Hank, a woman and a small boy.

"That's your wife?" Sophia moved closer, struck by something in the way the woman in the portrait smiled. Her heart skipped a beat and then pumped faster the closer she got to the picture. "What did you say her name was?"

"Lilianna." Hank ran a hand through his hair, looking older than he had a moment before. "God, I miss her."

"Does she have a sister?"

"No, she was an only child. I met her in Mexico City while she was vacationing with friends."

"Did she die?"

"No." His voice grew terse. "She and my son were kidnapped a little over two years ago." He pointed to the toddler in her lap. "He was five on his last birthday."

Sophia couldn't mistake the deep sadness in Hank's voice, nor the overwhelming sense of something familiar in the woman's eyes and the way she held the child. As if a memory teetered on the edge of her consciousness, Sophia's eyes rounded. "What was your son's name?" She held her breath, knowing before he answered what it was, and she whispered it at the same time as Hank.

"Jake."

Hank stepped back as if she'd struck him, his eyes narrowing. "Why did you ask his name if you already knew?"

"It could be a coincidence." Her heart hammered against her ribs, her instincts telling her this wasn't a fluke. *Madre de Dios,* if it wasn't…

Her gaze met Hank's as she said, "I know them." Sophia clapped a hand to her stomach, the food she'd just eaten threatening to rise up to the sob stuck in her throat. "That's Anna and her son, Jake. I know them." Sophia ran from the room, racing for the bathroom in the hallway.

"Wait!" Hank yelled. "What do you mean?" He ran after her.

Behind her, Sophia could hear voices. One sounded like Thorn's, but she couldn't hold in the contents of her stomach, the truth of what she'd just learned making her insides riot. She flung open the bathroom door and made it to the toilet just in time to lose the sandwich and milk PJ and the housekeeper had insisted she eat.

Movement behind her made her moan. "Go away."

"You're going to have to try harder than that to get me to leave." Thorn's voice sent a wave of warmth over Sophia's suddenly chilled, trembling body.

"I'm sick. I'd rather you didn't see me this way." She heaved again, hating that she couldn't stop herself.

"Too bad." Work-callused fingers pulled her hair back from her face. "I'm not going anywhere."

"Stubborn man," she whispered.

He chuckled. "Hardheaded woman."

When she thought she could, she sat back on the cold tile floor and leaned her head against the sink cabinet.

Thorn released her hair and reached for a washcloth, running it under the tap. "Now, tell me what happened."

She closed her eyes, all the fight gone from her. "Where do you want me to start?"

Thorn pressed the cloth to her face, the warm, damp fabric a balm to her cool, clammy skin.

"Start with what you said to Hank," he prompted. "He looks like he saw a ghost."

Sophia looked up at the man who'd brought her and Thorn together.

Hank stood in the doorway, his face pale, his blue eyes intense. "What did you mean, you know Lilianna?" he demanded.

"Give her a moment." Thorn brushed the cloth across Sophia's lips.

Sophia clasped his wrist. "Let me." She took the rag from his fingers and pressed it to the side of her face as she stared up at Hank, her heart racing as she spoke. "I know them as Anna and Jake, but they are the same. Hank, I know where your wife and son are."

Thorn turned in time to see Hank Derringer take a step backward, his face blanching even more. "Please tell me you're not lying."

Sophia shook her head. "I'm not lying. Anna was the one who set me up with Hector. She helped me escape *la Fuerte del Diablo.*"

Hank ran a hand over his face. "Dear God, they're alive?"

"They were when I left Mexico." She couldn't vouch for anyone at the moment.

Thorn looked from Sophia to Hank, and back to Sophia. "Are you well enough to take this conversation to another room?"

She nodded and tried to rise. Before she could, Thorn scooped her up and carried her into the large living room where PJ stood beside Chuck, who held Charlie in his arms.

"Are you okay, Sophia?" PJ asked.

Sophia nodded. "I'm okay." She stared up at Thorn. "You can put me down. I can stand on my own."

Thorn slowly lowered her feet to the ground but refused to remove his arm from around her waist.

"You know Lilianna? She was where they held you hostage?" Hank grasped her hands in his.

Sophia squeezed his fingers. "*El Martillo* keeps her in his quarters. She's rarely allowed to go outside the walls."

"But she got you out." Hank's head moved side to side as he stared at their joined hands. "Why didn't she come with you?"

"I begged her to come, but she refused."

Hank frowned. "What?"

Sophia knew it would hurt Hank, but she had to tell him. "Anna told me she could never leave."

Hank straightened. "Why would she say that? I know my Lilianna. She loved me—she loved our home, our family and life together."

"I don't know why. When it came time for me to escape, she hugged me and told me to find you, that you would help me."

Hank's jaw tightened and he let go of Sophia's hands, his own clenching into fists. "Who is this *El Martillo?*"

"I never saw him. I only knew when he was there because everyone in the camp got nervous, even Antonio. The man came in the night by helicopter. He stayed in his quarters. Those closest to him went in and out, but he never did, leaving again under cover of night."

"He probably threatened to harm Jake." Hank slammed his fist into his palm. "The bastard!"

Thorn's arm tightened around Sophia, his attention captivated by the man who'd hired him. Knowing it was a huge risk and that the likelihood of being killed was high, he knew what had to happen. "We have to go after her."

Sophia stiffened against him. "Do you know what you're saying?" She stepped out of his arms and stood in front of him. "*La Fuerte del Diablo* is surrounded by members of the cartel. Those men were trained in the Mexican army. They're equipped with deadly weapons, and they don't hesitate to kill."

Thorn looked over her head to the man who'd taken him on when he hadn't been employed in two years, shown faith in him and given him a chance to start over. "If Hank's wife and son are in that compound, we have to get them out."

"Drennan's right." Chuck Bolton kissed his daughter and handed her to PJ. "She's been missing for more than two years. This is the first real lead Hank's had on her whereabouts."

"We have to move fast." Hank paced the living room floor to the fireplace and back, his head down and his body tense.

"Agreed," Thorn said, then added, "Before *El Martillo* realizes we know."

"If he hasn't already moved her." Hank strode from the room. "I'll call the other members of this team. We'll meet in the war room in the morning."

"What about the FBI and the border patrol?" Chuck asked.

The boss stopped and turned toward them. "None of this information leaves this room. Understood?"

Everyone answered as one. "Yes."

Hank spun, heading for the front door.

Thorn called out, "Where are you going?"

"I want to know if they caught up with the man responsible for the explosion and fires in town."

Thorn glanced down at Sophia. He wanted to know, as well.

"Go with them. I'll be okay."

"I'm not leaving you."

"And I can't step outside without being detected. I want to know if they caught Antonio. I won't be safe until they do."

"If you're sure." Thorn waited.

Sophia turned him around and gave him a gentle push. "I need a shower and some rest. If you're hanging around, I won't get either."

Thorn took off after Hank.

Chuck kissed PJ and Charlie. "I'll be back in a few minutes to take you two home."

"Take your time. I'm not even sure we have a home." PJ smiled. "And Charlie's about ready for a feeding."

Chuck caught up with Thorn and the two men stepped out into the fading light, crossing the yard to the long van the FBI had brought in as the base of operations. Two generators hummed loudly, providing power to the computers, lights and air-conditioning. Apparently only a skeletal staff had remained behind. One agent sat at a folding table outside the van, cleaning his M4A1 rifle. He glanced up as the three men approached. "Lehmann isn't here."

"Mind if I check with the computer operators?" Hank asked.

The man shrugged and refocused his attention on the rifle in his hands, sliding the bolt back into place. "Knock yourself out."

Hank stepped into the van first, followed by Chuck and Thorn.

"Any news on Martinez?" Hank asked.

The man at the computer nodded. "Had a sighting in Wild Oak Canyon right before the explosion, and then again near the house on the edge of town that got torched."

Thorn's fingers clenched. He wanted to ask if they'd seen Elena Carranza, but didn't want to draw any more attention to her plight than necessary.

The agent continued. "They think Martinez recruited a gang to help stage the explosion and fires."

That corresponded to what Sophia had related about the fire at Thorn's house.

"I take it they didn't catch him." Hank's words were a statement.

"No, but Lehmann was following a lead on one of the gang members. He should report in soon."

"What about the woman?" Hank asked.

The man shook his head. "Nothing yet. Seems to have disappeared. They probably split up to throw us off their trail."

Hank backed toward the door. "Thanks."

Thorn dropped down out of the van first. The man who'd been sitting at the folding table had disappeared.

Two long black SUVs rolled to a stop next to the van, and Grant Lehmann stepped out of the lead vehicle. "Hank." He nodded to the other two men, his attention returning to the ranch owner. "We've had a confirmed sighting of Martinez in the area. Again, I stress, he's dangerous. If you see him, don't hesitate to shoot. He's already put one citizen in the hospital."

"You think he set the explosion in town?" Hank asked.

"I don't only think it, I know it." Lehmann slipped his sunglasses off his face. "We canvassed the area and learned that a man fitting his description, along with two others, was seen around the back of the diner right before the explosion. They took off on motorcycles."

"Were they the same gang that burned the house on the edge of town?" Thorn asked, his teeth clenching.

The director nodded. "Thorn Drennan, right?"

Thorn nodded.

"That was your house, wasn't it? Sorry we didn't catch him before he torched it." Lehmann's eyes narrowed. "What had us puzzled was why he targeted your house. Do you have a connection to Martinez or his gang?"

Thorn kept a poker face, refusing to show any signs of emotion or indications that he was about to lie. He'd learned how to do this by some of the best and worst criminals. "Not that I know of. But I was sheriff for several years. Someone could have carried a grudge against me." That wasn't a lie. His wife's death had been because of a drug dealer's grudge. His training as an officer of the law made his gut clench at the thought of withholding evidence and the location of Elena Carranza, but something told him now wasn't the time to reveal her. His instincts had never been wrong.

"Seems strange Antonio would fill your house with bullets. He must have thought someone he wanted dead was inside." Lehmann pinned Thorn with his gaze. "Some neighbors down the street said they saw you enter with a woman."

"An old friend from college." Thorn gave him the story.

"Sally Freeman. She and I left the house to check out the explosion."

"The fire chief said you went back into the house after someone. Was there more than one woman inside?"

Thorn smiled. "As a matter of fact, there was. PJ Franks had loaned me her truck to check out the explosion. It wasn't until they dragged me out of my house that I learned she'd left before the shooting began and walked over to a friend's house."

Lehmann stared at him for a long time as if processing Thorn's story to see if it added up.

"Your man inside the van said you had a lead on one of the gang members with Antonio?" Hank asked, drawing the director's attention back to him.

Thorn released the breath he'd been holding.

"Yeah. Someone recognized one of the men on the motorcycle based on a snake tattoo on his arm. We did some digging and found a cousin of his on the south side of town in a trailer park. We were late by five minutes. The bikers had just left, Antonio with them."

"Any idea which direction they went?" Chuck asked.

"They could have gone anywhere." Lehmann rolled his neck, pressing a hand to the base of his skull. "They were all on dirt bikes. For all we know, they could have headed back across the border. CBP is sending a chopper out from El Paso. Hopefully we'll have a better chance of finding them from the air."

Hank snorted. "There's still a lot of ground to cover, and a dirt bike can go almost anywhere."

"It's all we have to go on for now…unless your team's come up with something to add to it." Lehmann's gaze traveled from Hank to Chuck, and then came to rest on Thorn.

"Nothing you haven't already discovered." Hank stuck

out his hand to the regional director. "Thanks for keeping us up-to-date."

Lehmann shook Hank's hand. "If you'll excuse me, I need to brief my agents and get out of here for a while."

"Not much to offer in town with the diner out of service." Hank nodded toward the house. "I could have my housekeeper make up some sandwiches for your guys."

Thorn waited for Lehmann's response. They'd have to hide Sophia if the FBI was traipsing through the house.

The director put one foot on the step to the van. "Thanks, but I'm pretty sure the men would prefer pizza. I thought I saw a place off Main."

"Joe's Pizza Shack stays open until nine," Chuck offered. "They make a mean pie."

Lehmann disappeared inside the van.

Thorn headed back to the house, anxious to get Sophia back in his sights. After what had happened with his house and the diner, he didn't want to risk leaving her for too long, even in as safe a place as Hank's security-wired home.

Once inside, he found PJ standing in the living room staring at Sophia playing with Charlie on the floor. "She's good with babies."

Thorn braced himself as he watched Sophia lying on her side on an area rug, propped up on her elbow. She was leaning over Charlie, tickling her.

Charlie giggled, her eyes sparkling, her dark brown hair sticking out in all directions in soft wisps. She batted at Sophia and giggled again.

Sophia smiled down at the baby and stroked her chubby cheek, her own cheeks flushed with pleasure.

Thorn's heart squeezed so hard he pressed a hand to his chest to ease the pain. PJ was right—Sophia looked natural playing with the baby girl. She would make a good mother.

Then it hit him. She'd thrown up the night he'd found her in the cabin and again today. She'd passed out when she'd been hungry, and she was desperate to get away from her abusive ex-fiancé. So desperate she'd risk escaping out from under the cartel.

Thorn's lips pressed together to keep him from blurting out the question foremost in his mind.

Charlie giggled once more and Sophia smiled up at PJ, her smile freezing when she spotted Thorn.

For a moment her eyes widened, then her smile faded and she looked away, her expression guarded. Sophia rose from the floor, lifting Charlie in her arms. "Did they find Antonio?" She kissed the baby's cheek and handed her to her mother.

"No," Thorn replied, his voice clipped, barely controlled.

Sophia looked at him again, her eyes narrowing. "Is something wrong?"

"You're pregnant," he blurted accusingly.

Sophia's gaze shot to PJ.

PJ hugged Charlie. "I didn't say a word."

Thorn glared at PJ. "You knew?"

"I figured it out when she was at the Hendersons'."

Chuck entered the house, calling out to PJ. "Ready to hit the road and see if we have a home to go to?"

"Good timing." PJ touched Sophia's arm. "You'll be okay."

Sophia's gaze followed PJ through the front door as she left, finally returning to Thorn when they were left alone.

Not wanting their resulting argument to go public, Sophia headed for the bedroom, assuming Thorn would follow.

He did, catching up to her as she entered. "We're not done here."

"I know." She waved him through the door.

Once he was inside, she closed the door and faced him, her gaze steady, her face inscrutable. "Yes. I'm pregnant."

Thorn closed his eyes as the flood of emotions washed over him. Pain, guilt, anger and, strangely, hope. "Why didn't you tell me?"

"I didn't want anyone to know." Sophia's finger twisted the hem of the clean shirt she was wearing. "The fewer people who know about it, the better. Should Antonio learn I'm pregnant with his child, he'll stop at nothing to get me back."

Sophia stepped up to Thorn. "I don't want to go back to *la Fuerte del Diablo*." Her hand lifted protectively to her abdomen. "I left to give my baby a better life. One where she's not afraid all the time." Her jaw tightened even as her eyes filled with tears. "Please…don't tell anyone."

Thorn's anger dissolved, and his hardened heart melted into her watery green eyes. *Damn her!* Damn her for opening him up to pain again. Having lost Kayla, their child and the house filled with memories, he couldn't do it again. He gripped her arms, anger bubbling over. "I won't tell anyone, but understand this—I'm not getting involved with you or anyone else." He shook her slightly.

Tears tipped over the edges of her eyelids. "I know, and I completely understand."

Thorn recognized the strength it had taken for her to come this far and her fierce desire to provide a better life for her baby, but he also knew how vulnerable she was and that she wouldn't last much longer on her own against a cartel out to kill her, with the FBI and CBP ordered to shoot on sight.

As much as he wanted to have Hank reassign him so that he didn't have to dig his own emotional grave deeper, he was stuck. He'd gone way past being able to hand her off to someone else. So far past that all he wanted was to hold her in his arms and keep her safe from anyone who wanted to hurt her.

"I can leave. You don't have to help me." Her fingers dug into his shirt, belying her suggested solution.

"You know damn well I can't let you leave." Thorn pulled her into his arms, crushing her mouth with his. He dragged her body close to his, melding them together in an embrace far more flammable than a lit match to a stack of dry tinder.

When at last he let her up for air, she sighed and leaned her cheek against his chest. "This should never have happened."

"No," he agreed, inhaling the scent of her floral shampoo. "It shouldn't have happened."

"And I don't expect it to continue." She pressed her palms to his chest and leaned back to gaze up into his eyes. "Once I leave here, I have to disappear."

A hollow feeling settled in Thorn's gut and spread to his heart. She'd been telling him the same information from the beginning. Sophia had no intention of sticking around once she was free to hit the road. Why, then, did it hurt more now?

He brushed the hair from her face, tucking it behind her ear. "We'll talk about that later. Right now, we have to keep you safe from Antonio and away from the FBI and border agents."

"Is that even possible?" She snuggled closer to him, a shiver shaking her body. "Antonio tracked me to your house in town. He has to know I'm here. It's only a matter of time. Why doesn't Hank turn me over to the FBI or the CBP? He wouldn't have to worry about Antonio, and maybe they would see the truth and not shoot me."

Thorn shook his head. "Rumor has it there's a mole in

the FBI, someone who's been allowing coyotes to move people and drugs across the border into the States. Hank doesn't trust anyone past his own inner circle of men."

"From what Brandon said, the regional director is Hank's friend."

"Maybe, but he's not part of Hank's inner circle—people Hank trusts with his life."

"I'm not part of his inner circle. How does he know I'm not lying?"

Thorn traced her lips with his finger, mesmerized at how they moved with each word she spoke. "He trusts his instincts."

"I don't know why," Sophia said. "I've done nothing to build his trust."

"You've given him hope." Thorn gave in to the temptation and brushed his lips across hers.

She closed her eyes and whispered, "As long as I am here, you are all in danger." Sophia pushed her hands against his chest until she could stare into his eyes. "Antonio will find me."

"Hank won't let him get to you." Like a moth to flame, Thorn was drawn to her as he grazed her lips with his, loving how soft, full and warm they were. "And I'll do everything in my power to keep him away from you."

"Even help me leave when the roadblocks clear?"

Chapter Thirteen

Sophia's arms twined around his neck, pulling him closer, her breasts pressing against his chest. Fire burned inside her as the ridge beneath his jeans nudged her belly. She wanted to be closer to this cowboy who'd saved her life and treated her with gentle respect. "You'll help me when I have to leave?" she repeated.

"If it comes to that." He buried his face against her neck and moaned. "Right now, all I can think about is how your skin feels against mine." His mouth touched the pulse pounding at the base of her throat and he moved lower, sweeping across the swell of her breast beneath the soft cotton of her T-shirt. He lifted the hem, dragged it up over her head and tossed it onto a chair.

Her heart thumped against her ribs as if it would break free of its restraints. Sophia stood in a black lace bra, the cool waft of an air-conditioned breeze feathering across her nakedness. Thorn's coarse hand skimmed down her waist and over the swell of her hip, disappearing into the waistband of her borrowed jeans to caress her bottom.

"If you just weren't so darned stubborn…and beautiful…and brave." He trailed the fingers of his other hand along the curve of her throat and across her shoulder, sliding the strap off.

Beyond frustrated and way past impatient, she reached

behind her and flicked the clasp free, releasing the garment to fall to the floor, her breasts bobbing free.

Thorn groaned. "I'm in so much trouble with you, Sophia."

"You are?" She felt empowered as she tugged his shirt free of his jeans and flicked the buttons open one at a time. "I'm on the run from a man. I sure as hell never planned on getting involved with another." She freed the last button and gripped the openings of the shirt, pulling him closer. "I'm not staying," she said, her words fierce, determined, more to remind herself than him.

"Okay, okay." He held up his hands in surrender. "You're not staying. I'm not in the market for a relationship. What's keeping us from doing this?" He bent to take one of her nipples between his lips and tongued the pebbled tip.

Sophia arched her back, pressing closer to his warm, wet tongue. She cupped the back of his head, holding him as close to her as she could get him. "Exactly," she breathed. "No strings, no expectations."

"Just mutual lust," he muttered around the nipple.

"The other L word." She guided his other hand to the second breast, then reached for the rivet on his jeans. "Think they'll miss us for a little while?"

"Hank's in the bunker." He nuzzled her cleavage while backing her toward the bed.

"It's too early for supper." She pushed the top button loose on his jeans and gripped the zipper tag. "Who else would care?" She didn't have family standing outside ready to criticize her actions, or a husband she was cheating on. All loyalty to her ex-fiancé had ended the first time he'd hit her.

Clothes flew off and Thorn swept her off her feet, laying her across the neatly made bed. "I thought you'd died in that fire." He came down over her, balancing, a hand on either side of her.

She gave him a crooked smile and cupped his cheek. "You'd have been free of your duties if I had."

"Don't." He touched a finger to her lips, his brows drawn together. "You have a baby to think about."

How well she knew. "Does that bother you?" Her gaze slipped to his neck, refusing to look him in the eye. Afraid he'd be hesitant to make love to a woman carrying another man's child.

"Hell, yeah."

Her heart cramped and she lay very still against the softness of the blanket. What did she expect? She'd been with another man and was pregnant with his child. What man wouldn't be bothered?

He lay down beside her, his hand smoothing over her cheek where the bruise had all but vanished. He trailed his fingers over the fullness of one breast and down to her still-smooth belly. "Scares the hell out of me."

"Because it's someone else's baby?" she asked, her breath catching in her throat as she waited for his answer.

"No." Thorn's lips clamped together in a thin line.

Even more softly, she whispered, "Because of how you lost your wife and child?"

For a long moment, he didn't answer. When he did, he spoke so softly that she had to strain to hear. "There was no reason for them to die." He stared at her belly, but he must have been reliving the past. Shadows descended over his eyes. "I didn't react fast enough."

She grabbed his hand, threading her fingers through his. "It wasn't your fault." She brought his hand to her cheek. "You didn't pull the trigger."

"I might as well have." His fingers tightened around hers.

"But you didn't."

"Now I'm expected to keep you safe." His gaze shifted to hers. "You're pregnant, just like her. Only this time, you're the target of an entire cartel and the U.S. government, not just collateral damage of a bullet meant for me."

"Again, whatever happens to me will not be your fault."

"Maybe."

"Do you still miss her?"

"Kayla?" His finger traced her collarbone. "I always will."

The tightness in her chest was expected, and she understood and accepted it. He'd loved his wife. That was one of the reasons she found herself falling in love with him. A man who loved his wife that much was a man worth giving your heart to. He'd never willingly break her heart if he loved her.

Oh, if only he loved her as much as he'd loved his wife. As quickly as the thought emerged, she pushed it to the back of her mind. Theirs was not a forever commitment. It couldn't be. "Kayla was a very lucky woman."

"Kayla died," he said flatly.

"I'm truly sorry for your loss. But she always knew you loved her. For that, she was very fortunate. Not all married couples can claim they still love one another."

"I'll never forget her."

"Nor should you." Sophia smoothed the frown from his brow and pressed a kiss to his lips.

"I'll never understand a man who hits a woman. Especially one he's promised to love." He pulled her into his arms and rested his chin on the top of her head. "Your ex hit you often, didn't he?"

"Yes."

Thorn's arms tensed around her. "I can't let anything else happen to you."

She pressed her palms against his chest, shoving him

away with a smile. Then she drew a line with her finger from the middle of his chest down his taut abs, to the line of hair angling downward to the thick, straight shaft jutting upward. "I was hoping something *would* happen."

Thorn grasped her hand and pinned it above her head, not so tight that it would scare her. "I think I've got this." With careful, deliberate moves, he kissed and nipped his way the length of her torso, stopping to feast on her breasts before moving downward. He pressed his lips to her belly, gently skimming over it to the triangle of curls at the apex of her thighs.

Sophia squirmed against the mattress, wanting more, faster. Never had she felt the amount of raging desire she experienced at Thorn's touch. The past few months with Antonio had been a nightmare of sexual demands she'd been forced to perform or suffer the consequences—a bruised cheek, broken rib, busted lip or swollen eye.

Thorn treated her body like a delicate flower to be held with the lightest touch, to be revered and cherished as if it would break with too much pressure.

When he parted her folds and stroked her core with the tip of his finger, she dug her heels into the mattress, arching her back off the bed.

The time of gentle persuasion was over. "Please, I want more."

He chuckled, his warm breath stirring her nether curls. "Patience." He dipped into her channel, stirring her juices, dragging them up to the sensitive strip of flesh between her folds, throbbing from his initial attack. "I don't want to hurt you."

"You won't." With his next stroke, her head rolled back and her thoughts winged away, lost in the haze of desire building inside.

When he replaced his fingers with his tongue, she

moaned, coming apart with each thrust, swirl and stroke until she exploded in a burst of sensations so intense all she could do was gasp. She grasped his hair, her fingers convulsing around the strands, holding him steady one moment, urging him on the next.

When she thought she could stand no more, he reached over the side of the bed, grabbed his jeans and ripped his wallet from the back pocket. He rifled through the contents until he came out with a small foil packet.

"I can't get pregnant because I already am."

"For your protection and peace of mind."

Her heart warmed. He cared enough to protect her and her baby.

He slipped the condom over his erection and settled between her legs.

As he hovered at her entrance, he bent to claim her mouth.

She swept her lips over his, her tongue pushing through his teeth to tangle with his.

As their tongues collided, he plunged inside her, gliding in, stretching and filling all the emptiness she'd endured over the year of her abduction.

Pressing her feet into the mattress, she rose up to meet him thrust for thrust, her hips rocking to his rhythm, her fingers digging into his buttocks, guiding him deeper.

As the heat increased and she neared the precipice, tingling started at her center and spread like wildfire throughout her body to the very tips of her toes and fingers. She grew rigid, holding on to the fevered euphoria of their most intimate connection.

Thorn impaled her one last time, remaining deeply rooted inside her. He dropped down on top of her, holding her close, crushing the air from her lungs.

Sophia didn't care. If she died right then, she'd die

happy, fulfilled and intoxicated with what making love should always be like.

After a moment Thorn rolled to his side, bringing her with him, allowing her to take a deep breath.

She lay for a long time in the haven of his arms, her eyelids fluttering closed, the deep exhaustion of pregnancy claiming her. Never had she felt so incredibly... loved. Her elation faded to despair as she reminded herself that this feeling was destined to be a one-time event. As she drifted into sleep, from the corner of her eye, a single tear dropped.

THORN LAY FOR a long time, drinking in the beauty of Sophia as she slept, her green eyes shuttered, the salty track of a tear like a scar on her perfect skin.

He wanted to take away her pain, to hold her until all the terror subsided, to keep her safe always. Inside, Thorn realized that until the cartel thug Antonio Martinez gave up his quest to reclaim his hostage, Sophia would be on the run, constantly in fear of discovery.

Thorn would have stayed cocooned in the sheets with Sophia had a knock not disturbed his perusal. He rose from the bed, slipped into his jeans and padded to the door barefoot.

When he opened it, Zach Adams, one of the men Hank had hired as a Covert Cowboy, stood with a grimace on his face. "Hate to interrupt, but Hank wants us in the bunker. Now."

Thorn nodded. "I'll be right there." He closed the door, found his boots and finished dressing in less than a minute. Then he bent over Sophia's bed and pressed a kiss to her forehead, careful not to wake her.

Pregnant, running from an assault and making love all in one day had drained her. She needed sleep.

He drew the curtains over the blinds, blocking out the last of the sun's rays. "Sleep, sweetheart. We'll figure this out together."

He left the room, closing the door softly behind him, and hurried to the bunker, his pulse speeding as his resolve solidified. Antonio Martinez couldn't continue to make Sophia's life hell. If the FBI and the CBP couldn't nail the bastard, it was up to him and the Covert Cowboys to do the job.

In the bunker, he found Hank, Chuck, Zach and Blaise Harding gathered around a large-screen monitor on the wall of the computer lab. Hank had called in all the new members of CCI.

Brandon manned the keyboard at his desk. "Based on Ms. Carranza's accounts and the amount of time she and her escort were on the run and the direction they came, I pulled satellite images from across the border in the Mexican state of Chihuahua, locating a small village called Paraíso." Brandon chuckled. "It translates to paradise, which is ironic, considering it's in the middle of a desert with nothing much around it."

Hank waved a hand impatiently. "Get to the point, please."

Brandon cleared his throat and clicked the mouse. The view on the big screen zoomed in on a location to the west of the town. The clarity of the satellite image sharpened until a fortified compound came into view.

"You think that's it?" Hank leaned closer. "Is that *la Fuerte del Diablo?*"

"Can't be absolutely certain, but given the parameters, I can't find anything else that remotely resembles a drug cartel fortress within a three-hundred-mile radius. And if you look closely inside the walls, there's a space large enough to land a helicopter. And to the south is a dirt landing strip for fixed-wing aircraft. The place is big enough to house a small army of cartel members and stage a boat-load of drugs for delivery. From what I can tell, there isn't a cow, horse or goat in the area. They aren't trying to disguise it as a ranch, meaning the Mexican government either doesn't have them on their radar or they're paid off to turn a blind eye. What better location to ship drugs into and out of the U.S.?"

"And what better place to hide hostages?" Hank's voice was low, angry. "How soon can we get our team in there?"

"They'll be heavily armed and possibly booby-trapped," Zach stated.

Hank turned to the man. "Is this the same place you were held captive and tortured?"

"No, I was captured by *Los Lobos,* archrivals of *la Familia Diablos.* But this compound is very similar, and the two cartels play for keeps. They shoot first and ask questions later."

"Trigger-happy," Chuck added.

"They have to be, or they die." Zach's jaw and fists tightened. "And they show no mercy to prisoners."

"Do you think we'll find Lilianna and Jake there?" Thorn asked.

"It's the only lead I've had on them in the past two years. I have to check it out."

"It could be a suicide mission," Zach warned.

Hank faced Zach. "If Jacie was kidnapped by *La Familia Diablos* or *Los Lobos,* would you leave her there?"

"I'd die trying to get her out," Zach responded, his face grim.

From what Thorn knew, Zach had been an undercover agent with the FBI seized by *Los Lobos,* along with his female partner over a year ago. Held captive for weeks, he'd been tortured for information regarding a government insider allowing *la Familia Diablos* cartel free rein across the border into the U.S. His partner had been tortured to death while Zach had been forced to watch.

When *la Familia Diablos* had attacked the *Los Lobos* hideout, Zach had escaped back to the States. If anyone knew the extent of suffering the cartels could impart, it was Zach.

Hank faced the gathering of Covert Cowboys, his six bodyguards and ranch security men. "Together, we have eleven of us."

Chuck blew out a stream of air. "Any idea how many are inside the fortress? What we'd be up against?"

"I asked Sophia. She said it varied anywhere from fifteen to thirty, depending on what was going on," Hank said. "Brandon's working on verifying numbers, but we have to go on limited intel for now." He looked into the faces of each man in the room. "I can't ask any of you to do this. Like Zach said, it's a suicide mission at best."

Zach stepped forward. "I'm in."

"Me, too," Chuck agreed. "I can't imagine if PJ was the one stuck in that hell for two years."

One by one, the bodyguards and ranch security team added their names to the list.

Blaise raised his hand. "Count me in."

"Me, too." Thorn moved forward.

"I can't let you go." Hank stared at Thorn. "We need you with Sophia. She doesn't stand a chance on her own, and with all of my ranch security on the team, this place won't be safe."

Thorn itched to be with the team storming *la Fuerte del Diablo,* but he'd promised to keep Sophia safe no matter what.

"What about me?" Brandon stood with the rest of them, his face set, his young body not nearly as intimidating as the hardened warriors of the Covert Cowboys and ranch security.

"I need you to man the computers and feed us information as you get it," Hank said. "We can lock down the bunker. It's fireproof and hardened, so a direct attack won't penetrate it."

"When do we start?" Zach asked.

And the planning began.

SOPHIA WOKE TO a dark room and reached out a hand for the warm, solid comfort of Thorn. As she touched the empty pillow, the loneliness of the empty room threatened to overwhelm her.

Who was she kidding? He was only obligated by his job to protect her, not provide comfort and emotional support. That's what family was for. In her case, it wasn't an option—she was on her own. And at that moment, it was a very lonely feeling.

She flicked on the reading lamp on the nightstand and stared around the room. Tall ceilings, walls painted a pale terra-cotta and rich mahogany furnishings made it as warm as an air-conditioned room could be. Without personal touches, it might as well have been a very nice hotel room.

Sophia would give anything for a photograph of her mother, father and baby brother. She missed them so much it hurt. What she wouldn't give to hear her mother's voice telling her everything would be all right, just like when she'd been a little girl and had fallen and scraped her knee.

The light from the lamp glanced off something black and shiny on the nightstand. Thorn's new cell phone that Hank had given him to replace the one that burned in his house. He wouldn't have gone far without it.

Hungry and in need of the facilities, Sophia rose from

the bed and slipped into the jeans and T-shirt Hank's housekeeper had unearthed from Lilianna's wardrobe. She opened the connecting door to Thorn's room, hoping he was there. He wasn't.

As she passed back through her room, the light once again glanced off Thorn's cell phone.

If Antonio already knew she was there, what would it hurt to call her parents? It wouldn't trigger him to find her because he already had.

And what was it Hank had said? He'd give anything to know his wife and son were still alive, to hear their voices.

All the time she'd been incarcerated in *la Fuerte del Diablo,* Sophia had dreamed of hearing the voices of her mother, father and brother, Ernesto. Had her family had the same dreams?

Did cell phones have reception this far out in the country? As wealthy as Hank was, had he had a cell phone tower installed nearby to enable his communication with the outside world?

Could she place a call to Mexico?

Her heart pounded as she took first one step, then another toward Thorn's phone. The closer she moved, the faster she went until she pounced on the device and held it in her hand.

Her parents' number was as clear in her mind as it had been a year ago. She dialed it and got a message that the number she had dialed was not a working number. Had they disconnected or changed numbers? Then it dawned on her that a call from the United States to Mexico would require the country prefix.

Her hands shook as she dialed the full number and waited.

"Hola." When her mother's voice sounded in her ear, Sophia almost dropped the phone.

Her throat closed, and she fought to push words past the sobs. "Mama."

A long pause followed, then a tentative, "Sophia?"

"*Sí*, Mama, it's me."

"Oh, dear God, Sophia!" Her mother's sobs crackled into Sophia's ear.

"I'm okay, Mama." Sophia almost regretted the call. To give her mother hope when she had very little herself of coming out of her situation free or alive.

"We thought you were dead." More sobs.

Sophia cut through them, unsure of how long she could talk or if it put her or her parents in further danger. "Mama, how's Papa?"

"Sick with worry about you and Ernesto."

Sophia's hand tightened on the cell phone at the mention of her younger brother. "What's happened to Ernesto?"

"He's gone, too!" Her mother hiccupped, her breath catching. "Where have you been? Why haven't you called?"

"I can't go into that now. Just know that I'm alive. Tell me what happened to Ernesto."

"He had gone to work for the bank where your father works, but he fell in with a bad crowd at a local night club. He went there last night. We haven't seen him since."

A deep voice sounded in the background of the call and Sophia's heart skipped several beats. Her father. He spoke in rapid-fire Spanish. Her mother answered, her mouth away from the phone. Sophia couldn't follow the conversation.

"Mama?" she said into the phone. "Mama!"

"Sophia?" Her father's deep voice filled her ear. "Where are you? Why haven't you called?" He spoke in Spanish.

After several days around people who only spoke English, it took Sophia a moment for her mind to process and reply back in Spanish. "I'm in Texas. I'm okay for now. What about Ernesto?"

"I just got off the telephone with someone who said that if you do not return to the fortress, they will kill your brother."

Like a punch to the gut, Sophia doubled over. The cartel had her brother. She should have known Antonio would be monitoring her home in Monterrey and that he'd use her family against her. He knew how much she cared about them.

"Did they say anything else?" she asked, barely able to force the words past her heartbreak.

"If you don't go immediately and alone, he will be dead by sunset tomorrow." Her father paused. "Who are these people? Why are they doing this to you and Ernesto?"

"Papa, I can't go into it. Just know this. I love you." She fought to make her voice strong when her entire body shook. "Tell Mama I'm going to make this right."

She didn't wait for his response, pressing the button that would end the call. Sophia tossed the phone to the nightstand, knowing what she had to do.

She had to return to *la Fuerte del Diablo.*

Chapter Fourteen

When Thorn went back to Sophia's room to check on her, he was surprised to see her out of bed, dressed and looking as if she was going somewhere.

"I thought you'd be sleeping," he said.

"I couldn't." She paced across the room, parted the curtains and stared out at the night. "Why are there men still moving around the barnyard?"

"Brandon located *la Fuerte del Diablo*. Hank's getting a team together to cross over and free Lilianna and Jake."

"I want to be with them," she said.

Thorn shook his head. "Won't happen. Hank's leaving me behind to keep you safe."

"I'm the only one here who knows what room they keep Anna and Jake in. They need me."

"The odds are against them as it is. You don't have the combat training most of those guys do." He gripped her arm and forced her to look at him. "Think of your baby."

Her gaze met his, tears swimming in her green eyes. "I need to be there."

"You have to trust them. If you go, they'll be worried about what might happen to you. They won't be able to focus on their mission. That could get more people killed, and they'll already be outmanned and outgunned." He gathered her in his arms and smoothed his hand through her hair. "Don't worry, I'll be here with you. Antonio won't have a chance to get anywhere near you."

"When are they going?"

"Hank's arranging for a team to be transported via airplane late tomorrow evening."

"Isn't he afraid tomorrow will be too late?"

"Given the numbers they'll be up against, it might be too soon. He needs time to charter the transport plane he'll need to drop the men in on the other side of the border."

Sophia lowered her head. "I need to eat."

"I'm glad to see you're feeling well enough. Your baby needs the nutrition as much as you do."

He escorted her to the kitchen, where Hank's housekeeper had left a tray of sandwiches in the refrigerator. After Sophia had eaten an entire sandwich by herself in silence, Thorn began to wonder what had her so preoccupied. Perhaps the thought of Hank's men storming the compound had her worried for Lilianna and Jake.

Sophia's face was pale throughout the meal, the shadows beneath her eyes deeper and her eyelids slightly red rimmed, as if she'd cried recently.

When they'd finished and cleaned up their plates, Thorn hooked her arm and headed toward their rooms. "I think you could use more rest."

She halted before they'd gone too far, bringing Thorn to a stop. "I'm not tired."

"Then what's wrong?" He faced her, tipping her face up to the light and brushing his thumb across her cheek. "Have you been crying?"

A film of tears washed over her eyes. "No."

"Liar." He touched his lips to hers in a brief kiss. "Were you upset when you woke up and didn't find me there?"

She pulled her chin away from his fingers and looked away. "A little."

"I wouldn't have gone, but Hank called a meeting to discuss the plan." He cupped her cheek. "If it helps to know, I'll be with you from here on out."

She stared up into his eyes, the tears spilling down her cheeks.

Not exactly the response he'd anticipated from his statement.

"Thorn," Hank called out from near the hidden door to the bunker. "Ah, Sophia. Good. You're awake." He waved them over. "Feeling better?"

Sophia wiped the tears from her cheeks and crossed to the ranch owner. "Have you learned anything else about where they're keeping Anna and Jake?"

He smiled. "I take it Thorn filled you in on what Brandon found?"

"He did."

He turned to the hidden door and pressed his thumb to the pad on the wall. "I'd like you to look at what we've been working on." The door swung open, revealing the staircase.

"Of course." Sophia followed him into the bunker, Thorn close behind.

Again, Thorn was struck with a sense of something not being quite right with her. Until she told him what it was, though, he'd only be guessing.

Hank led them into the conference room with the big screen at the end. Brandon was still there, his fingers alternating between the keyboard and the mouse. "I accessed records of the satellite images for the past few days and put together a day-by-day progression of activity I thought you might find interesting."

Hank held out a chair for Sophia and sat in the one beside her. Thorn sat across the table, the better to study Sophia.

Brandon clicked the keyboard several times and an image came up, very much like the one he'd seen earlier at the meeting of the team.

The compound sat at the center of the image, concrete walls surrounding it.

"It's a fairly large complex with several buildings." Brandon moved his cursor, pointing at the largest building in the center. "This appears to be the main residence." He moved the cursor to a large empty spot to the right of the big building. "Now watch this."

He clicked the keyboard, and another image that looked exactly like the first appeared on the screen. Only the empty space had something in it that resembled the shape of a helicopter.

Sophia leaned forward. "A helicopter landed at *la Fuerte* each time *El Martillo* paid a visit."

"This image was from two weeks ago." Brandon turned to Sophia.

Sophia's face blanched and her body trembled. "*El Martillo* was there two weeks ago. From what Antonio told me, he had four of his men executed for passing information to *Los Lobos*."

Thorn couldn't imagine what this *El Martillo* would do to her if she were captured and returned to the fort.

Brandon clicked the screen. The helicopter disappeared, and in its place a tractor-trailer rig materialized with what appeared to be boxes lined up to be loaded into the back.

"Drugs?" Hank asked.

"Probably." Zack entered the room and took the seat beside Thorn.

"And notice the men gathered around." Brandon zoomed in.

The image blurred, but Thorn could still make out men carrying what looked like AK-47s. "Well armed."

"And probably trained by the Mexican army. The cartels pay better," Zach added.

"There are roads into and out of the compound," Brandon continued.

"But we won't be taking those." Hank tapped his fingers against the hardwood tabletop. "In order for us to maintain the element of surprise, we have to come in cross-country."

"Are those the exact coordinates?" Sophia pointed to the numbers on the top right corner of the screen.

"Yes," Brandon responded. "Smack-dab in the middle of the desert, south of Big Bend."

Sophia focused on the screen, then she closed her eyes. When she opened them again, she glanced around the table to Hank. "I never saw the place from this angle, so I can't be certain, but from the layout of the buildings it looks like *la Fuerte del Diablo.* And If I'm not mistaken, you'll find Anna somewhere in the main building."

Hank captured her hand and squeezed it.

Thorn tensed. He knew how much Hank loved his wife, but seeing him cling to Sophia's hand like that sent a jab of jealousy through Thorn he didn't know he had in him.

"Thank you," Hank said.

Sophia's lips thinned. "Don't thank me until you get them out alive." She glanced across the table at Thorn. "If you'll excuse me, I'm very tired."

"Come on, I'll take you topside." Thorn rose and led Sophia out of the room. Once they'd climbed out of the bunker, he slipped an arm around her. "Are you sure you're okay?"

"Why do you ask?"

"You seem preoccupied." He continued walking with her toward the bedroom they'd shared a couple hours ago. "Having regrets?"

"About?"

"What happened?"

She stepped through the door and pulled him inside, closing the door behind him. "If there's anything I'm not regretful about, it's you." She rose up on her toes and planted a kiss on his lips, lacing her hands behind his head to deepen the contact.

When she broke it off, she dropped her forehead to his chest. "I don't know what I would have done without your help that first night. I'd most likely be dead or on my way back to *la Familia Diablos*." A shiver shuddered through her at the thought, knowing it was exactly where she had to go. She wouldn't let her brother die for the mistakes she'd made. Her parents had gone through too much already.

"Then why were you preoccupied at the meeting with Hank?"

Sophia glanced away. Lying had never been easy for her. With Antonio, her life had been a lie in order for her to survive his abuse. With Thorn, she couldn't look him in the eye and tell him an untruth. "I was remembering all the horrible things that happened while I was there. The brutal beatings of men who didn't follow orders exactly right. The executions of rival cartel members caught on the wrong side of an imaginary border. The cries of the women whose men were found with their heads cut off."

Thorn pulled her against him, his arms wrapping around her waist, his touch more comforting than sexual. Just what she needed at that moment.

She closed her eyes, trying to block out all that was the worst of what she'd endured. "I never wanted to go back." And she would never consider it, if not to save her brother from a similar fate. If going back to Antonio kept him from killing Ernesto, so be it. The only bargaining chip she held to keep him from beating her to death was the fact that she was pregnant with his child. Surely he wouldn't kill her until after the birth.

"You're safe with me," Thorn said.

"Yes, I am." She tipped her head up, inviting his kiss. As she'd told him, she wouldn't be around forever. This would be their last time together, and she planned to make it a memory that would last.

Sophia stepped away from him.

"Do you have to be anywhere anytime soon?" she asked.

Thorn's lips curled upward on the edge, and he reached for her. "No."

She dodged his hands and slipped out of the T-shirt and jeans, slowly sliding her panties over her hips.

Thorn stood still, his gaze following every move, the ridge beneath his fly growing with each passing second. When she stood naked in front of him, he growled and swept her up in his arms. "I thought you were tired."

She laughed and nipped his earlobe. "I was."

He carried her to the bed and laid her across the mattress, then straightened. "Then maybe I should leave you to your sleep." His eager expression belied his words.

Sophia climbed to her knees, ran her hands down her naked flesh then flicked a button loose on his shirt. "If that's what you really want…"

"No. It's not." He finished the buttons, tossed the shirt and shed his boots and jeans in record time. Then he slid into the bed beside her. "You know what I want?"

"I could guess." She climbed up over him, straddling his hips, his member nudging her behind. "But I'd rather you showed me."

"Seems you're the one on top of things." He tweaked her nipple. "Perhaps you'd rather show me."

Their casual banter made it easy to make love to Thorn, a far cry from their first few encounters rife with tension and distrust. Now all she wanted to do was lie with him, making love into the dark hours of the morning.

One kiss at a time, she showed him how much he'd come to mean to her in the very short time they'd been forced together. If only they had more days together. If she wasn't headed back to the very place she'd sworn never to return to. A place she may never leave again. A lump blocked her throat, and she fought the rising sob.

This was to be their last night together. Sophia wanted to remember the joy, not the impending doom and sorrow. She started with a kiss, her lips tasting his, her tongue seeking the warmth and strength of his. Her body moved over his as she rose up on her knees and came down on him, guiding his shaft to her entrance.

Their coupling was intense, fiery and beyond anything she'd experienced in her life. When she lay spent beside him, in the comfort of his arms, she wondered how she could walk away from him without dying inside.

Thorn held her curled into his side, his chest rising and falling in a smooth, even pattern of deep sleep.

For a long time, Sophia drank in the sight of him in the dim light managing to find its way through the drawn curtains. The cowboy was handsome, dedicated and had a heart of gold.

She'd miss him, but she had to go.

Carefully, she extricated herself from his embrace and eased out of the bed.

Thorn rolled over, his eyes opening slightly. "Where are you going?" he asked sleepily.

"To the bathroom," she whispered. "Sleep."

His eyes closed. "Don't be gone long."

"I'll be right back." She dressed in the jeans, shirt and the tennis shoes Hank had loaned her from his wife's closet. Carefully, she lifted the pistol Thorn had laid on the nightstand before he'd gone to bed. Then she slipped from the room into Thorn's and out the double French doors onto the wide deck, tucking the gun into the back waistband of her jeans.

Trying to remember where all the security cameras were, she stuck to the deepest shadows and headed away from the house, moving from the bushes to a tree and across to the fence.

A shadow moved near the edge of the house.

Sophia tensed and stopped, hunkering low to the ground, her gaze on the house, watching, waiting for whatever was there to move again. After a moment, a cat emerged from behind a bush and sauntered toward the barn.

With a sigh Sophia continued, hugging the fence and working her way back to the barn, slipping in the back entrance where the four-wheelers were stored.

Hoping the foreman kept them topped off with gasoline, she shifted one into Neutral and pushed it through the door and out the back entrance into the night.

Each of the ATVs was equipped with GPS. All she had to do was enter the coordinates she'd memorized from the screen Brandon had shown her and follow the trails through the canyons and across the Rio Grande back into Mexico. Nothing to it—as long as she could dodge the border patrol, evade the FBI and, most of all, escape the notice of the cartel members set on killing her.

For the first quarter mile she pushed the vehicle, the strain on her muscles nothing compared to the pain in her heart. Thank goodness the land around the ranch house was flat, no hills, or she'd never have gotten as far as she did.

For the first time in her life, she'd met a man she could trust. A man who had a huge capacity to love and knew how to treat a woman right. How she wished she'd had more time to get to know him better, to show him that she was worth the trouble of loving again.

She envied Kayla and she envied her friend Anna the love of their husbands.

Sophia had to placate herself with the knowledge that she had a baby to love. Someone she'd give her life to save. She had to focus on getting her brother out of trouble, then she'd find a way to remove herself from the cartel's clutches.

If she did manage to get back to Wild Oak Canyon, she'd look up Thorn. Yeah, and miracles happened to people like her.

At what she guessed to be a quarter of a mile away from the ranch, she climbed onto the four-wheeler, her hand hovering over the starter.

A shiver of awareness slipped across her skin, and she turned back to see if anyone had followed.

In her peripheral vision, a shadow moved. Her focus jerked to track it, scanning the horizon between her and the ranch. All she could see was one lonely, dwarf mesquite tree huddled close to the dry earth, its tiny leaves brushed carelessly by the breeze. Nothing else moved.

A nervous chuckle left Sophia's lips as she hit the start button. The engine cranked immediately. She pressed the gas lever, and the vehicle leaped toward her fate.

THORN WOKE IN the darkness and blinked several times before he realized where he was. The clock on the nightstand read five minutes after three.

Sophia had gotten up to relieve herself, saying she'd be right back. He hadn't checked the clock then. How long had she been gone?

His pulse quickening, Thorn rose from the bed and

slipped into his jeans. A quick peek into the bathroom and he was no closer to finding Sophia. The light was off—it was empty.

His heartbeat thumping hard now, he returned to her room and checked inside the connecting room. She wasn't there. Out of the corner of his eye, he noticed the curtain on the double French doors was stuck between the two doors, as if someone had gone out in a hurry.

A lead weight sank into his gut as he reached for the doorknob he'd locked earlier. The knob turned easily, opening to the outside. Thorn returned to Sophia's room, shoved his feet into his boots, grabbed his shirt and headed outside in search of his missing charge.

He'd have woken if she'd been abducted. Which meant she'd slipped out on her own. Perhaps to get some fresh air? He prayed that was the case. Deep down, though, he knew it wasn't. She'd always said she didn't want to put anyone else at risk.

One of Hank's night guards stepped from the shadows. "Halt. Who goes there?"

Thorn recognized him as one of the men Hank had hired straight from a gig in Afghanistan. The man had been a marine, fearless and determined. But he walked with a limp. Another stray Hank had collected to fight his good fight.

"Did you see a pretty blonde come this way?" he asked, hopeful the guy's keen sight had picked up her where-abouts.

"Just came on duty about an hour ago." He shifted the M4A1 to a resting position. "Only movement I've seen was the FBI director's SUV pulling away from the ops tent."

"Working late hours, isn't he?"

"There were some raised voices in there for a few minutes before the director left."

"I need help locating the woman. I think she might be in danger."

Hank stepped out on the porch wearing jeans, a T-shirt and slippers. "What's going on?"

Thorn gritted his teeth. "Sophia's gone." On his watch, and she'd gotten away.

Within minutes, everyone on the ranch staff, including the housekeeper, had been alerted and was now checking every nook and cranny for her. Every last bodyguard and security guard reported finding nothing.

The group gathered in the barnyard. Hank walked over from the Joint Operations tent, his face grim. "I spoke with the crew on duty, thinking maybe Ms. Carranza turned herself over to them." Hank shook his head. "They never saw her, and the director left alone."

"She ran," Thorn said. "She couldn't have gone far. All the vehicles are accounted for."

"Except one." Scott Walden, the foreman, stepped into the middle of the crowd. "One four-wheeler is missing from the barn. I followed the tracks out the back door into the pasture. Whoever took it headed south."

Thorn's heart sank. "She is going back to Antonio. Back to *la Fuerte del Diablo.*"

"Why?"

"She was worried that by her being away from there, others would be hurt and that Antonio wouldn't stop hurting people until he had her back." Thorn's fists clenched. Antonio would beat her, regardless of her pregnancy. Sophia and the baby might not survive. "I'm going after her."

Hank put a hand on his arm. "You can't."

He jerked his arm free. "Like hell I can't."

"More than Sophia's life will be at stake in the compound."

"You don't understand—she might not make it back to

the compound. Traveling at night in the Big Bend canyons, she could run off a cliff, be bitten by a snake, get attacked by wolves or, worse, cartel members."

"Each of my ATVs is equipped with GPS tracking devices. Let's get Brandon to pull up her location on the computer and see how far she's gotten."

Thorn fought the urge to jump on the next available vehicle and storm after her. "Okay, but I'm going after her."

"And you will, but with a better understanding of where she is and what's at stake." Hank led the way into the bunker.

Brandon was already at his computer, clicking away on the keyboard. One final click and a screen displayed a topographical map and a red dot in the middle. "There. I guesstimate she's close to two hours away from us, deep in Big Bend country."

"If you follow her now, you may or may not catch up to her," Hank said.

"But she could be hurt."

"Brandon will keep an eye on her progress."

"I can do better than that." Brandon jumped up from his desk and headed into another room, emerging with a handheld device. He clicked the on button and waited, then handed it to Thorn. "You can follow her progress on this."

"But it's only the progress of the vehicle. We don't know if she's the one driving it."

"It's the best we have," Brandon said. "Short of going after her yourself, you'll have to trust that she can make it back on her own."

Two hours might as well be two weeks. She'd cross the Rio Grande while still under cover of darkness. If he started now, he'd cross in daylight. Stronger chance of being discovered by the trigger-happy cartel or diligent border-patrol agents.

"Hank," Brandon continued, "I just checked with your guy at Charter Avionics. They've been so busy that he's been up all night. But he was pleased to let you know that you can have the cargo plane today."

"What time?"

"They're pulling the preflight now. It can be ready in one hour, and they've located a cargo to pick up in Monterrey. Say the word and they'll file the flight plan."

"Tell them we'll be there in an hour." Hank turned to his foreman. "Scott? Is your flying license still current?"

"You know it," Scott replied.

"He's a pilot?" Thorn asked. What else didn't he know about Hank and his team of mercenaries?

"One of the best." Hank clapped his foreman on the back. "Flew missions in Iraq."

"And now I'm a foreman. A long way from my duties in the air force." Scott grinned. "I grew up on a ranch. I prefer working with horses and cattle, but I keep current on my flight skills, thanks to Hank."

"Drennan, you ever jump from a plane?" Hank asked.

Thorn nodded. "I did back in college a couple times."

"Chuck will give you a quick refresher with the equipment we have. If all goes well, we could get to the fort before Sophia." Hank faced the team. "Our timeline has just moved up. We leave as soon as we gather our gear and weapons."

Chapter Fifteen

Sophia had the feeling again that someone was following her. Doing her best to stick to the shadows of bluffs, she still had several long stretches of open ground to navigate. Thankful for the full moon lighting her path, she pressed on, hoping and praying the four-wheeler wouldn't run out of gas or someone wouldn't stop her from reaching her destination.

Her brother's life depended on her return to *la Fuerte del Diablo*.

She'd found her way along the trail she'd taken a few days earlier with Hector and now faced the long, somewhat flat stretch leading to the low-water crossing they'd forged on their dirt bikes. With the recent rain, Sophia couldn't be sure the river would be low enough to cross on the four-wheeler. The best she could do was cross on the ATV. If it was too deep, she'd lose the bike and have to continue on foot, without the aid of the GPS.

She slowed as she neared the river, her gaze darting left and right, searching for movement. At this point she'd be exposed, out in the open for anyone to see, including the United States border patrol. Although she couldn't imagine why they'd stop her crossing into Mexico. Didn't they concentrate on people *entering* the United States?

She gunned the throttle, sending the ATV out across the

open expanse and into the water. Halfway across the river, the vehicle's forward momentum slowed and it started floating sideways.

No. Just a little farther. *Come on,* por favor.

The wheels hit a sandbar beneath the water's surface and sent the vehicle forward again and into shallower water.

When she emerged safely on the Mexican side, Sophia paused as the engine chugged and choked. Setting the shift in Neutral, she revved the throttle until the engine ran smoothly again.

As she reached for the shift to set it in Drive, something stung her shoulder. She clapped her hand to the sharp pain and felt warm, sticky liquid. When she held her fingers up in the moonlight, she knew. She'd been hit. Another shot kicked up the rocks in front of the ATV. The next shot hit the handlebar, missing her fingers by half an inch. The bullets were coming from the other side of the river.

With too much open space to navigate before she reached cover, Sophia knew she'd never make it. She threw herself off the vehicle on the shadowy side. As soon as she landed on the rocky ground, she lay flat and pulled Thorn's handgun from the back waistband of her jeans. If she remained still enough, maybe whoever was shooting at her would assume he'd hit his mark and killed her, then maybe he'd move on.

With nothing but the four-wheeler as cover, Sophia lay still, the minutes stretching by like hours. Then she heard it. The sound of an engine splashing in the river. Only one engine.

Carefully, so that her movements wouldn't be detected, she eased around the knobby tire.

A man with a rifle slung over his shoulder hydroplaned across the river on a four-wheeler much like hers. Only his ATV wasn't lucky enough to catch a sandbar. Instead, it was caught in the current and drifted down the river.

The rider jumped off, holding what looked like an automatic rifle that soldiers carried over his head.

Sophia waited until he was close enough, then she aimed the pistol at the man—knowing she had only one chance to get it right—and pulled the trigger.

The bullet hit him in the leg and flung him backward into the water. His rifle flew into the air, landing with a splash in the current.

Sophia leaped to her feet and ran to the man, who was flailing and grasping for a handhold as the current carried him farther downstream.

At last he scratched his way to the shore, dragging himself up on the Mexican side.

Sophia was there, waiting for him, and she pointed the gun at his head.

When he turned to look up, the moonlight glanced off his features.

Sophia gasped. "I saw you at the ranch. You're with the FBI."

He grunted, his face creased in pain. "Help me."

"Why should I? You tried to kill me." She refused to get close enough to let him grab her and take her weapon away.

"Please." He reached out a hand. "My radio went down with the four-wheeler. If you leave me here, I'll die."

"Don't the feds know you're out here?" Her heart fluttered and she studied the horizon, searching for more agents like him.

"No." He dragged himself farther away from the river, leaving a thick trail of blood on the rocks. When he'd gone a couple feet, he collapsed facedown, his voice muffled but clear. "I'm not one of them. I'm a mercenary, a sharpshooter for hire."

"Then why the FBI outfit?" She nodded at his official-looking coveralls with the FBI lettering on the shoulder.

"Lehmann wanted everyone to think I was one of them."

"Why? Don't they have sharpshooters in the FBI?" she demanded, none of this making any sense.

"Yeah, but they usually shoot criminals."

Her stomach clenched. "And you'll shoot anyone who'll pay the price." She stood back, her weapon trained on him. "Are you telling me Lehmann wants me dead?"

"You and Antonio Martinez."

"Why?"

"Something about loose cannons and knowing too much." He groaned. "I don't know. Ask Lehmann." He looked at her with pleading eyes. "Just don't leave me here to die."

"*Lo siento, señor,* you are on your own." Much as she hated leaving an injured man, she had her brother to think of. "I have to go." Weighted by guilt, she turned toward her ATV.

"It's not safe to go back to the cartel," the man called out.

"I know." She didn't have a choice. It had been made for her when they'd taken her brother.

She returned to her vehicle and looked it over carefully, locating a storage compartment behind the seat. Inside it was a flare and a long, thick strap.

With the gray light of dawn creeping in from the east, she didn't want to stay long lest someone stop her to ask what she was doing there. She couldn't afford to be arrested. Not now.

Hurrying back to the downed man, she dropped the flare and the strap close to him and stepped out of his reach. "Use the strap as a tourniquet and the flare once

I'm gone. If I have a chance to send help, I will. Not that you deserve it."

She'd done all she could afford to do. With a last look at the man now sitting up, applying the tourniquet to his wounded leg, Sophia started the four-wheeler, shifted into gear and shot off toward the coordinates on the GPS.

Hungry, thirsty and exhausted beyond caring, she passed through the small town she and Hector had avoided on their escape route out of Mexico. The road leading to *la Fuerte del Diablo* lay before her. It was the path to hell, but hopefully one that would free her brother and spare her parents more grief.

She'd only gone a couple miles, kicking up a cloud of choking dust, when two men stepped out into the middle of the road, AK-47s pointed at her.

Sophia pulled to a stop and reached into her back waistband. She tossed the gun to the ground, and with her hand raised high in the air she spoke clearly. *"Me rindo. Quiero ver a Antonio."*

The men grabbed her, shoved her into their waiting truck and sped toward the compound, stopping at the gates, where more guards with high-powered weapons awaited, one with a radio who called ahead, warning of her arrival. Once inside, they drove straight to the main building.

Led like a prisoner being marched toward the firing squad, Sophia was shoved forward to face the man standing at the entrance.

Wordlessly, Antonio grabbed her arm and flung her through the door.

Sophia hit the cold, hard tile, resigned to the fact that he would take out his anger on her. She climbed to her feet and cringed when Antonio backhanded her, sending her staggering into a wall.

"You have embarrassed me." He spoke in English, knowing she would understand but his men would not.

"Let my brother go, and I will stay," she said, wiping the blood from her busted lip.

Antonio laughed, grabbed her arm and shoved her down the long hallway. "You are not one to give orders."

"I only came back to save my brother."

"He is not my prisoner to free."

Sophia stood tall, her head thrown back, all the rage she'd been hiding over the year surfacing. "Let him go, or I will leave again."

"You are *mi novia,* and you will do what I say!" he yelled, flinging her into the room she'd shared with him for the past year.

One of his men called out behind him.

Antonio turned all his fury on the poor man. *"¿Qué quieres?"*

The man spoke fast in a hushed, nervous whisper.

Sophia couldn't hear everything, only the name *El Martillo* voiced in a fearful tremor.

A thundering rumble shook the roof, the sound Sophia related to the arrival of the cartel kingpin.

Antonio's face blanched and he kicked at the messenger, sending him running away. He grabbed Sophia's wrist and tried to haul her out into the hall. "We must leave."

She braced herself against the door frame and yanked her arm free of his grip. "Not without my brother." Backing into the room, she put as much distance as she could between her and the man she'd grown to despise.

"You do not understand." Antonio lunged for her, his lips curling into a snarl. "I did not take your brother. He is not my prisoner to bargain with."

Sophia dodged him and rolled across the bed to land on her feet on the other side. The wound on her shoulder was nothing compared to what Antonio would do if he caught her.

The popping sound of gunfire outside made Antonio glance away.

Sophia grabbed a wooden chair and held it like a weapon in front of her.

Antonio's eyes took on a wild, frantic look. "We are all as good as dead if we do not leave now."

"Afraid of the people you associate with?" she asked.

"Only one." Antonio yanked the chair from her grasp and sent it crashing against the wall. Then he grabbed her by the arm and dragged her from the room, stopping so suddenly, Sophia slammed into him.

"Going somewhere, Martinez?" A deep voice speaking in English and devoid of all emotion echoed off the walls.

Sophia looked around Antonio to see a man wearing a black suit and sunglasses.

"I'm glad you two are here at the same time. You've led us on quite the chase." The man held a dark gray pistol in one hand. With the other hand, he removed his sunglasses.

"Oh, thank God, the FBI." She tried to rush forward. "It's over, Antonio. You will not hit me ever again."

Antonio's hand shot out, stopping her from passing him. "It's over all right. We should have left immediately." His gaze never strayed from the bigger man's face. "He's going to kill us."

"No." Sophia shook her head. "I'm not a criminal. I didn't kill those DEA agents. I'm a prisoner."

"*El Martillo* knows," Antonio said, his voice flat.

A loud bang shocked Sophia's eardrums.

Antonio jerked backward. The hand that had been holding hers dragged her with him as he fell to the floor, a bright red stain spreading across his chest.

"Get up," the man with the gun demanded.

Sophia looked back at him. "You're with the FBI. I saw you at Hank's ranch. You have to help me get Hank's wife and son out of here."

The man's lips curved. "That's why I'm here." He nodded toward the end of the hall. "But we must hurry."

Sophia didn't hesitate. She freed her arm from Antonio's death grip, stepped over his body and ran.

The reassuring sound of footsteps rang out behind her as she reached the rooms where Anna and Jake were held. "They're in here. But the door is locked."

"Not for long." The man in the suit shoved a key into the lock and turned it.

Too late, Sophia realized her mistake as he pushed the door open and shoved her inside.

The key, Antonio's mention of *El Martillo*...

"You're *El Martillo,*" she whispered, her chest tight, refusing to allow air into or out of her lungs.

"Sophia!" Anna called out from behind her. "Oh, Sophia, you're back." The woman Sophia had seen in the portrait in Hank's house pulled her into her arms and hugged her close, along with her young son. "Leave her alone," she said over the top of Sophia's head, her tone fierce. "She's done nothing to you."

"On the contrary, she's compromised my operation. We're leaving now. Before they find us."

An explosion rocked the floor beneath them. Anna, Sophia and Jake dropped to their knees.

Anna linked her arm with Sophia's and then stood, pulling her to her feet, her face grim, a hint of a smile on her lips. "I think you're too late."

"Not as long as I have a hostage." He grabbed for Sophia, looping his arm across her neck and pulling her back against him, pointing his gun to her head. "Come on, Anna, you and Jake are leaving with me if you don't want to see your friend killed."

SCOTT DROPPED THEM from the sky far enough away from the compound that they wouldn't be seen drifting to the ground in their parachutes in the predawn gray sky. But that meant hoofing it to the cartel hideout on foot across the desert. When they got close enough, Hank sent two men forward to plant diversionary explosives to draw attention away from the rest of them advancing on the walled fortress.

Using an MK12 special-purpose sniper rifle, Zach took out the sentry on the northwest corner while Chuck nailed the man on the southwest corner and the rest of the team used grappling hooks and rope to scale the back wall while members of the cartel were responding to the explosion on the opposite side of the compound.

First inside, Thorn dropped to the ground, an HK MP5 submachine gun clutched in his right hand, six forty-round replacement magazines strapped to his body and an armor-plate carrier with an armor plate tucked inside, protecting his chest. On his head, he wore a ballistic helmet. Each man carried either an M4A1 or an HK416 carbine assault rifle, with a knife at his side and a Sig Sauer SP226R 9 mm pistol strapped to one leg. They were loaded with enough ammo to take down an army of cartel thugs.

With the submachine gun taking point and his knife in his other hand, Thorn kicked in a door at the back of the main building.

A man inside standing guard opened fire.

Thorn ducked back behind the door, giving the man time to spend a few rounds, then he dove in, rolled and came up shooting. He took the man out in a short five-round burst.

Yelling inside the building meant they only had a few minutes to locate the prisoners and get them to safety.

Thorn covered while Blaise kicked in the door the guard had manned. Inside they found a young Hispanic man in jeans and a Universidad Nacional Autónoma de México T-shirt. He held up his hands. *"No disparen!"*

"¿Dónde usted?" Zach demanded.

"Ernesto Carranza," the young man answered. "I speak English."

"Any relation to Sophia?"

"Elena?" He nodded. *"Sí."*

"Where are they keeping her?" Thorn demanded.

"I didn't think she was here. They grabbed me to get her to return."

A rush of relief washed over Thorn. So that's why she'd gone back to *la Familia Diablos.* Dread quickly followed. Antonio had used her brother to get her back. He'd never let either one of them leave alive.

"Stay here or follow and keep out of the way, but be warned, there will be bullets."

"I'm coming." He followed, leaving a good distance between them.

Thorn came to the end of the hallway and turned left. A body lay in the middle of the corridor. One he knew they hadn't shot.

A man in a suit emerged from a room with a woman in front of him, a gun pressed to her temple. He closed the door behind him.

Thorn recognized them immediately.

Grant Lehmann held Sophia at gunpoint.

"That's Antonio Martinez. He's dead, and I caught his accomplice." He nodded toward Thorn. "It's okay, you can put your guns down," he said with a smile. "Show's over."

"Don't trust—" Sophia gasped.

Lehmann's arm tightened, cutting off her words. "That's right, don't trust a cartel member. We need to get her back to the States and on trial for the deaths of the DEA team."

"Let her breathe, Lehmann," Thorn warned, his hand tightening on the submachine gun.

Hank came up behind Thorn. "Grant? What are you doing here?"

"I heard you were making a move into cartel territory. Couldn't let you go it alone," Lehmann said smoothly. Too smoothly.

"So where's your team?" Thorn asked.

"Handling things outside. I took lead on the inside to make sure the two most wanted didn't escape."

Sophia's eyes were wide and round. She clutched at Lehmann's arm around her throat, trying to shake her head.

"Let her go, Lehmann," Thorn said, taking a step closer.

"She's escaped you before. If I let her loose, she'll do it again."

Her face going from red to blue, Sophia sagged against Lehmann.

His heart in his throat, Thorn growled. "Let her go. Now." He raised his submachine gun and pointed it directly at the FBI regional director's head. "Or I'll shoot you."

Apparently Lehmann had loosened his hold when Sophia's body went limp. Color began returning to her face.

"Hank, call off your dog. He's not going to shoot while I'm holding his girlfriend." Lehmann's gaze narrowed. "I know you were harboring her, and you could be in a whole lot of trouble stateside should the word get out that you're a traitor."

Hank raised his pistol, leveling it at Lehmann's face. "I think I know a traitor when I see one."

"I don't know what you're talking about."

"You're the one who has been leaking information to *la Familia Diablos*."

"No," a muffled voice called out through the closed door. "He is *El Martillo,* leader of the *la Familia Diablos.* Don't trust him."

"Lilianna?" Hank stepped closer.

"Hank? Oh, God, Hank! It's me, Lilianna. I'm in here with Jake!"

"You!" Hank's face turned a mottled red. "You stole her away from me. All the time we were searching, you knew!" The pistol in Hank's hand shook, then steadied. "Bastard!"

Lehmann laughed. "And you thought I was your friend."

"You won't get away with this, Grant. You betrayed your country."

The FBI traitor snorted. "I've gotten away with it for years. How do you think drugs and human trafficking flowed so easily past the farce they call Customs and Border Protection? Not to mention beneath the noses of the FBI?"

"You arrogant bastard." Thorn's gut knotted. If he didn't get Sophia away from Lehmann, there wouldn't be anything left for him to save.

"Having a heart or a conscience doesn't make you rich, does it, Hank?" Lehmann's lip curled. "You stole the only thing I cared about when you took Lilianna away from me. Well, I got her back, didn't I?" His nostrils flared, his face reddening. "How did it feel?"

Thorn wanted to kill the man even if Hank didn't.

Hank stood with his fist wrapped so tightly around his pistol his knuckles turned white. "You know damn well how it felt. My life ended."

"You're through, Lehmann," Thorn said. "Your drug-dealing, human-trafficking days are over."

"You're a fool, Drennan. You and these broken-down

cowboys Hank's hired. Who do you think they will believe? It will be my word against yours. Besides, when all is said and done, there will be no witnesses." Lehmann stood his ground, the gun against Sophia's head. "Come any closer, and I'll shoot her." He struggled to hold her limp body in front of him.

Thorn refused to lower his weapon. He couldn't shoot for fear of hitting Sophia. And Lehmann would follow through on his promise to kill her.

Sophia's eyes opened and she blinked at Thorn, mouthing the word *now.*

At the angle she'd slid, she had a clear shot for an elbow to Lehmann's groin. She slammed her elbow back and ducked out of Lehmann's hold.

His gun went off, the shot going wide, hitting the other side of the hallway.

Thorn hit the trigger of the submachine gun at the same time Hank fired his pistol, both rounds clipping Lehmann in a shoulder, sending him slamming back against the wall. Lehmann slid, leaving two streaks of blood as he descended to the floor.

Thorn, his heart thundering, crouched beside Sophia, who lay facedown on the floor. "Are you okay?"

For a long moment she didn't respond.

He gently turned her over, and her eyes blinked against the light. "Thorn?"

"Yeah, darlin', it's me." He smiled at her. "You brave, stupid, hardheaded woman."

"Stubborn man." She gave a half laugh, half cough. "Did you get him?"

"Hank did." He brushed the hair off her forehead.

"Is he dead?" she asked.

"No. We need him alive to reveal the extent of his network."

"Ernesto?" She pushed against Thorn. That's when he noticed the wound on her shoulder.

"You're hurt." He pressed her back to the floor and ripped the sleeve away from the injury.

"Just a flesh wound." She smiled, but it faded quickly. "My brother…"

"I'm here, *mi hermana*." The young Hispanic knelt beside her and took her hand. "Mama and Papa…we thought you were dead." He carried her hand to his lips and kissed her fingertips. "I've missed you."

"Come on, we have to get you to a doctor." Thorn slipped his machine gun over his shoulder and rose, lifting Sophia into his arms and away from the front of the doorway.

Hank slid Grant Lehmann's gun into his back waistband and reached for the door. It was locked.

He aimed his pistol at Lehmann's head. "Where's the key?"

Lehmann clutched his arm and laughed. "Inside with her."

"Lilianna, get away from the door."

"I'm clear!" she called from inside.

Hank redirected his aim to the door handle and pulled the trigger. The door frame splintered. Hank kicked the door, and it flew inward.

In the next moment, he was engulfed in an embrace from the wife he'd almost given up on ever finding.

Thorn's heart swelled for the man who'd gone through hell. His own arms tightened around Sophia. For only knowing her the short time he had, he knew he didn't want to live another day without her. She was brave, caring and willing to sacrifice herself for the ones she loved.

"You'll never get back across the border with me," Lehmann said, his voice shaking, his face losing some of its color. "Who do you think they'll believe? An FBI regional director or a team of washed-up mercenaries?"

"He hired a mercenary sharpshooter to pose as FBI to kill me," Sophia said. "And he almost succeeded. He's back at the river crossing. And I'm sure he'd be happy to tell all for the price of saving him."

"I paid that man too much," Lehmann snorted. "I could have done a better job killing you. But still, it would be my word against yours. I have friends in high places."

"And so do I." Hank stood with his arm around his wife and son. He raised one hand to touch the high-tech helmet he wore. "I think they'll believe the video I've been recording since we stormed into *la Fuerte del Diablo*. It's being transferred back to my computer guy at the Raging Bull and by now is in the hands of my trusted friends in the FBI and the CBP. I'm sure they'll be waiting at the border with a welcoming committee. Especially since we'll be bringing *El Martillo* with us."

Lehmann's eyes closed, and his forehead creased as if in pain. "You'll never get out of here alive."

Hank held a hand up and squinted as if his attention had been redirected. After a minute, he spoke. "Thanks, Harding. I knew I'd picked the right men when I hired y'all."

Hank's gaze settled on his former friend. "While you've been bleeding and blabbing, my men reported in that they've subdued what *la Familia Diablos* members remain on the grounds. The rest ran. So much for loyalty, huh?"

Hank left the building, carrying his son and holding Lilianna close like he never wanted to let her go.

Thorn followed, hugging Sophia to his chest, Ernesto beside him.

"I can walk, you know." Sophia leaned into him and kissed his cheek.

"I like holding you." He scowled down at her. "At least I know where you are when you're in my arms."

"I had to come, or they would have killed my brother."

"I would have done the same. But promise me one thing."

Her arms slipped around his neck, and she feathered her fingers through his hair. "Anything."

"No more running."

"I promise."

"And when we get back to the States, I want to take you out."

"Out where?"

"On an honest-to-God date. I want to start over, get to know you, learn what your favorite color is, your favorite ice cream."

"Deal." She kissed his lips then pulled away. "On one condition."

"What condition?"

"You take me to see my parents first."

"That can be arranged."

She stared up into his eyes. "One more condition."

"No more conditions."

"Just one." She cupped his cheeks in both her palms. "Is there room in your heart to love another as much as you loved your wife?"

Thorn smiled down at her. "I'll never stop loving Kayla, but being with you has shown me that I could be open to loving another."

She looked away, her hand slipping to her belly. "How about two others?"

He laughed and spun her around. "I wouldn't have it any other way."

When he finally came to a halt and set her on her feet,

Sophia stroked the side of his face, her touch warming him through to the heart he'd thought dead forever. "Thorn?"

He turned his face into her palm and kissed the lifeline that had brought him back from the dead. "Yes, Sophia?"

"My favorite color is blue, I love chocolate ice cream and I believe I'm falling in love with you."

Chapter Sixteen

Hank Derringer leaned against the breakfast bar at the pregrand opening of the newly reconstructed and improved Cara Jo's Diner in Wild Oak Canyon, three months after it had burned to the ground. He'd helped Cara Jo with the costs of reconstruction, allowing her to expand the floor space, update the kitchen equipment and give the diner a shiny new appearance with a fifties, retro feel.

Clearing his throat, Hank began speaking. "I called this meeting of the Covert Cowboys not only to celebrate the reopening of Cara Jo's Diner but to thank you for all the good work you've done over the past months we've been in business.

"Grant Lehmann is awaiting his trial, but with the evidence we've accrued from his hired sharpshooter and other FBI agents seeking a plea bargain, he's sure to get a fat sentence and be off the streets for a very long time."

Everyone in the room clapped and cheered.

"Most of all, I want to thank everyone for helping bring Lilianna and Jake home safely." His voice cracked as he continued, "I owe you so much."

"Thanks, Hank." Chuck Bolton was the first to speak. "But none of us could have been as successful without the confidence and support you've given us." He stared down at the baby on his arm. Charlie, now six months old and tugging at Chuck's collar, giggled and cooed, obviously loving her father. "Some of us wouldn't be here today if CCI hadn't come along to save our sorry butts."

Blaise Harding snorted. "Speak for yourself, Bolton."

"Admit it, Harding—you wouldn't be engaged to Kate if you hadn't gone to work for Hank," Zach Adams said.

Blaise kissed Kate with a loud smack. "You got that right." He bent to lift Kate's daughter, Lily, into his arms. "And I wouldn't have my sweet Lily to give me hugs."

Lily wrapped her little arms around his neck and pressed a kiss to his cheek. "I love you, Daddy."

Blaise's eyes rounded and he leaned back, staring at Lily, then Kate. "Did you hear that?"

Kate smiled up at him. "She wanted to call you Daddy." The beautiful strawberry blonde nodded. "I thought it was time."

Blaise squeezed Lily to his chest until she squealed, "Let me down. Pickles is getting away."

He set her on the ground, his eyes shining with moisture as he watched his little girl chase after the black-and-white border collie.

Hank laughed as his son, Jake, raced after the two.

"I owe Hank my life for assigning me to find Jacie's sister." Zach pulled Jacie's hand through his arm and smiled at the pretty brunette cowgirl. "I'd probably still be wallowing at the bottom of a whiskey bottle if not for Hank and the Covert Cowboys. And Jacie."

Jacie laughed. "Instead he's making me crazy, following me around when I'm leading big-game hunts. When's his next assignment, Hank?" She winked and pinched Zach's arm.

Hank tipped his head toward Thorn. "How's the house comin' along?"

Thorn rested his hand on Sophia's thick waistline. "Should be finished in a month."

"Cuttin' it kinda close?" PJ smiled at Sophia. "You'll be havin' that baby before you move in."

Sophia laughed. "Thorn's got ten weeks to make that deadline."

"Do you know what you're having?" Kate asked.

Sophia glanced up at Thorn, smiling. "A girl."

Thorn's lips twisted. "Don't know what to do with a little girl."

Chuck laughed. "Trust me, they'll know what to do with you. Isn't that right, Charlie?" He lifted his baby girl high in the air.

"Hey, I'd like a little of that affection, too." PJ groused good-naturedly.

"Darlin', you know I love you," Chuck said.

"Oh, yeah?" PJ crossed her arms. "When are you going to make an honest woman of me?"

"Soon as you set the date."

Hank's bark of laughter got everyone's attention. He cleared his throat and nodded at Thorn.

"There's my cue." Thorn dug in his pocket, winked at Hank and dropped to one knee. "Sophia, love of my life, the only woman I can see myself shackled to for the rest of my days, will you marry me?" He held out an open ring box with a beautiful diamond engagement ring inside. "I already have your father's blessing, if that helps."

Sophia pressed her hands to her chest, tears welling in her eyes. "Really? You want to marry me?"

Thorn nodded. "We might have had a rocky start with you almost killing me, but I'm willing to take the chance if you are." He removed the ring from the box and held it out. "So what's it going to be? Yes or no? And please say yes, 'cause I can't wait much longer to make you my wife."

"Yes!" Sophia gave him her hand, and he slipped the ring on her finger. Then she flung her arms around his neck and kissed him.

Chuck tipped his head toward PJ. "So, is it going to be a double wedding?"

PJ smiled. "I'm in, but Sophia and Thorn might want the day all to themselves."

Sophia shook her head. "A double wedding will be twice as much fun as a single. Do you agree, *mi amor?*"

"I do." Thorn held her as close as he could without squishing her belly.

Tears welled in PJ's eyes. "I'm gonna have more family than I know what to do with."

Lilianna slipped an arm around Hank and leaned into him. "She's got a good heart, just like her father."

"Yes, she does. I'm about the luckiest man alive." He kissed his wife and hugged her close.

Slowly Lilianna had settled back into her old life. She'd be seeing a therapist for years to come, but she was happy to be home, and Jake was recovering from his two-year ordeal with the cartel. Hank had taught him to ride horses, and it was helping him to open up and be a regular little boy.

While the ladies gathered around Sophia, congratulating her on her engagement, the men circled Hank.

"So, Hank," Blaise said over the chatter of the women, "what's next?"

"I have assignments waiting for each of you, and I'm thinkin' of hirin' a couple more cowboys and maybe even a cowgirl." He stood straight, his arms crossing over his chest. "Y'all still in?"

As one, the cowboys yelled, "Hell, yeah!"

* * * * *

KILLER BODY

CAST OF CHARACTERS

Dawson Gray—Former special ops soldier. He reluctantly takes on the assignment of bodyguard to a potential murder suspect.

Savvy Jones—Bar waitress who can't remember killing a drug lord's son and then shooting herself. Was she a witness and then set up to take the fall?

Frank Young—Webb County district attorney who hired Dawson to protect the witness or keep tabs on the killer, whichever it turns out to be. He has his own secrets to hide.

Marisol De La Fuentez—Mexican national and seductress. Who occupies her bed and her schemes?

Jose Mendoza—El Martillo, the Hammer. Humberto Rodriguez's enforcer. He'd kill to protect the cartel.

Tomas Rodriguez—Playboy son of a Mexican drug lord, shot to death behind the Waterin' Hole Bar and Grill.

Humberto Rodriguez—Ruthless Mexican cartel leader whose son is murdered behind the Waterin' Hole Bar and Grill in the United States. He wants revenge and will stop at nothing short of death for the one who killed his son.

Liz Scott—Savvy's only friend, who found her lying in the alley with a bullet wound to her head.

Eb (Earl Bradford)—The Waterin' Hole's bartender. Does he know what happened that night Tomas Rodriguez died?

Edward Jameson—A rich man, whose daughter, Sabrina, has been missing for four months. He'll do anything to get her back.

Audrey Nye—Owner of the Lone Star Agency, responsible for assigning agents to investigate for or protect clients. Has a tendency to take in strays and give them a second chance.

Jack McDermott—Dawson's friend, sent by the boss to replace him on the bodyguard gig.

This book is dedicated to my family—my husband, daughters, son, grandson, mother, father, sister, brothers and all my extended family.
Because...family is everything.

Chapter One

Dawson Gray clutched the phone in a death grip to keep his hand from shaking. "I'm not right for this job. Isn't there a surveillance gig I could cover? What about Jack? Can't he do it?" This was just the kind of job his buddy Jack was best at. Dawson didn't want to disappoint his new boss, but he didn't want to be responsible for anyone's life other than his own.

Private investigation was what he'd signed up for when he'd joined the Lone Star Agency. Taking pictures of cheating spouses, he could handle. Protecting someone from an unknown enemy, never again.

He stared at Laredo's Doctors Hospital from the parking lot, dreading the visit. The last two times he'd been in a hospital had left him with the permanent need to stay clear. When he was in the military he'd had to stand at the bedside of the young corporal he'd been responsible for and watch him slowly bleed to death of wounds from an IED roadside explosion. Then he had to witness his wife's death, or rather he missed saying goodbye to the only woman he'd ever loved. She'd died before he'd arrived.

"The D.A. in Laredo needs someone today. I'd send Jack, but he's not available. You're the only agent not tagged at this time." Audrey Nye sighed over the line and pleaded with him. "I need you to do this. A woman's life depends on you."

His boss's words made his stomach knot and his palms sweat against the steering wheel. Who was he to provide protection to anyone when he'd already lost too many of the people he cared about? How could Audrey give him this assignment when he'd only been sober for two months? Two months wasn't enough to make him qualified to blow his nose in public, much less watch over the welfare of a woman who'd been left for dead in an alley? He opened his mouth to tell his boss he couldn't take the job, but she beat him to the punch.

"Dawson, you can do this. I wouldn't have assigned the case to you if I didn't think you could handle it. Laredo itself isn't bad, but the city's so close to the border that a lot of the drug-war fighting happening in Mexico bleeds across the Rio Grande. You're trained in special ops. You know how to use a weapon. I know you're right for this job. You're there, so you might as well check it out. If you still don't think you're up to it, I'll find someone else, even if I have to take the case myself."

When his female boss, with no military training whatsoever, volunteered to take on a potentially violent bodyguard gig, he knew he had a problem. Dawson's jaw tightened and he drew in a deep breath. "I'll take care of it."

"Thanks, Dawson. I knew you would." Before he could comment, she continued, "The D.A., Frank Young, is scheduled to meet you at the nurses' station on Savvy's floor. He'll fill you in on the details. Tell them you're her fiancé or they won't let you in. Don't let on to anyone you're anything else. The D.A. wants this all to be low-key. Got that?"

"Yes, ma'am." As long as it stayed at the pretend level. Dawson wasn't in a position to be anything other than a hired protector. Since his wife's death two years ago, he'd been nearly suicidal. Brokenhearted, he'd volunteered for the most dangerous of missions in Iraq, taking risks no one in his right mind would dream of. He hadn't been in his right mind. Not since Amanda's death. After nearly getting killed three times and a mandatory psych evaluation, his commander had shipped him home and Dawson had gotten out of the service.

He shifted his truck into Park, pulled the keys from the ignition and pushed the door open. Heat hit him like a steamroller. The glaring Texas sun beat against the black asphalt.

Thankful for the thick soles of his cowboy boots, Dawson stepped out of the truck and stood.

An image of his wife lying across sterile sheets with tubes and wires attached to her sent a shiver over his body despite the oppressive morning heat. His heart thundered against his chest and he couldn't quite catch his breath as he approached the door to the hospital lobby. The sudden craving for whiskey hit him so hard he wanted to drop to his knees.

A woman carrying a baby stepped through the sliding doors on her way to the parking lot. She smiled at him and held the door open. "Are you going in?"

He nodded and hurried forward to hold the door for her so that she could grab hold of a toddler while she juggled the baby in her arms. "Thanks."

Dragging in a deep breath, he stepped inside the cool interior of the hospital and marched toward the information desk.

An older woman sat behind the desk, peering over the top of her glasses. "May I help you?"

"I'm looking for Savvy Jones's room."

The woman touched her finger to a keyboard, one letter at a time.

Dawson bit his tongue to keep from groaning. That ubiquitous hospital scent of disinfectant filled his lungs and made him feel nauseous.

The woman smiled up at him. "Are you a relative?"

Dawson forced the words past his constricted throat. "I'm her...fiancé."

The woman directed him to the fourth floor, giving him a room number and pointing out the elevator.

After he stepped into the elevator and selected the floor, Dawson's fingers curled into tight fists. He watched the numbers change above the keypad. The elevator stopped on the third floor; a young nurse stepped in, her eyes widened and her gaze swept over him. "Hi." She smiled and tucked a strand of long blond hair over her shoulder. "Visiting?"

He barely cut her a glance. "Yeah, my fiancée."

Her shoulders slumped and she sighed. "The hunks are always taken." She flashed another smile and held out her hand. "I'm Dani. Call me if things don't work out."

"Things *will* work out." If he had anything to do with it, they would. He'd perform his protective duties until a suitable replacement could be found, then he'd be on his way back to San Antonio and his next assignment. He nodded toward the door opening on the fourth floor. "Getting off here?"

She shook her head. "I wish, but no."

Dawson stepped out into a hallway, read the signs on the wall and followed the one toward Savvy's room. At the nurses' station he stopped. Audrey had said that the district attorney who'd contracted for a bodyguard would meet him there.

A man stood with his back to Dawson, a cell phone pressed to his ear. His voice was barely a murmur. Tall, with sandy-blond hair and wearing a tailored business suit, the guy had to be the district attorney.

He turned, spied Dawson and nodded. "Check on it, will you?" he said into the phone. "If she is who this guy thinks she is, we have to handle things carefully. Call me later with what you find out." He disconnected and faced Dawson with his hand held out. "You must be Dawson Gray. Ms. Nye told me all about you."

"Not much to tell." Dawson accepted the man's hand. His grip was firm, if somewhat cool.

"Frank Young, Webb County district attorney." He dropped Dawson's hand and nodded toward a corner. "Ms. Jones's room is down that hallway. The nurse says the sedative should be wearing off soon."

"Ms. Nye said you'd fill me in on the case."

Young nodded. "Last night Ms. Jones was found in the alley behind the Waterin' Hole Bar and Grill, where she works, with what appeared to be a self-inflicted gunshot wound to her left temple. Fortunately for her the injury was only a flesh wound. The unfortunate part is that the gun found beside her and that she supposedly used to shoot herself happens to be the same gun used to kill Tomas Rodriguez."

Dawson gritted his teeth. "Are you telling me she killed Mr. Rodriguez?"

"I can't tell you anything. When she woke up this morning she was so doped up the nurses couldn't get anything coherent out of her. When they asked her questions, she swore she couldn't remember anything."

"About the shooting?"

Young shook his head. "Anything, as in even her name."

Dawson glanced toward the hallway. "Amnesia?"

"That's what the doctors are saying. It could be temporary, or it could be permanent. Only time will tell." Young crossed his arms over his chest.

"Are you sure it's not just a convenient stall? She can't testify in a trial if she can't remember."

The D.A. nodded. "That's very true."

"What about her other mental faculties? Can she talk?"

"Yes, she asked the nurses for water and told them that she was cold and wanted a blanket. No slurred speech or problems following simple directions."

"Why hire a bodyguard? Why not post a policeman on her?"

"With all the trouble from across the border, the police force is shorthanded. And I'm not so sure I can completely trust the force to handle this matter as delicately as is needed."

"Why?"

"Why?" The D.A. stared at Dawson as though he expected more from him. "Do you know who Tomas Rodriguez is?"

Dawson shook his head. "Name sounds familiar."

"I suppose the border troubles don't always make national news. Make no mistake, though, people around here know the name." The D.A. looked left then right before going on. "Tomas Rodriguez was the son of Humberto Rodriguez, one of the most powerful leaders of Nuevo Laredo's drug cartel."

Dawson stared at the closed door. "Which paints a bright red bull's-eye on Ms. Jones." Great, he was in for a rough time of protecting a potential murder suspect from being killed by an avenging father with an army of mercenaries.

"Exactly. Once word gets out that Tomas is dead, which it probably has by now, Rodriguez will be gunning for her and I'm not so sure the police force will stand in the way."

"Are they that corrupt?"

"No, it's just that they have families to worry about. Some of them have family on both sides of the border. If they want their loved ones to remain alive, they have to stay out of it. Anyone standing in the way of Rodriguez's desire for vengeance on the person responsible for killing his only offspring will suffer consequences."

The woman had her death warrant signed before Dawson had even shown up for work. "If she killed Tomas, why don't you lock her up?"

"Another fact I just learned a few minutes ago when I talked to one of the nurses has me worried, something I haven't shared with the press or anyone else."

"I thought you said Ms. Jones doesn't remember anything."

Frank Young gave a mirthless laugh. "She doesn't. But some things you don't forget even when you forget your name."

Dawson crossed his arms over his chest, impatient with the other man's dramatic pause. "Enlighten me."

"The prints on the weapon match the prints from her left hand. Since she shot herself after she supposedly shot Tomas, she had to have used her left hand."

"Your point?" Dawson snapped, the smell of disinfectant making him eager to get to the crux of the matter so that he could get the hell out of the hospital.

"She used her right hand to eat breakfast this morning. Ms. Jones is right-handed." As if sensing the importance of the D.A.'s words, the busy hallway stilled. No nurse pushed through a door, no patient ventured out. Silence filled the space after Young's announcement.

"She's right-handed?" Dawson's eyes narrowed as he stared at the district attorney, the full impact of those words sinking in.

The D.A. nodded. "Exactly. Why would a right-handed person shoot herself in the head with her left hand?"

"You don't think she shot herself." It was a statement, not a question. "You think that whoever killed Rodriguez shot the woman and made it look like murder-suicide." The pulse in his temple throbbed and he pressed his fingers to the growing ache.

"Right."

"And whoever tried to kill her the first time will most likely try again."

"Right, again. Murderers don't normally like loose ends."

"She's the only one who saw the crime take place?"

"As far as we know. No one else has stepped forward." The D.A. nodded toward her door down the hall. "She hasn't actually pointed any fingers. Since she probably didn't shoot Rodriguez, I can't put her in jail."

Dawson scoped the hallway again with new purpose, his gaze narrowing at every person passing by. "Whoever killed Tomas Rodriguez won't want to give her the chance."

A DULL ACHE THROBBED against the side of her head. She struggled to open her eyes and adjust to the fluorescent light in the hospital room. She lifted her hand to press it against her temple, but her hand was tied to something.

An IV was taped to the top of her hand. She vaguely remembered the tubes from the last time she'd woken, when the nurses had insisted on cranking her bed into an upright position to eat a breakfast she couldn't taste. What had happened? Why was she lying in a hospital and why did her head hurt?

What else was wrong with her? She tested movement of her toes. The sheet near the end of the bed wiggled and she let out a sigh. She wasn't paralyzed. She attempted to sit in the bed and made it halfway up before collapsing back. The effort was exhausting.

Again, she tried to remember what brought her here. Had she been in a wreck? Where was her family? A sudden emptiness filled her chest, pressing hard against her heart. Did she have a family? She glanced around at the sterile room. No flowers, no get-well cards, no signs of anyone caring whether she lived or died. She didn't know which was worse: that she couldn't remember who should care about her, or that she didn't actually have anyone who cared about her. For the life of her, she couldn't picture anyone, couldn't name a name, not even her own.

Her heartbeat jumped, her breath coming in low shallow gasps. The more she tried to remember, the more she realized she couldn't. Where had she been, what was she doing? How had she gotten hurt?

A violent shiver shook her body, having nothing to do with the temperature in the room and more to do with the fact she couldn't remember her name or even what she looked like.

She tried again to sit up in the bed, this time succeeding. An uncontrollable urge to run hit her. Before she could think, she yanked the tape off her hand and pulled the IV needle out. Cool air raised chill bumps on her legs as she slid them from beneath the sheets and let them drop over the side of the bed.

She slipped off the mattress, her bare feet touching the cold floor. For a moment, she thought *no problem.* Then her knees buckled, her muscles refusing to cooperate. With a dark sense of the inevitable, she cried out as she crumpled to the floor.

She lay still for a few moments, willing the air to return to her lungs.

The swoosh of a door opening and closing made her turn toward the sound.

"Help," she called out.

No one answered.

Irrepressible fear gripped her so firmly she couldn't breathe. A hospital usually meant a safe place where people went to recover from their injuries. Why then did panic seize her and squeeze the air from her lungs?

Footsteps neared, rounding the corner of the bed.

She shrank back, looking up at a man wearing green-blue staff scrubs.

"Savvy Jones?" he asked through the matching mask on his face, his words heavily accented.

"I d-don't know," she whispered.

The man's dark brown eyes narrowed, his bushy black brows dipping low on his forehead. He lifted a pillow from the bed. "Let me help." Instead of reaching out to lift her, he bent beside her.

"I can get up myself," she said, although she doubted she could. "If you'll just move back. Please."

The man didn't move back. He reached out, his dark-skinned arms covered in tattoos of vicious red devils and blue-green dragons.

Alarmed by the violent nature of the pictures on the man's arms, she scooted backward until her head bumped into the table beside the bed. "Leave me alone."

"I will," he said, his voice cold, menacing, "once I take care of you."

The pillow came down over her face, pushing her head against the cool tiles of the floor.

She fought and screamed into the pillow, her struggles useless.

The man held her down with minimal effort, his body bigger, stronger—his goal, murder.

Chapter Two

"I have a court case at ten," District Attorney Young said. "I left an officer at her door, but he knows he can leave as soon as you arrive. I'm counting on you to keep the woman safe. Can you handle it?"

Despite his self-doubt, Dawson nodded.

The D.A. handed him a business card. "As soon as she's coherent, give me a call. I'll be here. Hopefully she'll wake up soon, this time with her memory intact so we can get down to the business of catching a killer."

A killer who could be very anxious to finish the job. Dawson accepted the card and turned it over in his hand as the man in the suit walked away.

Okay, so he had his work cut out for him. One witness to a murder, one drug lord on a mission to kill the person who killed his son. A stroll in the park, no doubt.

He walked to the corner in the hallway. As he turned and spotted an empty chair outside the room Ms. Jones was supposed to occupy, the skin on the back of his neck tightened. Where was the cop? Had he gone in to check on the patient? Had he left his post?

Dawson jogged the remaining distance to the door, his hand raised to knock against the wood. He was probably worried for nothing. The cop had to be inside.

A muffled thump carried through the solid door. Dawson shoved the door open and raced inside, his first impression one of an empty bed.

His first day on the job and he'd already lost his client.

Movement caught his attention on the floor around the other side of the bed. A figure wearing blue-green scrubs hunched close to the floor, a pillow in his hands, devils and a dragon tattooed on his forearm. Beneath him slim, curvy legs flailed and kicked.

"Hey!" Dawson grabbed the man by the shoulder and yanked him off balance. He threw the guy to the floor, away from the woman he assumed to be Savvy Jones.

Savvy shoved the pillow aside and gasped for air, her face red, her eyes wide. "He tried to k-kill me!"

The man masquerading as a member of the hospital staff rolled to his feet and swung a tree-trunk-size arm, backhanding Dawson.

Dawson raised his hand to block, but the force of the man's swing sent him slamming against the wall. He stumbled and righted himself, but not soon enough to stop the attacker from racing for the door. Nor did he get a good look at him; his face was covered in a surgical mask. Dawson threw himself at the man, catching him by the ankle before he cleared the door.

The big man tripped and fell into the swinging door and out into the hallway, crashing into a nurse passing by with a cart filled with medication. The cart upended, the nurse hit the floor and pills scattered. The perpetrator scrambled to his feet. In one awkward leap, he cleared the nurse and ran for the stairwell.

Dawson followed, skirting the nurse and cart. Before he got halfway down the hallway, he realized he couldn't go after the man. If he did, that left Savvy Jones unprotected. He stopped just past the spilled cart, his fists clenched, his heart pounding. Then he turned and helped the nurse to her feet. "Call the police. Tell them someone just tried to kill one of your patients. The man is headed down the stairwell."

The woman nodded and limped toward the nurses' station.

A man dressed in a Laredo police uniform rounded the corner and ground to a stop, his eyes widening. Then he ran toward Dawson, pulling a pistol from his holster. "Stop, or I'll shoot!"

Anger surged through Dawson and he advanced on the man.

The man's eyes widened and he pointed the gun at Dawson's chest. "I'll shoot."

"Then make it count." In a flash, he knocked the pistol from the cop's hand, sending it clattering across the floor. His next move had the cop slammed face-first against the wall, his arm locked behind his back in a painful grip. "Were you the officer assigned to guard Savvy Jones?"

"Yes," he gasped. "Let me go, or I'll bring you up on charges."

"And I'll have your badge," Dawson said. "I'm the bodyguard the D.A. hired to do the job you obviously couldn't."

"What do you mean?"

"You left your post."

"I got called away to handle a shooting in the E.R." He didn't struggle. "It turned out to be a false call."

"And you left Savvy Jones unprotected." Dawson jammed the man's arm up higher. "She was almost killed."

"I'm sorry."

Dawson shoved the man away. "Get out of here."

The officer retrieved his weapon, holstering it. "I'll have to clear this through the D.A."

"Then clear it. I have a job to do," Dawson said.

"As do I. Step aside." A man in green scrubs, with a

stethoscope looped around his neck, hurried toward Savvy's door.

"Stop right there." Dawson's tone brooked no argument.

The man in scrubs held up his badge. "I'm Savvy Jones's doctor."

Dawson scanned it, his eyes narrowed. "No one goes in here without my permission."

The doctor crossed his arms over his chest. "And what clearance do you have?"

He patted his chest where his Glock usually rested in the shoulder holster beneath his jacket and moved to block the doorway. "I'm Ms. Jones's bodyguard. If you need any more clearance than that, contact the D.A."

"Don't worry, I will." The doctor performed an about-face and marched toward the nurses' station. A gathering of orderlies and nurses keeping at a distance from Dawson's threatening stance parted to let the doctor through.

Dawson had been away long enough. He entered Savvy's hospital room and dodged around the end of the bed to find a slim young woman lying on the floor, gasping for air. Her hospital gown had hitched up in the struggle, exposing a significant amount of peaches-and-cream skin and a silky slip of forest-green panties. Strawberry blonde hair spilled down her back and across the floor in long wavy strands. A bandage covered the left side of her head with a white band of gauze wrapped around her forehead to keep it in place.

"What's going on?" She pressed a hand to her eyes, dragging in deep breaths.

"Someone doesn't like you much."

She groaned. "I don't think I ever want to see another pillow. Especially if it's over my face."

"Are you okay?" Dawson squatted next to her. "Want me to call the nurse?"

"No, as long as I can breathe, I'm okay." Deep green eyes blinked open and widened. "Who are you? You aren't armed with a pillow, are you?" She leaned to the side to peer around him.

"No pillow, just me, Dawson Gray." He held out his hand. "I'm your bodyguard, and if anyone asks...your fiancé."

"Bodyguard? Fiancé?" Her green eyes widened. "Which one is it?"

"Officially, your bodyguard."

Savvy shook her head. "And I didn't think this day could get weirder. Well, thanks for coming to my rescue." Her forehead crinkled into a frown and she winced. "Ouch. Remind me not to frown. It hurts." She looked at the outstretched hand but didn't take it. "Should I know you? I mean, you being my fiancé and all."

"No. We're meeting for the first time."

"Good, because I don't remember you. Still, how could you be my fiancé if I've never met you? Am I a mail-order bride or something? I'm confused." She pushed up on her elbows and closed her eyes. "Is it me, or is the room spinning?"

"It's definitely you." He nodded toward her head. "You've got a head wound and someone just tried to smother you. I'm sure neither is helping. Other than that, are you sure you're okay?"

"I think so. Although my legs didn't give me any warning before they gave out." Her lips twitched.

"Give yourself a break. You've been through a lot, by the looks of it." He shook his head. "If it's all the same to you, maybe we could get you into the bed." He scooped his hands beneath her legs and lifted, straightening. For as tall as she was, she couldn't weigh much over a hundred pounds.

"Hey!" Her eyes widened and she wrapped an arm around his neck. "Not so fast."

"Sorry." He laid her back against the pillows and adjusted the hospital gown around her, his fingers brushing against the silky skin of her thigh. What was he doing? Dawson snatched his hand away and stuffed it into his pocket.

Savvy lay still, her face pale. She didn't say anything for a few seconds.

The urge to protect hit him so hard, he stepped away. He had no right to be her protector. Qualifications for this job included a proved success rate.

His record stunk. He'd lost his wife, lost a soldier and almost lost his mind. Dawson turned toward the door, retreat foremost in his mind. "Excuse me. I have a call to make."

"Please," she called out in a small, scared voice.

The one word halted his forward progress and made him turn back. Big mistake.

She leaned toward him, her wide-eyed gaze darting from him to the door. "Do you have to leave me—" her voice faded, and she shrank back against the sheets "—alone?"

With his hand in his pocket already fishing for his cell phone, he paused. "I'll be right outside the door. I won't let anyone past me."

"Please…" Her fingers plucked at the hospital gown, bunching it, causing the hem to inch up her legs. "I don't even know how I got here."

Dawson clutched his cell phone, his brain telling him to leave. Now. But his misguided instincts pulled him back toward the bed and its occupant. "You don't remember how you got here because you were unconscious."

Savvy shook her head slowly and winced. "No, it's

worse than that." Her full, bottom lip trembled and she turned away from his gaze.

Dawson's chest squeezed tight and he forced himself to hold back—not to reach out to her. The woman needed someone to talk to. That someone was not him. "How so?"

"I don't remember where I was." She looked to him with those trusting green eyes. "Can you tell me?"

Dawson sighed. He couldn't leave her when she looked at him like a lost puppy. Calling himself every kind of fool, he retraced his steps to the foot of her bed. "You were found in an alley behind a bar."

She reached up to brush away a tear slipping from the corner of one eye, her shoulders straightening. "What bar?"

"The one where you worked."

A frown lined her forehead and she pressed a hand gently to the bandage on the side of her head, closing her eyes. "I don't remember working. Are you sure I worked at a bar?" Eyes as green as a forest of pine trees blinked up at him, the shadows beneath them making her appear more like a waif than a fully grown young woman.

"So they say." Dawson tore his gaze away from those eyes and glanced toward the door. God, he didn't want to be responsible for another living soul. The way things were going, Savvy would threaten more than his confidence. The curves of her calves, the swell of her thighs peeking out from the edge of the cotton hospital gown, the way her eyes glittered with unshed tears spelled disaster to everything male and primal inside him.

She leaned forward and touched his arm. "Tell me something, please."

"What?" he growled, anxious to get outside the room, away from Savvy and her green-eyed gaze. He had to make a call to Audrey before he made the biggest mistake of his life.

A soft sniff made him freeze.

Two fat tears rolled down Savvy's cheeks and plopped onto the sheet. "I know *your* name is Dawson Gray." Her fingers tightened on his arms convulsively. "Do you know *mine?*"

SHE HELD HER BREATH and waited for his answer.

Dawson's gaze dropped to where her hand clutched at his sleeve. "Savvy," he said, his voice hoarse, gravelly, as though he had to strain to say the one word. He cleared his throat. "Your name is Savvy Jones."

"Savvy." She let go of his arm and lay back against the pillow, her frown deepening. "Savvy." She rolled the name off her tongue, closing her eyes and willing her memory to return. The more she tried, the more her head pounded. At last, she dragged in a deep breath and admitted, "I can't remember." She opened her eyes and stared at him through a glaze of moisture. "I can't remember anything before waking up in the hospital."

"You've had a head injury. The memory lapse could be temporary. At least you didn't forget the basics."

She snorted softly. "Basics? I don't remember my entire life. How old am I? Are my parents alive? Where did I grow up? Am I—" Her gaze dropped to her ring finger and her breath caught in her throat. Was the skin around her ring finger a shade lighter than the rest of her hand? Or was it her imagination? She stared up at him, her heart a big lump in her throat. "Am I married?"

Dawson shrugged. "I don't know. The D.A. didn't mention it."

"The D.A.?" She stared up at him.

"District Attorney Frank Young." Dawson frowned, clearly uncomfortable with her questions. "The man who hired me to protect you."

"Why is the district attorney interested in me?"

"He should fill you in when he comes to see you." He reached in his pocket. "He asked me to call him when you came out from under the sedative."

"Do you think he'll know all about me?" She twisted the fingers of her right hand around her left ring finger as though she'd done it before when a ring had been there. "I could be married and not remember it." Her hands shook and she could barely drag air into her lungs. "I might have family out there worried about me."

"The D.A. should know."

Savvy shook her head. "What if he doesn't?"

"You worked in the bar. Someone there would have to know your family. They would need to be notified about your condition."

"Yeah…" She eased back against the pillow, her heart slowing to a regular pace, the lump in her throat still a problem. "They would have notified my family…if I had any."

"Maybe you should rest." He glanced toward the door.

Savvy wasn't ready to let him leave; she had so many questions needing answers she refused to let Dawson out of her sight. "How did I get injured?" She touched her fingers to the bandage on the side of her head. "What happened?"

Again, he glanced toward the door. "Let me get the doctor."

"No!" She grabbed for his sleeve. "Stay with me. Tell me what you know."

"Look, lady, all I know is that I was hired by the district attorney to play bodyguard to you until you could remember what happened."

"Did the D.A. tell you what happened?"

"Only that you shot—" Dawson clamped his lips shut

for a second before continuing "—received a gunshot wound to the head. You should ask him for the details."

Savvy gasped, her heart slamming against her chest, beating so fast the wound at her temple throbbed. "Gunshot?" She tried to remember, tried to picture herself in an alley, but couldn't. She didn't think she'd ever worked in a bar. And to be shot in an alley behind one? It didn't feel right. "Who shot me?"

Dawson shifted ever so slightly, but just enough that Savvy could tell he didn't want to respond. "I don't know."

"You know something, or you wouldn't have hesitated when you answered." What was he hiding?

Dawson dug in his pocket and pulled out a cell phone. "I really need to make a call. Do you mind?"

"Yes, I *do* mind." She pinned him with her stare. Now, *that* felt natural, as if she'd been in some position of authority at one time. "Are you or are you not my bodyguard?"

He hesitated. "The D.A. hired me to protect you." He glanced down at his phone. "But I'm not the right guy for the job." He stared at her with chocolate-brown eyes she could fall into. A thick, dark strand of coffee-colored hair fell down over his forehead.

She wanted to reach out to push it back. Instinctively, she trusted him. She had to; she didn't know anyone else, and he didn't want to be her bodyguard. "Why?" she asked, her voice softening. Something had him tied in a knot. Worrying about him helped keep panic about herself at bay. "Why do you think you're the wrong man for the job? You managed to save me from being smothered."

His hand tightened on the cell phone, his jaw clenching so hard the muscles twitched. "That guy should never have made it into your room."

"But, then, you weren't here yet. And once you got here, you took care of him." She raised her brows, challenging him to come up with another excuse, which she was certain he would.

"I've never been a bodyguard."

That didn't matter to her. He knew how to fight and defend. He had to have learned it somewhere. "Were you ever a cop, FBI agent, in the military?"

"Military," he said tightly.

Savvy pressed on. "Soldier or staffer?"

"Soldier." He dragged in a deep breath and huffed it out.

She crossed her arms over her chest. "If you were a soldier, you know how to use a gun. You know how to defend yourself and others."

He grunted, his brown eyes darkening to an inky black. "I'm not the right man for the job."

"I ask you again, why?" She waited, refusing to let him leave without a reasonable answer, and to her, there wasn't one.

"Because, damn it, I'm no good at it!" He swung away and stomped toward the door.

"Dawson," she called out. Savvy's voice caught on his name, her stomach flip-flopping as the only man she felt she could trust was leaving.

His hand smacked against the solid door, absorbing the force needed to swing it open. "I'm not the right man for this job."

"Please," she whispered. "You're the only person I can trust in a world of strangers."

"Why me?" he said, his back to her.

"Because you've already proved yourself. You've saved me once."

"But that doesn't mean I can do it again."

"Maybe not, but I know you'll try." Why wouldn't he turn and face her? What made him so certain he couldn't handle this job? "I don't know anyone else," she said, not too proud to plead.

He turned toward her, his face blank, emotionless. "You don't know me."

"Right now, I don't know anyone." How could she convince him? The thought of Dawson walking out the door and leaving her alone left her feeling so scared she couldn't think straight. "I'll take my chances with you."

For a long moment, he stared at her, his eyes fierce, his body stiff. Finally, he shrugged. "It's your life."

Chapter Three

Dawson paced the length of the tiled floor, careful to keep his footsteps quiet while Savvy slept the afternoon away. With each pass beside her bed, he studied the woman.

Strawberry blonde hair splayed out in a tangle across snow-white sheets. Auburn lashes fanned across pale cheeks where a dusting of freckles gave her the youthful appearance of a teenager. That was all that reminded him of a teen. The proud tilt of full breasts couldn't be hidden completely by the shapeless hospital gown. Those legs— long, silky smooth and toned—made him think of how they'd feel wrapped around a man's waist. Lush coral-colored lips could inspire kisses from even the most devout bachelor.

But not Dawson Gray. When he'd lost Amanda, his high school sweetheart, his wife, the mother of his unborn child, he'd sworn never to walk that path again. He refused to expose himself to that kind of agony again.

Savvy Jones could only ever be a job to him. He'd do well to remember that and not allow her *attributes* to blind him to the danger surrounding her or the unrest raging in the border town of Laredo.

Dawson stopped in front of the window as the sun slowly sank over the city skyline. A dusty red haze clouded the air as the plump orange globe melted into shades of pink and gray.

District Attorney Young had called to inform him that he'd be by shortly to question the witness.

Dawson glanced over his shoulder at Savvy. He didn't have the heart to wake her. The police had come and gone, asking Savvy a barrage of questions of which she'd had few answers. The doctor had made his rounds after consulting with the D.A., still prickly from his run-in with Dawson. But he'd informed Savvy that she would heal quickly, and that she was lucky it had only been a flesh wound. No damage to her skull except for the lump she'd acquired when she'd fallen to the pavement, resulting in a mild concussion. Nevertheless, the hospital staff kept a close eye on her to watch for any brain swelling. If all went well, she'd be allowed to leave the hospital the following morning.

Which introduced a whole new set of complications for Dawson. Where would Savvy go? Would she insist on him tagging along to babysit her? Could he let her step outside the hospital without him to face whatever threat lurked in the shadows of the city?

He'd waited until she was truly asleep before attempting to place a call to Audrey. Despite Savvy's confidence in him, he still wanted out.

Audrey wasn't answering her cell or returning Dawson's call. The assignment stuck until he could get through to the boss and arrange a replacement.

"You didn't leave," a gravelly voice said behind him.

Dawson spun in Savvy's direction. She lay against the pillows, her eyes open, studying him.

"No. I can't leave until I find a replacement."

"Thanks." Her pretty lips twisted. "Nice to know I'm such a burden." She blinked and stretched, her left arm only going as far as the IV would allow before she dropped it to the sheets. "Would you do me a favor?"

Realizing he was staring, Dawson nodded. "Depends on what it is."

"I need to see if I can stand on my own two feet." She pushed the sheets aside and slowly sat up, dragging the IV tube with her.

Dawson hurried forward and gripped her elbow to steady her. "Are you sure this is a good idea? Shouldn't you wait for a doctor or nurse?"

"No, I need to do this on my own." Although her face paled several shades, she shook her head. "Just let me get my head on straight." She leaned against his arm for several long moments, breathing in and out with even, measured breaths.

Dawson stiffened and would have pulled away, but she held on to him, a reminder that she needed help to balance and that he couldn't release her or she'd fall.

"Okay, I'm ready." With a little scoot that raised her hospital nightgown daringly high up her thigh, she eased off the side of the bed. "I have to warn you, the last time I tried this, I dropped like a rock." She laughed, the sound as shaky as the hand she slipped into his.

Hell. Dawson switched hands and wrapped his arm around her waist, the skin peeking through the openings at the back of her hospital gown disturbingly soft and smooth against his forearm.

He helped her find her feet and held her up until she stood flat-footed on the cool tiles.

Her pink toenail polish shone brightly in contrast to the plain white flooring. A sweet, girlie color Dawson wouldn't expect on a redhead or a strawberry blonde, but it suited her.

"Got it?" Dawson asked.

She nodded and smiled, her overbright eyes shining up at him. "Funny what you take for granted when you have it. I never would have thought I'd need help standing on my own two feet." Her smile slipped. "But don't worry. It's one step closer to getting you off the hook." Her mouth pressed into a thin line and she attempted a step forward.

"How's that?" Dawson moved alongside her, letting her lean into him as much as she needed.

"As soon as I can get around on my own, you won't need to hang around."

Dawson frowned. "What about the bad guys trying to kill you?"

"I gave it some thought." Her gaze shifted away from him to the window. "Once I'm out of here, I'll be extra careful. I'm sure I can manage just fine."

"Yeah." Dawson admired independence, but bravado was just plain stupid. "You think you could fight off a guy like the one who paid you a visit earlier? The one with the pillow and the body mass of a refrigerator?"

Savvy's entire body shook and she staggered on her next step.

Dawson pulled her close to keep her from falling flat on her face. She felt right against him, her narrow waist snug in his grip, the top of her head fitting just below his chin. Not too short and not too thin. Amanda had been quite a bit shorter than him. So small he'd treated her like a fragile porcelain doll, afraid he'd break her. In the end, he had. She'd been too small to deliver their baby. Both Amanda and their baby had died in childbirth.

Dawson's hands tightened. The guilt he'd lived with for the past two years weighed more heavily than the woman in his arms.

"Hey, you don't have to hold me so tight. I think I have

it now." Savvy pushed against his chest, leveraging herself into an upright position.

Dawson jerked his hands free and stepped away from Savvy as if she were a red-hot poker, heat rising up his neck from the collar of his shirt.

Savvy cried out, "Wait!" Her knees buckled and she would have fallen if Dawson hadn't reached out and dragged her back into his arms.

She slammed against his chest, her face buried in his shirt, her hair tickling his nose, soft and silky despite its tumbled disarray.

A low laugh rumbled from her chest, pressing her breasts into him. She finally glanced up. "Guess I wasn't as ready to be on my own as I thought." Her fingers bunched in his shirt and she sighed. "I'm still a little light-headed, but I'll be ready by morning."

He stared down into eyes so green they rivaled the forests of east Texas. With her body smashed against his, he couldn't hide the effect she had on him. The hard ridge pushing against his fly nudged against her belly. "Where will you go?"

Savvy's eyes widened and a peachy-rose flush spread across her cheeks. "I don't know." She laughed, a sound completely devoid of humor. "I don't remember where I live…"

"Oh, good, she's conscious." Frank Young blew through the door without knocking, sliding his cell phone shut with one easy, practiced move. "Do you think you can answer some questions for me?"

Dawson slowly turned Savvy around where her bare backside faced the window, not Frank Young's prying eyes.

Savvy nodded.

Frank's eyes narrowed and he got right to the point. "Well, then, what do you remember from last night?"

Savvy deadpanned. "Nothing."

"Nothing whatsoever?" Frank's brows rose.

"Until Dawson told me, I didn't even know my name." If Dawson hadn't already witnessed the effect of her memory loss on her, he might have missed the quaver in her voice.

The D.A. missed it completely. "I'll have a talk with the doctor. There has to be a way to get your memory back."

"Let me save you the effort." Savvy's shoulders pushed back, her spine stiffening beneath Dawson's hand. "He said the amnesia could be temporary or could just as easily be permanent. Only time will tell."

Young's eyes narrowed and he stared hard at Savvy. "Are you sure you don't remember anything?"

Savvy glared at the D.A. "Why would I lie about a thing like that?" She waved at the hospital room. "How would you like to wake up in a hospital room, with strangers and no idea who or what you are? Try it sometime, although I don't recommend it." She nudged Dawson's arm. "I need to sit." The hand on his arm shook, but Savvy's face remained firm and unwavering.

"My apologies, Ms. Jones." Frank Young's head dipped toward her. "You might not understand just how important it is that you remember what happened."

"Since I can't remember, maybe you can tell me why it's so important."

"Ms. Jones, a man was killed in that alley, by the gun the police found in *your* hand."

Dawson's arm tightened around Savvy as he fought the urge to plant a fist in the district attorney's smug face.

Savvy leaned into him, her face waxy white, making the freckles stand out across her nose and cheeks. "They found a gun in my hand?" She stared down at her right hand and then reached up to touch the gauze circling her head. "Why would I have shot someone? Was he shooting at me?" Her fingers found the lump of bandages over her left temple.

"That's what we need to know. Why would you shoot Tomas Rodriguez, and then shoot yourself?"

Savvy stared up at Dawson, her brows furrowed. "I shot someone, then I shot myself?" She shook her head. "Is this true?"

Dawson grabbed her cold hands and held them in his, wishing the D.A. would back off. "That's the way it appeared."

"Why do you think I shot someone and myself? There has to be a reason...evidence."

"When your coworker found you, she reported that you had a gun in your hand." The D.A. crossed the room and stood directly in front of her, his gaze intense, drilling into hers. "The same one used to shoot yourself in the head and to kill Tomas Rodriguez. The only fingerprints on the weapon are yours."

Her eyes widened and she stared at Young. "I don't remember." She sucked in a deep breath and let it out slowly, her head swinging from side to side. "I don't remember anything."

Frank Young's lips pursed into a tight line. "I suggest you do something about getting your memory back, Ms. Jones, or you could be tried for the murder of Tomas Rodriguez."

Savvy looked to Dawson, her eyes searching for answers. "How can I be tried for a murder I can't remember committing?"

"The evidence is circumstantial," Dawson said in an attempt to reassure Savvy.

"If my fingerprints are on the murder weapon, the evidence isn't just circumstantial, it's damning." She turned to the D.A. "What can I do?"

"Stay in town." Frank Young brushed a speck of dust off his fancy suit before looking up at Savvy again. "No formal charges have been brought against you, as yet. That could be only a question of time. In the meantime, you and Mr. Gray have bigger problems than the federal court system."

Savvy laughed, the sound verging on hysterical. "What could be worse than being accused of murder?"

"Tomas Rodriguez was Humberto Rodriguez's only child." Dawson stared down into her face, his hands holding hers firmly in his. What else could he do? He couldn't shield her from the truth any longer. She needed to know what she was up against. "Humberto Rodriguez is the kingpin in the Mexican drug cartel in Laredo's sister town, Nuevo Laredo, and some say even here in Laredo. He's also known for his ruthless and vindictive streak."

Savvy pulled her hands free of Dawson's, a frown tracing furrows in her forehead. "Does he think I killed his son?"

"The local news media got hold of the story." Young glanced up at the empty television screen. "Everyone in South Texas and the northern regions of Mexico knows Tomas Rodriguez is dead. It's been all over the news stations. Once Humberto gets wind that you were the one holding the smoking gun, we've no doubt he'll be after you. Based on the earlier attack I was informed of, it sounds like he already knows who and where you are."

Savvy lay back against the pillows and pinched the bridge of her nose. "Great. Everyone knows who I am but me."

The Dawson of a couple months ago would have headed for the nearest bar to escape his troubles. And frankly, the call of whiskey had him licking dry lips. One glance at the pale, defenseless woman lying in the hospital bed dispelled any lingering desire to drown his worries in booze. The police force hadn't protected her. Young had been right, someone who didn't have a stake in the region needed to handle this job.

"Knock, knock." A dark-haired woman poked her head through the door and smiled.

Dawson stepped between the door and Savvy's bed, shielding her from any possible threat.

"This is Savvy Jones's room, right?" The woman eased through the doorway, her brows dipping low on her forehead.

"Yes, it is, Ms. Scott." Frank Young closed the distance between them. "Please come in. Maybe if Ms. Jones sees a familiar face, it will jog her memory." Young cupped the woman's elbow and drew her toward the bed. "Savvy, do you remember Liz Scott? She's the coworker who found you in the alley."

SAVVY STARED UP at the slim woman with the long dark brown hair hanging down around her shoulders.

She wore faded jeans and a white cotton blouse with the sleeves rolled up. "Hi, sweetie," Liz said in a soft Southern drawl as she set a bud vase with a single yellow rose on the nightstand beside the bed. "I brought you some clean clothes for when they release you." She held up a canvas bag, tears pooling in her eyes as she forced a shaky smile. "How are you feelin'? You gave us all quite a scare."

Panic swelled in Savvy's chest as she looked up at the woman and tried to remember her. She looked nice, and she acted as if she knew her, but nothing triggered in her memory to remind her who she was. "Do I know you?"

Tears tipped over the edge of Liz's eyes and she forced a laugh. "Yes, honey, you do. We work together at the Waterin' Hole. You're the only one there who keeps me from walloping the customers. And you babysit my Charlie sometimes." Liz glanced across at the D.A. and back at Savvy and shrugged. "What did the doctor say about the memory loss? Does he think it's only temporary?"

Savvy shrugged. "We won't know until the memories return…or not." She leaned forward and grasped Liz's hand. "I'm sorry, but could you tell me more about…me?"

"I'll tell you everything I know." Liz's lips twisted into a wry grin. "Which doesn't amount to a whole hill of beans."

"Why?" Savvy asked, anxious to recover her past and frustrated about the lack of information forthcoming. "Am I a bad person?"

"Oh, no, not at all. You've been the best thing since sliced bread to me and Charlie." Liz held her hand and perched on the side of the bed. "You're not just my co-worker, you're my friend and have been since you came to live in the same apartment complex four months ago."

"Where?" Savvy gulped, drinking in everything the woman said, wanting so badly to fill the empty spaces in her memory. "Where do we live?"

"In the Oasis Apartments complex close to the Waterin' Hole. You're in 212 and Charlie and I are in 215. Which reminds me…" She dropped Savvy's hand and stood, digging in her back pocket. She pulled out a folded sheet of paper and handed it to Savvy. "Charlie sent this."

"Charlie…" Another name she couldn't put a face to. She fought back tears as she accepted the paper and unfolded it. A large purple heart drawn in crayon filled the page. In the center, written in a child's bold print, were the words *We love you, Savvy.*

A familiar ache filled her chest as she stared down at the crinkled paper. Familiar and yet forgotten in the depths of her muddled mind. "Charlie is…"

"My seven-year-old precocious daughter." Liz patted Savvy's arm. "She worships the ground you walk on."

Savvy stared up at the woman, her eyes blurring with tears. "I don't remember her." Her tears fell on the page she held, a sob rising up her throat. "I don't remember whether or not I have a family and, I'm so sorry, but I don't remember you." More tears followed until her body shook.

Liz rubbed her back, her hand warm and comforting. "Oh, sweetie, it'll be okay. You'll get it back."

The D.A. moved closer. "Yes, and when you do, I want to talk to you. I—we need to know who else was in that alley with you and Tomas Rodriguez. It could mean all the difference in your defense."

Her eyes widening, Liz stepped between the D.A. and Savvy. "Savvy didn't kill that man. She wouldn't do that."

Could she really be tried for murder? Did they really think she'd killed a man? Savvy raised her hands. The most frightening question yet was could she have done it? *Think, Savvy, think!* She squeezed her eyes closed and pressed the bridge of her nose with her fingertips. The more she tried to remember, the more her head ached. When she opened her eyes, the two men stared at her. The D.A. hovering like a vulture ready to pounce on roadkill. Dawson with pity and concern written into the lines creasing his forehead. God, she didn't want to think, and didn't want anyone's pity, especially from this man who claimed to be her bodyguard, albeit a reluctant bodyguard. Her chest ached and her eyes burned. Savvy didn't want to cry but couldn't hold back much longer. She reached out and gripped Liz's hand. "Please, make them go away."

Through her tears, she could see the slight narrowing of Dawson's eyes. He turned to the D.A. and took his arm, steering him toward the door. "Look, you said you didn't think she did it. Give her some space. Maybe she'll remember who did."

Frank hesitated. "But I have more questions."

"Questions she obviously can't answer. Let the woman rest. She's been through enough for one day."

With that, Frank Young let the bodyguard herd him out of Savvy's hospital room, the door swinging closed behind them.

"There, now." Liz smoothed the hair out of Savvy's face and smiled at her. "They're gone. Is there anything I could do for you?"

"Yes." Savvy gulped back the ready tears and scrubbed the end of the sheet across her cheeks. "You can tell me who I am."

Liz squeezed her hand. "Well, now, I can tell you this… You showed up four months ago at the apartment complex, looking for a furnished apartment. I remember that day because you looked kind of sad and desperate. All you had with you was a small bag filled with clothes. You didn't have a job and only carried enough money in your pocket to pay the first month's rent. The apartment manager almost didn't let you rent because you didn't even have a driver's license, credit card or any other form of identification on you."

"None? But where did I come from? Why did I go there?"

"You said you'd driven until you'd run out of gas and very nearly ran out of money." Liz's lips twisted. "You never told me why. I think you were running away from something or someone."

Savvy's forehead crinkled, pulling at the bandage at her temple. The pain reminded her that she was awake, alive and not dreaming this horrible nightmare. *Who am I?*

"I hope you don't mind, but after the ambulance carried

you away to the hospital, I checked through your purse, hoping to find information about next of kin, but didn't find a driver's license, medical insurance or any other form of identification." Liz shrugged. "I'm not sure if you have someone somewhere who could be getting worried about you. I've been your friend for four months, but I don't know much about your past."

Savvy shook her head, pulling her hand from Liz's warm fingers. "It's as if I don't exist." Her chest tightened, making it harder for her to breathe. The room seemed to shrink in size as she stared at the sterile white walls of the hospital room, her heartbeat increasing its pace until it pounded against her ribs. "I need to get out of here."

Liz frowned. "Has the doctor released you? Are you cleared to leave?"

"I don't know and I don't care. I have to get out." She pushed the sheets aside and slid her legs over the side of the mattress, ready to walk out, until she remembered her previous attempts and how weak she'd been. She hated being dependent on anyone, but knew she might end up reinjuring her head if she fell again. "Will you help me?"

"Of course, but should you be getting up?" Liz gripped Savvy's elbow and helped her to her feet. "I mean, you've had a head injury."

Determination to do this on her own filled Savvy and stiffened her legs. This time when her feet hit the floor, she remained standing. Whether she trembled from the effort or from the lingering effects of the drugs still wearing off, she didn't care. "That's good. I can do this." Now what? She couldn't waltz out of here in a hospital gown.

"I don't know about this." Liz held on to her arm, her gaze darting for the door as if hoping the two men would return and rescue her. "You should stay until the doctor says you're good to go."

"I can't. I have to get back to familiar surroundings. Maybe that will help me to remember."

Still holding her arm, Liz stepped in front of her. "You're pushing it, Savvy. You need to take care of yourself." She cupped her face with her hand. "Honey, you could have died."

"I might as well have never lived. I don't remember anything. Do you even have a clue how that feels? My mind is completely blank. Nothing. *Nada*." Savvy threw her hand in the air and teetered.

"It'll take time, sweetie. You might not get your memory back in a day." Liz stared at the door. "You're not ready to go out there. It's crazy."

"I'm spinning my wheels here in the hospital, getting nowhere. Nothing here triggers a single memory. Nothing. I need familiar territory. I want to go to my apartment to see if anything comes back." Savvy's hand rose to Liz's still cupping her face. "If you're really my friend, you'll help me."

For a long moment, Liz stared into Savvy's eyes, then she glanced at the bandage swathing her head and finally she sighed. "Do you need help getting dressed?"

"No, I think I can manage." Relief flooded Savvy. Tightrope-like tension followed immediately. She let go of Liz and took several tentative steps toward the bathroom. Although wobbly, she managed on her own. At the bathroom door, she grabbed for the handle.

"Hey, you'll need these." Liz eased past her and set the bag of clothes on the floor inside the bathroom. "Don't be a hero. I can help. All you have to do is ask."

Savvy gave her a shy smile. "Thanks. I will." She closed the door between them and leaned on the bathroom sink. Taking a deep breath, she raised her head and stared into the mirror, hoping that seeing her own face would trigger her missing memories.

Hope died when she gazed at the woman in the reflection. A white bandage covered her left temple, held in place by a strip of gauze wrapped around her head. Strawberry blonde hair, matted with specks of blood, fell over her shoulders and down her back. Deep green eyes looked back at her...eyes of a stranger. Nothing in the mirror made her remember this woman, or her past.

A sob rose up her throat and she choked it down. She couldn't cry over her loss—she wouldn't. If she wanted to recover her memory, she had to go to familiar places, touch her things, live the life she'd been living to get it back, memories and all.

Since her face didn't jog her memory, she'd have to go to the places she'd lived and worked. If they didn't find evidence of another suspect, she'd be arrested and charged with the murder of Tomas Rodriguez. The sooner she remembered, the sooner she could clear her name, before the authorities decided to toss her in jail.

A sense of urgency filled her as she dug into the gym bag Liz had brought. She found clean jeans, a blue Dallas Cowboys T-shirt, panties, a bra and white tennis shoes, a hairbrush and a toothbrush.

Careful not to disturb her wound, she washed her face and dressed, stopping now and again when her head swam with the effort. Clothed and feeling a bit steadier on her feet, she tackled the gauze circling her head, peeling it off, round by round. When she pulled the bandage away, a two-inch square white gauze bandage peeked out of the edge of her hairline near her temple.

Using a clean washcloth, she dabbed at the dried blood and residual orange-colored disinfectant used around the bandage. Gently working the brush through her hair, she restored it to some semblance of order, draping the hair over the wound as best she could, hiding most of it. Pale and shaky, she stepped from the bathroom, having accomplished the tasks in less than five minutes. "I'm ready. Can you give me a lift?"

Liz held out her arm. "If you insist. I'm still not sure this is a good idea."

"I have to do it. Someone has to be trying to frame me. Until I remember what happened, I'm the prime suspect. My memory is the only thing standing between me and jail."

"Savvy, you may or may not get your memory back." Liz smiled sadly. "What then?"

"I'm taking this one bit at a time." Savvy pushed through the door to her room and out into the hallway, walking right into Dawson's chest.

Oh, yeah, she had to convince her court-appointed bodyguard to let her leave the hospital.

Chapter Four

Dawson gripped Savvy's arms and steadied her. "Why are you out of bed?"

She straightened and pushed away from him. "I'm going home." When she tried to pull free of his hands, his grip tightened.

"Not until the doc releases you, you aren't."

She stared up at him, her mouth thinning, tears awash in her eyes. "I have to. Don't you see? I can't remember anything here. I have to be around my own things."

"You can wait until tomorrow."

"No." She reached up to pry his hands loose, her weakened state making her attempt ineffectual. "I can't wait until tomorrow. Not knowing is driving me crazy. Let me go." A single tear tipped over the edge of her eyelid and slid down her cheek. "Please."

He could have resisted if she'd yelled and screamed at him, but the one tear and her anguished plea jerked at his heart, reawakening the dormant organ. How could he resist those eyes staring up at him as if she held her world in his hands? For a moment, he wavered. "No, it's not safe out there."

Savvy's lips twisted in a half grin, her eyes shimmering. "And it's safe here?"

She had a point. The attack that morning had almost

ended his assignment before it had begun. "It's easier to protect you inside a building than out in the open. The avenues for attack multiply exponentially once you step out the hospital doors."

"Either I get attacked outside or I go crazy stuck in my room. I prefer to take my chances." She brushed away the moisture from her eyes and laid a determined hand on his arm. "Are you with me? Because, if not, I'll go without you."

Electric impulses shot up Dawson's arm where Savvy's hand touched him. The low sexy voice, the eyes glittering with unshed tears threatened to bring him to his knees, if he let it. With a hard-won deep breath, he shook off her hand, unwilling to let himself care more about her than the job warranted. "It's your funeral." He turned, and without offering her any assistance, he marched toward the exit.

Liz leaned close and whispered in a not-so-quiet voice, "A bit uptight, if you ask me. But very sexy in that he-man kinda way." She gave a soft wolf whistle.

Dawson shook his head. "I heard that."

A bright pink flush rose up from Savvy's collar and flooded her cheeks. "I wouldn't know. He's just a bodyguard to me, and for the sake of whatever, he's my fake fiancé." Her gaze connected with his as if daring him to refute her statement.

"Not your real fiancé?"

"No. It just makes it easier for him to get past the nurses."

Liz's cheeks dimpled. "In that case, would you mind if I made a pass at your guy?"

Savvy's fingers clenched into fists at her sides, and she bit down hard on her lip. "He's not mine. Do whatever you like." She pushed a long strand of strawberry blonde hair over her shoulder and closed the distance between herself and Dawson.

He'd bet behind that tough-gal exterior, her legs shook and she teetered on the verge of collapse. With her shoulders flung back, she didn't let a single sign of weakness shine through. She probably thought that if she did, Dawson would have her back in the hospital so fast her head would be spinning more than it already was.

Damn right he would. But he couldn't help admiring her pluck. He preferred it over the tears.

Pausing at the glass door, Dawson performed a three-hundred-sixty-degree turn, his gaze going to every corner of the lobby before he stared out at the street quickly growing dark. A gathering of fifty or sixty people stood in front of the emergency entrance. Scattered among them were news reporters and camerapersons; at the center stood the D.A.

Savvy peered through the glass. "Why is there a crowd?"

Though her voice came out weaker than a whisper, Dawson heard it.

Dawson's jaw tightened. "Looks like the D.A. is giving a statement."

"The news report about Tomas's death generated quite a stir." Liz grinned. "The people out there are actually here to thank you for shooting Tomas Rodriguez."

Savvy's hand rose to her throat and she tried to swallow. "But why?"

"Tomas had a nasty habit of raping young women on both sides of the border," Liz answered.

"If people knew this, why wasn't he caught and prosecuted?" Savvy asked.

Liz's lips twisted into a frown. "The rape victims never brought charges against him. Word is that he threatened to kill family members if the victims turned him in. These people are here to thank you, Savvy, for saving their young girls from that monster."

"I don't remember shooting anyone," Savvy said quietly.

A chill snaked its way down Dawson's spine as he stared out at the women and children standing outside the hospital holding up signs written in Spanish and English. The one sign he could make out from behind the glass doors of the hospital said Thank God and Thank Ms. Jones. A lead weight settled in his gut and he backed away from the door, intent on taking Savvy with him. "There are too many people out there. This is a bad idea." Dawson faced Savvy, blocking her path to the door.

"I'm going home." Savvy touched his arm. "Don't worry, if something happens to me, I won't blame you."

He stared down at the hand on his arm, the gentle touch searing his skin. "You won't have to. I'll blame myself." His glance rose to her face. "Give it another day."

"I can't." She shook her head without breaking eye contact. "Besides, I want to hear what the D.A. has to say."

With a sigh and a cold sense of dread, he faced the door. "Then at least stay behind me. If someone wants you dead, they'll be waiting for a clear shot."

"Wow, you've got me convinced." Liz's eyes darted left and right. "You don't think someone will try to hurt her out there, do you?"

"Someone wants her dead in a bad way," Dawson responded without taking his gaze off the crowd. "Ready?" He looked around at Savvy's pale face. "It's your call."

She nodded, straightening her spine. "I'm ready."

He had to hand it to her. She might be stupid to step into the line of fire, but she had nerve. Dawson pushed through the glass doors. "Stay close."

SAVVY WALKED OUT into the heat of South Texas behind Dawson, hovering so close to him that when he came to a stop, she bumped into his back. "Sorry."

"Don't be. The closer you are to me, the less of a target you'll make."

She swallowed. "But what about you?"

A low chuckle rumbled inside his chest, shaking the hand she rested on his warm back. "Don't worry, if I get hurt, I won't blame you."

Wouldn't blame her? How could he not blame her? Savvy second-guessed herself. Neither she nor Dawson would be hurt if she did as he'd asked and stayed in the hospital for at least one more night.

A quick look behind her firmed her resolve. No. She couldn't go back in there. She'd always think of the hospital as a plain white void where she'd woken to nothing. No memory, no past, no family. She gritted her teeth and clutched the fabric of Dawson's shirt in her fist. She couldn't go back.

Savvy touched Dawson's arm, urging him to stop so that she could listen to what the D.A. had to say.

"Did Savvy Jones really kill Tomas Rodriguez?" A reporter held a microphone in the D.A.'s face, her camera-person behind her.

"At this point Savvy Jones is just a person of interest. An investigation is being conducted. As we learn more, we'll keep the media informed."

A man with shaggy brown hair, carrying a pocket-size camera, pushed his way through the crowd of reporters. "What do you know about Ms. Jones?"

The D.A. frowned. "That she lives in Laredo and works as a waitress at the Waterin' Hole Bar and Grill."

"Is Savvy Jones her real name?"

"Rest assured," Young said, "we're conducting an investigation on all persons involved in the incident, including a thorough background check on each."

"Is it true Ms. Jones has only been in Laredo for the past four months?"

"Yes." Young's eyes narrowed. "Do you have a particular direction you're going with this line of questioning?"

The man looked all innocence. "No. Just checking."

Savvy leaned forward. "Why is that man asking so many questions about me?"

A woman in the crowd pointed at Savvy and shouted, "It's her!"

Then as if surrounded by quicksand, Savvy was quickly engulfed in a swarm of hot bodies and grasping hands. A large woman pushed her way between Dawson and Savvy, cutting her off from her lifeline.

Savvy reached out for Dawson but couldn't quite get past the determined woman, who had grabbed her hands, pressing kisses to the backs of her fingers. *"Gracias, señorita, gracias!"* She stuffed a photograph into Savvy's hands and, curling her fingers around the tattered edges, she kissed her hands again and moved away.

Jostled from one person to another, with flashbulbs blinding her, Savvy fought to breathe in the crush.

A young woman who couldn't be more than sixteen hugged her neck, tears running down her face. "Thank you, Ms. Jones. Thank you," she said in heavily accented English. She released her to let someone else through.

Savvy panned the crowd, frantically searching for the tall Texas bodyguard. It didn't take long to spot him, but not until her gaze met his chocolate-brown stare did her heart slow.

Dawson towered over the women, pushing his way back through the mob to get to her. When he reached her side, he slid a hand around her shoulders, tucking her beneath his arm, effectively blocking access to her.

"*Por favor, señor,* we wish to thank the *señorita* for taking care of Tomas Rodriguez for good."

Dawson shook his head and said in a voice loud enough to be heard over the crowd, "Tomas Rodriguez's killer has not yet been identified." With one arm around Savvy and the other clearing a path, he pushed his way through the crowd toward the parking lot.

Before they'd moved more than a dozen feet from the hospital entrance, the shaggy-haired man with all the questions shoved his pocket camera in her face and a flash blinded her. "Ms. Jones—if that's really your name— where did you live before Laredo? Does the name Jameson mean anything to you?"

Savvy held up her hands to block more of the blinding flashes. "I don't know anyone by that name. And I don't know the answers to any of your questions. Please, leave me alone."

Another reporter held a microphone in her face. "How do you feel about the death threats from the drug lord, Humberto Rodriguez?"

Dawson's brown eyes blackened and a storm cloud of a frown dug into the lines of his face. "Move."

"I just want a minute of your time, Ms. Jones," the man with the little camera called out over the other reporter's question.

With her head ready to split wide open, Savvy leaned against Dawson's broad chest. "Let's get out of here."

Before the crowd could pen them in again, Dawson hooked an arm around Savvy's waist and half lifted, half dragged her through the throng.

The stitches on Savvy's head throbbed. She stumbled

and righted herself, a full-fledged panic attack pushing her toward the cars lined up in the parking lot.

A tremor shook her from head to toe. She could barely get herself out of the hospital parking lot. How had she thought she could survive in Laredo without Dawson's help? She was still weak. "I should have stayed put in the hospital."

"We can always go back," Dawson said, his voice low and intense, his eyes inscrutable in the gathering darkness. He slipped an arm around her waist and held her against him, his head swiveling right and left.

"Whoever tried to kill me earlier might try to hurt you, too."

"Don't worry about me. I'm in it until a replacement can be found."

Savvy's chest tightened. Dawson hadn't even *wanted* the job. "Maybe none of this would be happening if I could remember," Savvy whispered so low she didn't think he'd hear her.

Apparently Dawson heard her, because he replied softly, "Sometimes it's better if you can't remember."

Savvy's gaze jerked to his, but he'd turned his face away from her. Did Dawson have ghosts he'd rather forget? What could be so incredibly bad that you'd want to forget your past?

Curiosity burned inside her and she opened her mouth to ask him what he wanted to forget. "Dawson—"

The brooding man stopped in front of a pickup truck and yanked open the door. "Get in and stay low." His guttural growl effectively stemmed the flow of questions she wanted answered. With his help, she climbed up into the truck and adjusted the seat to lie back enough so that she couldn't see over the dash, and consequently no one could see her through the side windows.

DAWSON CLIMBED IN next to her. Without another word, he inched out of the parking lot, slipping out a side street. Not until they were two blocks away did the gravity of their departure hit him. He gripped the steering wheel, wondering if he'd made a terrible mistake taking her away from the hospital.

Adrenaline faded away, leaving him drained and in desperate need of a drink. With every ounce of resistance, he passed a corner liquor store, forcing himself to focus on his task. Until Audrey sent an agent to relieve him, he couldn't touch even a drop of alcohol.

Savvy reclined in the seat beside him. Her arm rose to cover her eyes, emphasizing the sensuous curve of her breast and the taper of her narrow waist. Dawson's groin tightened, as did his grip on the steering wheel. He should focus on the road ahead, not the woman lying beside him.

Several blocks and mind-clearing breaths later, he still couldn't keep himself from stealing another glance in her direction. The steady rise and fall of her chest reassured and alarmed him at the same time. This woman depended on him to keep her alive. For the past two years, he'd barely kept himself alive. What kind of life was it when a man buried himself in a bottle to escape his failures? Looking back, he realized he'd chosen the coward's way out. If the past could be undone, he'd go back in a heartbeat and fix all his mistakes.

Dawson stopped for a red traffic light, staring out the window at the light without really seeing it. If he could fix his past mistakes, would that have changed the outcome? Would Amanda and their baby still be alive? Would Corporal Benson have lived through the roadside bombing? Dawson shook his head. Going back wasn't an option. As Audrey had told him over and over, moving forward was the only way to forgive your past.

A horn honked behind him. The traffic light had turned green.

Dawson pulled his head out of the past and moved forward, reminding himself to focus on today, now, this woman who depended on him.

"Why do you want to forget your past?" Savvy said, her eyes closed, her arm still resting over them.

The question broadsided him and he answered before he could think. "My mistakes cost lives."

Her arm dropped to her side and those green eyes stared across at him.

Using the traffic as an excuse not to face her, he drove on, kicking himself for even giving her that much. Savvy Jones didn't need to know all the sordid details of his past failures. He made a turn at the next street and glanced in the rearview mirror. Another vehicle turned behind him, the headlights blinding him.

The car sped up until its bumper almost touched Dawson's heavy-duty truck bumper.

Adrenaline jolted through his veins and he pressed his foot to the accelerator to put distance between him and the dark car behind him.

"Did it involve a woman?" Savvy asked, adjusting her seat to an upright position.

"Don't," Dawson barked out, his mind on the car behind him and the narrow street ahead.

"I'm sorry. Is it too painful to talk about?" Savvy stared ahead. "Since I don't remember my past, I guess I'm curious about others."

"Savvy, now's not the time." Dawson prepared to make a sharp turn at the next street corner to see if the car behind him would do the same. If so, they had a problem.

She sighed. "I get it. You don't want to talk about it. I just feel so…empty."

Dawson's heart squeezed in his chest, but he couldn't respond, not when they might have a tail. He whipped the truck to the right, taking the turn so fast, the bed of the truck slipped sideways. The car stayed with them.

She sat up straight and glanced out the side mirror, holding her hand up to block the bright lights blinding her.

"Hold on, we're going to make another sharp turn."

She gripped the handle above the door frame as he spun the truck left at the next corner. "Do you always drive like this?"

"Only when I'm being followed."

Chapter Five

"Followed?" Savvy twisted in her seat to look behind them.

"Get your head down!" Dawson pushed her head down across the console.

"Okay, okay, I get it. You don't have to be so—"

"Damn!" Dawson slammed on the brakes.

Despite her bodyguard's warnings, Savvy had to see what was going on. She risked raising her head just enough to peer over the dash. A dark sedan stretched across the road ahead, completely blocking the way.

"Brace yourself." He jerked the truck into Reverse.

Savvy tucked her head down and wrapped her arms around the back of her neck, prepared for impact.

They hit the car behind them, the impact throwing her forward, the shoulder strap whipping her back against the seat at the last moment.

As quickly as they hit, Dawson shoved the shift in Drive, his hands on the wheel, spinning it to the left toward a narrow alley between buildings. The passenger-side mirror scraped the bricks with a long screeching sound that made Savvy grind her teeth. But the alternative could be worse.

Savvy clamped her lips closed and held on. "I'm beginning to see the merits of having stayed in the hospital," she muttered as the truck skidded sideways onto the next street, coming within an inch of hitting a solid brick wall.

A low rumble erupted from the man clinging to the steering wheel next to her. A smile tilted the corner of the lip she could see from her side of the truck. Was that laughter?

His rugged face lit up, making him look like a whole new man. As quickly as it had come, the smile left and his frown returned. The car that had been blocking the other road skidded to a stop in front of them, blocking them yet again.

Despite the dire situation, Savvy couldn't help but wish Dawson would smile again. "You really should smile more often."

"Remind me when I'm not being chased by two homicidal maniacs." He grunted as he leaned into another turn, racing down an alley behind businesses.

At the end of the alley, Dawson gunned the accelerator, whipped around the corner to the right and sped into the alley ahead on the left. He cut his headlights and removed his foot from the brake, slowly picking his way past Dumpsters and stacks of empty wooden pallets. When he reached the next street he eased out enough to see around the corner of the building.

Savvy turned and peered behind them. No headlights, no signs of the car that had been tailing them. "I think we lost the one behind us."

"Yeah, but for how long?" Dawson checked his rearview mirror and glanced at the empty street ahead before crossing to another side street. He drove for several minutes, weaving in and out of secondary roads, his headlights off, using the brakes as little as possible.

Savvy kept a vigilant watch behind them. "Being chased by bad guys is exhausting." She lay back against the headrest, her lips twisting. "I know, I know, I should have stayed in the hospital. But even there, I wasn't totally safe."

"I would have looked out for you."

"Dawson, even you have to sleep sometime." At the rate they were going, neither one of them would sleep until Savvy was cleared of the connection to the murder of Tomas Rodriguez. The gravity of her situation weighed even more heavily on her. "I'm sorry I got you into this mess."

"It's my—"

"I know. It's your job." Irritation surged, pushing aside her exhaustion and serving only to add additional pain to her already-throbbing temple. Savvy pressed a hand gently to the stitches, applying pressure to alleviate some of the soreness. "Are we going to my apartment?"

"Against my better judgment." His lips clenched into a thin line. "I don't expect it'll be easy."

"We could park a couple blocks away and walk in."

Dawson shot her a measuring glance. "Are you up to it?"

If she wasn't, she wasn't going to tell him. She'd already caused enough trouble for one day. "Yes." Her legs and head had better cooperate.

She stared at the city streets of Laredo, hoping something would come back to jog her memory. After a while she shook her head. "I don't remember any of this."

"I wouldn't sweat it." He flicked on his headlights and negotiated a turn onto a busy four-lane road, slipping into traffic.

Savvy glanced behind them every minute or two, her neck aching with the effort.

"You don't have to keep turning around. I'm watching our rear in the mirror."

Savvy sighed and leaned back. "This entire day has been a lot to digest."

"I'll bet."

She stared at the GPS display mounted in the instrument panel of the truck. "Do all bodyguards have GPS devices in their vehicles?"

"Those who work for the Lone Star Agency. The boss insists on the best."

So the tall, dark and pensive man *could* share a little about his life. Savvy suppressed a smile, forcing her voice to be casual. If she wanted to know more about Dawson Gray, she had to ease it out of him. "You like working for the agency?"

"I'll let you know. I've only been with them for a couple months."

That's right. Dawson had a life before the bodyguard gig. "In what branch of the military did you serve?" she asked.

"Army." The one word came out in a short, sharp syllable. The harshness of his tone making her think twice about asking more questions. She could wait. Apparently they were going to be together for a while longer. She had time. If she wasn't shot by the murderer or Humberto Rodriguez's henchmen first.

Dawson pulled the truck behind a building and parked it in the shadow of a Dumpster. "Your apartment building is two blocks over. Are you sure you're up to it?"

Savvy nodded, unclipping her seat belt. Her heart pounded in her chest, not so much from the possibility of facing more bad guys but of what she'd find in her apartment. Or perhaps she feared that she wouldn't find anything to remind her of who she was, where she'd come from and why she'd chosen Laredo as her stopping point.

Dawson climbed down from the truck and opened the door behind his. A large gym bag sat on the floorboard.

Savvy's heart skipped a beat when Dawson unearthed a shoulder holster and a gun.

He slipped the leather straps over his shoulder and put the gun into the holster beneath his left arm. Back to the bag, he grabbed a blue chambray shirt and a leather jacket. He pulled the shirt over his shoulders, concealing the holster and gun. Then he closed the door and rounded the hood to open her door for her.

With a deep breath, she slid down into his arms, careful not to make contact with the gun. His hands gripped her elbows, steadying her. She looked up into eyes as dark as a starless night. "Thank you." She wanted to say more, but their closeness stole her breath away.

He smiled down at her. "Here, you'll need this." He held out the large leather jacket with a Harley logo painted across the back.

"What do you want me to do with it?"

"Wear it."

"But it must still be in the high eighties."

"Think of it as a disguise." He held it open. "Go on, get in."

Savvy eyed the jacket. "A jacket? In this heat? Don't you think the baddies will figure it out?"

"I have something else that will help."

She frowned at him, but slipped her arms into the sleeves. When he settled the jacket on her shoulders, she felt ten pounds heavier. "I'm not so sure I like this."

"Humor me." He reached for her hair, pulling it out of the back of the jacket.

Savvy stepped back, his nearness making her twitchy in all the wrong places. "I can do that."

"For now, just—"

"Humor me," she finished for him and chuckled nervously, wondering what to do with her hands. She wanted to rest them against his chest, but knew that would send the wrong message. Finally, she let them drop to her sides.

Once Dawson had her zipped into the jacket, Savvy thought that would be the end of it and he'd move away. Instead, he pulled the long tresses up and twisted them on top of her head.

"I'm not going to a fashion show, you know. It's just an apartment."

"You are the target of one of the most ruthless men in Mexico."

A chill swept through her and her voice locked in her throat.

"Just another part of the disguise." He held the knot of hair on top of her head and reached into his back pocket, pulling out a folded baseball cap. He plunked it on her head and stood back. "There. Now you're ready."

Feeling like a little kid in her brother's hand-me-down clothes, Savvy let Dawson lead her through the backyard of a run-down ranch-style house, quickly crossing the street a block over.

He didn't stop until they came to a tall, overgrown hedge lining a parking lot. An apartment complex loomed above the bushes, filling the block with its featureless, stuccoed walls.

"That's it?" Savvy's feet dragged as Dawson led her toward a gap in the shrubbery. The shadows of the street-lights couldn't disguise the faded rosy-brown paint. Cars in front of the building had seen better days, some rusted, others dented and dinged, an occasional cracked wind-shield or a trunk held down by a frayed bungee cord.

"I live there?" Savvy whispered. This setting didn't feel right. She couldn't picture herself in such a run-down place. Where were the wide porticos, Grecian columns and the porters waiting to carry her luggage?

She ground to a complete halt, her hand slipping from Dawson's. Was her world one of lavish riches? Or was she dreaming of the life of a princess because hers was straight from hell? Savvy closed her eyes and tried to bring back the Grecian setting she'd first imagined when she'd seen the chipped stucco of the weathered apartment building. Why had the image emerged? Why?

A hand on her arm broke her concentration. "Are you remembering something?" Dawson's voice pierced the darkness.

Savvy shook her head. "No. I thought—" A waitress in a bar didn't live in a lavish villa on some faraway Greek coast. She sighed. "No." In the heat still radiating off the parched Texas soil and the oppressive weight of the Harley jacket, another cold chill racked Savvy's body. None of this felt right…natural…familiar. "I don't remember this at all."

"We don't have to go in if you don't want to." Dawson reached for her hand again, peeling back the jacket sleeve to find it. He wrapped his warm, strong fingers around hers.

When she tried to pull her hand free, he held tight. "I need to go inside." She had to see for herself. Anything could trigger a memory.

"It's not safe. The people who want you dead could be waiting for you there."

Her gaze swept the street in front of the building. A car pulled past the spot where they hid by the hedges. "Liz said I live in apartment 212 and she lives in 215."

Dawson glanced up at the doors with the faded numbers and shook his head. "It's way too exposed for you to take the risk. We shouldn't go in at all."

"But I have to get in."

He scanned the cars, the roof and the area surrounding

the building. "Then I'm going in first. You stay hidden behind the hedge."

Savvy opened her mouth but a large warm finger pressed over her lips. Dawson leaned close enough to her face she could smell his aftershave. Any words she might have said withered, forgotten with the intimate sensation of his finger touching her lips.

"Please stay." Dawson removed his finger.

Savvy remained breathless, her heart galloping through her chest. "Okay."

For a long moment, he stared into her eyes. Then, as if he'd finally seen what he wanted to see, he nodded. "I'll be right back." He slipped through the gap in the bushes and moved through the cars like a shadowy panther stalking its prey.

Dawson disappeared into the shadows of the staircase leading to the second floor. Savvy held her breath, her head twisting from side to side, her ears straining for any sound of someone approaching her or Dawson. When he emerged on the second-floor landing, he quickly negotiated the lock with the key Liz had given her. He stepped to the side of the doorway and let the door swing open. For a moment he didn't move, then he ducked into the dark entrance.

For an interminably long few seconds, Savvy held her breath, waiting for Dawson to reappear. Just about the time she stepped through the gap of the hedges to go after him, he appeared at the door and waved for her to come on.

Savvy let her breath out and, following Dawson's lead, crept through the parked cars, keeping low, crossing the open areas quickly and silently.

When she reached the steps, Dawson waited at the bottom, ready to lend her a hand up to the second-floor landing.

"Someone beat us to it," he whispered into her ear as they reached the top. "The place is a mess."

Disappointment warred with fear, but Savvy squared her shoulders. "I don't care. I need to go in."

"Then make it quick. You're a sitting duck as long as you're here. This would be the first place I'd look if I were one of the bad guys."

"Thanks." She gave him a tense smile and stared into the apartment. "Nothing like a little pressure."

"Close the door and close the curtains before you switch the lights on." He held the door open and then stepped back. "I'll stay out here to keep watch."

Savvy stepped across the threshold, closing the door behind her, all the while wishing Dawson had come inside with her. She groped on the wall next to the door, searching for a light switch. When she found it, she flipped it, illuminating the room.

She gasped.

Every piece of furniture had been overturned, broken or shredded. Books lay in tattered ruins, the pages ripped out and scattered across the worn beige carpet. Across the wall large shaky letters scrawled out the words *La señorita debe morir.*

Savvy pressed a shaking hand to her throat. Her breath caught and held for so long, her vision blurred. The young lady must die.

The words on the wall reverberated through her head several more times until she realized she'd translated them. *I understand Spanish.* But how? Had she grown up in South Texas?

The young lady must die. *I'm the young lady.* That thought got her feet moving. She scanned the contents of the room, searching for photographs, diaries, keepsakes... anything that might bring back her memory.

The tiny living area yielded nothing. She hurried into the closet-size bedroom with its full-size mattress stripped bare and ripped down the middle. The faded floral bedspread lay shredded across the floor next to equally distressed pillows. A line of spray paint twisted across the wall with the same message she'd found in the living room.

After a quick but thorough search of the floor, drawers and beneath the bed, she could find nothing at all that triggered even the most remote memory. The bathroom, too, was ransacked; clothing, scant as it was, lay in ragged strips on the floor. She couldn't even grab a change of underwear from her dresser.

Angry tears clogged her throat, making breathing virtually impossible.

"Savvy?" Dawson stood at the threshold to her bedroom, his body filling the frame, his shoulders almost as broad as the width of the doorway. Not even his stalwart strength could make this better.

The walls closed in around Savvy, the air too thick. She had to get out. Like her memory, her apartment had been shattered. Panic welled up inside, a panic so intense she wanted to scream. She pushed Dawson out of the doorway, tripped over a couch cushion on her way to the front door. She flung it open and ran out onto the landing, sucking in air as fast as she could.

"Savvy!" Dawson chased after her.

She couldn't face him, couldn't stand the pity in his eyes. This was her world. She had to make sense of it, but right now she couldn't. With an urgent need for space, she ran for the stairs, intent on putting as much distance between her, the apartment and Dawson as she could before she broke down.

With each step, she slowed, her legs dragging, feeling more and more as if she waded in molasses. Questions tumbled through her head like a recording stuck on Re-play. Who was Savvy Jones? Where had she come from? Where did she go from here?

"Savvy?" A black-haired child stood in front of her, curls hanging down her back in wild disarray, her pale blue eyes wide and fearful. "What's wrong?"

"I—" Savvy ground to a halt and stared down at the beautiful little girl wearing jeans and a graphic T-shirt. Something in her heart pinched so hard it made her breath catch. "I— Oh, God, do I know you?"

Chapter Six

Dawson hurried after Savvy. On the landing outside the apartment, Savvy froze, her body trembling.

A little girl stood in front of her, holding out her hand. "Don't you remember me, Savvy? I'm Charlie. You're my best friend." A tear slipped out of the corner of her baby-blue eye and slid down her cheek.

Dawson's chest clenched. If his child had lived, she'd be two now. Pain wrenched his heart as he relived his loss all over again.

Savvy dropped to her knees and took the child's hand. "I'm sorry." Her voice caught. "I can't remember anything."

Dawson pushed aside a sudden desire to lift Savvy into his arms and hold her until all the hurt went away, both hers and his. He forced himself to glance around, scoping the parking lot for enemy threat. After all that had happened, anywhere in the open was a bad place to be, yet he couldn't bring himself to break up the reunion between Savvy and the little girl who obviously recognized her. Maybe this was what Savvy needed to remember who she was. The best he could do was keep a watchful eye out for her.

"Charlie!" Liz Scott ran out of a door farther down the landing, her eyes wide and frantic until she spotted Charlie and Savvy. "Oh, Charlie!" Liz ran up behind the child and dropped down behind her. "Don't go outside without me, do you hear?"

"Yes, Mama." Charlie's gaze swung to her mother and back to Savvy. "Savvy doesn't remember me."

Liz gave Savvy a weak smile. "I know, honey. Savvy has a boo-boo on her head. It made her forget everything."

"Everything? Even our secret handshake?" Charlie held out her hand to Savvy.

"I'm sorry." Savvy lifted hers to Charlie's and her fingers wrapped around the little girl's in a regular handshake, then they slipped through until the tips of their fingers curled around each other. They balled their fists and punched knuckles.

Charlie's smile lit the night. "You remembered!"

Savvy laughed, the sound weak but hopeful. "I did." She glanced up at Dawson, the wonder in her eyes making his heart skip several beats. "I remembered."

"We should get inside." Dawson looked from Liz to Savvy. "It's not safe out here."

"Come with us." Liz herded Charlie into the open door of her apartment.

Dawson helped Savvy to her feet. Using his body as a shield, he covered her back, guiding her into Liz's apartment. Once inside, he closed the door behind them.

Liz met Savvy with a tight hug. "I was getting worried when you two didn't show up right away. What happened?"

"Someone followed us," Savvy answered, a shiver shaking her narrow frame.

"Holy smoke." Liz pushed the curtain aside on her window and peered out into the parking area below. "Do you think they'll come here?"

"They've already been here." Savvy's dull response made Liz drop the curtain and return to the redhead's side.

"They were?"

"My apartment is ruined. All the furniture, my clothes..." Savvy waved a hand. "Everything."

"Oh, Savvy." Liz wrapped her in another warm hug.

Dawson found himself wanting to be Liz. The look of utter defeat on Savvy's face made him want to punch someone, to inflict a lot of pain on the people responsible for hurting her. Reminding himself that she was just another job didn't make a dent in the anger simmering beneath the surface.

"You still have us, Savvy." Liz patted Savvy's back.

Savvy shook her head. "I don't know you. I can't remember."

"But we remember. We can help you." Liz pulled Charlie into the circle of her hug with Savvy. "Won't we, Charlie?"

"Yes, Mama. We can teach her how to read bedtime stories to me again, can't we?"

Savvy smiled at the child, her lips trembling. "Did I? Which was my favorite?"

"Your favorite is 'Beauty and the Beast.'" Charlie grinned up at her, her youthful enthusiasm hard to resist. "My favorite is 'Cinderella.' I like that she married a rich prince."

"Marrying a rich prince isn't always a dream come true, you know. Being with someone who really loves and cares for you is more important, no matter how much money you have." Savvy frowned. "I wonder what made me say that?"

"You told me that before," Charlie said. "Remember?"

Savvy shrugged, running a hand over the child's hair. "Maybe I did."

Dawson observed the scene, remembering how he and Amanda had dreamed of reading bedtime stories to their child. They'd talked of the things they'd teach her and the places they'd go together as a family when he returned from his rotation to Iraq. Memories shook him, bringing back the pain he thought he'd buried in the bottle.

"Stay here," he said, his voice a little more gruff than he intended. "I want to search your apartment again. There has to be something there."

Savvy looked up at him, her eyes red rimmed, the green irises brilliant with more unshed tears. "Thank you."

He stared at her longer than he should have, sinking into the incredible depths of those eyes. Eyes that seemed to mirror her lost soul. Then he turned and flung himself out of the apartment, making sure to lock the door behind him, his determination to be reassigned renewed and even more urgent. He dug the cell phone from his pocket and hit the speed-dial number for Audrey, bracing himself for the possibility of getting her answering machine instead of her voice.

The ringer chirped four times before a breathless Audrey answered, "Dawson!"

"Audrey, I—" Unprepared for the boss to answer after so many failed attempts, Dawson almost forgot what he wanted to speak to her about.

She saved him by jumping in. "I got your messages. All four of them." She laughed. "Jack McDermott is finishing up his current assignment. I can send him out tomorrow afternoon, if that's what you want."

Dawson's hand tightened on the phone, an image in the forefront of his mind of Savvy lying on the floor of the hospital after the man with the tattoos tried to kill her. "Yes…that's what I want." Why did he hesitate? He'd never wanted to be a bodyguard. He didn't want the responsibility of another person's life on his hands or the guilt of failing them.

"Then I'll have him report to you tomorrow. I have the

perfect private-investigation assignment for you if you want it."

"You might hold off on that. No matter who provides the protection, we need to find out more about the Rodriguez cartel. Savvy—Ms. Jones is still the only suspect and possibly the only witness to the murder."

"Jack would be great for the investigation piece. He speaks fluent Spanish and he has connections in that area. Can you hold out until he becomes available?"

"Yes."

"I'll see what I can do to free him up."

"Good. Oh, and do a search on the name Jameson. I don't know what it has to do with Savvy, but see if there is any connection."

"Will do," Audrey replied.

Dawson closed his cell phone, slid it into his pocket and continued down the landing toward Savvy's apartment.

Why was he second-guessing his request for reassignment? Why did he hesitate when offered a replacement? Hadn't protecting a witness to murder proved to be exactly what he didn't want? He could be out spying on a cheating spouse, no life-or-death crisis to avert. No red-haired woman with green eyes would look to him to keep her alive while she ran around Laredo searching for clues to her past and a murder she couldn't remember committing.

His hand hesitated on the doorknob to her apartment. A movement caught his eye among the cars below. He eased out to the edge of the railing and peered over. For a long moment, nothing moved in the night. Then a dark shadow darted between two cars and Dawson released the breath he'd been holding. A cat. He shook his head as he entered Savvy's apartment. Better to be punchy than to miss something.

Scanning the mess with Savvy's perspective in mind,

Dawson fully understood why she'd been so upset. She'd hung a lot of hope on finding something that would jog her memory.

Room by room, Dawson worked his way through, scouring the debris for anything of use. The living room was a bust. But once inside the bedroom, he found a shirt that had missed being ripped and a pair of jeans at the bottom of the closet that hadn't been completely ruined. Only a rip in one knee marred the faded denim. At the back of the closet on the highest shelf, he found a shoe box. One filled with receipts and pay stubs from the Waterin' Hole Bar and Grill. At first he thought it was another bust, but when he turned the box over, emptying the meager contents, he almost missed a photo as it slipped out onto the cluttered floor.

He lifted the picture from the floor, swallowing hard. A strawberry blonde baby with springy curls framing her cherubic face stared up at him. Worn edges and moisture stains on the picture spoke of someone holding this photo, possibly crying over it. The face in the picture could have been Savvy at one and a half or two years old. But the date on the back indicated a more recent time, eight months ago, to be precise.

Did Savvy have a baby? Was she married? If she had a baby, why would she leave it behind? What mother could leave a child? He stared down into eyes as green as her mother's. She had to be Savvy's.

His fingers tightened on the photograph. The picture had created more questions than answers in regard to Savvy's past. Questions he found himself wanting to know the answers to. He slipped the photo into his pocket and continued his search with renewed determination. What more would he find out about Savvy? The more disturbing question was why did he care, when he'd be replaced on this assignment soon?

SAVVY SAT ON the couch with an energetic Charlie beside her handing her book after book.

"And this is the story you read to me when I'm scared." She slipped another book into Savvy's lap. "This is the story you bought for me after I lost my first tooth. It's about tooth fairies."

"Charlie, let Savvy breathe. She's still recovering from her injury." Liz set a steaming cup of tea on the scuffed coffee table. "Here, maybe this will help calm your nerves. Today has to have been absolutely crazy for you."

Savvy smiled her thanks and lifted the cup of tea. "It has. I feel like such a burden to everyone. Even to myself. I really hoped something in my apartment would trigger a memory."

Liz grinned at Charlie. "Well, you did get one memory back. You remembered the secret handshake."

Savvy smiled at the little girl. "But that doesn't help me find out who I am."

"No, but it's a start. If you got that back, maybe more memories will come with time."

"I can't wait, Liz." Though she'd only known Liz for a handful of minutes, she felt comfortable sitting and talking with the woman who called herself her friend. "I have to know who I am, where I'm from, what I'm capable of..." Her voice faded off, her hands trembling on the teacup. Her greatest fear being that she had really committed the murder of Tomas Rodriguez.

"Stop it." Liz took Savvy's teacup and set it on the table. "You might not remember much, but Charlie and I remember the important things about you." She gripped Savvy's hands. "You're smart. You help me keep my checkbook

balanced since I don't have a head for numbers. You're
kind. Even the most obnoxious customers at the bar like
you because you don't give them lip. You smile no matter
how awful they are to you. You're patient with Charlie,
which qualifies you for sainthood in my eyes, since she
can be such a handful."

Savvy pulled her hands free of Liz's and ran one over
Charlie's head again, loving the silky-soft hair, the feeling strangely familiar, as if she'd smoothed a child's hair
in her past. She sighed. "I wish I remembered."

"You will. Charlie, be a big girl and take your books to
your room. You can read them yourself."

Charlie smiled at Savvy. "I'll save this one for you to
read to me tonight before bed." She held up a battered book
that had obviously been read countless times.

Savvy smiled back, unwilling to disappoint the child.
She doubted she'd be back that evening to read to her. But
maybe when she sorted out the mess of her life, she'd get
that chance. And she wanted it. More than she had memories to justify.

After Charlie left the room, Liz turned to face Savvy. "I
know you can't remember much, but let me tell you what
else I know about you. You told me once you didn't want
to live your other life anymore. It hurt too much. You said
you didn't want to end up like your father, who was too
worried about the almighty dollar to see what really mattered. Family."

"I talked about my father?" Savvy sat forward. "Did I
say who he was?"

"Sorry, that was all you gave me." Liz shrugged. "When
I asked what you meant, you clammed up. That was the
only time you talked about your former life." Liz gave her
a gentle smile. "You were so sad, like you'd lost someone
you loved a lot. Because you've been my friend for the past
four months when I didn't know whether or not I could go

on being a single mother, providing for my sweet Charlie alone, I didn't push for answers."

The sadness Liz spoke of squeezed inside Savvy's chest. Maybe she couldn't remember because she didn't want to. Like Dawson. It hurt too much.

Liz reached for Savvy's hands, holding them between her warm fingers. "Being with Charlie seemed to help. I think that our connection was Charlie and the lack of any other family. I don't have any other family but Charlie. You became my family."

Savvy's throat tightened. "It's nice to know I have you." Even if they weren't connected by blood, Savvy knew she wasn't alone in the world.

"You can count on me for anything." Liz's gaze met hers and she gave her hands a reassuring squeeze. "The most important thing you need to know about Savvy Jones is that she doesn't have a mean bone in her body. There's no way you killed Tomas Rodriguez. You couldn't squash a spider you found in your bathroom the other day. You came and got me to catch it and release it outside." Liz shook her head. "That doesn't sound like a person who could pull the trigger on a man."

Savvy stared down at their joined hands. "Thanks for your vote of confidence. But if I didn't kill him, why did I have the gun in my hand when you found me?"

Liz let go of Savvy's hands and retrieved her cup from the table. "All I can think is that you were framed. Someone wanted it to look like you killed Tomas to take the heat off the real murderer."

"That's what Dawson said. The gun was in my left hand." She shrugged. "It's kind of funny that I can't remember being left- or right-handed, but my hands seem to know."

A knock at the door made Savvy jump. "I guess that will be Dawson."

Liz beat her to the door. "Let me check first." She peeked through the peephole and let out a low whistle. "Man, oh, man. He's one fine-looking bodyguard." She unlocked the door and let him in. "I wish he were mine."

Dawson's brows creased as he stepped through the opening. "Who?"

Liz grinned. "Oh, nothing. We were just talking."

Savvy's cheeks burned. She couldn't even rebut Liz's statement. Not with Dawson standing right there. He wasn't hers. She was just a job to him, a job he didn't particularly want.

"We need to leave." Dawson's gaze raked over Savvy and his frown deepened, but he didn't remark on the blush that must be staining her cheeks. Would he guess Liz had been talking about him?

Savvy hoped not.

He held out his hands. "I found a pair of jeans and a shirt they missed."

She grabbed the bundle from him and clutched it to her chest. "Thanks."

"Ready?" He jerked his head toward the door. "The longer we stay, the more chance of placing Liz and Charlie in danger."

Savvy's eyes widened. "I didn't even think about that." She hugged Liz. "Please stay safe and keep a close eye on Charlie. I'd hate for anything to happen to either of you because of me."

"Don't worry about us. We'll be careful." Liz smiled, her blue eyes misty. "I'll miss you." She gave Dawson a fierce frown. "Take care of her."

He nodded, his lips pressed into a tight line. Then he turned and headed for the door without uttering another word.

Liz's brows rose, her gaze following the cowboy. When

she turned toward Savvy, a mischievous smile curled her lips. "Good luck with that with one, sweetie. He could be a keeper."

Savvy hurried after Dawson, Liz's words reverberating inside her head.

A keeper?

He was about the most handsome man Savvy could remember ever seeing. Given her limited memory, that wasn't much to go on. But she knew handsome, even if she couldn't remember any specific men in her past.

Even if Dawson showed interest in her, Savvy couldn't let herself be tempted. She couldn't start a relationship when she didn't know who she was.

She twisted her fingers around the ring finger of her left hand. No sign of a wedding ring. Liz said Savvy had been in Laredo for four months and she'd indicated Savvy had been without family for the entire time Liz knew her. Was she divorced? Separated? Widowed?

Even if she was attracted to Dawson, she couldn't do anything about it until she knew for sure. With that thought firmly in her head, she followed the man who'd inspired her to wonder whether or not she was free.

His hips swayed in the faded denim, conjuring more than professional interest. Dawson stepped through the door, his hand held out to the side to stop her from following. He stood for a moment, his head swiveling from side to side. Finally, he waved at her to follow. "Stay close."

Close? Savvy sucked in a breath and focused on Dawson's broad shoulders. "I don't like the idea of you getting shot."

"It's my job to protect you."

"Still…"

"Would you rather lead the way?" He kept moving until they reached the shadows of the stairwell.

She stiffened. He thought she was kidding. "Yes, I'd rather lead." When she stepped around him, he grabbed her hand and jerked her around.

Her foot caught on the step and she tumbled forward.

His arms closed around her as she plowed into his chest, face-first. She would have fallen but for his quick reflexes. Now she stood with her hands planted firmly on his hard, muscled chest, her mouth within inches of his.

"You're not going first." His gaze captured hers in the dim light filtering through from the streetlights, his expression unfathomable in the shadows.

Without conscious effort, her gaze dipped to his lips. "What if I want to?" Was that breathy voice hers? And what exactly was it they were talking about? She'd forgotten somewhere between the inky blackness of his intense eyes and the full, kissable lips temptingly close to hers.

"You don't get a choice in this." His arms tightened around her, his head dipping even lower until his breath warmed her mouth.

The scent of peppermint and denim swirled around her senses, clouding her mind with thoughts she shouldn't be thinking and a niggling spurt of anger over his cavalier comment. Before she could tell herself how wrong it was, she lifted up on her toes and pressed her lips to his.

The warm, soft feel of his mouth against hers sparked desire so powerful she couldn't pull away.

His arms tightened as he crushed her to him, deepening the kiss into something so savagely desperate, Savvy couldn't determine where she ended and he began. They fused as one in that searing, rugged connection. His tongue lashed out, stabbing against her lips until she opened her mouth and let him in.

How long they stood in each other's arms became irrelevant. Whether a moment or a lifetime, the kiss changed everything. Something that should never have happened became so real, so intense, Savvy forgot to breathe.

Dawson's fingers dug into the hair at her nape, dragging her head backward. His lips slipped from hers, sliding across her chin and down the sensitive column of her throat.

Savvy dragged in deep gasps of breath, her breasts rising up to meet his steady descent. How she wanted to feel his mouth on every part of her body. To lie naked beside him and explore every inch of him.

"Ms. Jones!" a man's voice called out.

Dawson jerked around just as the flash of a camera erupted in the darkness, blinding Savvy.

She raised her hand to block the light too late. Her night vision shot, she couldn't see the man holding the camera.

Chapter Seven

Frustration and anger fueled Dawson's temper. All the pent-up aggravation of the past twenty-four hours made him want to hit someone. Might as well be this creep seeking to sensationalize Savvy's story. He grabbed the man by the collar and jacked him up against the wall.

"Get the hell out of here." Dawson shoved the man again, letting him go as his gaze panned the parking lot. How could he have lost sight of his duty? His temporary lapse in sanity could have cost Savvy's life. Instead of a reporter shooting a camera, any gunman could have picked Savvy off in the time it took for one kiss.

His lips burned with the memory of that kiss. After two years of believing he could never want another woman the way he'd wanted his wife, he wanted Savvy. Guilt seared his chest, surging through his veins. He couldn't get involved with Savvy. Amanda had been his life, his only love. He couldn't dishonor her memory.

Savvy was nothing more than a job. "Let's get out of here." He hooked an arm around Savvy's waist, shielding her as much as he could with his own body, and set off across the parking lot to his truck.

"Ms. Jones!" The shaggy-haired man who'd asked all the questions at the hospital ran after them. "Could you answer a few questions?"

"No," Dawson shot over his shoulder as he opened the passenger door and lifted Savvy into the seat.

The man kept coming. "Did you really shoot Tomas Rodriguez?"

Dawson pressed the lock and slammed the door between the reporter and Savvy. He rounded to the driver's door and slid in beside Savvy.

"I don't know who shot Tomas Rodriguez," she told the man through the window.

"Is it true you have amnesia?" the man shouted.

She nodded.

"Do you know who you really are? Who your father is? Anything about yourself?" he persisted.

Dawson twisted the key in the ignition, ready to get as far away from the pesky reporter as he could.

Savvy shook her head. "No, I don't know," she whispered.

Damn the reporter. They never should have come to the apartment complex. Anyone could find out where Savvy Jones lived by asking. The bad guys already had. It was only a matter of time before they turned up here to finish the job they'd started. Dawson slammed the gear into Drive, pulling past the man.

The shaggy-haired man ran alongside the truck, banging on the window. "Ms. Jones! I might have information that can help you." The truck pushed past him but he kept yelling, "You can find me at the Desert Moon Hotel! Ask for Vance Pearson!"

"Dawson, stop!" Savvy spun in her seat, looking back at the man left standing in the middle of the street.

A dark green sedan moved past them, slowing as it came abreast. Dawson couldn't see in through the heavily tinted windows, but he wasn't taking any chances. "Forget it. We've been in one place too long already." He slammed his foot on the accelerator and the truck shot forward, leaving the man on foot and the green car behind.

"Please, Dawson," Savvy begged. "He might be able to tell me more about who I am."

Her hand touched his arm, making the skin beneath his shirt tingle.

Focus, Dawson. "Yeah, and he might just be after a story. We couldn't stay, even if I trusted him. That car we passed could be another hit man with a bullet your size. Who cares who you are if you're dead?"

"I'm as good as dead with no past."

"You aren't going to be dead on my watch."

"I might as well be. I have no memories to define me." Savvy turned away, facing the passenger window. She couldn't hide from him when her reflection showed the sadness as clearly as if she'd been facing him.

"Sometimes memories can be more painful than forgetting."

She faced him, her eyes large pools of deep green in the light from the dash. "Those painful ones help define who we are as a person. They make us stronger. We learn from our mistakes."

Dawson forced himself to keep his attention on the road, away from those liquid eyes, that pale, pleading face, so desperate to know who she was. "What if you get your memory back and don't like who you were?"

"Then I'd have a choice to change. We can't go back, but we still have choices. We don't have to make the same mistakes in the future."

"Some people would prefer to just forget."

"Like you?" she demanded.

"Like me."

Savvy sat for a while, twisting the seat belt in her hand. Finally, she asked in a low, quiet voice, "Who was she?"

Dawson's eyes burned. He blinked several times to clear

his vision and see the road ahead before he answered, "My wife."

Savvy remained silent beside him for a long moment.

Dawson hoped she'd drop the subject, wishing he hadn't told her anything.

"You must have loved her a lot."

He didn't answer as waves of guilt washed over him. That lingering feeling of having failed Amanda had yet to fade in his memory.

"Do you really wish you could forget?"

Dawson refused to face her. "Yes."

"What about the good times? If you loved her, there had to be good times. If you forgot everything about her, you'd be forgetting the good along with the bad. Do you really want that?"

"It hurts to remember things you no longer have."

"You can't even imagine how frighteningly empty it is to forget everything." She stared out her side window again. "Without our memories, we're nothing."

"With them, we're crippled." His voice came out harsh. He didn't want to remember, didn't want to talk about it and he didn't want to care about Savvy Jones.

Dawson had to remind himself yet again that Savvy Jones was a client. He couldn't afford to become emotionally involved, not when his replacement was on the way. His job was to keep her from being killed until Jack McDermott took over. Tomorrow couldn't arrive soon enough. At the rate he was going, Dawson was on the path to fail yet again. Just like he'd failed his wife. Like he'd failed the men in his unit. Like he'd failed himself. His grip tightened on the steering wheel.

Failure isn't an option.

He whipped the truck around a corner and zigzagged through narrow streets to lose anyone who might have followed them from the apartment complex. After several minutes driving with no headlights in his rearview mirror, he steered the truck toward the outskirts of town and a nondescript motel he'd passed on his way in.

Despite his determination to remain distant from the woman beside him, he glanced toward her.

Her shoulders remained stiff, her chin held high. The shiny reflection of a tear slid down her face, ripping through all his rationalization, leaving him raw and exposed.

Damn.

"WHERE ARE WE GOING?" Savvy's words cut into a silence so thick she could practically feel Dawson's thoughts churning. She wanted to ask more questions about his wife and their life together but didn't think he'd answer.

"To a motel."

Her heart skipped several beats before pounding back to life, shooting blood through her veins at supersonic speeds. Her and Dawson in a motel. Together. After that kiss? "No."

"You have a better suggestion?"

"I want to know if that man really has any information that could clue me in to my past."

"No."

Savvy's fingers clenched into fists, her backbone stiffening. "If you won't let me go after that man, then I want to go to the bar where I worked. I need to talk to the customers, the bartender, anyone who knew me and might have seen something last night."

"No."

"I *have* to do something. If I don't find out who really killed Tomas Rodriguez, then I'll have Tomas's father and every thug in his arsenal gunning for me, plus my own government could hit me up on murder charges."

She pulled in a deep breath and let it out, hoping to slow her heart rate. "Please."

He gave a short shake of his head. "It's too dangerous."

Her jaw tightened mutinously. "I'm willing to take that risk."

"You just got out of the hospital. You don't have all your strength back."

"I have you." She knew it was a cheap shot at his ego, but she had to get back to the Waterin' Hole and learn as much as she could about what had happened the previous night. After that, she'd hunt down the man with the pocket camera for any information he might have about her. She would shake it out of him herself, if need be. "Look, Dawson, I know you didn't want this job, but you're stuck with me until the real killer is identified. Think of it this way—the sooner we clear my name, the sooner I quit being a moving target for every gunslinger in South Texas and Mexico. Clearing my name frees you up to get on with your life."

As she said the words, her chest tightened. The thought of Dawson leaving left her feeling even more bereft than when she'd woken in the hospital, devoid of her past. Dawson was her rock, holding her steady in a world gone crazy. She didn't know what she'd do without him. Most likely, she'd survive. She didn't know much about herself, but deep down, she knew without a doubt that she was not a quitter. And maybe, just maybe, somewhere out there, she had a family worried about her. She'd find them.

"We're going to a motel where you can get some rest." He glanced at her. "You look like hell."

"Thanks. You really know how to poke a hole in a girl's ego." Her lips twisted. "You'd look like hell, too, if you'd been shot and left to die in an alley."

"My point exactly."

"Okay, we'll go to the motel long enough for me to get cleaned up. Then I'm going to the Waterin' Hole, with or without you."

Dawson grunted, refusing to respond.

Savvy crossed her arms over her chest. He'd see soon enough that she meant business. She couldn't find the real killer while hiding away in an obscure motel.

When a yawn sneaked up on her, Savvy quickly hid it behind her hand. She had to admit, she wasn't up to running full steam ahead. Only that morning, she'd had trouble standing on her own.

Wow, had it only been that morning? So much had happened in the short time she'd been awake. Any normally healthy person would be exhausted by the events. She sneaked a glance at Dawson.

Was he tired? He looked as stalwart as ever.

He had to help her find the killer. Once they found the person responsible for Tomas's death, Savvy was off the hook and Dawson could leave.

If they found the person responsible. A terrible thought occurred to Savvy. What if she really had shot Tomas Rodriguez? What if she was a murderer? How would she feel if Dawson was right and she didn't like what she learned about Savvy Jones? Could she live with herself knowing she had shot a man? A chill that had nothing to do with the truck's air conditioner slithered across Savvy's skin.

Her entire focus revolved around regaining her memory. Either the memories cleared her or they condemned her.

She pinched the bridge of her nose. What had her mind blocked from her? What secrets could be so horrific her brain refused to reveal them? Her pulse throbbed behind the bandage at her temple. Had she shot herself because she couldn't live with the knowledge that she'd killed a man? Left-handed?

Think, Savvy, think. The harder she concentrated, the more her head hurt until tears pressed at the backs of her closed eyelids.

A large warm hand closed over hers. "Don't, Savvy."

Blinking back the tears, she stared up at Dawson. "I have to remember."

"The memories will come back. Give your brain time to recover from the shock."

She clutched his hand in hers, staring out the front windshield. "I don't have time."

"Forcing yourself to think isn't helping, is it?" He let go of her hand to return his to the steering wheel, negotiating a turn into the parking lot of a seedy motel with faded paint and few cars parked in front of the rooms. A sign below the name indicated rental by the night or by the hour and a vacancy sign blinked in faded neon red.

Savvy's heart sank. Lovely. "No. Nothing seems to help." She sighed. "I didn't find a thing in my apartment that hinted at who I am. No pictures, no letters, nothing. It's as if I never existed."

"It'll all come back. Don't force it." He pulled around the far end of the motel and parked his truck.

Savvy couldn't see the main road from where they parked, which meant no one would see the truck from the road.

Dawson pulled the keys from the ignition, turned in his seat and gave her a narrow-eyed stare. "Will you promise me that you'll stay put while I get a room?"

Savvy snorted. "It's not like I can drive off in your truck without the keys. Besides, like you said, I'm not totally recovered. I wouldn't get far."

"You didn't answer my question."

Savvy nodded. "Yes. I'll stay put."

Dawson hesitated a moment. "Keep low. Don't let anyone see you." He climbed out of the truck and disappeared around the corner of the building.

After he left, Savvy laid the seat back until she was certain no one walking by would see her lying there. Every sound made her jump, every glare of headlights made her duck lower in the seat and wish Dawson would hurry back. She didn't like being alone in the dark. Not after all that had happened. As much as she hated relying on Dawson, at least he made her feel safe. In her current circumstances, that sense of security went a long way to calming her.

In the dark, outside a motel, with nothing but her thoughts tumbling through her head, Savvy pored over what she knew so far about the night she'd been shot.

From what she'd been told, Liz had found her in the alley near Tomas Rodriguez's body with a gun in her left hand. She flexed her left wrist, trying to imagine the weight of a gun. It didn't feel right. She wasn't left-handed. Someone had to have forced her to hold that gun to her head. She couldn't imagine shooting herself. The sight of blood always made her queasy.

Her heartbeat quickened. How did she know that? She squeezed her eyes shut and tried to think of a time she might have seen blood.

A moment passed and nothing came to her.

Again, she retraced her steps through the day, recalling the man with the tattoos who'd tried to smother her. She couldn't identify his face because it had been covered by a surgical mask, but she would recognize his tattoos if she saw them again. An image of a blue-green dragon and red devils had seared an imprint into her mind. The sum total of her accessible memories consisted of the ones she'd made over the past eighteen hours.

The one that stood out most, aside from terror of the tattooed man attempting to smother her and being followed by the two mysterious cars, was the memory of Dawson's kiss. Try as she might, she couldn't clear it from her head. "What do you expect?" she muttered to herself aloud. "It's not as if I have many memories to go through." Despite her efforts to push that particular recollection to the back of her mind, she found herself reliving the way his lips had ground against hers, his tongue thrusting inside her mouth. How rough and urgent it had been.

Her body warmed all over, hot liquid pooling low in her belly, the juncture of her thighs pulsing to the remembered strokes of his tongue. She sat up straight, her breath rasping in her throat, her hand pressed to her tingling breasts. What was she thinking?

A dark face appeared in her window.

Savvy shrieked.

Dawson yanked the door open and pulled her into his arms. "Are you okay?"

No, she wasn't okay. In the throes of remembering their last embrace, she couldn't shake off the longing, the need to be held by one man. And now, here she was in that man's arms.

"Yes, I'm fine." She pushed against his chest until he stood back, his hands falling to his sides. "Really. It's just…" She scrambled for an excuse. "You scared me," she finished. A half-truth. He hadn't scared her so much as she'd scared herself with the intensity of her desire. Generated by a mere memory! The real man standing within touching distance, warm, living, breathing and deliciously rugged, had her shaking with the uncontrollable urge to let nature take its course.

He grabbed the gym bag from the back floorboard. "Come on, I got a room on the back side."

Clutching her spare clothes to her chest, Savvy moved as far away from Dawson as she could. Almost worse than her desire for the man was her fear of him figuring it out. Could he see the lust in her eyes? She titled her head toward the ground.

When they stopped in front of a door, she finally looked up. "Is this my room?"

"Yes." He stuck the key in the lock and turned it, pushing the door open.

The room was barely big enough to be classified as a closet. A full-size bed took up the center space, covered in a worn floral bedspread that had seen more than its share of washings. She couldn't expect more from a motel that rented rooms by the hour. Savvy stepped inside, squared her shoulders and forced herself to face Dawson. "Where will you be staying? Not far, I hope."

"Not far at all." His lips quirked up on the corners. "I got *a* room, not rooms."

Savvy's pulse sped up, her face heating. "What do you mean?"

"We're sharing this room," he said.

Even before Dawson finished the last word, Savvy's head shook from side to side. "No. We can't." She stared at the four walls instead of his face. "Don't they have another room?"

"Yes, but none that connect." He shut the door behind him, his body filling the closet-size space.

Savvy's breaths came in short, shallow pants. Afraid she'd pass out, she backed up and sat on the corner of the only bed in the room. "You can't stay here." She popped up when she realized what she was sitting on and how suggestive it might be to him. Heck, it led to all kinds of wicked thoughts in her own head, so what must it be doing inside his? Especially after that kiss.

She turned away, pressing a cool hand to her heated cheeks. "It's not right. We only just met."

He set the gym bag on the dresser. "You're my responsibility to protect. I can't do that from another room."

She held her wad of clothes against her chest. "No. You can't stay. I'll be fine by myself. No one knows where we are."

"I'm not leaving you." His eyes narrowed. "I won't risk you dying on my watch. End of discussion." Those sexy lips pressed into a firm, hard line.

Savvy opened her mouth to argue but shut it again without uttering a sound.

Dawson tipped his head toward the open bathroom door. "You can have the shower first."

"How generous." She scurried toward the only escape she had, the minuscule bathroom, closing the door firmly behind her and turning the lock on the knob.

Then she collapsed against the door, willing her heart to slow and her breathing to return to normal. Maybe a shower would help her get her act together and cool the memory of their kiss.

She ripped the flimsy shower curtain aside and turned on the water, coaching herself as she went about cleaning the grime off her body and the desire out of her mind.

He's just a bodyguard. A man without any emotional involvement in her. There to do a job, to keep her alive. Nothing else.

She could get through one night alone with him, no problem. As she lathered her skin with soap and scrubbed around the injury on her head, she couldn't stop her body from reacting. She stood naked in the shower while Dawson no doubt paced the room on the other side of the door, only a few short feet away.

Savvy twisted the faucet setting to cold, rinsing the soap from her hair and body, wincing as some of the water soaked through the bandage to her stitches. Served her right for lusting after a man she'd met only that morning.

Clean and cold, she stepped out onto the bath mat and dried off, slipping into the jeans and T-shirt Dawson had salvaged from her ruined apartment. The clothing reminded her of yet another failed attempt to recall her past. Clinging to that depressing thought, she wadded up her dirty clothing in her hands, sucked in a steadying breath and emerged from the bathroom.

Dawson lay on the bed, his feet stretched out in front of him, his boots on the floor beside him, his holster and gun nowhere to be seen. "Better?"

He looked all too appealing with his shirt unbuttoned, exposing more of his chest than she had a right to see. Her lips pressed together, her eyes burning, suddenly overwhelmed with everything that was happening to her. She turned away from Dawson. "Yeah, I'm better."

The bed squeaked behind her.

"You don't have to be brave all the time, you know." His work-roughened hands closed around her bare arms.

"Yes, I do." His hands sent electrical impulses shooting throughout her body.

"It'll come back." His breath on her shoulder made her want to turn in his arms and kiss him.

Frustration burned inside her. She didn't know him. She didn't know *herself.* Savvy shook off his hold and faced him, ready to lash out to keep from falling into his arms. "What makes you so sure?"

He shrugged, running a hand through his hair. "I've seen it with injured soldiers. Their situations or injuries are so traumatic that their minds shut down those memories to protect them from going crazy."

"And their memories return?"

He shrugged. "Most of the time."

"That's no guarantee."

"You have to have faith in yourself."

"And that's what you have? Faith?" She wanted—no, needed—to put distance between them. She needed him to despise her so that she wouldn't have to fight her longing for him. "Where was your faith in yourself when you lost your wife? Is that why you don't want the responsibility of another person's life?"

His face turned to stone, his hands clenching at his sides. "I lost it."

"Well, me, too." Savvy clutched the dirty shirt and jeans to her chest as a shield to keep from reaching out to touch him, to take back her harsh words. "This is all I have. The only things left of my life before I woke up." Her voice caught on a sob. "I have nothing."

Her eyes burned, but tears wouldn't fall. She'd cried enough tears for a lifetime and they didn't help. They didn't solve the mystery of her past, didn't unlock her memories, didn't even make her feel better. She ran for the door, needing to get out of this box into the night. Panic pushed her away from him and her need to be held in his strong arms.

Dawson's hand on her arm stopped her.

She tried to jerk free, but he held tight.

"Let me go. I don't need your pity," she said through clenched teeth.

"That's not what I'm offering." He handed her a rumpled photograph. "Maybe this will help. I found it in your apartment."

"What…" She took the photograph from his hand and stared down at it. "Who…" Her lungs clenched, refusing to let air in or out. "My God." She'd thought she'd had no tears left to cry, but she was wrong. Sobs rose in her throat and giant drops spilled from her eyes. Through her tears, she looked up at Dawson. "Is she mine?"

Chapter Eight

Dawson shrugged. "I don't know. But she has your red hair and green eyes."

Savvy stared at the photograph, tears streaming down her face. "Why would I leave her to come here?"

A huge lump settled in Dawson's gut. From what he knew about Savvy's personality, wild horses couldn't have dragged her away. Nothing could make her leave a child behind. Nothing short of death.

Dawson stared around the dark and dingy motel room, his gaze landing on Savvy as she clutched the faded photograph, tears flowing down her cheeks. His chest hurt so badly, he couldn't stay. He couldn't stand by knowing what he felt to be true.

The only reason Savvy would leave a child behind was if that child was lost or dead.

Memories spilled into his mind, the walls closing in on him. Dawson couldn't get away fast enough. He jerked his cowboy boots onto his feet and headed for the door.

"Where are you going?" Savvy asked with a catch in her voice.

"Out." He paused with his hand on the doorknob, fighting hard to breathe. "Lock the door behind me, don't go out and don't let anyone in but me. Got that?" he barked.

"Yes," she answered, her voice small in the dark room.

He couldn't face her. If he did, he'd be forced to face his own losses. Dawson left, closing the door behind him, blocking the look of anguish on Savvy's face. The same anguish he'd felt when he'd come face-to-face with the deaths of his wife and their baby girl.

Once outside, he walked across the parking lot, past his truck, past the motel, until he found himself running. Not until he'd put five blocks between him and Savvy did he slow to a stop, his heart pounding, his breath coming in shallow gasps. The bright lights of a liquor store shone like a beacon, drawing him closer like a parched animal to a watering hole. His boots carried him to the door, but he couldn't cross the threshold.

If he bought a bottle of whiskey he could escape into a fog of blessed alcohol-induced oblivion. For a short time he'd forget about what he'd lost. Forget that he was too late to say goodbye, forget that he'd failed to be there when they'd needed him most.

A bottle of alcohol could give him the temporary amnesia he needed to make it past his memories and live another day.

An image flashed through his head of Amanda staring up at him, her eyes bright with happiness after she'd read the results of the pregnancy test. The look of joy on her face, the hum of her singing to herself as she crocheted a blanket for their first baby filled his chest with longing. More than anything she'd wanted to be a mother, to give him children, to have someone she could love when he went away to war. He'd never seen her happier than the day she'd learned she carried their child.

Do you want to forget all the good times? Savvy's words echoed in Dawson's head as he stared at the bright lights of the liquor store. Yes. He wanted to forget, damn it!

But did he?

The happy times were as painful as the bad times. They cropped up often enough to remind him of all he'd lost.

Dawson backed away from the door, dropped to the curb and buried his head in his hands. When had running away solved anything? He'd been running since Amanda died. But he could never run far enough.

Because he couldn't run away from himself. Amanda and their baby had died. He hadn't. No matter how many times he'd wished he had died with them, he hadn't. Life had gone on, with or without them or him. The life he'd led hadn't been much of a life at all. He'd stopped caring, tried to stop remembering, but mostly, he'd stopped living in a way that became worse than dying.

For some reason, only God knew why, Dawson had lived. Maybe He had a purpose for him. Maybe that purpose was here and now. To protect Savvy, to find the real killer, to be there when someone else needed him.

Lifting his head from his hands, he looked down the long road dotted with streetlights, seeing more clearly than he had in two long years.

If his purpose was to protect Savvy, he couldn't do it five blocks away. A police car passed on the street, slowing down.

Dawson could only imagine what the officer thought of a man loitering outside a liquor store. He jumped to his feet and walked steadily toward a twenty-four-hour pharmacy he'd passed in his rush to escape.

Once inside the store he loaded up with what food he could find and other items he'd need to keep Savvy safe and healthy. In less than five minutes he'd made his purchases and left the store. The entire time he wondered whether or not he'd find Savvy at the motel room when he returned, hoping like hell he would.

FOR A LONG TIME after Dawson left the motel room Savvy studied the photograph, memorizing every line and curve of the child's picture, from the sparkling green eyes to the soft strawberry blonde curls framing her cherubic face. A deep sense of sadness filled her, overwhelming her to the point she could barely breathe. Had this child really been hers? She tapped her palm against her forehead. Somewhere locked in her mind were the details of what had happened to her. The deep sense of loss filling her heart made her conclude there was a distinct possibility that the child had died.

Savvy lay down on the bed, placing the photograph on the pillow beside her. A chill settled beneath her skin and shook her until her teeth rattled. With painfully slow movements, she dragged the blankets up around her. Curling into a fetal position, she lay as still as death, her gaze glued to the child's smiling face.

"I'm sorry, baby." She reached out and stroked the picture. "I can't even remember your name." She swallowed hard. "Am I your mommy?" Had she carried this child in her womb for nine months? How could anyone forget that? Her hand went to her belly. She jerked the sheet down and pulled her shirt up. Faint lines of stretch marks laced across her flat abdomen. "I'm a mother." A sob rose in her throat and emerged in a keening cry. "And I can't remember."

She turned over on her back and stared up at the ceiling, willing her brain to unlock the doors and free her memories. Had losing her baby made her *want* to forget? Was the amnesia her mind's way of easing her pain? Would she ever get her memories back?

Savvy turned her head toward the photograph. Even if the baby had died, would she want to forget her? Forget how she felt in her arms, how she'd laughed and cooed, fed and diapered her? What about her first steps, her first word? Did she want to forget all the joys, all the love?

"Oh, baby, I want to remember everything." She lifted the photograph, stared into the happy green eyes and wanted to know more about this child. No matter how painful. What was her name? Where had they lived? Questions swirled in Savvy's tired mind, the answers as elusive as memories of her own childhood. She clutched the picture in her fingers, refusing to let go of the one clue to her past as she surrendered to sleep.

It couldn't have been long after she fell asleep when soft knocking woke her. Not until it became louder did she come fully awake, sitting up straight in the bed, her heart racing.

Another knock, louder this time.

Savvy threw the sheets aside and leaped out of bed. Her legs wobbled and her head spun dizzily. She sat back on the edge of the bed to keep the room from spinning out of control.

"I'm coming," she muttered, rising slowly this time. When she reached the door, fear bunched in her gut as she leaned in to look through the peephole.

At first, she couldn't make out the dark figure on the other side, which did nothing to slow her heartbeat.

Another knock startled her and she backed away from the peephole.

"Savvy, open up. It's me, Dawson."

Relief eased the tightness in her chest and she scrambled to unlock the dead bolt and safety chain, flinging the door open for Dawson to enter.

He slipped through the doorway, carrying two bulging plastic bags. With his foot, he kicked the door shut behind him. "You had me worried for a minute there."

"I must have fallen asleep." Savvy shot the bolt home

and took one of the bags from him, peering inside. "There wouldn't happen to be food in here, would there?" Her stomach rumbled.

"It's not much, but at least we won't starve." He set the other bag on the dresser and faced her. "Are you all right?"

She nodded, refusing to meet his eyes, her own misting over at his concern. "Yeah."

"Remember anything?"

She shook her head, not trusting herself to speak.

He pulled out plastic jars of peanut butter and jelly.

"Got a chef's salad in there somewhere?" she asked.

"Fresh out of health food." He smiled. "But I make a mean PB&J sandwich. Want one?"

"PB&J?" She liked it when he kept things light. That way she didn't think about the picture, her lost memories or the men trying to kill her.

"PB&J. You know, peanut butter and jelly." He held up both jars.

A smile tugged at the sides of her mouth. "Yes, please." She'd need her energy to stay one step ahead of the killers and she'd need to stay healthy to help her body and mind recover. "I *love* peanut butter and jelly sandwiches."

"You do? Is that something you remember?" He set the jars on the dresser and removed the twist tie from the loaf of bread.

Savvy tilted her head. "No…it's just something I know."

"There you go. Whether you think you're remembering or not, you remembered that you like PB&J sandwiches."

She pulled a package of plastic utensils out of the bags. "I guess so."

"Uh-uh." He removed the items from her fingers and set them on the dresser. "I'm the chef."

Savvy raised her hands, surrendering the plastic knife. "I wouldn't dream of taking away your fun."

He spread jelly and peanut butter on the slices of bread and folded them together, passing one to her. "For you." Fishing around in the bag, he unearthed a plastic bottle of apple juice and offered it to her.

"No, thanks." She wrinkled her nose and dug into one of the bags. "I thought I saw orange juice in there." When she found it, she opened it and took a long drink. "Better."

Dawson nodded, a smile playing around the corner of his lips. She could really fall for him when he smiled like that. "We're learning," he said in that low, sexy voice that wrapped around her like a glove.

"What do you mean?" She curled up on the edge of the bed and bit into her sandwich, trying to quell the longing his voice inspired.

Dawson didn't help by sitting down beside her, making their situation that much more intimate. "You don't like apple juice, but you do like orange juice. Did they give you apple juice at the hospital?"

"No." A trickle of optimism helped chase away her earlier sad thoughts and almost distracted her from Dawson's nearness. "I guess I remembered that, if only subliminally."

"A big word." Dawson's brows rose. "You must either be well read or well educated."

"Both. Harvard," she answered without thinking. Her eyes widened. "I went to Harvard." She straightened. "If I went to Harvard, there should be a record of my attendance, my address...my family."

Dawson pulled his cell phone out of his pocket and punched a button.

"You can't call Harvard." Savvy glanced at the clock on the nightstand. "The administration office will be closed until morning."

"I'm not calling Harvard. I'm doing better than that. I'm calling my boss. She'll check it out and trace it back to a home address." He sat with his ear to the phone. After several seconds, he whispered, "She's not answering." His attention returned to the phone and voice mail. "Hey, boss, Dawson here. Check out Harvard records for one Savvy Jones. See if they have her address and next of kin and let me know ASAP. Thanks." He hit the end button and shrugged. "She'll get someone on it. Should hear back tomorrow."

Hope swelled inside Savvy. For a moment she sat staring at her sandwich, afraid to take a bite because she knew she couldn't swallow past the lump in her throat. She'd gone to Harvard. Surely the records would lead her home.

Home. Somewhere besides Laredo. Maybe even in a different state. Away from Liz Scott and her daughter, Charlie, and… Savvy glanced up at Dawson, a sinking feeling blighting her brief ray of happiness. Away from Dawson, the one person who had anchored her since the moment she woke up in this nightmare. She bit into her sandwich, concentrating on the explosion of flavors, from the strawberry jelly to the rich texture of peanut butter.

"I've been thinking." Dawson wiped his hands on his jeans and reached into the grocery bag for potato chips. "Maybe you're right about checking out that reporter, Vance Pearson." He opened the bag and held it out to her. "Although I doubt he's much of a reporter. He didn't have much of a camera."

"If he really knows something about me, I want to know what it is." She stared across her half-eaten sandwich at Dawson. "When do you want to go?"

"I'd rather not go in the dead of night. You need sleep and so do I."

She nodded, munching on a potato chip. "When, then?"

"Later in the morning, after he's had a chance to leave his hotel room."

"Wouldn't that kind of defeat the purpose of talking to him?"

"I'd rather not expose you. If we go, we'll go incognito."

"Incognito?" She frowned. "Like before?"

"Yeah." He dug into another bag and pulled out a baseball cap. "Only, I have a new hat for you."

She grinned. "I've never heard of the Fighting Iguanas. Do they even play baseball?"

"Hockey."

She looked at him, her brows wrinkling. "In Texas?"

"San Antonio. I'll take you to a game someday."

Take her to a game? That would imply that he'd see her after this whole mess was over. Savvy's heart warmed.

He took the hat from her hand and settled it gently on her head, careful not to touch the bandages at her left temple.

Savvy stood perfectly still, breathless at how near he was, his body heat warming the air around her. She wanted to touch him, to feel his strength beneath her fingertips, to draw on that strength to help her through the next few days. "Shouldn't we also check in with the D.A. to let him know we haven't skipped town?" she asked, her voice breathy.

"Yeah. We'll do that tomorrow, as well. He's probably ready to put out an APB on you since your well-publicized escape from the hospital."

She smiled at his description. "I felt like I escaped from a prison." She sighed, the food in her stomach making her sleepy, exhaustion tugging at her eyelids. "Maybe I'll just take a nap." She leaned back against the pillow, her face breaking open in a wide yawn. "Wow, did you put sleeping pills in my PB&J? I can't keep my eyes open."

"No, you're just tired. Close your eyes. I'll take first watch."

"Mmm. Thanks." She stretched and settled on her uninjured side, snuggling into the blanket. "When are you going to sleep?"

He moved off the bed and stacked their food back in the bags. "When you're safe."

Her mind drifted off but came back long enough for her to say, "I thought you weren't coming back."

"Me, too."

"What changed your mind?"

"The voices in my head," he grumbled, a frown creasing his forehead.

She stared across at him, trying to keep her eyes open but failing miserably, blocking out his image. "The voices in your head…do they happen often?" Savvy opened her eyes just in time to see that sexy smile tugging at his mouth.

"Only since I met you." The huskiness of his voice made her pulse quicken and her sleepiness vanish.

"Dawson?" Savvy closed her eyes to the man who filled the room with his body and ragged soul and rolled onto her side, pulling the covers up to her chin.

"Yeah."

"Did you love your wife?" She held her breath, her eyes squeezed shut.

Silence stretched between them. Savvy couldn't regret asking. Something inside her had to know the answer.

"Yes." Dawson's answer was so quiet, Savvy thought she'd imagined it.

When she opened her eyes, she knew she hadn't. He stood beside the bed, staring down at the picture of the little girl, his face stony, but the look in his eyes raw with the same pain that had wrenched her own soul. "She died trying to give birth to our little girl. I lost them both that night."

Savvy sat up in the bed, all vestiges of sleep slipping away. "I'm sorry."

Savvy stood, leaning against his arm, one hand slipping into his. He couldn't forget his loss and she couldn't remember hers. Savvy stared at the picture of the child with the coppery curls.

Dawson looked down at their clasped hands, his fingers tightening around hers until they hurt. "Don't get involved with me, Savvy Jones."

Savvy welcomed the pressure, refusing to let go of his hand. She turned to face him, tipping her head back to stare into his eyes, defiantly. "Who said I'm getting involved?"

His nostrils flaring, Dawson stared into her eyes. Then he pulled her close, trapping the hand that she refused to let go behind her back. His other hand tangled in the hair at her nape, yanking her head back. "You don't know *what* you're getting into." His lips crushed hers in a kiss that shook her to her very core. The shock of his attack left her gasping, her lips parting to let his tongue thrust between.

Her body responded to his savage kiss, every cell on fire, the burning spreading fast and low. Her calf curled around the back of his leg and her free hand climbed up his chest, clutching at his shirt.

As if all the emotion of the day had culminated in the joining of their lips, Savvy fell into the embrace and, for the first time since she'd awakened in the hospital, she felt really alive.

He let go of her hand, his fingers sliding down over her hips and into the waistband of her jeans, cupping her butt, kneading the flesh.

Savvy couldn't get close enough, the urgency of her need past common sense, past any hope of reason. Only skin against skin would do. Sliding her hands between them, she unclasped the rivet on her jeans, tugging at the denim.

He helped push her pants down her legs until she slipped out of them. The shirt came off with his quick tug at the hem, though he slowed to carefully bypass the bandage at her temple.

Naked, she stood in front of him, her breasts peaked and aching for his touch. Her entire body pulsed with the need to feel his against hers, him inside her, filling all the emptiness.

He held her at arm's length, his gaze traveling over every curve until heat flooded her cheeks and she wondered if she had gone too far.

"You're beautiful," he said, his voice as rough as his kiss.

"You're still dressed." She boldly reached out, making quick work of undoing the buttons of his shirt, dragging the sleeves over his broad shoulders until it dropped to the floor. When she reached for the button on his jeans, he took over, removing a foil packet from his wallet before shedding the denim and stepping free, solving one of her unspoken questions. The man preferred to go commando, obviously feeling that underwear was an unnecessary addition to the wardrobe.

That throbbing place between her legs moistened even as her lips dried in anticipation. She spread her hands across his chest, reveling in the crisp hair sliding through her fingers. She tweaked the hard brown nipples, leaning close to take one between her lips, sucking on it until he groaned.

Savvy removed the foil packet from his fingers and tore it open with her teeth. Then, her gaze locked with his, she smoothed the sheath over him, loving the steely hard length of him, anxious to feel it inside her. She needed validation that this was not a dream she'd woken to, that she didn't die in that alley, that she was a live woman with wants and needs that only this man could fulfill.

Dawson's hands clasped her around the waist, his fingers sliding over her butt to her thighs. Then he lifted her and wrapped her legs around his waist, the tip of his member pressing against her opening. "This is wrong. I shouldn't be doing this."

"Did anyone ever tell you that you talk too much?" She covered his lips with hers, lowering her body to take him into her.

He was big, his girth pressing into her wetness, the delicious stretching making her cling to his shoulders, her breath catching and holding in her chest. Her head tipped back, her long hair hanging down her naked back adding to the erotic sensations flooding her body. She moved up and down, accepting more of his length until he could go no farther.

There he paused and held her body close to his. "This is too fast."

She shook her head. "Don't quit on me now."

"You deserve more."

"I want this."

"I want to do it right." Carrying her, he walked the two steps to the bed and lifted her off him, laying her down on the sheets.

She didn't want to let go; her hands clung to his neck.

He plucked them free and stood back.

"Please," she said, hating herself for begging. Her legs fell open, her fingers sliding down over her belly to that swollen aching nub.

Dawson sucked in a deep breath, his gaze moving over her inch by inch until she thought for sure her skin would ignite.

When she couldn't stand it a second longer, he lay down beside her.

Savvy let go of the breath she'd been holding, her body melting against his. "I wasn't sure…" Her hand moved across his chest, tentatively at first, afraid he'd leave if she came on too strong again.

He leaned up on one elbow and brushed a strand of her hair away from her face. "Why me?"

Her hand paused at his belly button, tangling in the dark line of hair angling toward his hard, stiff member. "You make me feel alive. Like I'm somebody."

He didn't respond with words. But his hands moved over her like a master musician strumming a treasured instrument. He made her body sing with longing. As his lips followed his fingers on a slow path downward, her back arched off the bed. She wanted to be closer to have him inside her—now.

But Dawson had other plans. His fingers led the way down to the patch of strawberry blonde curls at the juncture of her thighs, where he parted her folds. He slipped between her thighs, draping her legs over his shoulders. Then he touched his tongue to her, sending her into a cataclysmic spasm of sensations, sparking a flame that burned out of control, sending her up and over the edge. Her hips rose off the bed as his tongue flicked over her again and again.

Savvy's fingers clutched at his hair, dragging him deeper until she cried out, the tension beyond breathing. When she could take no more of his sweet torture, she tugged his hair, urging him up her body until he lay on top of her, pressing her into the mattress.

As his lips claimed hers, the taste of her sex mingling in their mouths, he slid inside her, thrusting deep.

Skin slapped against skin in a wild frenzy of coupling,

both their voices crying out in the dark as they burst over the edge.

Bathed in sweat and the scent of their lovemaking, Savvy fell back to earth, a peaceful lethargy invading every limb, every muscle of her body, especially her eyelids.

Dawson rolled them onto their sides, their connection still complete.

She liked it this way, snuggling close to him, her cheek resting against his naked chest. "Dawson?"

"Yeah, babe?"

"Promise me something?" she said, a yawn taking over on her last word, her eyes closing.

He stiffened. "If I can."

"Promise you won't regret this in the morning."

When he didn't respond, Savvy sighed, refusing to let his silence dispel the afterglow of what had happened. "I didn't ask for forever."

Chapter Nine

His nose tickled, so he wiggled it, but the tickling sensation didn't go away. Reaching up, he brushed his finger beneath his nose only to discover the source of the irritant. He opened his eyes.

A long strand of strawberry blonde hair curled across his chin.

Dawson jolted from dead asleep to wide-awake and immediately turned on.

Shortly after Savvy had fallen asleep, Dawson had risen, pulled on his jeans and then sat against the headboard, meaning to stay awake and hands free of his client. Sometime during the night, exhaustion had claimed him and for once he'd slept without any dreams to plague him. His head had found its way down to the pillow, his body stretched fully across the bed.

Savvy snuggled at his side, her hand resting against his chest, one of her trim, naked legs draped over his denim-clad thigh.

For a moment he remained still, breathing in the clean, feminine scent of woman and the musky aroma of their lovemaking that lingered in the air. The soft skin of her breast pressed against his bare side. He couldn't budge his arm from beneath her head. He couldn't bring himself to wake her, when her breath warmed his shoulder and the delicate fingers of her hand rested on his chest, curled into his short crisp hairs. If he wasn't careful, she'd wrap her fingers around his heart.

He missed having a woman in his bed. Natural urges clamored for him to take her in his arms and make love to her all over again. As he touched her leg, his jeans tightened, reminding him that he was a man with the normal needs any woman could satisfy. But no woman he'd met since Amanda's death had sparked as much heat in him as Savvy did in her sleep.

He eased out from under her carefully, so as not to wake her. Once off the bed, he let out the breath he'd been holding and stared down at the woman.

Her chest rose and fell in a slow, steady rhythm, her lips slightly parted. At least while she slept, she didn't worry about who she was or what had happened to the child in the picture. A frown dented her smooth brow and she rolled onto her side, her fingers clutching the pillow, a soft hiccupping sob escaping her lips.

Before he could think, he leaned over and lifted a strand of her hair off her face and tucked it behind her ear. She didn't know how good she had it. If she'd lost a loved one, she couldn't remember the pain. But her tears over the child's photograph had been his undoing, had made him doubt his desire to forget.

In the cool light of morning, he tried to clear his head, to reestablish his sense of purpose. He pulled the sheet up over her luscious body. Even that didn't douse the fire burning in his gut.

Dawson turned away, promising himself he'd get through the day, protect Savvy and hand her off to his friend and fellow agent, Jack McDermott. Against his better judgment, he'd crossed the line last night, taking advantage of Savvy when she was vulnerable. Her life was messed up enough without a broken-down alcoholic in it.

Dawson glanced down at his watch. Jack would be there later that day. Until then, Dawson had to keep Savvy alive and out of sight. He crossed to the window and pulled the heavy curtain aside, letting a triangle of light fall across the floor. The parking lot stood empty, the harsh South Texas sunlight muted by morning with a fine layer of dust hovering in the air. Nothing stirred, no strange black sedans lurked, no gunmen were poised on the rooftops to pick them off.

The sheer stillness made Dawson twitchy. The longer they stayed in one place, the more time Rodriguez's thugs had to find them. And if they didn't check in with the D.A. soon, they'd be putting out an all-points bulletin on Savvy, thinking she'd skipped town when she was still the only suspect they had in the Rodriguez murder case.

Which didn't make much sense. Dawson scratched his head. Why had the D.A. allowed Savvy to go free? If they even remotely suspected her of killing Tomas Rodriguez, they should arrest her and lock her up. She'd be better off in a jail cell than roaming the streets, where the Rodriguez cartel could take potshots at her.

He'd have to check in with Frank Young and figure out the D.A.'s motives. Something smelled fishy, almost as though Young wanted Savvy to be a target, wanted Rodriguez to make a move on her.

Did he plan to use her as a way to draw out the drug lord? Or did he want her dead to cover up for the real murderer?

A quick glance behind him confirmed that the woman in jeopardy slept on, unaware of the direction of his thoughts. He pulled his cell phone from his pocket and entered the bathroom, closing the door between himself and Savvy. He hit the speed-dial number for Audrey at the Lone Star Agency.

"Good morning, Dawson, did you hear from Jack?" Audrey's crisp professional voice went a long way toward grounding Dawson.

"Yes, ma'am. He's supposed to be here sometime later today."

"Good," she said. "I have a P.I. job for you when you get back."

Dawson shook his head in an attempt to pull it out of Laredo and back to San Antonio and his next assignment. But try as he might, he couldn't shake the feeling he was missing something here. That he'd be leaving a job unfinished. "Could you run a check on D.A. Frank Young?"

"I did a little background check with the police databases as I do on all our clients and didn't find anything suspicious. He's a district attorney, after all."

"I know, but he's also human. Could you check into him a little more and see just how human? Maybe tap into his accounts, see if he's taking any payoffs. I don't know, just look."

"Why?"

"Call it a gut feel."

"Will do." Audrey paused. "When can I expect you back in San Antonio? I need to give our new client an idea of when we'll get started on the investigation."

"I'll let you know after I speak with Jack."

Audrey paused. "You know, Dawson, you can change your mind if you want."

"About the P.I. job?"

"That and your current assignment. If you want to stay, you can."

His hand tightened on the phone, thoughts of his upcoming handoff with Jack filled his mind, leaving him more convinced than ever he was doing the right thing. "I'll be coming back. I just don't know when."

"That's fine. Just know that you can change your mind."

"I won't." He sucked in a deep breath to loosen the tightness in his chest. "Let me know if you find anything on Young. If not me, Jack." He hit the end button without waiting for a response.

He faced the mirror and stared at his reflection without seeing it, his thoughts leaping ahead to the meeting between him and Jack.

How would Savvy feel about being left in Jack's care? Would she be relieved since she knew he had never wanted the job in the first place? Or would she feel betrayed, let down, failed by Dawson? Especially after what had happened between them last night.

No use borrowing trouble, Dawson's mother had always told him. He'd know soon enough. In the meantime, he could get a head start on the day. He jerked the faucet handles and grabbed his shaving gear from the gym bag he'd left on the counter the night before.

SAVVY LAY TRAPPED *inside a car, her seat belt restraining her in a choke hold against the back of her seat. She couldn't reach the release button with the door smashed in, pushing against her thigh. But she had to get out, had to check on the baby.*

"Help me," she yelled, hoping someone would hear her. She glanced over to the man sitting in the driver's seat.

Covered in blood, he lay crushed against the steering wheel. Blood coated his hair, the seat, the dash, every surface in view.

Savvy looked down at her arm. Everywhere she looked was blood. On her sleeve, her hands and the side of her face, making her hair stick to her skin. Was it her blood

*or his? She looked at the man beside her, her stomach
lurching. He didn't move, his chest neither rising nor falling. Dead. A chill slithered over her, shaking her body.
Who was he?*

*Shouldn't she know who he was? She'd been riding with
him. Surely she knew him. Over her shoulder, a whimper
alerted her to the occupant of the backseat. A baby's weak
cries wrenched her heart and made her try even harder to
get out of her seat to get to the child trapped in the back.*

*Her vision blurred, the light filtering through the bro-
ken windshield fading at the edges. "Don't cry, baby," she
called. "Everything will be okay," she lied, unable to help
herself or the baby. She drifted in and out of consciousness, trapped and unable to reach the belt's release.*

*A bright light lit the sky, shining down into her eyes,
and suddenly she was free of the seat belt, floating through
space, unable to get her feet beneath her. She drifted toward the bright light where a figure awaited her. A small
child with coppery curls held out her hand. She smiled
and waved, her chubby cheeks dimpling in her happiness.*

*Savvy reached out to the angelic child, her arms ach-
ing to hold her.*

*The tiny girl turned and toddled into the light, closing a
door between them with a soft click, the light extinguished
except for what escaped around the edges.*

Savvy sat up in bed, her heart pounding against her rib
cage, perspiration slick across her forehead. She searched
the room for the baby. Where was she? Where was the
coppery-haired child? Of the two doors in the room, light
shone from beneath only one.

Throwing the sheets to the side, Savvy leaped from the
bed and stumbled toward the door. With every step, the
room grew darker, her vision blurring. She had to get to
the baby. At last, she reached the door and flung it open.

Instead of a baby, a man stood in front of her, bare chested, his face covered in white foam, dark brown eyes widening.

She swayed.

He dropped a razor into the sink and reached out, pulling her against his chest. "What's wrong, Savvy?"

"Where's the baby?" She fisted her hands and pounded against his chest. "Where is she?"

"Savvy." His hands slipped around her back and he hugged her to him. "She's not here."

"But where is she?" Savvy banged her fists against his chest again, with less force, her body sagging into his. "Where is she?" Tears trickled down her cheeks, sobs rising from her throat.

"I don't know." For a long moment he held her in his arms. What else could he do? He couldn't answer her questions, didn't know who Savvy really was or what the child in the picture meant to her. "I saw her. She went through a door." Her cheek pressed into his chest, her moving lips soft upon his skin.

"You were dreaming, sweetheart."

"No. It was real." Her fists loosened and her fingers threaded through the hairs on his chest. "She was real, wasn't she?"

"I'm sorry, Savvy." He held her, his heart thumping against her ear. "The only person in here is me." His hand stroked down the back of her neck, smoothing over her hair and lower to capture her waist and pull her closer. "It's okay. Shh." He pressed his cheek against the uninjured side of her head.

"I was in a car wreck and I couldn't get to...to the child in the backseat. When I did get out of the car...she was... gone." A sob choked off her last word. "It felt so real." She looked up at him through moisture-filled eyes. "Do you think it was a memory?"

He reached out and brushed away one lone tear slipping down her cheek. "I don't know. Maybe."

"Was the child the baby in the picture?" Her voice dropped to a whisper and her chin dipped until she stared at his chest, hopelessness sweeping over her in waves. "Did she die?"

He didn't have the answers she wanted. How could he? His hands slipped to the back of her neck and he rubbed the skin, massaging away the tension.

"I know." Her lips lifted in a sad smile. "We just met. How could you know?" She stared at the hands resting against his naked chest, her eyes widening as she realized for the first time she stood in his embrace and she wasn't wearing a stitch of clothing. Heat rose from her chest all the way up to the roots of her hair. "I'm sorry."

She backed away, racing from the bathroom to the bedroom where she snatched at her clothing, slipping into her jeans and T-shirt. Once dressed, Savvy took several deep breaths before she faced the open bathroom door. Dawson rubbed the remaining shaving cream off his face with a towel.

Savvy couldn't meet his gaze, memories of their lovemaking filling every corner of the room. In the light of day, Dawson didn't seem at all affected by what had occurred between them.

She wrapped her arms around herself, her body trembling from the emotions the dream had evoked and the raw lust overwhelming her senses. "We should go."

The gulf widened between them. Knowing she should have welcomed the distance, both mentally and physically, Savvy's gut clenched and she missed the warmth of Dawson's arms around her, his body pressed against hers.

Her hands tingled; her arms ached to hold him. When she risked a look into his eyes, she staggered backward.

His gaze held hers for a long, electrifying moment. If he'd held out his arms, she'd have fallen right into them. But he didn't. "You're right," he said. "We should go."

WHILE DAWSON REPACKED his gym bag, Savvy closed herself in the bathroom, emerging clean faced with her hair tucked under the Fighting Iguanas hat.

Leaving her with McDermott was the only way to make his heart settle down behind his ribs. The only way he could regain any focus in this crazy world.

Savvy stood in the jeans, T-shirt and hat, looking like a kid lost in a grown-up world, afraid of everything, including him.

Dawson's hand tightened around the fabric handle of the bag. He wanted to tell her she shouldn't be afraid of him, but on second thought, he decided she *should* fear him. He feared himself and the tumult of emotions that had been spilling out of him since he'd met her in the hospital. The sooner they met up with Jack, the better.

Savvy moved toward the door. Before she could reach for the handle, Dawson stepped in front of her. "I'll go first." He clapped a cowboy hat on his head, tugging it low over his forehead. He pulled the curtain back on the window and checked the parking lot. After careful scrutiny, he let the curtain fall back in place. "I'll bring the truck around to pick you up. Lock the door after I leave, and stay here and watch through the window until I wave you forward. Got it?"

She nodded, rubbing her arms.

Dawson opened the door and stepped out into the morning sunshine, its heat already warming the pavement. He closed the door behind him and walked quickly toward the rear of the building where he'd parked the truck, his gaze darting in all directions. Not that he expected to see anything, but he couldn't be too careful after the attempts on Savvy's life.

When he reached the truck, Dawson performed a quick once-over, searching beneath the chassis, bed and hood before he opened the door and climbed in. Leaving Savvy for even a moment made him anxious to get back to her. What if in that one minute someone grabbed her? His heart sped up as he twisted the key in the ignition, firing up the truck's engine. He couldn't drive around town long with Savvy in the truck. The vehicle was too big to blend in, and was probably targeted by the cartel.

He shook his head, shifting into gear. What did he care? Savvy would soon be Jack's problem. He just hoped the agent arrived in a nondescript rental car, not easily traced to Jack or the agency.

As he pulled up to the door of their room, he panned the parking lot and the street beyond. He shifted into Park and climbed out.

The door to the motel room burst open and Savvy ran out, her face even whiter than before. "Go!" she yelled as she reached for the passenger door and yanked it open. "Go!"

Dawson jumped in and slammed the shift into Drive. As soon as Savvy sat in her seat, he gunned the accelerator, shooting them forward.

As the vehicle cleared the parking lot, its wheels spinning out onto the street, Savvy ducked in the seat and shouted, "Faster!"

Dawson obeyed, accelerating from five to fifty in seconds. He glanced in the rearview mirror.

Two dark sedans sat in the motel parking lot.

He cursed and took a corner too fast, slipping down another street. "What happened?" His attention alternated between the street in front of him and his rearview mirror.

"The hotel manager just phoned to say he'd received a call asking him if a Dawson Gray or Savvy Jones had checked in. He'd told them he wasn't allowed to give out that kind of information. Having had run-ins with the local cartels before, he thought he should let us know." Savvy's head came up and she peered over the back of the seat. "Did they follow us?" She pulled her seat belt over her lap and shoulder and buckled it into place.

"Not so far." He made another turn, speeding down the streets, putting as much distance between them and the seedy motel as he could before he felt they'd made a clean getaway. Not until then did he manage to take a steadying breath, letting it out slowly. He loosened his white-knuckled grip on the steering wheel and turned toward her. "Where to?"

"The Desert Moon Hotel."

Dawson wasn't surprised at her request. She'd follow any lead that could possibly reveal anything about herself, her past, her former life. He surprised himself by nodding without argument. "Right after we ditch the truck."

Dawson pulled up his GPS and searched for a rental-car dealer. Keeping to the side roads and off the main thoroughfares, he got them there without further incident, parking the truck in the back lot and driving away in a light gray sedan, so much like any other relatively inexpensive car filling the streets of Laredo.

He glanced at his watch. Noon. He had at most six more hours until he met with Jack. Six more hours of keeping Savvy alive before she became another man's responsibility.

She sat in the seat beside him, her gaze sweeping the

streets like a professional soldier on the lookout for the enemy. Her gaze swung to his and she blushed.

"What?" she asked.

"Nothing." For the next few minutes, he kept his eyes on the road, refusing to look at her. "When we get to the hotel, I want you to stay in the car."

She shook her head before he finished his sentence. "We already went through this. I'm no safer in the car than in the hotel with you. Rodriguez's men are everywhere. They'll find me."

He pushed a hand through his hair. "I hate it when you're right. Then again, we shouldn't go there at all."

He almost grinned when her gaze swung toward him, a fierce light burning in her eyes. "Then I'll go without you."

"Don't get your britches in a twist. We're here." He drove up to the back side of the Desert Moon Hotel, where delivery vans lined up along the loading dock. "Seems our Mr. Pearson has a rather large expense account. Stay close to me and keep that hair under your hat." Dawson parked the sedan between two similar cars in the employee parking area and got out, leaving his cowboy hat on the backseat.

Savvy emerged from the car, tucking loose strands of wispy strawberry blonde hair beneath the brim of her baseball hat. She moved ahead of him toward a back door.

Dawson caught up and laid a hand on her arm. "Let me take the lead." Once inside the building, they moved through the hallways where the staff worked. Dawson peered in several doors before he found the one he wanted, marked Laundry. "Wait here."

He parked Savvy behind a large rolling bin of soiled tablecloths and napkins standing in the outside hallway. Then he slipped through the doorway into the laundry room. Once inside, he worked his way across the room filled with washing machines, dryers and folding tables.

Two women worked with their backs to the door, moving from machine to table, swapping loads and folding in swift, efficient motions. When they had a load folded, they moved the clean linens to the shelves Dawson hid behind.

Dawson waited until they had a new load of linen to fold and made his move, snatching a maid's uniform, a restaurant waiter's shirt and a large white napkin.

He turned to make good his escape when another woman entered the room pushing a large bin of soiled linens, and parked it next to where Dawson stood. "Here's another load that needs washin'," she shouted over the constant hum of the machines in motion. Then she turned toward the shelves, gathering freshly laundered sheets and pillowcases.

The ladies at the table looked over their shoulders and nodded, returning to their folding without speaking.

Loaded with a stack of clean bed linens, the other woman left, the door swinging shut behind her.

The bin of soiled tablecloths looked just like the one he'd left Savvy hiding behind. Blood surged through his veins at the thought of Savvy roaming around the hotel without him.

Only halfway through the pile of clean sheets, the women continued folding, unaware of the man watching them.

Dawson made a dash for the door, but when he passed the bin of dirty laundry, it wiggled.

"Savvy?" he whispered in a voice he hoped the women at the table wouldn't hear.

"Dawson?" Savvy swam to the surface of the tablecloths. "Thank God it's you."

He shook his head and ducked low when one of the

women at the table glanced over her shoulder toward the spot where he stood. "What are you doing in there?" he said through the canvas of the laundry bin.

"It was either jump in or be escorted out for trespassing."

Dawson groaned and peeked over the top of the bin at the ladies. They weren't looking, so he stared down into the bin at Savvy. "What am I going to do with you?"

She frowned, her reddish-gold brows drawing together. "You could try getting me out for a start."

"Right." After another glance at the working women, he scooped his hands beneath Savvy's back and legs and lifted her over the top.

Savvy's arm slipped around his neck and she held on tight as Dawson dropped down behind the bin with her still in his arms.

Her hat fell to the floor, her hair tumbling down around her shoulders in large loose waves, sending wafts of fragrant floral scents beneath his nose.

Dawson inhaled, loving the feel of her against him, the soft warmth of her body molded to his. His groin tightened uncomfortably behind his button fly. Even when he tried to put last night behind him, his body refused to forget.

"It works better if you let me go," she said, her breathy voice doing all kinds of crazy things to the silent vows of abstinence he'd instituted just that morning.

He loosened his hold, but her arm didn't slide away from the back of his neck.

Her gaze locked on his mouth, her own parting enough to let her tongue slide out and sweep across her coral-colored lips.

Captured in her trance, Dawson couldn't look away from those tempting, moist lips. Of its own accord, his head dipped low, claiming her mouth beneath his.

Her arm tightened around him, the other rising to curl around the side of his face, bringing him closer still.

The sound of a dryer door banging shut jerked him back to the laundry room. He lifted his head and stared down into wide emerald-green eyes.

"What am I going to do with you?" Her whispered words echoed his of a moment ago. "I shouldn't, but I can't help it." She reached up and brought his face down to hers again, kissing him back, her tongue sliding between his teeth to tangle with his.

On his knees in a laundry room, holding Savvy against him, Dawson lost himself to the moment. For the second time in two years, he'd forgotten about Amanda and all he'd lost—and forgotten why he couldn't ever love again.

Voices grew louder until Dawson came out of the trance and realized the women were headed toward the last bin of dirty laundry. Clenching Savvy to his chest, he tossed the items he'd gathered on top of her, ducked low and slipped behind a shelf loaded with clean tablecloths, where he stood up straight, letting Savvy slide down his body to her feet.

The bin rolled away with the women, leaving the path clear to the doorway. The time had come for Savvy and Dawson to make their move.

"Here." Dawson handed Savvy the maid's uniform and the large white napkin. "Put that on and cover your hair with the napkin."

Savvy slipped the dress over her T-shirt and stepped out of her jeans, exposing long, pale legs, trim and sexy. She tied the napkin around her hair like a scarf, tucking the loose ends out of sight.

Dawson averted his gaze from her legs, his groin tightening uncomfortably as he remembered how those legs felt wrapped around his waist. He sucked in a deep breath in an attempt to calm his racing heart. Then he rolled up his sleeves and pulled the waiter's shirt over his shoulders, careful to cover the entire chambray shirt beneath.

Then, grabbing Savvy's hand, he raced for the doorway. A quick peek revealed an empty hallway, and they were on their way to find Vance Pearson's room, slowing as they reached the door leading to the kitchen.

Dawson winked at her. "Follow my lead." He stepped through the swinging doorway, grabbed a tray, a plate, a metal food cover and a set of silverware rolled in a white napkin.

Before the cooks or other waitstaff even knew they'd been there, they left, Dawson balancing the tray on his shoulder like a pro.

"You've done this before?"

"Spy stuff?" They reached the front lobby, where Dawson glanced left then right. With the coast clear, he made his way straight to the concierge's desk.

Savvy hurried alongside him, a smile twitching at her lips. "No, waiter stuff."

Dawson marveled at how she could smile when so many attempts had been made on her life already. She was tougher than she even knew herself. His chest swelled with an entirely different emotion than the earlier lust he'd been experiencing toward this woman. Admiration? For a woman he barely knew?

The concierge didn't look up until Dawson stood in front of him and cleared his throat.

"Yes?" He raised his brows and stared at him as if Dawson were a lowlife. "You must be new around here. Members of the kitchen staff do not belong in the lobby."

"Sorry. We're supposed to deliver this to Mr. Pearson's room, but I forgot the room number."

The concierge stared down at a computer monitor,

clicked a few keys on a keyboard and answered in a pompous voice, "Fourth floor, room 4212. And in the future, stay out of the lobby."

Dawson turned toward the elevators.

The concierge's voice called out after him, "Take the service elevator, for heaven's sake."

Guessing his way through the corridors, Dawson headed back toward the hallway leading to the kitchen.

"Here." Savvy pointed down a side hall where a service elevator stood open, its plain metal floor scuffed and dirty. They stepped in and pressed the button for the fourth floor.

The door closed before another member of the kitchen or cleaning staff could climb in.

As the elevator rose to the fourth floor, Savvy sucked in a deep breath, willing her pulse to slow from its mad pace. "I've never done this before."

"How do you know?"

"I don't remember. I just know."

"You'll know everything before long at the rate you're going."

She sighed. "I hope so."

The elevator door opened and they stepped out and through another door leading into the guest hallway. The room they wanted was halfway down the hall on the left.

Vance Pearson stepped out of the door, a cell phone pressed to his ear, headed toward them.

Savvy and Dawson ducked back into the service entry before Pearson could look up.

He passed by them to get to the guest elevators the next door down. As he paused in front of the car, his voice echoed softly off the hallway walls. "Yes, I'm sure it's her. She looks just like the picture. If you'll do a web search on Laredo's newscast from last night, you might catch a glimpse yourself...The D.A. assigned a bodyguard, so she should be okay for now…I will…No, I'll be here when you arrive…Yes, sir. We'll get her."

Savvy gasped, the sound covered over by the ding of the elevator arriving.

Dawson slipped his free arm around her waist and held her against him until the swish of the elevator door indicated Pearson had gone.

"Do you think he was talking about me?"

"Yes."

"What did he mean by 'we'll get her'?"

"I don't know." And Dawson didn't like not knowing. Having Humberto Rodriguez and his thugs after Savvy was enough of a challenge. What did Pearson want with her? "Let's check out his room."

A maid's cart stood outside the room next to 4212; the door was wide open and a maid was inside scrubbing the bathroom.

Before Dawson could protest, Savvy ducked through the open door.

Dawson waited outside, eavesdropping on her conversation.

"Could you let me into 4212? Mr. Pearson asked to have a tray delivered for when he gets in for lunch."

An older woman emerged, grumbling about carrying your own set of keys. Savvy followed, a hint of a smile lifting the corners of her lips.

Dawson had the uncontrollable urge to kiss her.

Once the older woman opened the door, she returned to the room she'd been cleaning.

Dawson and Savvy entered Vance Pearson's room, closing the door behind them.

"Make it quick," Dawson warned. "Otherwise the maid might decide to see what's taking us so long."

Savvy opened drawers quickly and quietly, rifling

through socks and underwear while Dawson checked the suitcase in the closet and the clothing hung on hangers.

Other than a newspaper from Boston and luggage tags marked San Antonio, Dawson found nothing.

Savvy stood beside the telephone on the nightstand, staring down at a blank pad of paper. She lifted it and tilted it to the side.

Dawson stepped up behind her. "Find something?"

"I don't know. Look." She held the notepad up to the light. "Are those indentations?"

Dawson took the pad from her and tipped it several times to catch the shadows from the overhead light. "Yeah. Let's get out of here."

He tucked the notepad in his back pocket, hooked her elbow and led her toward the door.

With his hand hovering on the door handle, Dawson paused and listened, peering through the tiny peephole. A man's voice, muffled by the soundproof door, grew louder as though moving down the hallway toward them.

Savvy touched his arm. "What's wrong?" she whispered.

"Someone in the hall," he answered quietly. "Get in the closet just in case."

Savvy slid open the closet doors beside Dawson and stepped inside. "What about you?"

"Leave a little space. I want to see who it is." As he said the words, a man's face appeared in the view of the peephole. The man glanced right then left before he looked down at the door-locking system.

Dawson slipped into the closet beside Savvy and closed the door all except a crack. "It's not Pearson, but he's coming in."

Chapter Ten

Savvy's breath caught and held as she stood behind Dawson in the darkness of the closet.

"Be ready," he said, his hand finding hers and holding tight.

Her heart pounded so hard against her ears she could barely hear the click of the lock disengaging.

Dawson leaned into the small opening he'd left in the sliding glass door. His shoulders tensed, his hand tightening on hers.

The soft *whoosh* of the door opening barely disturbed the utter silence. Savvy was afraid to breathe lest the man hear her and discover them hiding in the closet.

The room's air conditioner kicked on, providing a steady hum, drowning out the smaller noises, including the movement of the man's feet against the carpet.

A tense squeeze from Dawson's hand tugged her against him. He leaned into her ear, his breath stirring tiny tendrils of hair, tickling her neck. "Be ready."

Ready? Ready for what? An attack? Gunfire? Going to jail for breaking and entering, on top of a looming charge of murder? She wanted to ask but feared she'd make too much noise, so she kept her mouth shut and braced her feet for fight or flight.

"Now." Dawson silently slid the closet door open, peeked out and then made a dash for the door.

Savvy didn't see the man, but footsteps sounded on the tiles in the bathroom. She tiptoed after Dawson.

He pulled the door open and pushed Savvy through, following behind her.

"Hey!" a man shouted behind them as the door swung shut.

Savvy glanced back long enough to register the dragon tattoos on a burly arm. Fear almost stopped her in her tracks.

"Run!" Dawson urged.

Jerked out of her stupor, Savvy swerved around the maid's cart and raced toward the nearest stairwell, certain the elevator would take too long to open. She shoved through the door, Dawson pushing from behind. As quickly and quietly as she could, she took the stairs down to the lobby, never looking back, the image of a gun-toting bad guy firmly implanted in her head.

At the bottom of the staircase, Dawson held out a hand to stop her. "Wait." He paused and listened. No sounds of footsteps echoed in the stairwell. "If he followed us, he's not taking the stairs." He peeled out of his waiter-uniform top and rolled his sleeves down.

Savvy stared down at her dress. "I don't suppose we can swing by the laundry room for my jeans?"

Dawson shook his head. "Afraid not. We're better off getting out while we can. Stay here." He ducked out of the stairwell and closed the door behind him.

Savvy huddled in the corner, out of sight of the small window in the door, her ears perked, taking in every sound that could be a man chasing after them. The thirty seconds it took for Dawson to return stretched like hours. She'd become too dependent on him already and she didn't like being dependent on anyone. Her brows wrinkled. Another memory? She tried to picture anything in her clouded past that would make her resentful of dependency on others. Nothing. The vacant abyss of her former life stretched like an endless black sea.

The door swung open, shaking her from her depressing thoughts. She held her breath until Dawson's head peered around the corner.

She blew the air from her lungs, relief at seeing him outweighing the depression over her lack of memories.

"Ready?" He held out his hand.

So she was dependent on him. Was that a bad thing? She placed her hand in his, the warmth of his fingers curling around hers, filling her with hope and a sense of well-being she hadn't managed to manifest on her own since she'd woken up in the hospital. What if she never got her memory back? Would her next bodyguard be as good as Dawson? Would he keep her alive no matter who came after her? Would he stay with her until the real murderer was found? A chill shook her in the musty stairwell.

Some of her fears must have shown in her face, because Dawson leaned close and cupped her chin. "We'll be okay. Come on, let's get out of here."

It took less time to get out of the hotel than it had to sneak in. Within two minutes they reached the rental car.

Dawson settled into the driver's seat and turned the key, a smile pulling at the corners of his lips. "That was close."

"Please tell me you didn't enjoy that." Savvy slipped into the only pair of jeans she had left, tugging the maid's uniform over her head before she glared across at the smile on his face.

His grin widened. "I found it exhilarating."

Savvy shook her head, unable to keep her own lips from

twitching. When Dawson smiled, her insides flipped over. Her smile died away. "You should smile more often."

As quickly as it had come, his smile vanished. "Yeah? Why?"

She could have kicked herself for saying anything. If she'd kept her mouth shut maybe he'd still be smiling despite himself. "It makes you less scary."

"Smiling isn't part of the job description."

"It should be."

Dawson dug in his dash console and unearthed a pencil. "Let's hope this works." He laid the pencil flat on the paper and rubbed it back and forth over the indentations until letters and numbers appeared.

Savvy read the letters aloud. "E. Jameson." She looked up at him, her eyes narrowing. "Does the name ring a bell to you?"

"Maybe. It has a familiar ring." He looked around the parking lot before he shifted into Drive. "Let's go somewhere less public and I'll make a call to the boss to look up the name and number."

"E. Jameson." Savvy let the name roll off her tongue. Something tickled at the back of her mind. "I feel like I should know it." She closed her eyes and tipped her head upward, digging deep into the darkness of her damaged mind. The void stretched endlessly, and at last she sighed and shrugged. "It's as though all my memories are on the edge of my mind, waiting for a door to open and let them out. I know they're there, but they just won't come to me."

Dawson lifted her hand and squeezed. "They'll come back, in time."

"I'd hoped we'd find something. Mr. Pearson acted as though he knew something about me. And why did he ask if Jameson meant anything to me?"

"I have my boss checking on the name." Dawson pulled

into a back street, headed away from the hotel. "He could have been telling you anything to get an interview."

"Or he really could know something." Her lips pressed into a line. The urge to stay at the hotel made her ready to risk being discovered. Anything to learn more about her past. "Maybe we should have stayed and met with Mr. Pearson in person."

"No. It's too dangerous. The man snooping through his room was the same one who tried to smother you in the hospital. If Pearson really does know more about you, the man in his room could have been looking for that information to get to you again."

Savvy opened her mouth to argue, but before she could utter a word, Dawson raised his hand.

"We can come back later. We've been in one place long enough for now. Besides, we're scheduled to meet with another agent from the Lone Star Agency."

His cell phone rang as if on cue. Dawson hit the talk button. "Hey, Jack, about time. Oh, you're not? When?"

A lead weight settled in Savvy's gut. He didn't say it, but she knew. The man he talked with was Dawson's replacement.

Sinking back in her seat, Savvy felt more alone now than when she'd woken up without a memory in the hospital. Not that she blamed Dawson. As he put it, he never wanted to be a bodyguard. He didn't want the responsibility of keeping anybody alive.

Her gaze slid sideways to where Dawson sat in the driver's seat talking with Jack. She'd miss Dawson's quiet strength and determination…and his broad, muscular shoulders. Her gaze traveled upward, pausing at his lips, moving to form words, her imagination taking her back to the night before. A slow burn drove deep inside her, angling low in her belly. The juncture of her thighs ached for more of the intimacies they'd shared.

A replacement for Dawson might be just what she needed to keep her mind and hands off the man. She needed to focus on saving her own skin.

DAWSON ARRANGED a meeting time and place that would kill two birds with one stone later that day, then hit the off button on his cell phone. Now that release was close at hand, Dawson wasn't as relieved as he had anticipated.

If he made the switch and Jack took over the job of safeguarding Savvy, Dawson could resume his life as a private investigator with nothing more pressing than catching a cheating spouse in the act. No bullets fired, no sleeping in the same room with a sexy witness to a cartel murder. *If* he made the switch.

No, *when* he made the switch.

A glance at Savvy made his gut tighten.

Huddled in the corner of the seat, hugging her arms close to her body, the baseball cap barely containing the mass of strawberry blonde hair, she gave him the impression of a lost child. Her green eyes stared out the windshield, the shadows beneath more pronounced than earlier.

Did she know he planned to leave her? If he went by the tightness of her lips and the shadowed gaze...probably. Did she care? After last night?

"What are you looking at?" she asked, giving him the full benefit of her frowning countenance. For a moment she just stared at him, her head tilted at a challenging angle, then she turned away, looking out the passenger-side window.

She knew, all right. "Jack's an excellent agent. I'd trust him with my life."

"That's *your* life." She kept her face averted, her jaw tight.

"He's been a bodyguard a long time."

"Yeah, I know. It's a job." She sighed, her voice dropping to little more than a whisper. "I'm just a job."

"No. You're more than that."

"To whom?" She snorted softly. "To the drug lord's thugs, I'm a hit job. To you and your friend Jack, I'm an assignment. To the D.A., I'm a witness or a suspect." She shrugged. "Just leave it, Dawson. You don't have to pretend to give a damn."

He sat in silence, fighting the urge to pull off the road, take this stubborn fighter into his arms and tell her that he cared. More than he'd expected, more than he'd wanted to. But if he did take her in his arms, something told him he might not let go. And he had to let go.

He kept his hands on the wheel, his eyes aimed forward, and drove to the Webb County Justice Center in the heart of Laredo, where the district attorney's office was housed.

Jack had called from the outskirts of San Antonio, having just left the city behind. He'd arrive in Laredo in two and a half hours, tops.

In the meantime, Dawson needed to check in with his boss for further information on Savvy Jones. But first they needed to check in with District Attorney Frank Young before he or someone else on the local police force called out a warrant for Savvy's arrest.

He parked at the rear of the justice center on the second floor of the public parking deck between two other cars of equally indistinguishable markings. Then he unfolded his long length from behind the car's steering wheel, wishing for the space and comfort of his truck.

Savvy emerged from her side of the car before Dawson could get around it to open her door.

Dawson's brows rose. "In a hurry to be incarcerated?"

"In a hurry to report in so I can get on with the business of finding the real killer—with or without your help." She marched toward the stairwell leading to the third-floor pedestrian bridge connecting the justice center with the parking deck.

His brows dipping downward, Dawson followed, keeping a close watch on the vehicles and people moving in and out of the parking garage. Savvy's remark had struck too close to home, causing his chest to tighten.

Hadn't he been having second thoughts about passing her off to Jack? Her words only served to spread the doubt further. Dawson still believed he wasn't the right man for the job. Lost in the bottle a little over two months ago, he'd barely dried out. How could Audrey or Savvy consider him up to the task of fighting off an enemy like the Rodriguez cartel? Then again, could he walk away knowing the danger Jack and Savvy faced? Could he leave her to her fate? His gut knotted and anger surged through his veins. He refused to feel guilty. Savvy Jones didn't mean anything to him. Nothing. Or did she? "Leave the investigating to the police."

"And what has that bought me so far?" She entered the stairwell and held on to the railing as she climbed the single flight of stairs to the third floor.

Dawson followed behind her, noting how slowly she moved up the steps. "Investigations take time."

Savvy stopped halfway up the steps and leaned against the wall, drawing in deep breaths, her face paler than when she'd stepped out of the car. "I don't have time, in case you hadn't noticed."

Dawson stepped up beside her and slipped an arm around her waist, a reluctant smile threatening to spread across his face. "The kitten has claws."

"Not at all." She shrugged out of his hold. "I just call it as it is." With a lift of her chin, she pushed past him and climbed three more steps before stopping to catch her breath. A tendril of long coppery hair slipped from beneath her cap and down her back, softening the tough-girl image she was trying so hard to portray.

The woman would pass out before she asked for his help. Dawson suppressed his smile and hooked an arm around her waist again, refusing to let go when she tried to disengage. "Look, if you want to get up to the D.A.'s office, let me help."

"I don't need your help, so just leave me alone."

"Not a chance. Not until I'm good and ready."

"What, in two hours?" She faced ahead, but allowed him to steady her as they climbed the last steps to the landing. "You can leave me now. I'll stay at the D.A.'s office until Jack gets to town."

He looked left, then right, scanning the arched windows of the justice center, the rooftop and the parking deck behind him. "Just shut up and make the crossing fast, will you?" He guided Savvy forward, cocooning her body with his until they'd made it across the open area and into the building.

Not until they were safely through the door did Dawson relinquish his hold on her.

Savvy turned toward him, her face peachy pink, her color back and heightened. "Really, I can find my way from here. You can just leave."

"I can't and I won't until—"

She waved her hand. "Until you have a replacement."

He captured her hand in his and stared down into her eyes. "Until I'm good and ready."

"Fine." Savvy pulled her hand free. "Then just stay

back while I meet with the D.A. I'm the one he wants to throw in jail."

She made her way to the elevator and read the signs on the wall indicating the location of each of the offices in the building.

Dawson pressed the up button for the elevator and the door slid open. "He's on the fourth floor."

"I was getting to that." Twin flags of color bloomed in her cheeks as she stepped past him into the empty car.

They rode up one floor in silence, the only sound that of the *ping* indicating they'd reached their destination.

When Savvy would have exited first, Dawson's hand held her in place. "I still have my job to do."

She stepped back, her arms crossing over her chest. "Then by all means, do it."

Dawson left the elevator, his hand over the door to keep it from closing behind him. He looked left, then right. Men and women dressed in everything from suits to jeans moved up and down the hallway. None of them looked dangerous, but Dawson couldn't rely on looks to see Savvy through this ordeal. Most important, none of the men or women seemed to be carrying weapons.

He turned back to Savvy. "All clear."

She rolled her eyes as she marched past him and to her right.

"Where are you going?" Dawson's lips twitched.

Savvy stopped, her shoulders stiff, her head held high. "He's back the other way, right?" she said without turning to face him.

"Right."

"I knew that." Spinning on the ball of her foot, she performed an about-face and marched past him and through the door marked District Attorney Frank Young.

"May I help you?" A pretty young assistant looked up

from behind a smooth mahogany desk lined with a computer, an in-box and a nameplate inscribed with the name Delores Sanchez.

Savvy ducked down to read the nameplate before speaking. "Miss Sanchez, I'd like to see the district attorney."

The woman studied Savvy, her brows dipping then rising into the sweep of hair draped over her forehead. "Oh, you must be Ms. Jones." Delores rose from her seat and rounded the desk to take Savvy's hands in hers. "I saw you on the news report last night. I almost didn't recognize you with the hat." She shook her head. "Between you and me, there isn't a man, woman or child in this city that doesn't appreciate you for what you did."

Savvy's brows drew together and she pulled her hands out of the young woman's grip. "I don't remember what I did."

The young woman bobbed her head. "Tomas Rodriguez was bad all around. He got away with raping women on both sides of the border." She shot a look over her shoulder. "Frank plea-bargained charges of drug possession last year, but I think he wishes he hadn't."

"Can we see him?" Savvy asked, nodding toward the closed door behind Delores's desk.

Delores's mouth twisted. "He's been asking for reports on your whereabouts. I know he'll want to see you. But he's got someone in his office right now. If you'll have a seat, he should be free shortly." The woman indicated a leather couch in the corner of the office.

Savvy sat as far over as she could on the couch.

A twinge of irritation made Dawson sit in the middle instead of taking the opposite end. He didn't like waiting. Not with a drug lord gunning for Savvy and informants on both sides of the border willing to do anything to stay on the right side of such an influential man.

He'd been mistaken to think she was safe, even here in the justice center. Sooner or later, they'd have to leave, and that's when she became most vulnerable. Dawson half rose from his seat, determined to get her out of the justice center as soon as possible.

Before Dawson could rise to his full height, the door to Frank Young's office burst open and a beautiful, well-dressed blonde in tailored pants, matching jacket and shoes marched through, pausing with her hand on the doorknob to turn back, her blue eyes shooting sparks. "You might as well hand over your bank accounts, Frank. There's not a court in the district that will side with you. Not with the evidence I have." She laughed, the sound mirthless and harsh. "I thought being district attorney meant upholding laws and morals." She snorted delicately. "Guess they don't count when it applies to you."

Frank Young strode toward the door. "Be reasonable, Diana. There's no need for divorce. You know my work. I have business meetings with clients. There's nothing going on." His gaze landed on Dawson and Savvy in the outer office and his mouth tightened into a straight line. "We'll discuss this at home."

"Right. And maybe you can explain why you buy expensive lingerie for business purposes." Diana tucked her mock-croc leather clutch under her arm. "There's nothing to discuss."

Dawson's gaze left the retreating woman in time to catch fury blazing from Young's eyes before the attorney turned a tight smile on Dawson and Savvy.

"You picked a remarkable time to check in." He waved his hand toward his office.

Dawson ushered Savvy into the man's office and closed the door behind him.

Young took a seat behind a large mahogany desk and stared across at Savvy. "Remember anything yet?"

"Not a thing," she replied.

Young's eyes narrowed. "Nothing about the shooting? Who you are? Your father, your family?"

She shook her head. "No."

"Are you sure you don't remember anything about your past? Where you lived? Anything?"

Dawson frowned. "She said she didn't."

Savvy touched his arm. "It's okay." She turned to Young. "No. I don't remember anything about anyone or anywhere that I might have been. Why?"

He shrugged. "Seems no one knows much about you around here, Ms. Jones." He pressed the tips of his fingers together in a steeple. "I've been running queries, even looked through some missing-persons reports."

Savvy leaned forward. "Did you find anything?"

"Maybe." He stared across the desk at her, his eyes narrowing. "As soon as I get some confirmation, we'll talk."

"If you know something, please tell me."

His brows rose. "I will, as soon as I know for certain. No use getting your hopes up if it's a false lead."

Savvy bit hard on her tongue, but didn't push.

Dawson hooked a hand through her elbow. "We can't stay. The longer we're here, the more likelihood of someone setting up a trap to get to Ms. Jones."

Young's brows rose. "Any problems?"

"A few. I won't go into detail. Just know that she's not safe in Laredo."

The D.A.'s lips thinned. "I'm counting on you to keep Sab—Ms. Jones alive. She's valuable to me…uh, to the case." Young stood, straightening the already-straight papers on his desk. "Now, if you'll excuse me, I have work to do."

"Can you tell us anything about the investigation?" Savvy moved forward. "Have they found any evidence there was another person in the alley when Tomas Rodriguez was killed?"

The district attorney shook his head. "So far, nothing. If in fact someone set you up to take the fall for Rodriguez's murder, he did a good job cleaning up behind himself."

"Did you perform a trace on the weapon?" Dawson asked.

"We did. It belonged to a man who'd reported it stolen from his home in Laredo two months ago."

Savvy's shoulders sagged. "If you don't find the killer, will I go to jail?"

"Based on the left-handed issue, I have the district court judge convinced to hold off arresting you for the murder of Tomas Rodriguez. But I don't know how long that will last. He'll be happy to know you haven't skipped town." He gave Savvy a pointed look. "You realize that Mr. Gray is part of the deal to keep you out of jail. Without him protecting you and also keeping tabs on your whereabouts, I'd be forced to arrest you and lock you up until we find out who really killed Tomas Rodriguez."

Dawson tugged on Savvy's arm. "Well, then, if it's all the same to you, we need to get out of here."

"Certainly." The district attorney waved toward the door. "Keep in touch, and take good care of our girl."

"You have my number." Dawson urged Savvy toward the door. "Until evidence is discovered that someone else shot Rodriguez, we're going to stay beneath the radar. Call me only in case of emergency."

"Will do." The D.A. hurried around the desk. Opening the door to his office, he stood back while Savvy and Dawson exited. As Savvy passed by, his eyes narrowed and he stared at her as if memorizing her features.

On the way down in the elevator Savvy stood silent, her hat drawn down, shadowing her eyes and masking her expression. She let Dawson lead the way out of the elevator and the building, head down, keeping her thoughts to herself.

Once inside the car, she sat with her face turned away, her fingers interlaced in her lap.

Dawson should have welcomed the silence. The less she said, the easier it would be for him to leave her. The closer he came to the meeting with Jack, the less he liked the idea of handing off the task of keeping her alive.

Dawson eased out of the parking garage, scanning the street to the left and right before pulling out into traffic.

Before they'd gone ten yards, a rusted-out heap of a car swung out of a side street and bore down on them, tires squealing against heated pavement.

"Get down!" Dawson reached out to shove Savvy's head down, but she'd beat him to it, tucking her head low in her lap.

He grabbed the steering wheel with both hands as the car drove up beside him, commanding the inside lane of oncoming traffic.

Dawson slammed his foot on the accelerator, ducking as low as possible while still being able to see over the dash.

Cars honked and swerved, but the junker kept up with the rental car.

The passenger window slid downward.

This can't be good. Dawson's heart slammed against his ribs. He didn't have time to think, only react. "Hold on!"

Chapter Eleven

Savvy glanced up as the passenger window of the junker slid downward and a steel-gray, metal barrel poked through the opening and a man with a pockmarked face glared at her.

"He's got a gun!" she shouted.

Dawson slammed on the brakes, bringing the car to a screeching halt.

Savvy lurched forward and her head bumped against the dash, a sharp pain slashing through the wound at her temple. Dizzying lights flashed across her vision.

A loud bang erupted from the car running alongside them, followed by a thunk against their rental's metal car frame.

"Tell me they're not shooting at us," she cried.

"Okay, I won't tell you. But you might want to hang on." Dawson shoved the gearshift into Reverse, spinning the car around.

Savvy looked up, glancing through the seats to the rear window as cars all around them screamed to a halt, barely missing them.

Brake lights shone on the rusty car, and then white lights.

"They're backing up!" Savvy yelled.

Dawson jerked the steering wheel to the left, swinging the sedan into the traffic going the opposite direction.

The driver of an SUV swerved to avoid them, hitting his horn in protest.

Undeterred, Dawson gunned the accelerator, the rear tires spinning against the hot pavement. Once the tires got traction, the car shot forward, headed straight toward a building on the opposite side of the street. Dawson hung on to the steering wheel, turning left, his knuckles white, muscles bulging. The car hopped the curb up onto the sidewalk. Pedestrians scattered, screaming obscenities and shaking their fists.

Savvy prayed they didn't hit someone; at the same time, she prayed they'd live through yet another attack.

The rusty car made a similar turn, only it wasn't so lucky and crashed into a power pole.

The blessed wail of sirens filled the air, giving Savvy hope this particular chapter in her nightmare had come to an end.

Apparently even the shooters in the rusted-out car didn't relish a run-in with the local police force. After several attempts to start the engine failed, the junker's doors flew open and two men bailed out of the car and hit the pavement running, disappearing down side roads.

Savvy's body jerked back and forth as the car bumped off the sidewalk onto the pavement. The first police car rounded a corner, lights blazing and sirens earsplittingly loud, followed closely by an identical cruiser.

Dawson eased to the side of the road to allow the two cruisers to pass. Then, as casually as any other rubbernecker, he pulled back into traffic and drove away.

Savvy sat up, a hand pressed to her chest, her heart beating so fast she thought she'd pass out. "That was close."

"Too close." Dawson stared straight ahead, the rugged

lines of his face hard, as though carved of granite. The only indication of the emotions running through him was the tic in his jaw.

With a shaky laugh, Savvy shook her head. "I'm starting to feel like a runner doing sprints over and over." Savvy sucked in a deep breath and blew it out. "Every time I dare take a breath, we're running from the bad guys again."

He nodded. "We could use a little help here."

"Maybe a little." Savvy tried to laugh, failing miserably. "Do you get the feeling all of Laredo is out to kill me?"

Dawson glanced across at her, a smile lifting the corners of his lips. "I have to admit, you're holding up better than I would have expected."

"I was raised to be tougher than I look."

"By whom?" Dawson asked.

"I don't know." As soon as Dawson had asked the question, Savvy's mind had shut down, refusing to give her a reason why she should say such a thing. "Wow, I don't know."

"I'll bet my paycheck your memory will come back before the week's out."

"I hope it comes back sooner." She stared out at the cars moving by, searching for more men with guns ready to take her out. "I've only been out of the hospital for a day. I can't imagine dealing with this kind of stress for an entire week."

Dawson nodded but didn't comment, his forehead drawn into a deep frown.

"Even without the drive-by shooting, the meeting with the D.A. was strange. Do you think he really knows more about me than he's letting on?"

Dawson shrugged. "I don't know. I don't trust the man."

"What did you make of Young's wife?" Savvy asked, casting a glance at Dawson.

"She seemed pretty mad."

"Think he's cheating on her?"

"It happens that way." Navigating a turn gave him reason not to provide further comment.

Savvy didn't give up easily. "Didn't you say you only did private investigations?" she asked. "What kind?"

"Missing persons, embezzlement, cheating spouses. I haven't been at it long, though." He glanced her way. "Why?"

"Do you ever get a gut feel about cheating spouses?"

"I try to keep my opinions to myself until I get evidence one way or another."

"Very noble." She sat beside him, her fingers tapping against the armrest.

"Don't borrow trouble, Savvy."

"Because I have enough already?" Her lips twitched on the beginnings of a smile.

"Exactly."

She tapped her forehead. "Why can't I remember?"

When he opened his mouth to say something, she shook her finger at him. "And don't tell me it takes time. You and I both know I don't have time."

"What do you want me to say?"

"Anything, something." She flung her hand in the air. "Nothing."

"I've learned you can't make things better by wishing."

"No, but we can by doing."

Dawson stopped at a traffic light, his head swiveling, taking in everything from all angles. "What do you suggest that doesn't involve breaking and entering?"

"Take me to the bar where I worked—work."

"It's too dangerous." His jaw set in granite, his mouth pressed into a thin straight line.

"Dawson, I can't keep running." She laid a hand on his

arm, the contact giving her a jolt of awareness she'd rather not be feeling for a man who wouldn't be around much longer. She jerked her hand back. "I have to get answers."

"Whoever is after you will have someone staking out the place." His gaze remained on the streets surrounding them. Not once did he look into her eyes.

"Then we sneak in the back door, and I wear my cap."

Dawson shook his head. "No."

Savvy held his gaze. "If you don't take me there, I'll find my own way."

"No. You can't go there."

"Okay, then." She turned away, grabbed the door handle and opened the car door right as the light turned green.

Dawson reached for her and missed.

She was on the pavement swinging the door shut before he could do anything about it.

The car behind them honked.

"Get in the car, Savvy."

"Not unless you'll take me to the Waterin' Hole." She leaned down to look him in the eye, ignoring the angry gestures from the man in the car behind her.

Dawson glared at her, the tic working in his jaw, but he didn't respond to her demand.

The horn sounded again, blasting against her eardrum. "Goodbye, Dawson."

Dawson yelled, "I'll take you, damn it. Get in."

Calmly, she turned to the man behind them and mouthed the word *sorry,* then climbed into the car and strapped on her seat belt. "Now, was that so hard?"

"God save me from hardheaded females." Dawson hit the accelerator, shooting the car through the intersection.

"And God save me from stubborn men. There are way too many in this world, as it is." She knew that because she'd been around far too many. That memory came through strong and clear along with an image of a white-haired man with green eyes.

The image hit her so unexpectedly Savvy gasped.

Dawson hit the brakes. "What's wrong? Did you hurt yourself?"

"No. I had a memory flash of a man with white hair and green eyes." She closed her eyes, scrunching her forehead, trying to recall him, to bring him back in her mind. "I can see him, but I can't remember his name."

"Are you sure it wasn't one of the doctors at the hospital?"

"Positive. Most of them had dark eyes and hair." Squeezing her eyes tight, she blocked out the sunlight, the buildings they passed and tuned out the sounds, willing her mind to latch on and hold the image of the man. "The man in my mind wore a suit, not scrubs."

"A white-haired man in a suit. Do you think he might have been the killer?"

She shook her head. "No. I didn't see him with a gun in his hand. I don't think he was the killer." She opened her eyes and stared around at the cars moving along the street. "Why him? Why would I remember a man in a suit with white hair and green eyes and nothing else?"

"Think about what we were talking about. Maybe something we said triggered the image."

Savvy huffed. "We were talking about stubborn men. I bet he was one of them. But who?" She buried her head in her hands, wincing when she encountered the bandage on her left temple. "No, the man in the memory didn't do this. I'm almost certain."

"Well, that's good. At least you know it's someone from your past and that he could be a stubborn man." Dawson grinned.

She frowned at him. "Are you laughing at me?" She

swatted at his arm, liking that he teased her; it eased the tension she'd felt since they'd made love in the motel room last night. "So the great Dawson Gray has a sense of humor? Who'd have thought?"

"Only when I'm around hardheaded females." He handed her his cell phone. "Bring up the browser on my cell phone and look up the address of the Waterin' Hole."

Savvy's heart skipped several beats. "You're really going to take me there?"

"Against my better judgment." He pulled off the road and parked behind a shop advertising Western wear. "After we improve your disguise a little. That hair is going to get us in trouble."

Her hand went to the cap barely holding all her hair up inside. "I could cut it."

Dawson shook his head. "Not an option."

So Dawson liked her hair. An unbidden wave of feminine satisfaction swept over Savvy. Followed closely by an internal reprimand. She was being stalked by a killer. Why should the fact that Dawson liked her hair be in the least important at a time like that?

WHILE SAVVY SLIPPED into a plain white shirt and jeans in the dressing room, Dawson ducked out the back and switched license plates with an employee's car in the back lot. One more precaution to driving around the streets of Laredo. Whoever shot at them earlier had been waiting for them to emerge from the justice center and probably knew their license number by now. If they were involved with the Rodriguez cartel, word would have spread. Every thug this side of the Rio Grande would be looking for their sedan with that license number.

At the very least, trading licenses would buy them a minute or two. Maybe.

Already, he regretted his promise to take her back to the bar where she'd worked and behind which she and Tomas Rodriguez had been gunned down.

On his way to the store's back door, his cell phone vibrated against his side. Jack.

"Hey, man, I'm in town."

"Change of plans, Jack. I'm taking Savvy to the bar where she worked. I need you to meet me there."

"You sure that's wise? Don't you think the Rodriguez cartel will be watching that place?"

"Yeah. I'm going to sneak her in." He sighed. "If I don't take her, she's hell-bent on going alone."

Jack chuckled. "Not only beautiful, she's got a mind of her own."

"You know what she looks like?" Dawson stood outside the shop, staring through the window in an attempt to catch a glimpse of the woman in question.

She stepped out of the dressing room and glanced around, presumably for him, her eyes wide and wary. When she spotted him through the window, her shoulders rose and fell as if on a deep sigh.

"Yeah," Jack said. "I saw a clip of her last night on the local news in San Antonio. Pretty as well as lethal, isn't she?"

"You don't know the half of it." Dawson thought of last night and how she'd felt in his arms, the smooth texture of her skin, the way her legs had wrapped around him, holding him inside her. Definitely lethal to his ability to keep her at a distance, both mentally and physically.

"I'll have my work cut out for me."

Dawson's hand tightened on the cell phone. "We need to talk about that when you get to the Waterin' Hole."

"Plan on it. I'll see you in a few." Jack hung up.

As he tucked the cell phone in his pocket, Dawson

glanced around at the busy streets, then he ducked back inside the shop.

Savvy met him, in the shirt and jeans, wearing a new pair of cowboy boots and carrying her old clothes. "I'll pay you back as soon as I can." She handed him the sales tags.

Dawson's glance ran from head to toe. "That'll help. But you need a bigger hat to hide the hair and face." He reached up and lifted a straw cowboy hat, inspected the size and settled it gently on her head. With her strawberry blonde hair hanging down around her shoulders, her makeup-free face exposing a sprinkle of freckles across her nose, she looked like the girl next door. Or a cowgirl on her way to a rodeo, not the woman leaving the hospital yesterday.

Savvy smiled up at him. "How do I look?"

Good enough to kiss. Dawson frowned at the thought he'd almost spoken aloud and the reaction he'd had to her in the cowgirl getup. He wanted to find the nearest stack of hay and tumble in it with her. His jeans tightened uncomfortably and he forced himself to turn away from her smile. "You'll do."

She flipped her head upside down, gathered her hair in a knot and shoved it into the hat. The brim hid her hair and shadowed her face enough to hide the color of her eyes.

Dawson would prefer her to be completely invisible when they walked into the Waterin' Hole. As it was, she'd been marked by someone for extermination. Someone with the power and money to get the job done.

He paid for their purchases and whisked her out of the store and into the sedan. The sun faded into the west, making the haze of dust turn pink over the streets of Laredo. The GPS he'd salvaged from his truck pointed the way back toward Savvy's apartment building and farther west toward a seedier business district where the brick-and-stucco buildings needed paint and repair more so than those found around the justice center.

The Waterin' Hole nestled between two taller buildings as though the alley had been filled in to create yet another building on the tightly packed street. Several pickups and a few SUVs lined the street in front of the bar and grill. Dawson would have preferred to enter when the place was empty, but the evening crowd had already started filtering in.

Dawson drove past the vehicles and the row of buildings, turned down another street. He parked a block behind the Waterin' Hole in an alley, hiding the rental car behind a stack of weathered wooden pallets and rolls of chain-link fencing.

Savvy reached for the door handle.

"Wait," Dawson said. "Let it get a bit darker before we go in."

She sat beside him, her hand on the door handle, her gaze panning the alley and as far as she could see beyond. "Do you think we'll have trouble?"

He pulled his pistol from the shoulder holster hidden beneath his leather jacket. "Count on it. Don't let your guard down for a minute."

She nodded.

Dawson glanced at her. "Want to change your mind?"

Savvy shook her head. "No. I need to find out more about that night."

"Let me do the asking, then. If you start talking, someone will be sure to recognize you."

"If I don't ask the questions, my memory might not be triggered."

"Hang back and let me do the talking. You can sit close by and listen."

She chewed at her full bottom lip, the subconsciously nervous act making Dawson crazy.

A sudden urge seized him. The urge to lean over and kiss away her worries, to take that bottom lip between his own teeth and bite down gently until she surrendered her lips to him.

Savvy pulled the photo of the child from her shirt pocket and stared down at it, her fingers smoothing over the child's smiling face. "Liz said I'd told her I didn't want to live my other life. I didn't want to end up like my father—whoever he is. Do you think I was running away from something when I came to Laredo?"

All traces of desire faded, to be replaced by a hard knot in his gut. The picture and her quietly voiced question reminded him of all he'd been running away from, himself. "Maybe."

She stared across the seat at him, her green eyes dark beneath the brim of the hat. "I want to know who she was."

"Even if it hurts?"

"Yes." She stared down at the picture. "I have to know."

Dawson gazed out at the darkening sky. "Then let's go." He shoved at the door and unfolded his long length from the car. If he sat another minute beside Savvy, he knew he'd take her in his arms and hold her until the hurt in her eyes faded.

Damn it. She was getting under his skin and he couldn't afford to let that happen. Not when her life depended on it. If he was honest with himself, he'd admit this woman threatened him like no other. He'd thought the wall he built around his heart was impenetrable after Amanda's death. Savvy and her single-minded determination to remember had a way of chipping away at his defenses, removing the barriers.

Savvy joined him at the rear of the vehicle, settling the hat lower over her forehead. "Shall we?"

When she stared ahead at the street but didn't move, he gave her a gentle nudge. "Keep your head lowered. I've got your back."

"Okay, here goes." With a deep breath, she set off toward the alley where she'd been found shot in the head.

Savvy paused in the shadows of a Dumpster, the white of her shirt hazy blue in the shadows. Would this place trigger the return of the rest of her memories?

Chapter Twelve

A dark shadow flitted across Savvy's memory as she crossed from the Dumpster to the back door of the bar and grill. A tingling sensation snaked across the back of her neck followed by a flash of memory skittering through the recesses of her mind, too fast for her to process or decipher. All she got out of it were faceless bodies moving through this very alley.

A jolt of fear spiked her adrenaline and sent her running toward the back door of the bar in a hurry to put the alley behind her. Was this why she couldn't remember? Was the incident too raw, too violent to recall? Was her mind protecting her from the shock of what had happened by shielding her from the reality of the situation?

Dawson stepped up behind her, his hand reaching for the doorknob before she could. "Wait." He stared into her eyes. His eyes were impenetrable pools of inky black in the poorly lit alley.

She trembled.

"We don't have to go in," he said. "We can leave and never come back. I have a bad feeling about this place."

"You and me both." Savvy shook her head. Despite her fear, the urge to push past him and into the bar had almost grown to a full-fledged panic attack. If he saw that, he might make her leave, refuse to let her go inside and ask the questions that might lead to clearing her of murder charges. "No. I'm fine." She forced a smile to her stiff face. "Really."

His sooty brows dipped toward his nose and he stared at her for a few seconds longer. Then he leaned forward and kissed her hard on the lips.

Surprised by the move, Savvy's lips parted on a gasp, allowing his tongue full access to her mouth. Before she could think of what she was doing, her hands slipped around his neck, dragging him closer, deepening the kiss until she didn't know where he ended and she began, bringing back every detail of their lovemaking of the night before.

As quickly as it had begun, the kiss ended and Dawson set her away from him.

Without an apology, he twisted the knob and pulled the door open. "I'll go in first." After a quick glance at the empty alley, Dawson stepped inside, tugging Savvy in behind him, his big warm hand clasped around her smaller, colder fingers. He turned and flicked the lock mechanism to secure the door behind her and keep anyone else from entering that way. "Stay here. I'll be right back."

She nodded, her mouth still tingling from the unexpected kiss, her mind swimming with random thoughts, one surfacing more prominently than the rest. She'd wanted the kiss to last longer. She wanted to repeat it until all the bad guys went away and nothing remained in the world but her and her bodyguard.

He left her standing there in the dark hallway and she was thankful for the brief moments away from his overwhelming presence.

Glad he'd agreed to bring her here in the first place, Savvy obeyed his directive. She tried not to think about the doorway at her back leading to the alley where this nightmare had begun. But a chill settled over her. She fought the desire to put as much distance between herself and that alley where Tomas Rodriguez had died and she'd been left for dead.

Even though she couldn't specifically remember what had occurred there, she knew it was bad. Perhaps she remembered, or maybe the story of how she'd been found filled in more blanks than actual memories. Being this close to a place of death made her skin crawl.

What felt like an aeon passed, and Savvy had just taken a step forward when Dawson reappeared at the end of the hallway.

"Jack isn't here yet, but the room appears to be clear. There are a few customers in the bar, but they don't look like killers, as far as I can tell. None of them look to be packing."

"Packing?"

"Carrying a weapon."

"Thanks. I feel so much better knowing that." Savvy tried to lighten the mood with her words, but she shook inside. She took a determined step forward.

When she faced him, Dawson checked the angle of her hat, pulling it lower over her forehead.

"If you pull down the brim much farther, I'll be walking into walls. Do you *want* me to draw attention or not?" She tilted her head back, her brows rising on her forehead, a quirky smile daring to lift the corner of one lip.

Dawson gazed down into her eyes, his own brown ones turning a smoky black. He leaned forward and planted another kiss on her lips, surprising the heck out of her for the second time that day.

She pressed her hand to her lips and stared up at him. "What was that for?"

Dawson frowned and turned away. "To shut you up. Remember to let me do all the talking. I don't want to give anyone the chance to figure out who you are." He pulled at the sides of her shirt, tugging the hem from the waist-band of her jeans.

"Excuse me, but is it necessary to undress me in the hallway?" Savvy couldn't help the little bit of breathlessness that came across in her tone.

With Dawson's fingers brushing against her waist, she couldn't help wondering what it would feel like for him to brush them against her bare breasts. When that image crossed her mind, Savvy fought to keep her hand from flying to her lips and struggled to keep from gasping out loud at her own naughty thoughts. Why in the heck was she thinking about a hired bodyguard when she should be more concerned about finding the person or persons who'd set her up to take the fall for murder?

With her breath refusing to make it fully in and out of her lungs, Savvy allowed Dawson to steer her through the tables, away from the bar and into a booth in the corner closest to the back exit. The dim lighting worked in her favor. Not one of the customers scattered around the room looked away from the game on the television screen.

Savvy slid onto the vinyl seat and picked up a menu, not that she intended to eat or drink anything. The menu gave her additional cover and something to do with hands that had decided to shake.

"What can I get for you?"

Savvy started when a woman wearing a faded denim miniskirt, a white blouse tied around her midriff and crazy high heels stopped beside their table, a round tray balanced on her hand.

Savvy opened her mouth to ask the woman's name.

"Two light beers," Dawson answered before Savvy's question could be voiced.

The woman nodded and left.

Savvy leaned forward. "I don't like beer."

His brows rose. "You're remembering."

"Yeah, I guess I am." She sat back against the seat, a dull ache forming behind her eyelids as she fought to remember even more. "But that is such an insignificant memory. Why can't I remember the important details?" She fumbled with a paper napkin, folding it into an intricate pattern, then unfolding it again.

Dawson reached across and laid his larger hand over hers. "Don't push it."

"I know, I know, it'll come back." She loved the strength of his touch. It grounded her when she felt adrift in a sea of uncertainty. Savvy pulled her hand free and shifted her gaze to the retreating waitress. "I don't remember her. Should I?"

"I don't know. Maybe the manager hired her recently."

"Perhaps." She shrugged. "I guess it doesn't matter. I'm here to find out more about what happened the night I was shot." Her gaze panned the room and landed on the man behind the bar, wiping the counter clean between drink orders. "Maybe the bartender could shed some light." She scooted toward the edge of the seat.

"Oh, no, you don't." Dawson shot to his feet and blocked her path. "You promised to let me do all the talking."

Savvy's lips twisted into a frown. "I did, didn't I?" Already she regretted her decision to let him ask all the questions. Her desire to learn the truth burned in her gut. The sooner they started the better. "Then get to it, will you?"

Dawson grinned. "Pushy, aren't you?"

"I've been called worse." Her eyes widened. "And not around here." A frown sent her eyebrows toward her nose. "Now, why would I remember that?" She glanced around. "I could use a trip to the ladies' room."

Dawson scanned the bar before he let her rise from the table. "I'll walk you there."

"You'll attract attention."

Dawson grabbed her elbow in his grip. "Anyone ever tell you that you argue too much?"

"I don't remember, but there's a good possibility." She let him escort her toward the restroom sign in the opposite corner of the bar. The short dark hallway didn't have any other doors other than the bathrooms. Dawson nodded toward the ladies' room door.

"Sit down. I'll be fine."

Dawson scanned the room again. A movement at the entrance to the bar caught his attention. "There's Jack."

Savvy strained to make out the features of the man who hesitated inside the doorway, looking around. "The new bodyguard?"

"Yeah."

Savvy's heart dropped into her stomach. Dawson had said all along he'd protect her as long as he needed to, until a replacement could be found. "Your replacement."

Dawson didn't comment; instead, he opened the men's room door and looked inside, then he opened the ladies' room door. "Empty. It's all yours."

"Go on, Jack is looking for you." It was hard to make her words sound normal when what felt like a sock clogged her throat. "I'll be right back when I'm through here."

Dawson frowned, his gaze going from her to Jack and back. "Okay, but don't take too long."

"I won't."

"Lock the door behind you."

"Check." She stepped inside and twisted the lock on the door, her fingers shaking. With a door between her and Dawson, she couldn't hold back anymore. She didn't have to put up a front. The stress of the past day crowded in on her, quickly swamping her with the enormity of the situation. Someone was trying to kill her. If not for Dawson, she'd be a dead woman by now. And he was going to pass on the responsibility of protecting her to another man.

Even though he was a stranger when she'd woken up, Dawson was the only rock in her world right now. The only person who made her feel safe, who had kept her alive. The man who'd made love to her into the night and made her forget why she wanted to remember. When he left, she'd be on her own again, as far as she was concerned. She didn't know Jack or what he was capable of providing. She only knew Dawson. Wanted him, too…as more than just a bodyguard.

Tears welled in her eyes. She brushed them away and paced across the small tiled floor. No, she wasn't alone. This new guy—Jack—would take care of her and help her find out who really killed Tomas Rodriguez.

Or would he?

Neither Dawson nor Jack was being paid to solve a murder. They were only being paid to keep her alive. They had no obligation to clear her of charges.

Trapped by her circumstances, Savvy fought to breathe as her lungs tightened and panic set in.

As she saw it, she had two choices: wallow in self-pity or do something. Though she couldn't remember what she'd been like in the past, deep down she knew she'd never wallowed in self-pity. It didn't feel right. She had to do something, even if it put her in the line of fire. If Dawson planned on giving up on her, she'd just have to handle this mess herself.

Savvy marched to the sink, pulled off her hat and jerked the cold-water knob until water sprayed into the porcelain sink. Then she doused her face until all remnants of tears had been washed from her eyes and cheeks. Tough girls didn't cry. Tough girls got down to business. Her father didn't raise her to be a wimp.

Her hands halted in midswish, water dripping from her fingers. An image of a taciturn white-haired man flashed into her mind. The same man she'd pictured when she'd thought

of stubborn men. Was he her father? Had he been the one to
tell her tough girls don't cry? She stared hard at herself, her
eyes clashing with the woman in the mirror. Red hair, green
eyes and freckles. Nothing in her reflection reminded her of
the white-haired man, except the green eyes. But that didn't
mean anything. She could have taken after her mother. Despite the lack of similarity in appearance, the man resurfac-
ing in her memory had to be someone she'd known well.

Savvy dried her hands and straightened her shirt, letting the tails hang over her hips, hiding her shape the way
Dawson had wanted. It gnawed at her insides. She wanted
her clothes to fit well, even if the material was of an infe-
rior make and material.

How did she recognize the lack of quality? Had she only
purchased the best fabrics? Based on the hand-me-down
specials she'd had in her apartment, she doubted she'd had
designer clothes at any point in her life.

She thought hard until her head ached with the effort.
Then she wadded up her hair and stuffed it into the cowboy hat, pushing the brim down low over her forehead.
She'd think later. Right now she had questions for anyone
who might have been in the bar and grill two nights ago.

DAWSON WAITED until he heard the reassuring click of the
lock shooting into place. As long as she remained locked
in the bathroom, Savvy should be all right. From his seat
in the booth, he could keep a close watch on the door and
anyone moving toward the hallway. He stepped back into
the main room and waited for Jack to see him. Without
waving or acknowledging the other man's presence, he
returned to his seat and waited for his friend to join him.

"Dawson." Jack slipped into the seat where Savvy had
sat a moment before and lifted the beer the waitress had

left on the table while Dawson and Savvy had been arguing outside the bathroom. "For me?"

"All yours." Dawson lifted his own beer and swished the cool liquid around inside the bottle. The temptation to drink made him ache with thirst. In the past, he'd have given in to temptation to dull the pain. Now the need to keep Savvy safe outweighed his desire to dull the pain. He had to keep a clear head to keep Savvy alive. It was his responsibility to provide her protection.

Only a short time ago he'd been adamant about being relieved of his current assignment. Now he couldn't imagine leaving Savvy's fate up to anyone else. The woman needed a keeper, someone who anticipated her every move to help her avoid stepping squarely into trouble.

Jack took a long drink, set his beer on the table and stared around the room. "Isn't this the place they say Ms. Jones shot Tomas Rodriguez?"

Dawson's hand tightened around the beer bottle. "This is the place, but as for what actually happened, the jury's still out."

Jack grinned across the table at Dawson. "Changed your mind about the job?"

"What do you mean?" His back stiffened as Dawson prepared to battle his friend. Or was he bracing himself to fight his own internal battle?

"On the phone you said we'd talk about the handoff. Have you changed your mind? Do you want to continue the assignment?"

For a long moment Dawson stared at the bottle of beer in front of him. Jack would provide a more unbiased approach to protecting Savvy. He didn't have a junked-up past of guilt and failure to hold him back. Maybe Savvy would be better off with Jack. When Dawson opened his mouth to tell his friend that he could have the job, the words lodged in his throat. How could he walk away? Savvy trusted him with her life when she didn't trust anyone else in the world. Hell, she didn't know who to trust.

Jack leaned forward. "I'm ready to take on the task. Just say the word and Savvy Jones becomes my responsibility. No need to feel guilty. It's business."

Dawson's fist slammed against the table. The two beer bottles rocked. "No, it's not business."

"Are you in too deep already, man?" Jack shook his head. "Women have a way of making you crazy. Maybe you should step back and let it go."

Was that it? Had Savvy made him crazy enough to lose judgment? Had that long red hair and those deep green, trusting eyes, haunted by the loss of everything she knew from her past, edged through his defenses? Was it so bad to forget who you were? Forget what you'd lost?

Dawson gripped the neck of the bottle, his fingers tightening until they turned white. "I can't let go."

Jack sat back against the seat and studied his friend. Finally he nodded. "Okay, so what now? Audrey sent me to help in any way I can."

Dawson leaned toward Jack. "I need someone to find out everything there is to know about the Rodriguez cartel. I need to know who wanted Tomas dead, who had the most to gain by it. Since you speak Spanish fluently, that makes you the best man to do the job."

Jack nodded. "I have a few connections here in Laredo from a previous job. Anything else?"

"Frank Young."

Jack's brows rose. "The D.A. that hired the bodyguard for Ms. Jones?"

"The one and only. Why is he so determined to keep Savvy—Ms. Jones out of jail but protected? What's in it for him? What's he hiding?"

"You think he's using her as bait?"

"I don't know, but something isn't sitting right." Dawson's gaze shifted to the restroom hallway. Why was she taking so long?

"Will do." Jack's brows rose and a grin slid across his face. "When do I get to meet the woman who's got you all tied in knots?"

Dawson glared at the hallway. "She should be out by now." He rose halfway out of his chair before he found her.

Savvy stood by the bar speaking to the bartender.

"Damn. I told her to let me do all the talking."

"The one by the bar?" Jack asked. "I'll meet her later when we're not so conspicuous. As soon as I learn something, I'll get back with you."

"Anything—as soon as you learn anything."

A man rose from a nearby table and moved toward Savvy, his back to Dawson. He didn't appear to be carrying a weapon. Still, he could pose a potential threat.

Dawson's fists tightened into hammers as his feet ate the distance between himself and Savvy.

SAVVY LEANED OVER the bar, careful to keep her head down, relying on the hat brim to shield her face. "Can I have a glass of merlot?" she called out to the bartender.

"I'll see if we have any. Most folks around here drink beer or whiskey." He ducked behind the counter and unearthed a bottle. "Aha. I thought I had a bottle. I kept it here for one of my waitresses. She had expensive tastes." He glanced up, his eyes narrowing. "Savvy?" he whispered.

Savvy gave up any pretense of hiding her face and smiled crookedly across the bar at the older man whose care-lined face should have been familiar and was, if only a little. "I'm sorry, I can't remember your name."

"Earl. Earl Bradford."

He stared into her eyes as if looking for something. Recognition?

Savvy shook her head, sighing. "Sorry, still not ringing any bells."

"Most people who know me call me E.B."

"E.B." There was something familiar about it. "Yeah. That rings a little bit of a bell. More than Earl."

His smile broadened. "How are you? Will you be coming back to work soon?" Then his smile slipped and his face grew serious. "We thought you were dead." His eyes glistened and he bent his head, intent on wiping away an imaginary spot on the counter.

Savvy gulped back a wad of tears clogging her throat. "Sometimes I think I *am* dead, but don't have the good sense to realize it."

E.B. dropped the cloth, pulled a glass from the rack above his head and sloshed merlot into it. "Well, you're not and I'm not believin' any of that horse manure about you killing the Rodriguez kid."

"Thanks, E.B." A warmth filled her chest. So far she had two people who stood behind her. Three, if you counted the hired bodyguard. She risked a glance behind her to find Dawson marching across the floor toward her, his fists knotted, his brown eyes stormy.

Her breath quickened and she turned back to the bartender. "E.B., did you see anyone with Tomas Rodriguez that night, before he was shot?"

E.B. stared into the dark interior of the bar as if looking into the distance. "All I remember is Liz runnin' in yelling for me to call 911."

A man stepped up to the counter and tossed bills on the wooden surface. He glanced at Savvy, his eyes narrowing.

She bent her head, hoping her hair hadn't slipped free of

the hat. Just in case, she raised a hand to the cheek closest to the man, hiding her face in as casual a manner as possible.

Dawson eased up to the bar, the only indication that he was mad the silent tic twitching in his jaw.

The other man, who'd been staring at her with such intensity a moment before, dropped his gaze and headed for the door.

Not until the door closed behind the man did Savvy let go of the breath she'd been holding.

Dawson jerked his head toward the rear exit.

Savvy feigned ignorance and leaned over the counter, intent on answers. "E.B., did you hear anything concerning the Rodriguez cartel or Tomas in particular?"

"All I know is that Tomas was being his usual dumb, cussed self, pinching the waitresses and talking loud to anyone who would listen. He was standing right where you are now."

"Can I get another beer? Draft will be fine," Dawson interrupted.

Savvy fought back the urge to walk over and elbow him.

"Sure." When E.B. reached beneath the counter for a mug, Dawson glared at Savvy and mouthed the words *Let's go.*

She ignored him and continued with, "What did he talk about?"

E.B. pulled the tap, tilting the mug to minimize the foam as he filled it. "The band was loud. I don't recall." He released the lever and closed his eyes. "Tomas was spouting off to a woman about how he didn't trust someone. I think someone close to his father." E.B. opened his eyes and walked to the end of the counter to set the beer in front of Dawson. When he returned, he added, "You think whoever he was talking about might have knocked him off?"

"Maybe. I need to find out. Otherwise, I'll take the blame for Rodriguez's murder."

E.B. crossed his arms over his barrel chest. "You couldn't have done it. Anyone who says so is a flat-out liar."

Savvy smiled at the older man. "Thanks, E.B. If only the jury could see it that way."

"You couldn't even step on a cockroach, much less pull the trigger on a man."

"Do you remember the woman Rodriguez was talking to?"

"I've seen her here a couple times. Pretty woman. I think she goes by the name of Mari or Marisol. Usually comes in with the wealthier customers. I guess the Rodriguez kid could be classified as wealthy. Well, at least his drug-dealin' daddy is."

"If you think of anything else that might help, will you let Liz know? I'll be in touch with her."

E.B. nodded. "Sure will. Any idea when you'll be able to come back to work?"

Savvy shook her head. "I can't right now. I'd just be bringing you more trouble."

"Hey, one more thing." E.B. tossed the bar towel over his shoulder. "There was this guy here earlier today asking questions about you."

Savvy leaned forward. "A guy? What did he look like? Did he give you a name?"

"Did better than that, he left his card." E.B. reached into his shirt pocket and pulled out a card, handing it across the counter to her.

Savvy looked down at the name Vance Pearson and his professional title, private investigator, her stomach lurching. "What did he want?"

"At first he was looking for you. Then he asked if I'd seen or met a woman named Sabrina…Jameson, or something like that. He seemed to think you might know where this woman could be found."

Gooseflesh pebbled Savvy's arms. There was that name again. Sabrina sounded familiar. She closed her eyes and tried to force the memories forward in her mind. Savvy shook her head. "If I did know who she was, I don't now." She smiled at E.B. "Can I keep this?"

"Sure. I don't need it." E.B. reached across the counter and patted Savvy's hand. "For what it's worth, none of us think you killed Rodriguez."

"Thanks, E.B. I appreciate your vote of confidence." She pocketed the card.

"We miss you around here," E.B. continued. "You class up the joint."

Dawson appeared at her side, cupping her elbow. "We need to leave," he said, his voice strained, urgent.

E.B.'s eyes narrowed. "Hey, buddy. Leave her alone."

"It's okay, he's with me." Savvy tried to shake off Dawson's grip, but he wasn't letting loose.

She shrugged and cast a wry grin toward E.B. "I think this is my cue to leave."

Before Savvy and Dawson reached the hallway leading to the rear exit, Savvy pulled free of his grip. "Why the heck did you have to go and drag me away? E.B. might have more information."

"Just move."

Savvy planted her feet firmly on the tiled floor and refused to budge. "Not until you tell me what's going on."

Dawson opened his mouth to explain but didn't get the chance.

The front door burst open and two men rushed in, brandishing automatic weapons and firing at random.

Dawson shoved Savvy into the hallway, shouting, "Get down and stay down!"

Chapter Thirteen

Dawson hit the floor and rolled to the side, yanking the Glock from his shoulder holster.

The sharp report of weapons fire echoed off the walls, the acrid scent of gunpowder warring with the lingering scent of alcohol.

He slid behind the jukebox and chanced a glance around the corner in Savvy's direction.

She crouched against the hallway wall, covering her ears to block out the noise of bullets being fired.

"Run, Savvy," he called out as quietly as he could and still be heard over the sounds of customers yelling and chairs being overturned as they scrambled to get away from flying bullets.

"I can't," she said, her voice shaking.

"You damn well better. I'll be right behind you." He rose on his knees in a flash, unloaded four rounds and dropped back down before the attackers had time to get a bead on him.

He somersaulted to a position behind a large speaker near the stage.

A bullet hit the speaker, knocking it into Dawson's shoulder and showering him with black plastic shards.

A movement out of the corner of Dawson's eyes captured his attention.

One of the gunmen was working his way through the maze of tables and chairs toward the back hallway where Savvy hunched against the wall. He couldn't see her from where he stood, but it wouldn't be long before the shooter would have a direct line of fire.

Run, Savvy. Dawson willed her to move. But she stayed hunched over, her hands pressed to her ears, her eyes squeezed shut.

Dawson rolled to the side and sprang to his feet long enough to fire off another round at the two men with the automatic weapons. He dived for the hallway, sliding across the smooth tile floor. "Let's get out of here." He grabbed Savvy's hand and, as he rose, yanked her to her feet. Shoving her in front of him, he raced for the back door, turning around long enough to empty his clip, aiming at the two faces appearing at the other end of the hallway.

Savvy unlocked the door and fell out into the alley, crashing to her knees on the rough concrete stoop.

Bullets whizzed past Dawson's head where he stood. He dropped to cover Savvy's body with his own, and reaching out with his heel, he kicked the door shut behind them.

More bullets pierced the door's thin metal, blasting through the air to chip at the brick on the building behind the bar.

Dawson shoved Savvy to the side, out of range. He scrambled to his feet and wedged a metal trash can beneath the doorknob about the time something heavy hit the door, rocking it open an inch. The trash can held, but it wouldn't hold for long.

"Time to go." Dawson slipped an arm around her and lifted her to her feet. In seconds, they were running. They ducked between two buildings and across the street. When they reached the alley where they'd stashed the car, they could hear the shouts of the gunmen.

Savvy lunged for the sedan, diving into the passenger seat as Dawson slipped behind the steering wheel. With a flick of the key in the ignition, the engine roared to life and Dawson shifted into Reverse. He backed the car out of the alley, pulling into a hard turn when he reached the street.

The two men holding the guns stood in the middle of the street, settling their weapons against their shoulders and aiming for the rental-car windshield.

"Stay down," Dawson said, his voice low, controlled.

"How can you be so cool when they're aiming at you?" Savvy ignored his warning, unable to turn away from the men ready to put a bullet through her head.

"Because I'm not going to let them hit me. Please duck down." He grabbed her head and shoved it into her lap, then stomped on the accelerator, sending the car fishtailing backward, away from the attackers.

The windshield exploded in front of him, but he ignored the spray of glass and shot backward until the bullets no longer reached them.

The men ran after the sedan, but Dawson had sufficient distance that he risked spinning the car in a 180-degree turn. Then he shot forward, away from the attackers and flying bullets.

After he'd gone a mile, zigzagging through the streets of Laredo, he was certain no cars followed. He glanced down at Savvy hunkered low on the seat, rocking back and forth. "You all right?"

She shook her head and continued rocking, silent sobs shaking her shoulders.

His foot lifted from the pedal. "Were you hit?" He tried to remember which way it was to the hospital. "Do you need a doctor?"

"No." She lifted her head. "I'm fine. Really."

She didn't look fine. Dawson wanted nothing more than to take her into his arms and hold her.

She blinked back another tear and asked, "Is it safe to sit up?"

"For the moment." Dawson pressed his foot to the pedal and glanced in the rearview mirror for the hundredth time since leaving the Waterin' Hole.

Savvy sat up and scrubbed a hand over her cheeks, wiping away the moisture. She glanced over her shoulder. "I hope E.B. is okay."

"He dropped behind the bar when the shooting started. I bet he's fine. But I'm not so sure about you."

"I don't think I've ever been so scared in my life." She reached across and laid a hand on his arm. "I'm sorry I froze back there."

"You'd have to be made of stone not to be frightened after something like that."

"Yeah, but I could have gotten you killed."

"Not happening." He touched his chest and smiled. "See? No wounds."

"Shouldn't we wait for the police?"

"And give the bad guys another chance to shoot you? Or give the police another reason to throw you in jail?" He shook his head. "No. You're not safe staying in one place. I should take you up to our San Antonio office and keep you there until this is all over."

"You can't. I was told to stay in town. If it's all the same to you, I'd rather not go to jail for something I didn't do." She sighed and stared out the window at the passing houses as they moved through a subdivision. "Besides, I need to be here, close to the real killer until I can figure it out."

"Your investigating days are over," Dawson said, his tone hard, unbending.

"What?"

"You heard me. I was paid to protect you. So far, I'm not doing such a good job." He held up his hand to stop her from commenting. "And you're not helping."

Savvy bit into her bottom lip. "Sorry. I shouldn't have put you at risk."

"To hell with me. What kind of bodyguard lets the woman he's supposed to be protecting walk right into a dangerous situation?" He shook his head. "I should have let Jack take over."

Savvy stared across at him. "What did you say?"

"Doesn't matter," he grumbled, taking a turn and avoiding her look.

"Yes, it does. You said you should have let Jack take over." A smile curled the corners of her lips and a light shone in her eyes. "Does this mean you aren't turning me over to Jack?"

His lips pinched together and he didn't answer her.

She sat back in her seat, the smile stretching across her face. The first real smile he'd seen on her since he'd met her. And it nearly knocked him out of his seat. It was a given that Savvy Jones was a knockout, but when she smiled…her face rivaled the sunniest sky. Then she frowned. "Watch out!"

Dawson pulled his head back in the game and realized he'd just run a red light. "Damn woman. You'll be the death of me."

"Me? You're the one running stoplights." Though her words were tough, her smile returned. "What made you change your mind?"

"About what?"

"About giving the case to Jack?"

"You're too much trouble. I can't wish that on a friend."

"Yeah." She nodded. Despite the gruffness of his response, her cheerfulness didn't fade. "Where to?"

"We need to find a safe place to hide you until the people I've got doing some checking get back to me."

Savvy twisted in her seat. "You're serious? We're going to sit and wait?"

"That's right."

"But—"

He raised his hand in a sharp gesture. "No buts."

Savvy slumped in her seat, her arms crossed over her chest, refusing to look his way.

Good. He didn't need those liquid green eyes boring into his soul any more than they already had. He didn't want to own up to the reason he'd stayed on the job instead of letting Jack take over. Because if he did, he might have to come to grips with the fact that the woman was growing on him. That her lips were soft and kissable and that he wanted a whole lot more than a kiss from her. And…he shut down at that point, forcing such crazy thoughts to the back of his mind. He'd push them out altogether, if he could. Except that one strawberry blonde with deep green eyes sat beside him, making it impossible to ignore her effect on him.

SAVVY ENTERED the motel room before Dawson, a sense of déjà vu settling over her. Hadn't they done this less than twenty-four hours ago? Only this time was different. They'd already made love and knew how good it was. The memory flooded her mind. With so few memories to fall back on, she couldn't manage to push it back.

Nervous and at a loss for what to do with her hands, Savvy jammed hers into her pockets, her fingertips curling around Vance Pearson's business card. She pulled it out and stared down at the bold writing. "So Vance Pearson is a private investigator."

"That explains a lot about why he's here. But why is he investigating you?" Dawson set their bag of groceries on the dresser and turned to face her.

"I want to know who this Sabrina woman is and why

he thinks I might know where she is." Savvy glanced up, her gaze colliding with Dawson's. Now that they weren't running from bullets, Dawson probably wanted to confront her about what had happened at the back of the bar. Savvy prayed he wouldn't. What would she say? He'd initiated the kiss, but she'd responded. She closed her eyes, afraid he'd see the desire flaring in hers.

Warm, strong hands curved around her cheeks; two thumbs brushed over her lips. "You feel it, too, don't you?"

She gulped, trying to force down the lump in her throat. "Feel what?" Even to her own ears, she sounded breathless. And why wouldn't she be when she couldn't get enough air into her lungs, not with Dawson standing so close she could smell the musky scent of denim-clad male? Her body swayed toward him, but still she refused to open her eyes.

"Open your eyes, Savvy."

She squeezed them tighter. "No."

He chuckled. "I wouldn't have figured you for a coward. Open your eyes and tell me you don't feel it, too."

She sucked in a deep breath with every intention of telling him that she felt no such thing. But when she opened her eyes, his dark brown eyes stared down into hers, his full, sensuous lips only a breath away.

"It's okay. I didn't mean for it to happen, either." Then his lips covered hers, the warmth burning through to her core.

Savvy whimpered, wanting to deny him, wanting to tell him she couldn't commit to a relationship with him until she knew who she was. Nothing escaped her lips but a sigh as she fell into his arms, giving as much as he gave in that one kiss. Their tongues lashed out, meeting and tangling in a frenzy. His hands slipped down her throat and over her shoulders.

Her fingers inched up his chest and around his neck, twisting into the longer hairs at his nape. This was where she'd wanted to be since last night when she'd discovered how much she craved him. Since he'd saved her life in the hospital, she recognized something true and noble about him, making her want more than a protector. She wanted to be with him as an equal.

His fingers bunched the tail of her shirt, sliding it up her torso, as his mouth slipped across her chin and down her throat.

Her nipples beaded into hard little nubs, pressing against the smooth cotton of her shirt, as if begging him to taste them through the fabric. Heat pooled low in her belly, spiraling downward into her core, making her hot and liquid.

One hand slipped low over her buttocks, drawing her closer until she could feel exactly how aroused he was.

The hard ridge behind his fly pressed into her belly.

Electric currents skittered across nerve endings, making her gasp, her heart beating like a crazed drummer. It wasn't enough. Nothing short of having him inside her, sliding in and out of her hot, wet channel, would ease this ache deep within.

Her fingers rose to the buttons on her cotton shirt and one at a time, she flicked them open, mindless of the consequences. Mindless of anything but the man in front of her and her need to be with him, fully, completely....

When her fingers reached the button over her breasts, his big hand stopped her.

"We need to slow down."

"What?" She couldn't believe he'd called a halt. All the air in her lungs whooshed out, leaving her chest hollow, her head spinning. She forced herself to take a breath, then another before she stepped back, drawing the edges of her shirt together over her chest.

"You're right." With a shaking hand, she raked her hair back from her face, still unsure about what had just happened.

"I'm sorry, Savvy." Dawson reached for her, but she

backed farther away. "If it were just you and me, I wouldn't have been able to stop."

She held up her hand. "You don't have to explain. And I have no excuses."

"I had no right to kiss you." He stared down at her, as if he struggled not to kiss her again.

Lord help her, she wanted the same. "And I had no right to kiss you back."

Dawson's cell phone rang, vibrating across the dresser.

Savvy welcomed the interruption and took the opportunity to breathe. She was in way over her head with Dawson. He was essentially a stranger. Then why did her chest hurt? And why did she want to be with him when he wasn't there? Was the fear of someone trying to kill her the only reason she wanted Dawson close? How would she know until the nightmare ended?

She shook her head and forced herself to concentrate on Dawson's end of the conversation.

"What do you have, Audrey? Wait. Let me put you on speaker so that Savvy can hear, as well." He punched a button on his cell phone and a woman said, "Can you hear me, Ms. Jones?"

"Yes, ma'am."

"Hi, dear. I'm Audrey Nye of the Lone Star Agency. I checked Harvard today and I'm sorry to report, they have no record of a Savvy Jones. They've had many Joneses come through in the past ten years, but not one that's close to Savvy."

Savvy's brows pinched together. "I can picture the hallways and some of the professors. I know I attended."

"Maybe you attended under another name?" Audrey suggested.

"You mean my name might not even be Savvy Jones?" Savvy said, her voice barely above a whisper. Not only did she not know who she was, even the name everyone knew her by could be a lie.

Dawson curved his free hand around her waist and pulled her back to rest against the solid wall of his chest. His warmth helped to chase away the chill filling her. She wanted nothing more than to turn in his arms and let him shoulder all her burdens, make the uncertainty go away, let him protect her from whatever she'd run away from. But she couldn't. She had to figure out this mess for herself.

"What about the phone number we found in Vance Pearson's hotel room? And by the way, he's not a reporter. Apparently he's a private investigator." Dawson's chest rumbled against her back.

"It's unlisted and the security around it is pretty tight." Audrey sighed over the phone. "I've got some of my contacts loosening some strings. I should have that to you within the next hour or two."

"The sooner the better."

"We're doing what we can at this end. Did you learn anything else?"

"The bartender at the Waterin' Hole said a man meeting Vance Pearson's description had been there asking questions about me," Savvy said, her words hesitant at first. "He wanted to know if I'd seen or heard anything about a woman named Sabrina Jameson. He wasn't certain about the last name, just the first—Sabrina."

"I'll add that to my search criteria and see what I get. Thanks, Savvy."

"I won't be taking Savvy back there anytime soon. We almost became target practice for cartel gunners."

"What happened?" Audrey asked.

Dawson filled her in on the shooting, his hand tightening around Savvy's waist as the story unfolded. "We've had several close calls. Between Rodriguez's father being out for revenge and the real killer wanting to keep his identity secret, the streets of Laredo just aren't safe for Savvy."

"But the D.A. wants her to stay local? I don't get it. Does he want the real killer to finish the job? And Rodriguez has to have loads of people at his disposal who would be willing to shoot their own grandmothers, much less someone suspected of killing their leader's son."

Savvy gasped, her heart fluttering unsteadily. She'd had the same thought, but to hear it spoken aloud was almost too much.

"Sorry, Savvy," Audrey said. "You need to stay low. Dawson, your main concern is to keep her safe. I wouldn't even let Young know where."

"That's my plan." Dawson's face was taut, as if his jaw was carved of granite. "I have Jack checking into District Attorney Young."

"You think he's corrupt?" Audrey asked.

"I don't trust him."

Dawson wasn't leaving anything to chance. A warm glow spread through her. Dawson was a good man, on top of his game and looking out for her.

Then again, she was a job.

She stepped free of the hand around her waist.

"I also have him tapping his connections in the area to find out anything he can about who would want Rodriguez's son dead and why."

"Good. I'm glad you're staying with Savvy. Jack can work his contacts there in Laredo."

"Right."

"In the meantime, hang in there, Savvy. And, Dawson, lie low and keep Savvy out of harm's way."

Dawson nodded, his gaze on Savvy. "I will."

Chapter Fourteen

"You need to get some rest."

Savvy sighed. "I'll need my strength to get through whatever comes next, right? Because I'm sure it won't be a cakewalk." She pinched the bridge of her nose between her fingers, squeezing her eyes shut. "My head is pounding. I don't suppose you have some painkillers in that bag of groceries, do you?"

"As a matter of fact, I do."

"I'll take two." She gave him a weak smile and held out her free hand.

She'd been a trouper, racing through the streets of Laredo, being shot, shot at and almost smothered, but she still had the strength to smile.

If Dawson wasn't careful, he could easily fall in love with a woman like Savvy. Beautiful, determined Savvy who wanted to remember as much as Dawson wanted to forget.

He placed two pills in her hand and closed her fingers around them. "This should help."

When he tried to withdraw his hand, her fingers curled around his.

"Thanks, Dawson."

"For what?"

She opened her eyes and looked up into his. "For saving my life."

"You wouldn't have been shot at today if I had refused to take you to the bar."

"You didn't have a choice. I'd have gone, with or without you, and you know it." Her smile widened. "So, thanks."

Her tender look and the light in her eyes melted his heart all the more, forcing a lump to rise in his throat. He'd loved Amanda, and nothing could ever change that. But the feelings he had for Savvy were different. With Amanda, she'd always clung to him, relied on him to be there for her. She'd hated that he was in the military, hated that he was gone all the time and begged him to quit more times than he could remember.

Savvy needed him, but was also determined to stand on her own. She wanted the truth bad enough she'd risk her life to get it.

"Do you like being a private investigator?" Savvy asked.

He shrugged. "It's a job."

"You liked the military more?"

He hesitated, his gut knotting, and then he nodded.

She tossed the pills to the back of her throat, washed them down with bottled water and then asked, "What is it about the military that you liked?"

"Why does it matter? I'm not in the military anymore."

Savvy reached out and grabbed his hand, tugging him closer to sit on the edge of the bed. "We've been through a lot together in the past two days, and we're not out of the woods yet." She held tight to his hand when he wanted to pull away. "Talk to me, Dawson. I won't take no for an answer."

A smile twitched the corners of his lips. "Pushy broad."

Her lips twisted. "We've established that. Now, tell me...what was it about the military that you loved?"

Dawson stared down at the scar on his hand where he'd been injured in the explosion that had claimed the life of one of the soldiers under his command. A young man, barely out of his teens, sent to a foreign country to fight a battle he barely understood. Regret lodged in his throat, making his words come out low and hoarse. "It's being a part of something bigger than just me. When you're in the military, you have a unit that becomes a family. The hardest times make the bonds between you all the stronger."

She nodded. "I think I understand. I've only known you a couple days, but because of what we've been through together, I feel like I've known you a lifetime."

He stared into her green eyes and nodded. "Yeah, it's something like that. You'll do anything for your family."

She leaned forward and wrapped an arm around his middle. "Does that include dying?" Her words came out choked.

Dawson nodded, words refusing to edge past his constricted throat. He reached around her waist. They sat for a while, comforting each other.

After a long pause, Savvy placed a hand on his cheek, turning him to face her. "You don't have to die for me, Dawson Gray. Do you hear me? I won't let you die for me."

Despite everything he'd learned from the loss of his first wife, he couldn't help the surge of longing he had for this woman who refused to let him die for her. "It's not your choice." And it wasn't always his choice who he fell in love with. He'd been intent on a career in the army when he'd met his wife. He hadn't planned on loving Amanda, but it had happened.

Savvy had been a job. Nothing more. But somewhere between being shot at and running for their lives, she'd become more than that. He leaned forward and kissed her lips. Gently at first. As the need surged inside, the kiss deepened until he pushed her back against the pillows, his hands digging into her hair.

Her arms circled his neck and she kissed him back.

He forgot that he'd be leaving when the job was done. Forgot that he was supposed to remain impartial to his client.

The connection became the culmination of all the raw emotion, frustration and wretchedness he'd lived with over the past two years. In Savvy's arms, all of that went away, cleansed of regret, absent of guilt, free of the burden he'd carried until he'd caved under the pressure.

Dawson came to his senses first, his heart lighter than it had been in a long time. Danger still lurked in Laredo, but so did a potential for happiness. But he had to ensure Savvy's safety and her release from suspicion before he could get on with life. With or without Savvy in it. If he had his preferences, he'd prefer that Savvy be in his life. He wanted another chance at love.

"Why did you stop?" Savvy blinked up at him.

"I need to stay on my toes. I'd like nothing better than to take you to bed and make love to you, but when I'm in your arms, I forget everything else."

She chuckled, running a shaky hand through her tumbled hair. "Is that such a bad thing?"

"If I want to keep you alive, it is." He sat up and stared down at her kiss-swollen lips. Damn, he wanted to kiss her again and make love to her until the sun rose in the morning.

Instead, he stood, distancing himself from her. From temptation. "Get some sleep while you can. We don't know when we'll get another opportunity."

As if mocking his words, his cell phone rang.

When he recognized Jack's number, he hit the speakerphone key and set the device on the nightstand. "You're on speakerphone."

Music thrummed in the background. "Hey, Dawson, Savvy. I'm striking out on who actually murdered Tomas Rodriguez."

"None of your contacts had a lead?"

"No one is talking. They're afraid of saying anything."

Dawson sighed. "Thanks for trying. Did you find out anything about Young's mistress?"

Jack chuckled. "At least on that count, I got a hit. I got better than a hit."

Savvy scooted to the side of the bed and stood, straightening her shirt and hair. "Who is she?"

"A Mexican national by the name of Marisol de la Fuentez."

Savvy's gaze locked with Dawson's. "Marisol."

"I take it the name rings a bell?"

"The bartender at the Waterin' Hole said he'd seen her talking to Tomas Rodriguez the night he was shot."

"Interesting," Jack commented. "It gets better. I followed Young across the border to Señorita de la Fuentez's home in Nuevo Laredo. He switched cars at the border for a plain sedan, complete with Mexican license plates, which he drove to Marisol's villa. He stayed a couple hours and then left. What was remarkable about the setup is the next visitor to Marisol's house."

Dawson's fists tightened. "Who?"

"José Mendoza. *El Martillo.*"

"The Hammer?" Dawson asked. "Rodriguez's strong arm? I've read about him in the paper."

"That's the one. My sources say he's Humberto Rodriguez's lieutenant in charge of riding herd on his army of thugs."

"Where are you now?" Dawson asked. He didn't like the idea of his friend crossing the border into Mexico. Not with the problems they'd had recently with drug cartels' shooting rampages.

"I'm on the Texas side of the border. It was pretty dicey for a while there, but I managed to follow Marisol back across the border to the Waterin' Hole. She's here now."

"You're inside the Waterin' Hole right now?" Dawson asked. "They didn't shut down after the shooting?"

"I have an in with the police."

"Stay put. I'm coming." Dawson pulled his weapon from his shoulder holster, ejecting the clip. "I'm sure the police will want a statement from me."

Savvy raced for the grocery bag and unearthed a box of ammo, handing it to Dawson. "I'm coming with you."

"No, you're staying here." His fingers closed around the box, but she refused to release it.

"Dawson, you can't leave her alone," Jack's voice called out over the speakerphone.

He knew that, but Marisol could have all the answers he needed to clear Savvy of the murder of Tomas Rodriguez. "No, I can't leave her by herself. But I can leave her with you." He tugged the box from Savvy's fingers, his gaze narrowing on her.

Savvy frowned, her lips drawing into a stubborn frown.

"I don't want to take my eyes off the de la Fuentez woman," Jack insisted.

Dawson stared at Savvy and then at the cell phone. "I need to be there."

"Then we both go." Savvy laid a hand on his arm. "Please."

"I don't want you anywhere near the Waterin' Hole after what happened there today," he told her.

"Yeah." Jack backed Dawson. "The fact that no one was

killed is nothing short of a miracle based on the number of bullet holes in the walls."

Dawson stared into Savvy's eyes. "It's as if they were aiming for us, but didn't want to kill us. Or at least they didn't want to kill Savvy."

"Since I'm talking to you both, I take it neither one of you was injured?" Jack asked.

"We're fine," Savvy answered. "Dawson got us out, no harm done. Do you know if E.B., the bartender, is all right?"

"He's fine. A little scratched from the broken mirror behind the bar, but none the worse for having been shot at."

Savvy's shoulders rose and fell on a sigh. She'd been worried about her friend more than herself. All the more reason for Dawson to resist the urge to interview Marisol himself. Still, if the de la Fuentez woman had the answers to what really happened in that alley the night Savvy was shot in the head, Dawson wanted to know.

"I'm just sorry I missed the excitement," Jack said.

Dawson snorted. "I imagine it was as exciting as crossing into drug-cartel territory on the other side of the border. Are there any roads that aren't hot in Nuevo Laredo?" Dawson asked.

"It's crazy there. Most of the tourist gift shops are boarded up. It's like a ghost town. Those who've remained are afraid to leave their homes."

Savvy shook her head.

"Laredo is the gateway to riches for people, and the Rodriguez cartel is in it for the long haul."

Dawson made up his mind. He turned away from Savvy, refusing to meet her gaze. "Jack, we'll have to risk losing Marisol. I want you here to watch over Savvy."

"Are you sure?"

Savvy glared at Dawson. "I'm going with you."

"No. You'll stay here with Jack. I'm going to find out what I can about Marisol's connection to Young and *El Martillo*."

"You can't make me stay," she threatened.

"If I have to tie you up or have Jack hold you at gun-point, you will."

Dawson gave Jack the directions and hit the end button.

"I'm going." Savvy stood with her feet braced wide, her arms crossed over her chest. "I'm the one who could be tried for murder."

"It's not up for discussion." He knew of only one way to make her stay put while he interviewed Marisol. Dawson reached into his gym bag and pulled out a long, plastic zip tie, careful to block Savvy's view until he was ready. The hard plastic case of the GPS tracking device caught his eye and he grabbed for the tiny button-size tracking chip. Why he hadn't tagged her before, he didn't know—as many times as she'd threatened to waltz out of there on her own.

Zip tie and tracking chip in hand, he prepared for a fight. In order to protect her from others, he had to pro-tect her from herself. Hopefully, she'd forgive him later. If not, at least he'd feel better knowing she wouldn't be able to follow him into another situation where bullets flew.

When he turned back to Savvy, she'd crossed to the door and slid the chain free. "If you won't take me there, I'll get there myself."

By the time Dawson reached her, she'd released the bolt and flung open the door. But she didn't set foot outside be-fore Dawson spun her around, shut the door and pressed her up against it.

SAVVY'S BREATH CAUGHT in her throat and her heart ham-mered against her ribs. He held her wrists pinned above her head, his chest pressing against hers. "You can't hold me against my will." She tried for a tough stance, but her words were breathy and she couldn't seem to get enough air into her lungs with him standing so close.

"Wanna bet?" He hesitated for a long moment.

Long enough that Savvy hoped he'd change his mind. She stared up into his face, pleading with her eyes, praying he'd take her with him.

Then he kissed her hard on the lips, pressing the length of his body against hers, one hand holding her two wrists above her head, the other roaming down over her body to her bottom, sliding into her back pocket, pulling her snugly against him.

She wanted to resist, wanted to tell him to go to hell, but his lips softened, teasing her, his tongue skimming across the seam of hers until she opened her mouth willingly, letting him in.

She tugged at her captured hands, wanting to touch him, wanting to run her fingers through his hair, to explore the taut muscles of his chest, and lower.

In that one kiss, she lost track of time, lost track of why she was there and why she had to get away. In that moment of mindless bliss, she let her guard down.

That's all it took for Dawson to have her twisted around, her face pressed against the door and her wrists cinched tightly in a hard plastic restraint.

"What the hell?" She jerked her hands away from his, but it was too late. He had her bound snugly enough she couldn't budge the tight plastic zip tie. "Cut it, Dawson. Cut it now, or so help me…"

"You're staying."

She spun to face him, fury searing in her cheeks. He'd used her—kissing her senseless and tying her up all in the same breath. Her chest ached, her eyes burned with unshed tears and she wanted to hit him for making her think he cared, for making her want him when all he wanted was to leave her behind. "If you think this little bit of plastic is going to keep me from getting the answers I want, you're mistaken."

"No, I don't think this one zip tie will hold you."

Before she could guess his intentions, he bent and wrapped his arms around her legs, hefting her up over his shoulder in a fireman's carry.

She kicked her feet, squirming to get loose from his hold. "Put me down, Dawson Gray, or I'll scream."

"Go ahead."

Savvy screamed, realizing the futility of it. On the back side of the motel in a deserted area of town, who would come running?

No one.

He laid her on her side on the bed, gathered her flailing feet and zip tied them, as well. "One zip tie might not hold you, but two ought to do it."

"Dawson, you can't go to the Waterin' Hole without me. It's my life we're trying to straighten out. Surely I have a say in it."

"You do, but I have a say in protecting you." His jaw tightened into steel. "Taking you to the Waterin' Hole wasn't the way to do it. I almost got you killed. What if you have a child to go home to?"

She gulped back a sob, knowing deep down the child in the picture was gone, but that little bit of doubt made her all the more determined to get the answers she needed to know. "I would never have left my child for four months." The emptiness welling up inside her hurt so bad, she knew without a doubt that she didn't have a child to go home to.

He didn't comment, shrugging into his jacket and tucking his pistol into its holster beneath. He turned off the overhead light, plunging the room into darkness. Then he lifted the corner of the curtain and peered out into the parking lot. "Good. Jack's here." He dropped the curtain and faced her. "I'll be back."

She glared at him. "I won't be here."

Dawson frowned. "Don't give Jack a hard time. He really is a good guy." He crossed the room and leaned over her, pressing a kiss to her forehead. "I'm sorry, Savvy. I didn't see any other way to keep you safe."

So angry she wanted to scream and cry all at once, Savvy refused to say anything; she turned away from his kiss and didn't give him the satisfaction of knowing she would miss him and worry about him while he was gone. No. She didn't want him to know she'd wanted to go with him, not so much to learn what she could from Marisol de la Fuentez but to stay with the man who'd saved her more than once in the past two days. The man who had slipped beneath her skin while she was running around Laredo trying to find herself. Damn the man! Damn him to hell....

Dawson stepped out the door to greet Jack.

She'd find a way out of this. She wasn't her daddy's girl for nothing.

Savvy frowned. That white-haired man figured prominently in her memory right then. She couldn't remember his name, but his face was permanently etched in her mind. And he'd been the one who had taught her never to give up. She'd be darned if she'd start now.

Chapter Fifteen

Dawson hated tying up Savvy, hated leaving her with Jack. Not that Jack couldn't handle her. Jack was a top-notch agent and bodyguard, having been hired out to some of the most prestigious families in the state of Texas and beyond. He wouldn't let anything happen to her. Probably do a better job of protecting her than Dawson had up to this point.

Outside the Waterin' Hole, Dawson pulled his cowboy hat down low over his eyes. Police activity was light at this time.

A pretty woman meeting Marisol's description was near the entrance.

Dawson worked his way over to her. She was talking to a man wearing a nice suit, but he left as Dawson was approaching.

"So what's a pretty girl like you doing at a crime scene?"

She faced him. Her gaze roamed over him from head to toe. "What's it to you, cowboy?" she asked in a heavily accented and decidedly sultry voice.

"Just wondering."

Her eyes narrowed and her arms crossed over her chest. "Why?"

Dawson shrugged.

The man in the suit chose that moment to head back in their direction.

If Dawson was going to get anything out of Marisol, it would have to be quick. His gut told him that she knew something about the Rodriguez murder. If he wanted to find out how much she knew, he'd have to take a risk. "Do you know the district attorney?" He faced her squarely and gripped her wrist. "Or anyone known as *El Martillo?*"

Marisol's mouth curled into a sneer and she tugged at her wrist, trying to dislodge his fingers. "That's none of your business."

"I want to know if the D.A., you and a drug lord's enforcer are friends."

"I have a lot of friends," she told him.

"Does the D.A. know about the other men in your life, Marisol? Does he approve?"

The only indication of her displeasure was a brief and almost imperceptible dip of her brows before she forced a stiff shrug. "Of course."

"And if I were to tell him of your other conquests, do you think he'd be upset? If I told his wife of the woman he's cheating with, maybe he'd stop buying you expensive gifts."

Her body stiffened. "What do you want?" Her words were cold, clipped and razor sharp.

"I want to know who pulled the trigger on Tomas Rodriguez. Was it you?"

Marisol gasped. "I don't know what you're talking about."

Dawson tightened his grip on her wrist. "You know exactly what I'm talking about. Are you the one who set up Savvy Jones to take the fall for Rodriguez's death?"

She snorted. "And do you think I would tell you if I did?" The woman turned to the man in the suit as he arrived next to them. "Rex, *mi amor,* help me, will you? This man doesn't believe that I'm not interested in him."

Rex glared at Dawson's hand on Marisol's wrist. "Let her go."

Dawson's teeth ground together. He'd handled that all wrong, but if Marisol knew who had pulled the trigger, she'd run to that man now and let him know Dawson was questioning her. If she'd killed Rodriguez, she might show her hand in an attempt to eliminate the person searching for the killer. Either way, someone would be coming after him and soon.

Dawson let go of Marisol and smiled at her. "Sorry. My mistake."

He backed away from the couple, more to give Marisol space and time to tip her hand.

Once he ducked out of sight, he stopped, counted to ten and then turned to see where Marisol would go.

She had ditched the man in the suit and stood with a cell phone against her ear and a hand pressed to her other ear.

Dawson would wait for her to leave, and he'd see who she met up with. He'd bet it would either be the D.A. or *El Martillo.* At that moment, he didn't trust Frank Young any more than the drug lord's henchman.

The cell phone clipped to his belt vibrated. His heart skipped a beat, his first thought of Savvy and Jack in danger. When the caller ID indicated his boss, Audrey Nye, he dragged in a deep breath and hit the talk button. "Gray."

"Where are you, Dawson?"

"I'm at the Waterin' Hole."

"I hope you don't have Ms. Jones with you. Not after what happened earlier."

"Jack's got her in hiding." He didn't want to go into too much detail. Not when he needed to keep his wits about him and his eye on Marisol de la Fuentez. "What have you got?"

"I did a web search on the name and phone number you

gave me for E. Jameson," Audrey began. "First of all, the number is unlisted. But I pulled a few strings and found out the E. Jameson at the other end of that number is Edward Jameson, multimillionaire and Wall Street mogul. There's a lot of controversy around his disappearance from the power scene since the death of his grandchild and son-in-law. There's also speculation on the whereabouts of his daughter. He won't go public, but insiders say she disappeared shortly after her child and estranged husband died in a car wreck six months ago. Jameson's been searching for her since."

A cold hand settled over Dawson's chest. "Would Jameson's daughter happen to go by the name of Sabrina?"

"Yes."

His chest tightened. "Do you have a picture of her? Do you know what she looks like?"

"I have her DMV stats from her New York State driver's license. Would that help?"

Dawson attempted to swallow past the sudden lump in his throat. Deep down he knew what Audrey would say before the words came across the line. And with each detail, a hammer pounded another nail into his heart.

"Five foot seven inches, red hair, green eyes."

He blew out the breath he'd held. "Savvy."

Audrey agreed. "That would explain why we can't find Savvy in the Harvard database. Bet we'd find Sabrina Jameson."

"She's in deep trouble. If anyone else finds out who she is…" Not only was she wanted by the drug lord for a murder she didn't commit, she had a rich father who'd pay a fortune to get her back. A fortune any motivated kidnapper would jump at, given half a chance.

"Do you think anyone knows her true identity, besides maybe Pearson?" Audrey asked.

"I don't know, but it explains why they didn't shoot to kill *her* in the bar earlier today."

"That girl doesn't need a bodyguard, she needs a damn army to protect her."

Exactly. "I have to go." Dawson hit the end button. He needed to get back to Savvy, ASAP.

A man approached him from behind. Vance Pearson. "So have you figured it out yet?"

Dawson wanted nothing more than to slug the man and move on, but he stayed and waited to hear what he had to say. "What's in it for you?"

"Edward Jameson paid me to find her. As simple as that."

"What's the going rate for finding poor little rich girls?" Dawson's fingers clenched.

"Look." Pearson's eyes narrowed. "I'm doing a job, just like you are. Don't get all altruistic on me."

Dawson's fists unclenched. Pearson was right. He'd come for the job. But now that he knew Sav—Sabrina's identity, he couldn't be unbiased. He couldn't stand back and leave his emotions out of the picture. "So where do you go from here?"

"I've already notified her father. He's en route as we speak, on his private jet. Should be here in—" Pearson glanced at his watch "—two hours."

"And what do you expect me to do?"

"Just don't get in the way when he gets here."

Dawson saw his world unraveling in front of him. Sabrina would be reunited with her father and he'd have his own army of bodyguards. Dawson's services would no longer be required. "What if she doesn't want to go with him?"

Pearson shrugged. "My job will be done. What Sabrina chooses is up to her and her father."

Sabrina's father's money would buy a lawyer to clear

her of the murder charges. They didn't have to risk their lives to find the real murderer. Quite possibly, the real murderer would go unpunished. Dawson shook his head. At least Savvy wouldn't go to jail.

Sabrina, he had to remind himself. Her name was Sabrina.

He'd never see her as Sabrina Jameson. She'd always be Savvy Jones to him. The spunky redhead with a fierce spirit and a burning desire for justice.

"Does anyone else around her know who she is?"

"Only the D.A. I asked him to put her in protective custody, even jail, if necessary, to keep her safe, but he thought a bodyguard was sufficient."

Dawson sucked air into his lungs and let it out slowly. "You told the D.A.?"

"Yeah. As soon as I was sure it was her. Edward Jameson would want his daughter to be safe."

Dawson turned to go. "I have to go."

"Why?" Pearson stared up at him, his brows high on his forehead.

"You might have sealed her fate with your meddling."

"I'm just doing what I was paid to do by finding a missing heiress." Vance Pearson gripped his arm. "Seriously, don't stand in the way of Edward Jameson. He can be a formidable opponent."

"I won't." How could he? Sabrina had been born and raised in the lap of luxury. He couldn't compete with that and he didn't want to.

He glanced around the parking lot. That's when he noticed that Marisol had disappeared. Marisol, who happened to be the D.A.'s lover. How much did the D.A. know about her? Did he know that she was also seeing a criminal known for meting out harsh punishment on his boss's enemies? Did he know that Marisol would probably sell her soul for a dollar? Had he confided in her about Savvy's true identity?

Dawson's raced for the door. Where had she gone?

Dawson had to get back to Savvy as soon as possible. He couldn't trust the D.A. to keep his zipper up and his mouth shut. He couldn't risk Savvy to the hands of a woman out for money no matter how she got it or the men she hung out with.

When he reached the rental car, he popped the locks and jumped in.

As he fitted his key in the ignition, a sharp rap on his window made him jump.

"Hey, Gray!" Vance Pearson stood beside the car.

Dawson didn't want to continue his conversation with the private investigator. Savvy might be in trouble. The longer he delayed his return, the more nervous he became. He hit the down button and the window slid downward. "What?"

"You're really stuck on her, aren't you?"

If he wasn't in such a hurry, he'd punch the guy. Instead of answering, he turned the key in the ignition. The starter clicked but the engine didn't start. Damn! What a time for the car to break down.

"Look, I'm sorry. I didn't realize you were that into her. But I have to warn you. She's way over your head. And Edward Jameson won't appreciate your interference."

Dawson turned the key again. He knew Sabrina was way over his pay grade, but Savvy fit right in. Nothing. The engine didn't even turn over. He turned the key again with no results.

Then his hand froze on the key and every nerve in his body sizzled. His instincts screamed, *Get out!*

Dawson flung the door open, knocking Vance Pearson back.

Vance staggered, holding his hands up in surrender. "Hey, man, I didn't mean to make you mad. I'm only sayin—"

"Run!" Dawson raced for the side of a brick building.

He glanced back to see Vance behind him, his eyes wide. "Why are we running—"

The world exploded in a fiery flash, throwing Dawson forward.

Chapter Sixteen

"I promise not to make a run for it," Savvy said. "Please cut these ties."

"No," Jack said.

"Jack, this is ridiculous." Savvy wiggled on the bed, tired of lying on her side and unable to roll over with her hands behind her back.

Jack glanced at his watch. "Dawson's been gone an hour. I suppose it wouldn't hurt to let you loose."

"Exactly." Savvy gritted her teeth and fought to control the need to scream at the man. Anger wouldn't change his mind. She'd already tried that, with no results.

Jack rose from his seat next to the bed, dug a knife out of his jeans pocket and flipped open a wickedly sharp blade.

Finally. Savvy held steady as he cut the zip tie binding her ankles. She kicked her legs free and twisted so that he could cut the tie on her wrists.

The stubborn man who'd followed his partner's wishes to the letter cut through the hard plastic, and her hands were free at last.

She wanted nothing more than to wrap them around Jack's neck and strangle him, but her fingers were numb and she was more worried about Dawson than hurting his friend.

Savvy slid off the bed and stood, her knees wobbly at first, but stiffening as the blood flowed into them.

Jack rose and blocked the path to the door. "Just because I untied you doesn't mean you can go chasing after Dawson. He can handle the situation just fine."

"I can make decisions for myself." She strode across the room to stand nose to nose with the man. "Move out of my way."

Jack had the gall to grin. "No can do."

With a quick sidestep, Savvy attempted to go around him.

The large man moved surprisingly fast, grabbing her by the wrist and whirling her around to twist her arm painfully behind her back.

"Damn it, Jack! Dawson could be in danger. Don't you care about him at all?"

"Think about it, Savvy." Jack's voice softened. "Much as you'd like to help, Dawson would be in more danger if he was worrying about you. He'd lose his focus."

She hadn't thought of it that way. She stopped struggling and stood still. "He's a target as long as he's protecting me."

"Right." Jack loosened his hold, dropping his grip on her wrist.

She stepped away, absently rubbing the red marks left over from the zip ties. Savvy faced Jack. "He didn't want the bodyguard job in the first place."

"No, he didn't." Jack scratched his head.

"Why?" Savvy asked.

"He didn't tell you?"

"No."

"Then maybe it's not my place to tell."

"I think we've been through enough together that I have a right to know why."

Jack shrugged. "If he asks, it didn't come from me. Before he started with the Lone Star Agency, he was on a path to self-destruction."

Savvy's brows furrowed. "Dawson?"

"Yeah. He was involved in a roadside bombing that left one of his men dead. While he watched his man die in the MASH hospital, he got word his wife was in labor and not doing so well. By the time he got back to the States, she'd died. The baby, too."

Savvy's hand rose to her belly, her stomach clenching at the thought of losing a child. "He blamed himself, didn't he?"

Jack nodded. "Not long afterward, he processed out of the military and went on a drunken binge. If I hadn't pulled him out of a barroom fight, he'd likely have ended up in jail or dead."

"Is that why he didn't want to be a bodyguard to me?" Savvy asked.

"I think he didn't want the responsibility of another person's life, having let too many others down in the past."

Savvy shook her head. "But he's been nothing but wonderful keeping me safe. He's a good man." A man who would do anything to help her, even lay down his life. He was a man she could learn to trust and even love, if she let herself.

Savvy's chest tightened. She suspected she might already be halfway in love with the man she'd only met two days ago.

"I know Dawson is a good man and our boss recognized it, as well. That's why she took a chance on a recovering alcoholic and gave him a job. Dawson is the only one needing to be convinced." Jack smiled. "I have a feeling you're the one to convince him."

Savvy drew in a deep breath and let it out. "I have to go to him, Jack. I can't let him do this alone."

"And I can't let you go." Jack crossed his arms over his chest. "I guess that means we're in a standoff." His cell phone buzzed in his pocket and he grinned. "Maybe that's our man now."

Savvy held her breath as Jack slid his phone open.

He shook his head. "Sorry, it's one of my contacts." Jack pressed the phone to his ear. "What'd you say? The line has too much static...Get out? Why?" He frowned and then his eyes widened.

"What did he say?" Savvy demanded.

"He said someone knows where we are and that we need to get out of here. Now!" Jack reached for the gun in his shoulder holster and was turning toward the door when a loud crash slammed the door inward.

Two armed men rushed in with guns. The first one through the door shot Jack.

Savvy screamed as the bodyguard went down, blood soaking the floor beneath his right shoulder.

The second man through the door grabbed her and pushed her toward the door.

She kicked, screamed and put up such a fight, the man wrapped both arms around her and lifted her off the ground. As he carried her through the door, she braced her feet against the door frame.

"Madre de Dios!" Much bigger and stronger than she was, the man jerked her to the side, flinging her legs through the door.

Savvy knew if they got her into a car, she'd be lost. Jack lay on the floor of the motel room, probably dying, and Dawson wouldn't know where to find her. With her life on the line, she wasn't giving up easily. She screamed and screamed until a huge hand clamped down over her mouth.

She bit into the meaty palm and the man's grip loosened enough that she fought free, dropping to the ground. Before she could take more than two steps, he hit her in the head with something hard.

Bright lights flashed briefly before Savvy's world blacked out.

DAWSON STAGGERED to his feet, his head ringing, his hearing muffled. A fire burned behind him where his rental car had been. Flashbacks of Iraq and the roadside bomb that had taken one of his men crowded into his thoughts. That same sense of impending doom he'd felt as he raced down the hospital corridors to get to his wife spread throughout his body like a heavy weight, pulling him downward. His breathing became erratic and his heart pounded against his ribs. If he didn't get a grip soon, he'd be no use to anyone.

At the back of his mind, an image of Savvy Jones with her long strawberry blonde hair and green eyes surfaced like the rising sun, pushing back the darker images of his failures and losses. She was his reason for living.

Savvy. He had to get to Savvy. Dawson shook the gray fog from his vision and glanced around.

Windows in the surrounding buildings had been shattered and police emerged from the Waterin' Hole, pointing at the fire.

Vance Pearson lay on the street between him and the burning car, groaning.

Dawson crossed to the downed man. "Can you move?"

"I feel like I've been run over." He heaved himself to his knees.

"Anything broken?" Dawson asked.

Pearson patted his body and head. "I don't think so, but you sound like you're speaking to me from a cave."

"I'll get you an ambulance. What I need is a car. Where is yours?"

Still on his knees, the man took a moment to process Dawson's question. "I parked a street over from the bar. Why?" He looked up at Dawson, his gaze glassy.

"I have to get to Savvy—Sabrina. I don't have a good feeling about this."

"Yeah, man. Whoever did that to your car might want you out of the way." Pearson dug in his trousers' pocket and pulled out his keys. "It's a dark blue Nissan Sentra with a rental-car sticker on the back, a block behind the bar, parked along a side street."

Dawson took the keys from his hands and called out to some of the bystanders. "We need an ambulance here."

"Don't worry about me. I'll be okay. Just find Sabrina."

With a last glance down at the man on the ground, Dawson took off at a run in the direction Pearson had pointed. If he was a little unsteady, he pushed past it, focusing on his goal. Get to Savvy before someone else did.

When he reached the sedan, he slid behind the wheel and shifted into Drive. He pressed his foot to the floor, giving it all the power he could while he reached for his cell phone. The screen was cracked, but he punched the speed dial for Jack.

After the fifth ring, Dawson's fingers tightened on the steering wheel, his knuckles turning white.

"Yeah," a shaky voice answered. It didn't sound like Jack. Had he entered the wrong number?

"Jack?" Dawson asked.

"Yeah, it's me." The voice strengthened and sounded more like his friend.

The air left his lungs and his foot eased off the accelerator. "What's wrong?" The dizziness he'd experienced right after the explosion threatened to make the edges of his world gray and fuzzy all over again. Dawson shook his head to clear it. "What's happened? Where's Savvy?"

"They got her."

His world spun and he pulled the car to the side of the road until his senses steadied. "Who got her?"

"A couple of guys busted in the door, shot me and took her."

Dawson pictured his friend bleeding to death. Just like the man from his unit he'd been powerless to save. "Are you all right?"

"It's only a flesh wound. The impact knocked me down. I must have hit my head on the dresser in the fall."

Disbelief made him gun the accelerator and shoot the car in the direction of the motel. "You gonna make it?" Dawson wasn't so sure he would make it himself. He hadn't been this stressed since the explosion in Iraq.

"You bet." Jack sounded more confident than Dawson felt. "Nothing a couple of aspirin won't cure."

Dawson fought back the panic. "I'm calling an ambulance."

"No, Dawson. The bleeding has stopped. My head aches like a boulder fell on it, but I'll live. It appears no one was aware of the break-in."

Skeptical yet somewhat reassured, Dawson moved on to his most pressing problem. "We have to get her back."

"Where are you?"

"Two blocks away."

"Do you know who might have her?"

"I can guess, but I have another way of finding her."

"And how are you going to do that?"

"I bugged her before I left her with you."

Jack chuckled and groaned. "Don't make me laugh, it hurts my head."

"Grab my gym bag and meet me outside the motel."

"I'll be there."

DAWSON CALLED 911 and reported the kidnapping, describing Savvy and giving his phone number as a contact. When the officer asked him to come to the station to file a report, Dawson disconnected. He didn't have time to file an official missing-persons report. Savvy's life depended on him finding her as quickly as possible.

As he pulled into the motel parking area, Jack stood with the gym bag in hand and a towel pressed to his shoulder.

Dawson barely slowed to pick up Jack. He gunned the accelerator, sending the car shooting out onto the street before the passenger door was closed. Savvy couldn't wait.

Jack unearthed the GPS tracker and turned it on. After a long moment in which Dawson died a thousand deaths, the map appeared on the screen with a red blinking dot in the center.

"They're crossing the World Trade Bridge into Mexico."

Dawson slammed his hand against the steering wheel, muttering a curse. They were at least ten minutes from the bridge. At this time of night, the crossing into Mexico would take less time than during the day if they ditched the car and went on foot. As they drove toward the border, Dawson filled Jack in on what he'd discovered about Savvy, aka Sabrina Jameson.

Jack let out a long whistle. "Well, that's a relief."

"Relief? She's been kidnapped by dangerous men. How can that be a relief?"

Jack smiled. "They won't kill her until they get their ransom money."

Somehow Dawson didn't find any relief in Jack's remark. Assuming they found her, they still had to extricate

her from the clutches of a man known as The Hammer.
People could die in the process. People like Jack and Savvy.

Dawson parked Pearson's rental in a large parking area
on the United States side of the Rio Grande outside the
World Trade Bridge border crossing. There was light traffic in both directions, coming from and going into Mexico.

"You should stay here." Dawson held out his hand for
the GPS device.

Jack didn't give it up. "I'm going with you. Besides,
I think I know where they're going. I can get you there
faster."

"Where?"

"Marisol de la Fuentez's villa."

Dawson reached into the gym bag and pulled out a clean
white T-shirt and a black one with *Sturgis* written in big
block letters across the back. "You'll need the wound ban-
daged and a fresh shirt before we cross. We can't afford to
waste time answering questions."

Not only would they waste time answering questions
but also, if Jack lost more blood, he'd be more liability than
help in freeing Savvy from her captors.

In less than a minute, Dawson had ripped the white
T-shirt into long strips, field dressed the wound and helped
his friend into the clean shirt. Once finished, he stepped
out of the car.

Jack climbed out the other side and circled around to
stand beside Dawson. "Ready?"

"Let's go."

With little interruption, Jack and Dawson crossed into
Mexico, moving into the shadows of boarded-up buildings.

Jack led the way. They flagged a taxi and Jack gave directions to a location a block away from Marisol's villa.

As they sat in the backseat, Dawson stared at the GPS
device and the red blip on the screen, imagining Savvy's

fear. Once again, he'd let down a person he cared about. And he cared about Savvy more than he wanted to. More than a bodyguard should care about a client. If he lost her, he didn't know what he'd do. He wouldn't be able to live with himself.

"I was right. That's where they're taking her—to Marisol's villa on the outskirts of Nuevo Laredo off Highway 85. That's where our friendly D.A. was earlier today."

"If they hurt one hair on her head—" Dawson said, his voice catching on the lump in his throat.

"Hey, we'll get there in time. Remember, she's worth more to them alive than dead."

"What makes you think they'll let her go once they get their money?"

"At the very least, the negotiations will take time. Time we can use to make our move."

"Unless you haven't noticed, we don't have much in the way of weapons. We had to leave them behind in the rental car." They never would have made it across the border carrying pistols. "Armed with little more than pocket knives, what chance do we have of storming Marisol's villa to free Savvy?"

"We're former special ops. We'll come up with something," Jack said, staring out the window.

Dawson racked his brain for a plan during the taxi ride across Nuevo Laredo.

A block away from the villa, they paid the taxi driver and disappeared between the houses, moving in the direction of Marisol's villa and Savvy.

As they passed a concrete wall surrounding an upscale home, Jack put out his hand, stopping Dawson from stepping out into the street. "There it is," he whispered.

A concrete wall ringed another villa and bougainvillea climbed the walls, making dark shadows across the white

432   Killer Body

of the wall. A guard stood at the gate beside a cedar bush, holding an automatic weapon in his hand.

"I'll check the rear. Don't be a hero until I get back." Jack backed out the way they'd come and made a wide circle around the villa and the building beside it, moving through the shadows like a ghost. If Dawson hadn't been watching for him, he would never have seen him.

Savvy was inside that house, behind the solid concrete of the surrounding wall, probably held at gunpoint.

The urge to storm through burned in Dawson's gut, but he held his ground. Unarmed and with an equally unarmed backup, they had to tread lightly.

Lost in his thoughts, he didn't hear movement behind him until the cold blade of a knife pressed against his throat.

Dawson froze.

"Man, have you forgotten all your training?" Jack whispered in his ear. "Get your mind off the woman long enough to take out the guards, will you?"

Jack had made his point. He had to focus on the task at hand. "How many are there?"

"One on each side of the building. But there is only one entrance and you're looking at it."

The wall appeared to be seven feet tall. He could just see the terra-cotta tiles of the single-story roofline. If they took out a guard on one side, they could scale the wall and drop down on the other side.

"The guy on the west side is asleep," Jack said.

"Then we go west." Dawson backed away from the corner of the wall. He let Jack lead the way to the west side of Marisol's villa. Just as Jack had said, the guard sat slumped against the wall, his weapon lying across his lap, sound asleep.

Jack and Dawson slipped up beside him. Dawson

knocked the man out cold with one punch before the guy could cry out.

Jack cupped his hand. "You go." Dawson stepped into his hand and hefted himself to the top of the wall. He reached down for the automatic weapon Jack had taken off the disabled man, set it to the side then reached a hand down to pull Jack up beside him.

They peered down into the side yard of a sprawling villa. The manicured gardens burst with blooming plants of all kinds and smells. Dawson's teeth ground together and he dropped softly to the ground, ready to storm forward.

Jack dropped down beside him. "I see movement through the window."

Dawson spied a man brandishing a pistol and kicking at something on the floor. He lunged forward, stopped only by his friend holding him back.

"You can't just barge in there."

He strained against Jack's hold. "It's Savvy."

Chapter Seventeen

"Wake up," a voice called to her in a heavy Spanish accent.

Someone kicked her in the ribs, the pain jerking her out of the darkness into a brightly lit room. Savvy blinked her eyes open to see a body lying beside her, blood pooling across the floor.

She screamed and sat up straight, pushing away from the dead man. As her vision cleared, she screamed again. Frank Young in his tailored suit lay sprawled at an awkward angle, his eyes open, staring blankly at the ceiling.

She scooted away from the dead man, bumping into a pair of legs. When she looked up, a man with deep pockmarks scarring his face stared down at her. A man she'd seen before, pointing a gun at her from a car window and... The memory of a dark alley and a man with a scarred face flashed into focus. Fear rocked her, pulling all the air from her lungs. "You!"

A smile curled upward on one side of his face. "You know who I am?"

"I don't know your name, but you're the one who shot Tomas Rodriguez. I remember." She shook her head. As though a gate had been opened, memories flooded in, threatening to overwhelm her senses. "I was putting out the trash. You killed him and then—" She stared up at him, her eyes widening. "Then you tried to kill me."

"A little late to be remembering, don't you think?" He tipped his head back, looking down his nose at her, his arrogant posture designed to intimidate. "They call me *El Martillo*."

"José Mendoza. The Hammer." Savvy shook her head, refusing to let this man see her fear at the name. An image of Tomas Rodriguez's body flashed through her mind, his white shirt stained with dark red blood. Before she could stop herself, a chill shook her body. "Why? Why did you kill him?"

"He was causing too many *problemas*. He was, how you say…spoiled, no good, out of control."

"But you shot him down in cold blood."

"He would have run to his papa crying."

"And you were afraid his father would side with his son instead of you?"

The man shrugged. "No matter. He is dead and I have you to take the blame. Señorita Sabrina Jameson."

Savvy's breath caught in her throat at the mention of the name. Sabrina Jameson. *She* was Sabrina Jameson, not Savvy Jones. As with the recollection of the shooting, all the memories of her past flooded in, her reason for leaving behind her father's home, leaving everything she knew.

A hot wash of tears flooded her eyes as she felt for the photograph in her pocket. The child had been hers, her baby, her beautiful Emma. She'd died six months ago in a car wreck with Savvy's estranged husband. Savvy had almost died in that same wreck, but she'd lived.

Emma would have been two this week.

Lost in a torrent of emotions, Savvy didn't see it coming until a hand slapped the side of her face, yanking her out of her past and into the very real danger of her present. Pain shot through her temples. "What do you want?" she asked, clutching the sides of her head in both hands.

The man called The Hammer handed her a cell phone. "Call your papa. Let him know you are alive and that if he wants you to stay alive, he will give me twenty-five million dollars by tomorrow morning."

Savvy gasped. "Twenty-five million. He can't get that much money by tomorrow morning." She wasn't even sure he'd want her back after the horrible things she'd said to him when she'd left. She'd called him a money-hungry heartless fool. A man who cared more about his business than his family.

"He will or you die."

Savvy's hands shook as she dialed what she hoped was her father's cell-phone number. It had been such a long time, and her memory was only just returning. On the third ring, a man's voice demanded, "What?"

"Daddy?" Savvy recognized the harsh tone, the abrupt speech of a man used to getting his way or demanding an explanation why he couldn't. She'd left her home in New York City to get away from him and the lifestyle of the rich and uncaring to start over. To build a life of her own, free of his demands and her memories.

Edward Jameson had chosen her schools, chosen her husband and dictated her life in every way until she'd had Emma. Not until she had a child of her own did she grow a backbone. Then she'd learned that money wasn't everything and happiness wasn't doing as Daddy said. Soon after her marriage, she'd learned that her husband was just like her father. She'd divorced, but had stayed in the area so that Emma could be close to the father who rarely had time for her.

They had been on their way to her father's country estate, riding together and arguing over money, when her ex-husband had lost control of the vehicle.

Savvy tried to swallow past the lump of tears in her

throat as scenes from the car accident resurfaced. She'd lived, but her ex-husband and child had died in the wreck.

"Sabrina?" Edward Jameson's voice cut through her flashback. He sounded different now, changed from harsh taskmaster to old man, his voice shaking across the line. "Oh, God, Sabrina, where are you?"

"I don't know."

"I'm so sorry about everything, Sabrina. I've missed you terribly."

Tears welled in her eyes and lodged in her throat. Despite the bad feelings she'd left home harboring, she couldn't help the feeling of longing to see him again. "I missed you, too."

"Please let me come get you. Let me bring you home to stay."

"I can't." She could never go home to stay. Even if she was free to. "I'm being held hostage."

"By whom? What do they want? I'll give them anything. Just name it." These words coming from a man who always demanded the upper hand in any negotiations, willing to do anything?

He'd changed. Tears slipped from Savvy's eyes. She'd changed, too.

José ripped the phone from Savvy's hands. "You will bring twenty-five million dollars to Mexico at sunrise *mañana,* or your daughter dies. Meet me with the money in Nuevo Laredo at the church at the Plaza Hidalgo." He hit the off button and stuck the phone in his pocket. "We will see how much love Señor Jameson has for his daughter."

"My father will not negotiate with a murderer," Savvy said.

"*El Martillo* does not negotiate." He laid his pistol against her cheek, his eyes scraping over her body. "If he doesn't want you, I will have my own fun with the pretty lady, and then I will kill you."

A shiver shook Savvy from head to toe. She'd die before she let him touch her.

"TAKE THE GUARD on the front. I'll get the one at the rear." Dawson glanced at the lights spilling from the windows. He hadn't seen Savvy since José had moved her from the original room deeper into the villa. It made him tense, anxious and ready to go into battle. "See you inside."

They split up, circling the house. Dawson crouched in the shadows of a hibiscus bush and watched for the guard to make a mistake, and he did when he lit a cigarette. The flash of a match provided just the distraction Dawson needed. In the time it took for the man to light his cigarette, Dawson had grabbed him by the throat and knocked his head hard against the ground. He dragged him behind the hibiscus bush and slipped through the front door into a marble-tiled foyer. On the floor in a corner was the body of a man in a business suit.

Dawson eased around the room and peered down at the dead man lying in the shadows. Frank Young's face stared up at him, his eyes vacant, his skin gray and waxy.

Dread filled him. Whoever had Savvy didn't hesitate to kill no matter who it was. The death of the D.A. would raise a furor stateside. This man didn't care. Would he let Savvy live long enough to collect a ransom from her father? Dawson hoped so. At least long enough for him to get her out.

Voices drifted to him from rooms down a side hallway and he moved toward them, carrying the automatic weapon he'd taken from the guard at the front door. He'd given the other to Jack.

His friend appeared at the other end of the hallway, nodded to Dawson and pointed to a room halfway between the two men. They hefted their weapons to the ready and eased up to the doorway.

Dawson held up three fingers and mouthed the words *one, two, three.* On three, they burst through the door and pointed their weapons at José Mendoza, who had his pistol trained on Savvy's face.

"Dawson!" Savvy's eyes brightened, and she moved to get up from the floor. José grabbed a handful of her hair and yanked her to her feet in front of him.

If the killer hadn't placed her between them, Dawson would have shot him, nailing him with a bullet for each infraction he'd committed against Savvy.

El Martillo smiled, emphasizing the deep scars on his face. "Welcome, *amigos.* So good of you to join our party."

"Let her go," Dawson said through clenched teeth.

"Or what? You'll shoot me?"

"Yes."

Mendoza laughed. "You will not shoot me because you might hit the pretty *señorita.*" He pulled harder on her hair until she gasped.

"What do you want?" Dawson demanded.

"What Señorita Jameson will bring on the open market. Isn't that right, *mi amor?*" He slid his pistol along the side of her face.

"Shoot him, Dawson," Savvy said. "He's a monster. He won't let me live even if my father pays the ransom. He can't. I know he killed Tomas Rodriguez. Shoot him."

Dawson clenched the weapon in his hand, his fingers turning white. He wanted nothing more than to put a bullet into Mendoza's black heart for what he was putting Savvy through. "No."

"If you don't shoot him, he'll kill me anyway and you, too." Tears sprang to Savvy's eyes and slipped down her cheeks. "Shoot, damn it!"

Her tears ripped Dawson apart. "I can't."

Jack stepped forward. "Then let me." He lifted his weapon and aimed it at Mendoza.

"No!" Dawson raised his hand. "Don't shoot. You might hit Savvy."

Mendoza's mouth twisted into a wicked grin. "So that is how it is. The protector has fallen in love with the client? Most *irónico*." He jerked on Savvy's hair, pressing the barrel of the pistol to her temple. "Drop your guns."

Jack held his at the ready, unwavering. Dawson fought the urge to shoot and keep shooting. Was this how it would all end? Still, he held the weapon pointed at José Mendoza, and subsequently Savvy.

"Do as he says or you both get a bullet in your backs." A hard female voice sounded from behind Dawson. Marisol.

Dawson didn't have a choice. If Marisol shot them in the back, they'd be of no use in getting Savvy out of Mexico.

Dawson laid the automatic weapon on the floor; Jack followed his lead.

"*Por favor,* take them outside to kill them." She waved her pistol at the men. "I don't want more stains on my floors."

"You'll take them nowhere." A deeply accented male voice echoed off the walls.

A man Dawson recognized as Humberto Rodriguez from news reports stepped into the room, carrying a pearl-handled Colt revolver, flanked by four large men carrying shiny new automatic rifles.

He nodded toward José and spoke in rapid Spanish.

At first José glared at him, a sneer lifting the side of his mouth. As the older man continued, José's face paled.

Humberto paused and glanced at Savvy. "Let her go."

"No!" Marisol stepped forward. "She's worth a fortune in ransom."

Humberto's brows rose and he stared pointedly at the hand José had twisted in Savvy's hair.

The man let go and shoved Savvy away from him, pointing his pistol at the drug lord.

"No!" Marisol pointed her gun at Savvy. "You can't have the money!"

Humberto's eyes narrowed. "Consider it payment for murdering my son. *La familia es todo.*"

"Get down, Savvy!" Dawson yelled.

Humberto fired before José or Marisol had the chance.

At the same time, Jack dived for the automatic weapon he'd dropped to the ground.

Dawson dived for Marisol, knocking the gun from her hand. He hit the floor, sliding across the tile after Marisol's gun. He grabbed the pistol, rolled to the side and came up on his feet in a crouch. Humberto aimed at Dawson, but Dawson fired first.

Humberto's Colt fell to the smooth tile with a loud crack. Jack, automatic weapon in hand, hid behind a marble column, firing at Humberto and *El Martillo*'s guards.

As quickly as it had begun, the noise stopped.

José Mendoza and Marisol lay sprawled across the floor, their bodies riddled with bullets. Humberto and two of his men lay as still as death. Two others dropped their weapons to the floor and clutched at wounds that spilled blood onto the smooth white tile. "*Por favor,* don't shoot," one said, falling to his knees.

Dawson stood, taking Savvy by the hand and helping her to her feet. He checked her over for wounds before he could finally breathe. Then he pulled her into his arms. "God, Savvy, I thought I'd lose you." He held her close for a long moment, resting his head on the top of hers. "Are you all right?"

"I am now." She wrapped her arms around his middle and held him tight.

Jack kicked the weapons out of reach of the two wounded gunmen. "What should we do with these guys?"

"If we wait for the Mexican authorities, we may never get back across the border."

Jack cleared his throat. "Well, then, let's go. I've done enough sightseeing."

Dawson laughed shakily and bent to kiss Savvy full on the lips.

She smiled and kissed him back. "I remember everything."

Dawson kissed her again. "I'm sorry about your baby."

Savvy's eyes got a faraway look. "Her name was Emma."

Dawson kissed her again before he pulled back. "Ready to go home?"

She looked up at him. "I really don't have a home."

"What about your father's house?"

"I have to see him and make amends." She shook her head. "But I can't go back for more than a visit. His house holds too many memories of Emma and a life I don't want to go back to."

"Now that you remember, do you miss the good life?" he asked.

"No. It wasn't all that good. My father didn't have time to spend with his family. My ex-husband was just like him. The only person who made it bearable was Emma, and she's gone." Her breath hitched on the last word. "I can't go back there. It hurts too much."

Dawson pushed her hair behind her ear and kissed her temple below the healing stitches. "Then how about San Antonio?"

She frowned. "San Antonio?"

"That's where I live."

"Are you asking me to come live with you?"

"Not yet. I think we need to get to know each other first." He tucked her hand in his and pulled her toward the door. "First, we have to get out of Mexico. Then we can give it a week or two. Maybe go on a few honest-to-goodness dates. We'll know by then."

Savvy leaned her head against his arm, knowing she'd already made up her mind. Dawson was the man for her. But she'd give him the benefit of the doubt and the time to make up his mind before she told him. But not too much time. "I'll give you a week. After that, I call the shots."

"Pushy broad." He hugged her to him as they followed Jack out of the villa and into the streets of Nuevo Laredo. "I like the way you think."

The stars shone brighter than the few streetlights cutting through the gloom. But Savvy's smile rivaled the glow of the moon in Dawson's eyes. She'd lived. He hadn't failed her and she wanted to be with him. In his eyes, that was as close to heaven as a man got.

* * * * *

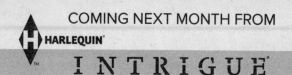